ACCLAIM FOR THE GARDEN OF BURNING SAND

Also by Corban Addison

A Harvest of Thorns
The Tears of Dark Water
A Walk Across the Sun

THE
GARDEN
OF
BURNING
SAND

HARPERCOLLINS PUBLISHERS LTD

Published by HarperCollins Publishers Ltd

First published in Canada by HarperCollins Publishers Ltd
in an original trade paperback edition: 2013
First Harper Perennial trade paperback edition: 2014
This mass market edition: 2018

This book is a work of fiction. Names, characters, businesses, organizations, places and events are either the product of the author's imagination or are used fictitiously. Any resemblance to actual persons, living or dead, events or locales is entirely coincidental.

Excerpt of Isaiah 35:7 is from The Holy Bible,
English standard version ®
(ESV ®) Copyright © 2001 by Crossway, a publishing ministry of
Good News Publishers. Used with permission. All rights reserved.

HarperCollins books may be purchased for educational, business, or sales promotional use through our Special Markets Department.

HarperCollins Publishers Ltd
Bay Adelaide Centre, East Tower
22 Adelaide Street West, 41st Floor
Toronto, Ontario, Canada
M5H 4E3

www.harpercollins.ca

Library and Archives Canada Cataloguing in Publication
information is available upon request

ISBN 978-1-44345-457-5

Printed and bound in the United States of America
QUAD 9 8 7 6 5 4 3 2 1

For the children of Africa
who meet suffering with song.

And for people of goodwill in every land
who have not forgotten them.

A person is a person through other persons.

—*Desmond Tutu*

The burning sand shall become a pool.

—*Isaiah the Prophet*

PROLOGUE

I am the end of the tunnel lost in my beginning.
—*Dambudzo Marechera*

An African Night

Lusaka, Zambia
August, 2011

T he girl walked alone on the darkened street. Lights
moved around her as cars drove by, their headlights
shining on the dusty roadway, but no one seemed to notice
her or care that she was alone. Her gait was steady, but her
steps were irregular, for one of her legs was shorter than the
other. She was wearing a thin dress that offered little protection against the late winter chill. She felt the cold on her skin,
but it concerned her less than the empty flat she had left.

She looked back at the building where she lived. Lights
were on in the windows. She could hear the blare of televi-
sions over the sounds of traffic. She held her doll by the arm

and stared at Auntie's flat through the thick lenses of her eyeglasses. She didn't understand where Bright and Giftie had gone or why they had left her by herself. She didn't understand why they had forgotten to close the door.

She turned back to the road and started off again, swinging her doll like a metronome. She heard music in the distance, and for a moment it distracted her. Then she saw a group of young people across the road. They were smoking cigarettes and talking loudly. Remembering Bright and Giftie, she took a step toward the tarmac, wondering if the smokers knew where they went. But a horn blast from a passing car stopped her in her tracks.

She clutched her doll to her chest and glanced around again, rocking ever so slightly on her feet. Everything looked strange in the dark. Sometimes Giftie took her to another building to play, but she couldn't remember which way it was. The street didn't appear the way she remembered. She began to cry. She wanted the sun to rise and the strangeness of everything to go away. The night made her afraid. People lost their kindness when darkness fell.

The girl saw him then—a boy playing with a ball in an alley. She focused on the boy and started walking again. Bright and Giftie had many friends. Perhaps the boy was one of them. She strolled along a wall rimmed with razor wire, her feet scuffing the dirt. As she approached the alley, she heard a popping sound, like fritas frying in a pan. She glanced over her shoulder and saw a truck pull up behind her, its tires grinding the earth. The truck stopped beside the wall and its lights pierced her eyes. She turned away and looked for the boy with the ball. He was gone.

The girl entered the alley and listened to the boy's voice echoing off the walls around her. She heard another voice— a woman's voice—rise above it, sounding cross. The girl caught a glimpse of the boy running. Seconds later he disappeared and the woman's lecture stopped. The girl walked deeper into the shadows, holding her doll and searching for a break in the wall—whatever the boy had passed through. She stumbled on a pile of rocks and tears gathered in her eyes. Even the ground was unfriendly at night.

She looked at the buildings beyond the walls. They were tall, like the building where she lived, but they were strange. The fear came upon her in a rush, and she decided to go back to the flat. Auntie would return soon, and Bright and Giftie would come home.

She was about to turn around when she heard the popping sound again. At once, light filled the alley. Then just as quickly darkness descended. The girl looked toward the street and saw the truck that had stopped beside the wall. It was driving slowly up the alley, its headlights off. A man got out of the truck and stared at her. There was something in the shape of the man's face that made her comfortable and uncomfortable at the same time.

The man knelt down and held out his hand. She saw a sweet in his palm. Her mother had given her sweets whenever she had asked her to sleep in the bathroom. After a moment, the girl reached out and put the sweet in her mouth. She smiled at the man, deciding he must be a friend.

What happened next made no sense to her. She had no idea why her legs grew weak and her fingers lost hold of her doll, why the night spun out of control and pain shot through her head. Her eyelids drooped, then opened again. She saw the shadow of the man hovering over her. He bent down and lifted her off the ground. She had lost her glasses, but his face was close as he carried her and she saw his eyes. They were large and round, like a cat's. Her mother had told her stories about cats—the cats that lived wild in Africa.

She heard a click like a door latch and felt the man's hands push her into a cramped space blacker than the sky. Her last impression was the rumble that began beneath her and grew louder until the world fell away and the night itself vanished in darkness.

A Hearing in the Senate

Washington, D.C.
May, 2012

The lights above the dais were blinding to Zoe, a string of miniature suns staring back at her, exposing every imperfection in her face—her slightly offset ears, the mole at the crest of her left eyebrow, the freckles that dotted the fair skin around her nose—and reaching deeper still, as if to make public her thoughts. Having watched her father on the campaign trail first in his race for the Senate twelve years ago and now in his quest for the White House, Zoe knew that all politics were theater and that privacy had no place on the stage.

She closed her eyes against the glare and pictured her mother's face—the way her smile had dimpled her cheeks and wrinkled the skin around her eyelids, the look of earnestness and secret pleasure that had turned skeptics into supporters across the globe. Catherine Sorenson-Fleming had been irresistible in life, a force of indefatigable optimism about the world that could be—a world in which the poor were not an afterthought. Africa was her great love affair, and she had passed it on to Zoe. It might as well have been written into her will as a bequest.

How would you have handled this, Mom? Zoe thought, wrestling with the dilemma before her. She remembered something her mother used to say: *"Speak the truth, consequences be damned."* But that didn't resolve the question. The truth was only part of the story.

Zoe opened her eyes and regarded Senator Paul Hartman, Chairman of the Foreign Relations Committee, who had taken his seat at the head of the dais beneath the great seal of the United States. Around him in the wood-paneled chamber aides scurried, brandishing sheaves of paper. Hartman placed a binder in front of him and glanced around the room until his eyes settled on Zoe. He smiled slightly, as if sharing an inside joke, and Zoe felt the ice inside her begin to crack. His kindness deepened her dilemma. He had no idea of the secret she carried, or the anger.

Senator Hartman was the reason she was here. He had read her article in the *New Yorker* and issued the invitation. She had been intrigued and skeptical at the same time.

"Is my father aware of this?" she had asked when they had first spoken on the phone.

"I haven't shared my thoughts with him, no," Hartman replied.

"What are the chances he'll come to the hearing?"

"With the election so close, I'm not sure. But your presence could shift the balance."

"In other words, the hearing is for show," she said, testing his motives. "A political ploy in support of the President less than two months before the polls open."

Hartman hesitated. "Was your article for show?"

The question caught her off guard. "I wrote it because it needed to be said."

"Call me old-fashioned," Hartman said, "but I feel the same way. As you put it, generosity itself is on the gallows."

"And you think a Senate hearing will make a difference?"

"The public loves a good controversy. Whether you meant to or not, you created one. If we take advantage of it, people might actually learn something."

It's a gamble, Zoe thought, *but it might just work— for him and for me.*

"I've talked to Frieda Caraway," he went on.

"Is she on your witness list?" Zoe asked. Caraway was an actress on Hollywood's A-list and something of a legend in humanitarian circles. AIDS, trafficking, conflict minerals, Free Tibet, her causes were as numerous as her screen credits, yet only the most cynical questioned her intentions. Her grandparents had died at Auschwitz.

"Not yet," Hartman said, "but I'm working on it."

The Senator's words had thrilled and terrified Zoe. The opportunity was too enticing to decline. "You get Frieda on a panel with a couple of experts from the development community, and I'll be there."

Hartman had chuckled as he hung up the phone. A week later he called her back with good news and a hearing date. He also passed along Frieda Caraway's email address.

"She read your article, too," he told her. "She can't wait to meet you."

"The nonprofit lawyer from Zambia or Jack Fleming's daughter?"

Hartman laughed. "You have your mother's tongue. She wants to meet the Zoe Fleming who took on the African justice system and changed the life of a girl with Down syndrome."

Five weeks later, Zoe had boarded the South African flight from Johannesburg to Washington, D.C. It was the first time she had returned to the United States in three years.

A chorus of voices outside the hearing room made Zoe turn her head. As spectators gawked and cameramen angled for a shot, Frieda Caraway made her entrance, her security detail in tow. Like Zoe, the actress was dressed in a conservative pantsuit and an open-collared blouse, but Hollywood glittered in her diamonds—at least ten carats between her earrings and the pendant on her necklace.

Zoe stood as she walked to the witness table. Frieda's almond brown eyes lit up. "My dear Zoe, such a *joy* to finally meet you."

Although they had exchanged emails and spoken once over Skype, Zoe was unprepared for the hug that followed Frieda's greeting.

"Looks like the sharks have gathered," Frieda whispered. "Are you ready for this?"

Zoe watched the cameramen take their positions in the space between the dais and the witness table. Behind them Senators shuffled papers importantly, but their eyes strayed toward the actress, revealing their true interest. Only one seat had yet to be filled—her father's.

"It's a bit of a circus," Zoe replied, trying to affect a nonchalance she didn't feel.

"Ignore it," Frieda replied. "The only thing that matters is what we're here to talk about."

Zoe took her seat again as Frieda shook hands with the other witnesses at the table: Bob Tiller, computer mogul, philanthropist, and masthead of the largest foundation in the world; and Susan Moore, chairwoman of the Organization for International Development, a global NGO. It was a star-studded panel. In a presidential election year, Hartman had pulled off a coup.

Zoe looked down at her notes, then back at her father's chair. She checked her watch. It was four minutes past two o'clock: the scheduled start-time for the hearing. If he didn't show up, the dilemma would resolve itself and the truth that had defined her life since she was seventeen would stay buried. She felt a sudden sense of relief. At moments she had convinced herself that the truth needed to come out. Yet the prospect of actually speaking it filled her with unease.

She glanced at her older brother, Trevor, sitting in the reserved seats. He nodded at her, a vision of ambivalence. She turned back to the dais and felt the guilt churning in her stomach. Trevor was one of her favorite people in the world and, until recently, the only man whose motives she trusted implicitly. Only a year apart in age, they under-stood each other as no one else did. In the years when they were raised by nannies—Jack off conquering Wall Street and Catherine gallivanting across the globe—Trevor had been her shelter. But he didn't know about the ghost that lived at the Vineyard house. He had left for Harvard, and she had never told him.

Zoe focused on Senator Hartman as he rapped his gavel, bringing the hearing to order. Suddenly, a door opened in the paneling behind him and Jack Fleming appeared, flanked by senior aides. Zoe took a sharp breath, barely conscious of the buzz rippling through the gallery or the cameras swiveling to capture an image of the candidate, fresh off the stump in Ohio. She hadn't seen her father in eight months. He looked older now, his hair grayer, his face fleshier, and his trademark pinstripe suit too tight around the midsection. He had always prided himself on his fitness, but the endless campaigning seemed to have weathered him.

He leaned down and whispered something into Hartman's ear—an apology, Zoe guessed—then took a seat on the left side of the dais without so much as a pad of paper in front of him. In spite of herself, Zoe almost smiled. When she and Trevor were children, he had sometimes allowed them to attend board meetings at Fleming Randall, the investment firm he had built into a Wall Street giant. Though they had been excluded from anything confidential, she had seen enough to understand the reasons for her father's success. Along with a dynamo personality and unshakable self-confidence, he had a photographic memory.

"Many thanks to Senator Fleming for his attendance," Hartman began, silencing the spectators. "I know his schedule is demanding. We have a distinguished panel to hear from, but before we give them the floor I'd like to say a few words about what brings us together today."

He looked at Zoe, then at Frieda, and commenced his remarks. "In the midst of the Great Depression, Franklin Delano Roosevelt articulated a vision of American society that has defined us for generations. 'The test of our progress,' he said, 'is not whether we add more to the abundance of those who have much; it is whether we provide enough for those who have too little.' Now, in the midst of what some have called the Great Recession, that vision is in peril."

Zoe listened as Hartman recited an argument she knew by heart. She kept her eyes fixed on his face, willing herself not to meet her father's eyes. She heard Trevor's voice over breakfast that morning: "*He loves you, Zoe. Do you really want to hurt him?*" It was a question she didn't know how to answer. Their estrangement was a knot that seemed impossible to untangle. For what he did, she had never forgiven him. But he had never asked.

At some point, she raised her eyes to the seal behind Hartman's head, etched in relief upon the polished blond wood. "*E Pluribus Unum*," her mother had been fond of saying. "A motto for the world, not a nation alone." She thought of Kuyeya lying on the hospital table in Zambia, crying, and Dr. Chulu, at once grim and enraged, examining her. Suddenly Zoe's suffering seemed small, even petty, in the shadow of an evil so much greater.

She decided then that Jack Fleming deserved to be defeated. Not because he had betrayed her or because he was unfit to be Chief Executive—in many ways he was born for the Oval Office—but because in the name of fiscal austerity he would abandon children like Kuyeya. That was why

Senator Hartman wanted her father in the chair, why he had brought her in from Africa to tell her story. It wasn't about partisanship or election-year politics. It was about conscience.

At last she looked at her father and touched the ring on her finger, the ring the Somalis had salvaged from the wreckage of her mother's plane. *You know what I'm thinking, don't you? August 19, 2000. I know you remember.*

He angled his head and she thought she saw a flash of fear in his eyes. At that moment Zoe did something she had never expected. She smiled.

The Rule of Achilles, Dad. You taught me.

No one is invincible.

PART ONE

The night comes with its breath of death.
—*Anonymous*

Chapter 1

Lusaka, Zambia
August, 2011

The music was raucous, but it was always that way in African clubs. The beat of the drum—the backbone of village song—had been replaced in the cities by the throbbing insistence of electronic bass, amplified until everything around the speakers picked up the rhythm—people, beer bottles, even the walls. On Zoe's first trip to the continent—a brief jaunt to Nairobi when she was six years old—her mother told her that Africa is the keeper of humanity's pulse. It was a truth she remembered every time she stepped foot in a Zambian bar.

The place was called Hot Tropic, the club *de jour* in a city constantly reinventing its nightlife. The decor was all fire and glitter, neon lights flashing red against the walls and dazzling disco balls turning everything to sparkle. The place was packed with bodies, most of them African twenty-somethings, bouncing to the beat.

Zoe was seated at a table in a corner of the bar where the decibel level was slightly buffered. She was dressed in jeans and a Hard Rock London T-shirt, her wavy blonde hair pulled back in a clip. At the table with her were three African friends from work—two men and a woman. Most Saturdays Zoe hosted a barbecue, or braai, at her flat, and afterward those who had not satisfied their appetite for beer and conversation went clubbing. Tonight, the subject on everyone's minds was the September election, pitting Zambia's President, Rupiah Banda, against the aging warhorse Michael Sata, and the energetic upstart Hakainde Hichilema, or "H.H."

"Banda is finished," Niza Moyo was saying, her dark eyes aglow with indignation. "As is his party. They've run the country for twenty years and what have they given us? Mobile hospitals that take doctors away from the real hospitals; police officers that have no vehicles to investigate a crime; roads that only the rich can drive on; and corruption at every level of government. It's a disgrace."

Like Zoe, Niza was a young attorney at the Coalition of International Legal Advocates, or CILA, a London-based non-profit that combatted human rights abuses around the world. She was feistier and more outspoken than most Zambian women, but she was Shona, from Zimbabwe, and her father was an exiled diplomat known for challenging authority.

"I sympathize with your position," said Joseph Kabuta, an officer with the Zambia Police Victim Support Unit. Solidly built with close-cropped hair and wide perceptive eyes, he reminded Zoe of the young Nelson Mandela. "But Banda is still popular in the rural areas, and Michael Sata isn't well. Zambians don't want another president to die in office."

"The press reports about Sata's health are overblown," Niza rejoined.

"What I can't figure out," Zoe interjected, "is why you don't throw out the guys with one foot in the grave and elect the best candidate. Everybody loves H.H. He's a born leader and he has no political baggage. But everybody says he can't win. Where's the logic?"

"It's the way people think," said Sergeant Zulu—who everyone called Sarge. Strategically brilliant and compulsively affable, he was the lead attorney at CILA and the mastermind behind the organization's campaign against child sexual assault. "In Africa, presidents are like village chiefs. People vote for the gray heads."

"So what you're saying is that reformers don't stand a chance until the old guard dies?" Zoe asked. "No wonder progress is like pulling teeth here."

Sarge smiled wryly. "Each generation has to wait its turn." He held up his empty bottle of Castle lager. "Anyone else need another beer, or am I the only one drinking?"

"I'll take a Mosi," said Joseph, draining his bottle and pushing it to the center of the table. Suddenly, he frowned and reached into the pocket of his jeans. He pulled out his cell phone and glanced at the screen. "It's Mariam," he said, giving Sarge a quizzical look.

Zoe perked up. Mariam Changala was the field-office director at CILA and the mother of six children. If she was calling Joseph in the middle of the night, it had to be serious.

Zoe watched Joseph's face as he took the call. His broad eyebrows arched. "Is Dr. Chulu on call? Make sure he's there. I'm ten minutes away." He put the phone away and glanced around the table. "A girl was raped in Kanyama. They're taking her to the hospital now."

"How old?" Niza asked.

Joseph shrugged. "Mariam just said she's young."

"Family?" Sarge inquired.

"Not clear. They found her wandering the streets."

Zoe spoke: "Who picked her up?"

"Some people from SCA."

"She's disabled?" Zoe asked. "SCA" stood for Special Child Advocates, a nonprofit that worked with children with intellectual disabilities.

"Presumably," Joseph said, throwing on his jacket. "Sorry to break up the party." He gave them a wave and headed toward the door.

Zoe decided on a whim to follow him. Child rape cases usually appeared on her desk in a weeks-old police file. She'd never learned of an incident so soon after it happened. She tossed an apology to Sarge and Niza and weaved her way through the crowd, catching up to Joseph.

"Mind if I come with you?" she asked. "I've never seen the intake process."

He looked annoyed. "Okay, but stay out of the way."

Zoe followed him into the chilly August night. Thrusting her hands into the pockets of her jacket, she looked toward the south and saw Canopus hanging low over the horizon. The brightest southern stars were visible above the scrim of city lights. Joseph walked toward a rusty Toyota pickup jammed in between cars on the edge of the dirt lot. Only the driver's door was accessible. Zoe had to climb over the gearshift to reach the passenger seat.

Joseph started the truck with a roar and pulled out onto the street. Since Hot Tropic sat on the border between Kalingalinga, one of Lusaka's poorer neighborhoods, and Kabulonga, its wealthiest, street traffic on a Saturday night was kaleidoscopic, a colorful blend of pedestrians, up-market SUVs, and blue taxi vans crammed with revelers.

"How did the people at SCA find the girl?" Zoe asked as they left the club behind.

He stared at the road without answering, and she wondered if he'd heard her. She observed him for a long moment in the shadows of the cab. She knew almost nothing about him, except that he had been a police officer for over a decade, that he loathed corruption, and that he had recently completed a law degree at the University of Zambia.

She spoke his name to get his attention. "Joseph."

He twitched and took a breath. "One of their community volunteers found her," he said. "A woman named Abigail. She saw blood on the girl's leg and called Joy Herald." Joy was the director of SCA. "Joy called Mariam at home."

"It happened in Kanyama?"

He nodded. "East of Los Angeles Road, not far from Chibolya."

She shuddered. Kanyama lay to the southwest of Cairo Road—the city's commercial center. A patchwork of shanties and cinderblock dwellings, most without toilets or running water, it was a haven for poverty, alcoholism, larceny, and cholera outbreaks. In an election year, it was also a cauldron of political unrest. But at least Kanyama had a police post. Chibolya was such a cesspool of lawlessness that the police avoided it altogether.

They left the well-lit neighborhoods of Kabulonga and headed west along the wide, divided highway of Los Angeles Boulevard. Skirting the edge of the Lusaka Golf Club, they took Nyerere Road through a tunnel of mature jacarandas whose dense branches slivered the light of the moon.

"Were there any witnesses?" she asked.

He sighed and shifted in his seat. "I have no idea. Are you always so full of questions?"

She bristled and thought: *If I were a man, would you be asking?* She considered a number of barbed responses, but in the end she held her tongue. CILA needed her to build bridges with the police, not wreck them.

Five minutes later, they passed through rusting gates and parked outside the pediatric wing of University Teaching Hospital, the largest medical facility in Zambia. Zoe climbed out of the cab and followed Joseph into the lobby. The air in the room was pungent with bleach. She saw Joy Herald, a matronly Brit, sitting on a bench with an elderly Zambian woman and a girl with mulatto skin who looked no older than ten. Zoe's heart lurched. The child's innocent eyes, framed by epicanthal folds, flat nose bridge, and tiny ears, revealed her extra chromosome.

She had Down syndrome.

Joseph spoke. "Where is Dr. Chulu?"

"He's on his way," Joy replied.

"Has the child been examined by anyone else?"

Joy shook her head. "The doctor's assistant is collecting the paperwork."

Before long, Dr. Emmanuel Chulu walked briskly into the lobby, his white medical coat billowing behind him. A giant of a man with an owl-like face and a deep baritone voice, he was the chief pediatric physician at UTH and also the founder of a clinic for the victims of child rape—"defilement" in Zambian parlance.

Dr. Chulu spoke to the old woman first, mixing English and Nyanja, the most common indigenous language in Lusaka. "Hello, mother, *muli bwange?*"

The woman returned his gaze but didn't smile. "*Ndili bwino.*"

"Are you a member of her family?" he asked.

The woman shook her head. "I am Abigail, the one who found her."

The doctor knelt down in front of the girl and gazed into her eyes, his large frame utterly still. The child was rocking back and forth and humming faintly under her breath. "I'm Manny," he said, searching her face for a sign of recognition. "What is your name?"

The child's hum turned into a moan. Her eyes grew unfocused and her rocking increased.

The doctor spoke to her in a number of different languages, trying to make contact, but she didn't reply. "Hmm," he said, visibly perplexed.

Zoe fingered her mother's ring, empathizing with the girl. She couldn't imagine the physical pain the child had endured, but she understood the horror.

All of a sudden, the child's moaning diminished, and her eyes focused on Zoe's hands. It took Zoe a moment to realize that she was looking at

Catherine's diamonds. She slipped the ring off her finger and knelt down in front of the girl.

"This was my mommy's," she said. "Would you like to hold it?"

The girl seemed to think for a moment. Then she reached out and clutched the ring to her chest. Her moaning ceased and her rocking grew less agitated.

Dr. Chulu looked at Joy, then at Zoe. "Ms. Fleming, right?"

Zoe nodded. "Yes."

"CILA hasn't sent a lawyer before. Our good fortune to have you." He looked around. "Has anyone seen my assistant? I can't do the exam without the forms."

At that moment, a young Zambian woman emerged from a door labeled "Administration," holding a clipboard and a stack of papers.

"Nurse Mbelo, just in time," he said, taking the clipboard. He looked at Abigail. "Mother, Officer Kabuta needs to ask you some questions, but first he needs to witness the examination of the child. Can you wait?"

Abigail nodded.

"Ms. Herald," said the doctor, "I presume you and Ms. Fleming can handle the child."

The intake room was small and poorly ventilated. The fluorescent light cast by two discolored bulbs created a haze at the edge of Zoe's contact lenses. After seating the girl on a narrow table, Dr. Chulu began the examination. His touch was gentle and his bedside manner as tender as a father with a daughter.

Zoe leaned against the wall and watched the doctor's face as he conducted the exam. She found the sterility of the intake room unnerving, as if the medical procedure, in its sheer scientific orderliness, could sanitize the rape of its obscenity. She searched Dr. Chulu's eyes for a shadow, a cloud in his professional calm, and felt empathy when his jaw went rigid. He placed a swab he was holding back in its clear container and sealed it in a plastic bag.

It was stained with blood.

The process of sample collection took thirty minutes. Afterward, Nurse Mbelo wheeled a robotic-looking instrument called a colposcope to the bed, and Dr. Chulu used the built-in camera to photograph the girl's injuries. The child endured the colposcopy for less than a minute before she rolled over and began to make a loud vibrato sound—part cry, part groan.

Dr. Chulu looked at the nurse. "How many images did you get?"

"Five," she replied. "All exterior."

The doctor conferred with Joseph. "Do you think it's enough for the Court?"

"I'll sign the report," Joseph replied quietly. "The magistrate will listen to us."

Dr. Chulu nodded and turned to Joy. "I need to keep her overnight to monitor her. But I can't put her in the ward without knowing her HIV status. I need you to keep her still while I conduct the test."

"Do you have any music?" Joy asked. "It might soothe her."

The doctor gave her a puzzled look. "I have a CD player in my office."

"I have an iPhone," Zoe interjected, taking it out of her pocket. "What about Thomas Mapfumo?" she asked, referring to the celebrated Zimbabwean artist.

"Try it," Joy said. "Your ring worked like a charm."

Zoe selected a song from the album *Rise Up* and pointed the speaker toward the girl. At the sound of the traditional Shona thumb piano the girl's protests lost their shrillness and she began to bob her head with the rhythm.

Joy looked at Dr. Chulu. "Do what you have to do."

The doctor reached out for one of the child's hands and cleaned the middle finger with a cloth. He put pressure on the fingertip and pricked the skin with a lancet. The girl stiffened, but the doctor held her finger firmly, dabbing drops of blood with a pad before collecting a sample in a vial. He handed the vial to his assistant who placed a drop in the window of the test display.

"Non-reactive," the nurse said.

"At last some good news," Dr. Chulu replied. "Get me ten-milligram bottles of Zidovudine, Lamivudine, and Lopinavir in suspension and some pediatric Tylenol."

Nurse Mbelo returned a minute later with the pain medication and what Zoe guessed were antiretrovirals—ARVs—designed to prevent the transmission of HIV.

Dr. Chulu looked at Joy. "If I give you the medicine, will you administer it?"

Joy nodded and helped the girl to sit, speaking softly in her ear. "I have some juice to give you. I need you to open your mouth. I know you can do it."

When the doctor handed her the first medicine dropper, Joy showed it to the girl and then gently inserted it between her lips, squeezing out its contents. The child swallowed the liquid easily. Joy repeated the procedure with the remaining three droppers, all of which the child took without complaint.

She understands medicine, Zoe thought, feeling a surge of affection for the girl.

Dr. Chulu took Joseph aside and Zoe joined them. "I'll contact Social Welfare in the morning," he said. "I need you to find her family."

Joseph nodded. "I'll go to Kanyama tomorrow. Someone will know her."

Zoe took a deep breath, debating with herself. "If it's all the same to you," she said, "I'd like to stay with her tonight."

The doctor stared at her. "That's not necessary. We can sedate her if we need to."

"I understand," she said. In truth, she had deep misgivings about spending hours in the sickness-laden air of the admissions ward, but she couldn't imagine leaving the girl alone after the trauma she had suffered.

Dr. Chulu smiled wearily. "If you want to give up sleep, I'm not going to stop you."

Chapter 2

The hours of the night felt like days in the admissions ward, and Zoe never quite fell asleep. She sat on a metal chair beside the girl's iron bed and rested her head against the wall, trying to ignore the cloying odor of the place. The girl slept fitfully, troubled by nightmares Zoe could scarcely imagine. The night nurse—a middle-aged Zambian—stopped by on occasion and brought Zoe a glass of water. She drank hesitantly, hoping the water had been boiled or taken from a bore-hole. Even after a year in Lusaka, her stomach had yet to conquer the witch's brew of bacteria and parasites that thrived in the city's water system.

At seven in the morning, Dr. Chulu reappeared holding a stuffed monkey. Zoe had been dozing when she heard his heavy footsteps.

"I bought this for my daughter," he said. "It's not much, but maybe she'll take to it. I imagine you'd like to keep your ring."

"I got it back," Zoe said with a yawn, turning to look at the child. She was lying on her side, her eyes closed and her knees tucked under her arms. "She made sounds for a long time during the night. But an hour ago she fell into a deep sleep."

Dr. Chulu stepped to the bedside and felt the girl's carotid artery. "Her pulse is thready, but not weak enough to trouble me. She's going to be uncomfortable for a while, but she'll heal. She's one of the lucky ones."

Zoe looked at the doctor, and he answered her unspoken question.

"I had a child rape case last month," he said. "The victim was an eight-year-old with mental retardation. She was severely underweight and had all kinds of complications from malnutrition. Her parents weren't feeding her. I see it all the time. Eighty percent of kids with disabilities die before the age of five." He pointed at the girl. "At least someone's been taking care of her. And now she has you."

Zoe nodded, feeling a bond with the child that she could not explain. "What about HIV?"

He shrugged. "It's a possibility, assuming the perpetrator was positive. But the likelihood of infection is low. We'll keep her on ARVs and test her again in six weeks." He gave Zoe a compassionate look. "I bet you could use some sleep. Why don't you go home?"

She stretched her arms and felt the ache of sleeplessness in every muscle. Still she hesitated.

"I'll get my CD player," he said, anticipating her concern. "She'll be fine."

"Okay," Zoe conceded. "I'll give you my mobile number in case anything happens."

After giving the doctor her information, she took a last look at the child and slipped out of the hospital. She inhaled the dry Zambian air and smiled at the rising sun. Even after years of visiting Africa's highland plateaus, she still found the near-perfect climate a gift.

39

She took out her phone and called Maurice Isaac, a driver for CILA who lived nearby. He dismissed her apology and promised to pick her up in ten minutes. She called Joseph next. He answered on the second ring.

"Did you sleep?" he asked, sounding groggy.

"Not a wink. What's the plan for today?"

He hesitated. "The plan?"

"Your trip to Kanyama. I'd like to be part of the investigation." When the silence lingered, she decided to press. "Look, I'm not Joy Herald, but I care about this girl. I can call Mariam if you like."

"That's not necessary," he replied. "I'm just concerned about your safety. The compounds are unstable with the election coming up." He took a breath and gave in. "All right. I'll pick you up at fourteen hundred."

With the shades drawn in her bedroom, Zoe managed to sleep until noon. She woke again to the ringtone on her iPhone—the chorus from U2's "I Still Haven't Found What I'm Looking For." She shook her head and blinked a few times, seeing only the blur of her mosquito net. A curse of Fleming genetics, she had inherited her father's near-sightedness. Without corrective lenses, she would have been legally blind.

She threw aside the net and found her contact lens case on the bedside table. As soon as she could see, she checked her phone. She thought the caller might have been Dr. Chulu, but instead she saw Mariam's name on the screen. The field-office director had left a voicemail.

"Good morning, Zoe," Mariam said. "Joseph told me you plan to accompany him to Kanyama. Be careful, please. We'll have a response team meeting in the morning."

Zoe pulled back the curtains from her second-story window and admired the red leaves of the poinsettia tree in the courtyard. The poinsettia had been her mother's favorite African plant, a symbol of the continent's exoticism and fecundity. She took a fast shower—there was never enough hot water in the tank for a long one—and dressed in jeans and a lavender Oxford shirt.

Heading to the kitchen, she fixed herself a breakfast of eggs, toast, and papaya and ate on the porch overlooking the gardens while rereading Proust's *Swann's Way*. It was a regular pilgrimage, the closest thing she had to religion after her years at Stanford. Like Proust's narrator, she saw the past everywhere she looked, as if it were a layer of reality just beneath the present. In this, too, she was her father's daughter. Along with his failing eyesight, she had inherited his extraordinary memory.

The text from Joseph came at quarter to two. She gathered her backpack off the dining-room table and crossed the courtyard to the gate. The guard—a recent recruit whose name she couldn't recall—let her out onto the street. She saw the VSU officer behind the wheel of his truck, wearing aviator sunglasses and a jean jacket. As soon as she climbed in, Joseph pulled away from the curb, accelerating quickly down the tree-lined road. The sky was spotless, not a hint of cloud.

"How was your morning?" Zoe asked.

"Fine," said Joseph.

"Do anything fun?"

He raised his eyebrows. "Why do you ask so many questions?"

She suppressed her annoyance. "I figured if we're

going to work together, we should be friendly. You seemed to have no trouble talking at the bar last night."

He cleared his throat. "If you have to know, I spent the morning working on this truck. It is—what do you call it?—a money pit. I bought it from a cousin who's a mechanic. I'm convinced he gave me a good deal because he knew it would be a steady source of income."

She chuckled. "Glad to see you have a sense of humor."

He gave her a sideways glance. "I have five siblings. You learn to laugh."

She whistled. "Your mother must be a saint. What does your father do?"

"He owns a textile company."

She frowned. *And you've spent the last ten years taking breadcrumbs from the government?* "Why did you become a police officer?"

His answer was cryptic. "One has to start somewhere."

She sensed a deeper truth beneath his vagueness, but she decided to leave it alone. "Where are we going?"

"To talk to Abigail. She's going to introduce us to her neighbors."

They entered Cathedral Hill and took Independence Avenue toward Cairo Road. Sunday traffic was light, but pedestrians were everywhere on the jacaranda-lined shoulders of the road. Zoe sat back and watched Lusaka pass by. Designed as a garden city in colonial times, its leafy boulevards, stately Edwardian architecture, and quiet bungalows had in the decades after independence suffered the encroachment of grit and urban decay. The poor had come from the villages in droves, and the wealthy had responded by barricading themselves behind walls rimmed with glass shards and razor wire.

Crossing Cairo Road, they skirted the edge of the bustling City Market before entering the ramshackle sprawl of Kanyama. Vendors stood on both sides of the dusty thoroughfare, hawking tires and tarpaulin and talktime for mobile phones. More established merchants tended booths set back from the road. Everywhere Zoe saw signs of the presidential election: banners, flags, T-shirts, and posters, almost all of them green—the color of the Patriotic Front. The air, too, was clogged with electioneering. Bands of young men prowled the lane with makeshift bullhorns, castigating President Banda and the ruling Movement for Multiparty Democracy.

One of the young campaigners gave Zoe an angry look before shouting something in Nyanja. "What is he saying?" she asked, feeling a twinge of nerves.

"Roll up your window," Joseph said, inching forward through the mob.

She complied quickly. "Was he talking about me?"

Joseph nodded. "He doesn't like foreigners."

Eventually, they turned left onto a tributary lane crowded with shabby cinderblock dwellings, their corrugated roofs scaled with the rust of many rainy seasons. Children of all ages scampered about, pointing at the truck and staring at Zoe. A few old people sat on chairs, watching the children. Missing from the street were young adults— the parents of the children. Some were working, no doubt, but Zoe knew their absence conveyed a darker truth: many of them were dead.

They rounded a bend and Joseph slammed on the brakes, barely avoiding a head-on collision with a pickup truck swarming with young Zambians in green T-shirts. The driver of the truck— a young man wearing a green bandana—honked loudly while his comrades beat the sides of the truck like drums. Zoe caught a hateful look from a lanky youth standing in the flatbed.

"*Muzungu! Muzungu!*" he shouted.

She felt a surge of fear. "What are you going to do?"

Joseph nosed his truck to the side of the road. "If I were alone, I might teach them a lesson. But I'm not alone."

As the vehicles edged past one another, the young hooligans pounded the roof of Joseph's truck. Time dragged on amid the thunder of hands and shouts. Zoe felt the urge to yell at them, to put them in their place, but she knew it would only exacerbate the situation. At last, the other truck accelerated up the lane, leaving them in a cloud of dust.

"*Bastards!*" Zoe exclaimed. "Who do they think they are?"

Joseph glanced at her but didn't respond. He made another turn and took them deeper into the labyrinth of unmarked lanes. Most of the homes they passed had no doors or windows, and many of the alleys were piled high with burning trash. After a few minutes, Zoe lost all sense of direction. The undifferentiated mass of slum-like buildings was dizzying. Joseph, however, seemed to know exactly where he was going.

In time, he pulled the truck into an alley not far from a weather-beaten house graced with a flame tree in the front yard. Grabbing her backpack, Zoe stepped out of the truck and was instantly mobbed by bright-eyed children. They pulled at her shirt, begged her for kwacha, and asked her to take pictures of them. She patted their heads and greeted them in Nyanja. "*Muli bwange? Muli bwange?*" It wasn't long before she forgot about the trouble-makers in the pickup.

She followed Joseph down a breezeway lined with flowerpots toward the door of the house. Abigail was waiting for them behind a curtain of lace. She invited them in and gestured for them to take seats on a couch covered with a sheet. Abigail sat opposite them on a worn recliner. She spoke hesitantly in English, pronouncing the words with care.

"How is the child?"

"She's recovering," Zoe said simply. "We need to find her family."

Joseph took a digital camera out of his pocket and showed her the screen. "I have a picture of her. Perhaps it will help with the neighbors."

Abigail stood, wrapping a shawl around her. "Come," she said. She led them out the door and down the road to a shanty dwelling that barely resembled a house. "Agnes," she called out.

An old woman appeared. Her skin was heavily wrinkled and most of her teeth were missing. She and Abigail exchanged words in Nyanja, and Joseph showed her the photograph of the girl. Agnes shook her head. She looked at Zoe and asked about the "*muzungu*"—foreigner.

Joseph chuckled. "She says your hair looks like gold. She wants to know if it's real."

Zoe smiled. In a country where almost all women wore wigs or hair extensions, she had been asked that question countless times. "Tell her I was born with it," she said, leaning down so the old woman could touch it. "Does she know anything?"

He shook his head. "She's never seen the girl before."

Abigail bid Agnes goodbye and led them to the next house. A rotund woman was hanging clothes on a line. She smiled at Abigail but eyed Zoe with suspicion. The exchange between the women ended almost as quickly as it began.

"Her family was asleep at midnight," Joseph explained.

Zoe thrust her hands in her pockets and took in her surroundings, trying to imagine the street as the girl had seen it. *I bet it was almost deserted*, she thought. In the compounds night was the handmaiden of violence. Those who were wise stayed indoors.

In the next half-hour, they spoke to two widows, a young mother nursing an infant, and a group of adolescent boys lounging under a tree. All of them denied having seen the child, and a couple of the youths made wisecracks about the girl's appearance.

Zoe turned away, angered by their callousness. "Let's get out of here," she said.

Suddenly, a boy spoke up. "Hey, *muzungu*, why do you care what happens in Kanyama?"

She stared at him. "Where were you at midnight last night?"

He shrugged. "I was watching TV."

"So you were awake?"

He elbowed one of his friends. "Do *muzungus* watch TV in their sleep?"

The joke elicited a chorus of guffaws.

She ignored them. "Did you see anything unusual? A person, a car you didn't know?"

The boy glanced down the street, then crossed his arms. "I saw a truck."

She caught her breath. "What color was it?"

"Silver. Like this." He reached in his pocket and produced a foreign coin, no doubt the largesse of a tourist or an aid worker.

"Was it parked or driving?"

The boy flipped the coin in the air and caught it. "It was driving."

She traded a look with Joseph. "Will you show us where you saw it?"

The boy considered this. "What's it worth to you?"

She didn't blink. In Africa everything had a price. "Fifty pin. But only after you tell me everything you know."

The boy's eyes lit up. Fifty thousand kwacha was the equivalent of ten dollars. He stood up and his friends joined him, their banter gone. "*Bwera*," he said. "This way."

He led them down the lane to a house with unpainted block walls and crumbling mortar. A gaunt woman wearing a sweat-stained shirt and *chitenge* skirt sat outside the door, holding a carton of cheap Lusaka beer. The boy pushed aside the curtain and sat down on a torn couch in the cramped living room, displacing a half-naked child who jumped up to make space for him.

"The truck drove by," said the youth. "I was sitting here. I saw its lights."

"What kind of truck was it?" Joseph asked.

"I think it was a Lexus. It went that way."

"Was it an SUV?" Zoe asked, realizing the vehicle had been traveling toward Abigail's house.

The boy nodded.

"What direction was the girl walking last night?" she asked Abigail.

The old woman pointed down the street in the same direction.

Zoe turned to the boy again. "You said you saw its lights. Did you see brake lights?"

He shook his head.

"What about the driver? Did you catch a glimpse of him?"

He gave her a blank look. "I saw nothing else."

She examined his face and decided to believe him. Unzipping her backpack, she took out the money she had promised him. "What's your name?" she asked.

"Wisdom," he replied.

"Wisdom is the finest beauty of a person. It's a proverb. It applies as much to *muzungu* ladies and little girls with funny faces as it does to Zambian men. Think about it."

She handed the boy the kwacha.

"We need to find someone near Abigail who saw the truck," Joseph said.

She nodded. "I was thinking the same thing."

They retraced their steps, questioning the people they had met and a few others who appeared on the street. None had seen the silver SUV. Zoe checked her watch. It was nearing five o'clock. From the way Abigail was walking, it was clear she was growing tired. Zoe was about to suggest that they take her home when Joseph led them toward Agnes's shanty and knocked on the door. The old woman appeared, and Joseph spoke a few words in Nyanja. Agnes scratched her head and blinked a few times, then replied in the same language.

"What did she say?" Zoe inquired.

Joseph ignored her and asked Agnes another question. The old woman nodded and walked around the corner of her house, showing them an alleyway strewn with loose stones and litter. She gestured toward the road and spoke again in Nyanja.

"She heard a vehicle outside her house," Joseph said. "It stopped for a minute or two, and then it left. She didn't think about it until now."

Zoe felt a chill. "Did she hear any voices?"

He put the question to Agnes. "She didn't hear people," he interpreted, "but she heard something that reminded her of a drum." The woman spoke again, and Joseph clarified: "Two drumbeats. Perhaps they were car doors being shut?"

Zoe left the alley and stood in the lane, staring at Abigail's house thirty feet away. She imagined Kanyama huddled against the night, its narrow streets lit by porch bulbs and the glow of the moon. Then headlamps appeared in the darkness, followed by the flash of an upmarket SUV and the sound of an engine. The driver had pulled into the alleyway beside Agnes's house and left the girl. *It explains why no one has seen her before. She's not from around here.*

Her eyes wandered the scene and focused on a group of children playing a game in the dirt. They were the same children who had showered her with curiosity when she got out of Joseph's truck. She had an idea. She asked Joseph for the camera and walked toward the children. They looked up from their game. There were five of them, and they were seated around a circle drawn in the dirt. At the center of the circle was a pile of rocks.

"How do you play?" she asked the oldest boy while Joseph translated.

Instead of speaking, the boy gave a demonstration. He threw a ball into the air, grabbed a few rocks with his fingers, dragged them outside the perimeter of the circle, and caught the ball again with the same hand. The second time he threw the ball into the air, he moved all but one rock back into the circle, and placed the orphaned rock in a pile beside his knee.

"*Chiyanto*," Joseph said. "I played it when I was a kid."

Zoe held up the camera, showing it to the children. "Can I take a picture of you? I'd like to show it to my friends back home."

They began to talk excitedly. "Photo," said the oldest. "*Muzungu* lady take photo." They wrapped arms around each other, smiling and waiting for the camera to flash.

She laughed. "They've done this before." She captured the moment in the digital frame and showed the picture to the kids. The oldest boy asked her to take a photo of him alone, which she did. It was then that Zoe brought the camera down to the level of the youngest and displayed the picture of the girl. The children crowded around and stared at it without speaking.

"Have you seen her before?" Zoe asked. "She was on this street last night."

The oldest boy tilted his head and shrugged. He looked around, seeking confirmation. All of them shook their heads—except one. The child was no more than seven years old, and his eyes were too large for his head. He smiled at Zoe shyly. The oldest boy pushed him and said something in Nyanja, but the child continued to stare at Zoe.

"Girl," he said, nodding.

Zoe took a sharp breath. "Will you translate?" she asked Joseph.

"I'll talk to him," he replied.

He sat down beside the child and spoke to him softly. When the child responded, Joseph bobbed his head and smiled. Joseph's performance had the intended effect. The boy spoke without restraint, using his hands to emphasize his words.

Eventually, Joseph looked up at Zoe. "His name is Dominic. He lives there." He pointed at a green-painted house close by. "Last night he was in bed. But he had to use the latrine. He saw the truck when it stopped. He saw a man with the girl. The man got back into the truck and drove away. The girl walked toward Abigail's house. She looked like she was crying."

"Did he see the man's face?" Zoe asked excitedly.

Joseph shook his head. "It was dark. He said the man was tall—taller than his father."

"And the truck: did he see the license plate?"

Joseph translated the question into Nyanja. Dominic's eyes widened and he drew something in the dirt. Zoe stared at the sketch as it materialized. The boy had traced what looked like a misshapen rectangle with an X at the center.

"What is it?" she asked.

"I don't know," Joseph said. He talked with the child further, and Dominic drew a second rectangle to the right of the X. "He saw something like this beside the license plate. He doesn't remember anything about the plate itself."

She tried not to feel disheartened. Dominic was an extraordinary discovery, but his testimony couldn't be valued on the street. It had to withstand cross-examination.

Joseph pulled a pen and notebook from his jeans. He filled a page with notes and reproduced Dominic's sketch. Then he and Zoe followed the boy home and had a conversation with his father—a sturdy man with salt-and-pepper hair. Joseph punched his mobile number into the man's phone and patted the boy on the head.

"*Zikomo*," he said. "It is a good thing you have done."

The child smiled and scampered back to his *chi-yanto* game.

When the sun disappeared behind the corrugated metal horizon, they returned to the alley where Joseph had parked his truck. Zoe glanced at him and saw the disappointment in his eyes. It was obvious he had expected to learn more from an afternoon in Kanyama.

"This is a strange case," she remarked.

"Every case is different," he replied.

"Sure, but most of them follow a pattern. The perpetrator is a neighbor or family member. The crime happens near the victim's home. The suspect covers it up with threats and bribery. This is different in every respect."

"It's different in *some* respects," he corrected. "The girl could have known the perpetrator."

"Sure. But why go to the trouble of driving

into Kanyama at midnight? It's as if he wanted her to disappear."

Joseph nodded. "Or be violated again. The perfect cover for rape is another rape."

"My God," she exhaled, acknowledging the horrible symmetry of the idea.

"The question I have," he went on, "is how he snatched her so late at night?"

"We have to find her family."

He nodded. "They'll file a report eventually."

She was about to ask another question when she heard the squeaking of brakes behind her. She glanced over her shoulder and saw a pickup truck blocking the alleyway—a truck carrying young men in green T-shirts. The driver stepped out of the cab, and Zoe's heart lurched.

It was the hawkish boy in the green bandana.

The rest of his gang jumped out and surrounded them. Joseph made a move toward his truck, but a brawny kid stepped into his path. Zoe scanned the alley and saw that they were boxed in. The walls were too high to scale, and the neighbors were useless—they would never come to the aid of a stranger. *Why are they doing this?* she thought.

What do they want? Suddenly she knew. *They want me.*

"Let me handle this," Joseph said, stepping between Zoe and the bandana-clad leader. He spoke a string of heated words in Nyanja, but the young man just smirked, eyeing Zoe.

"What your name, *muzungu*?" he asked in heavily accented English.

"Don't talk to him," Joseph commanded her. He gave the boy a piercing look. "I'm a police officer. You touch us and I'll throw you all in jail."

The gang leader laughed as if Joseph had made a joke. "In Kanyama, police sleep. You sleep with *muzungu*, police?"

Zoe heard sniggering and glanced around. The gang had closed ranks. A wave of dread surged through her and spawned an equal but opposite wave of anger. She was certain Joseph was unarmed; Zambian police officers were rarely issued firearms. She searched the ground for a weapon but saw only scattered bricks ten feet away.

"Back off," Joseph said darkly. "You don't want to make an enemy of me."

The gang leader looked annoyed. "What you

do, police? You fight for *muzungu*? Rupiah Banda fight for *muzungus*." He glanced around at his companions. "Police is friend of MMD."

The allegation had its intended effect: the gang members began to grumble and curse. Emboldened, the gang leader tried to shove Joseph out of the way, but Joseph backhanded him across the face. The gang leader cried out and threw a wild punch, which Joseph easily ducked. He countered with a swift jab into the kid's stomach. The gang leader doubled over, and Joseph pivoted on his feet, searching for another target. He managed to land two more punches before three boys took him down.

Zoe screamed as strong hands grabbed her from both sides. She fought back instinctively, torquing her body to escape their grasp and lashing out with her feet. She drove her heel into the jaw of a reed-thin young man, and he collapsed in a heap. She kicked a stocky boy in the stomach and hit him in the side of the head with her backpack. A third gang member wrapped her in a bear hug, and she kneed him in the groin and crushed his nose with her palm.

But she was no match for a joint attack.

Two boys came at her from behind, lifting her off her feet. She kicked violently, screaming at the top of her lungs, as they pushed her into the dirt and held her down. She felt their rough hands yanking at her shirt, at her jeans. Time seemed to fragment like shattered glass. *No! Please, God, no!* Apparitions danced around her in the dusk. One of the boys sat on her thighs and another straddled her back. She began to lose touch with reality. *This can't be happening! Not again!*

Suddenly, she heard a voice rise above the din. "Get away from her!" Joseph screamed. "Get back or I'll *shoot!*"

The weight on her thighs relented, as did the pressure on her back. She blinked, squinting through the dust clouding her contact lenses. Joseph was standing over a heap of bodies wielding an AK-47 rifle. At the sight of the roving barrel, the gang members who were still on their feet stepped back, and one of them dropped Zoe's backpack. Joseph trained the gun on their leader.

"I told you not to make an enemy of me," he hissed.

In an instant, fear replaced the gang leader's bravado, and he ran to the pickup truck. His compatriots followed, the injured stumbling behind the able-bodied. As soon as the gang leader keyed the ignition, he floored the accelerator and sped off down the lane, nearly throwing two of his companions out of the flatbed.

When they were gone, Zoe stood slowly, her whole body trembling. She leaned against Joseph's truck, feeling a relief so overwhelming it found no expression in her conscious thoughts. She watched Joseph as he fought to catch his breath. His clothes were coated with dirt, and he had a large scratch on his neck. At last she managed to speak.

"I didn't know you had a gun."

"I keep it in the truck," he growled. "My brother was in the army."

Zoe shook her head, struggling not to think about how close she had come to being raped. Then it struck her: the girl at the hospital had walked by this alley less than twenty-four hours ago. A man driving a silver SUV had abducted her, raped her, and abandoned her to the night. No one had come to her rescue. Zoe pictured her sleeping in her hospital bed, Dr. Chulu's monkey beside her, and heard the doctor's words: *"Now she has you."*

Joseph picked up Zoe's backpack and dusted it off. "Where'd you learn to fight like that?" he asked, handing her the bag.

She let out a small laugh and felt some of the tension release. "I took self-defense classes in high school. I have a brown belt in tae kwon do."

He raised an eyebrow and managed a half-smile.

She opened the passenger door of the truck and climbed in slowly. "Can we stop by the hospital on the way back?" she asked when he joined her in the cab.

He gave her a baffled look. "Why?"

"The girl," she replied. "I'd like to see her again."

Chapter 3

On Monday morning, the five members of the CILA response team—Zoe, Joseph, Mariam, Sarge, and Niza—took seats in the conference room alongside Mwila, the director of rehabilitation. It was a few minutes after nine, and the all-staff meeting had just wrapped up. The shades were drawn against the sun, but light filtered in and burnished the scarred wooden table in front of them.

"Before we talk about the case," Mariam began, looking at Zoe, "I want to say how relieved I am—how relieved we *all* are—that nothing worse happened to you yesterday."

"I have Joseph to thank," Zoe said, glancing at him. The shock of the incident was still raw, but she was determined not to let it affect her.

Mariam nodded. "I'm going to mention it to the Deputy Commissioner."

"I'd rather you wait until I catch the perpetrators," Joseph said.

"You're going after them?" Zoe was surprised.

"When the time is right."

Mariam smiled. "On to business. There's a lot we don't know about what happened to this girl, but here is what we do know. Sometime before midnight on Saturday she was raped by an unknown assailant. Around midnight, he transported her to a remote lane in Kanyama and left her there. The child has Down syndrome and hasn't spoken since the incident. With counseling, she might be able to help us, but not yet. We have an eyewitness who saw the man abandon her. The only information we have at present is that the man is tall and was driving a silver SUV with something like this near the license plate."

Mariam held up a piece of paper showing a replica of Dominic's sketch.

"Reminds me of a railroad crossing sign in the U.S.," said Niza, leaning forward.

"Perhaps it's a political sticker," Sarge offered.

Joseph spoke up: "I called headquarters, but we haven't received a missing-person report matching the child. Even if a report was filed, it could take days to get entered into the system."

"Until we find her family," Mariam said, "we need to arrange for her care."

Mwila nodded. "I talked to Social Welfare about sending her to St. Francis. I don't trust anyone else to handle kids with special needs. I also contacted Dr. Mbao at the University of Zambia. I haven't worked with her before, but Joy Herald recommended her highly. With a referral from Dr. Chulu, she'll come to St. Francis for the exam."

"From a legal standpoint," Sarge said, "we can't bring a case until we have a suspect and some corroborative evidence. In addition, there is the question of the child's age. She looks a lot younger than sixteen, but that won't be enough for the magistrate."

"The family will tell us when she was born," Zoe said. "The real problem is corroboration. Even if we find a suspect, we need something linking him to the rape itself, not just to the girl. We need an eyewitness to the act. Or we need DNA."

"As always, a nice thought," Niza replied. "But this is Zambia. There's no lab and no money for it. So says the Ministry of Justice."

Zoe clenched her teeth. Niza was a first-rate lawyer, but she was also a cynic.

"There's a lab in Johannesburg," Zoe said. "And we have the money even if the government claims it doesn't. Once we have a suspect, all we'll need is a magistrate to order a blood sample and a profile. They do it all the time in paternity cases."

Mariam affirmed Zoe's intuition. "It's true. We have the evidence from the hospital. This could be the case to press for DNA."

"We have a long way to go before we can start thinking about that," Sarge said. "We need the family, we need a suspect in custody, and we need the support of the Director of Public Prosecution. In that order."

Mariam nodded. "Let's meet again on Wednesday. Perhaps Joseph will know more."

Zoe left the table and navigated the maze of corridors to her desk. A converted colonial-era bungalow, the CILA office had a bifurcated layout. The reception and rehabilitation staff occupied the front of the house, and the executive and legal staff occupied the back. Zoe's desk was situated in the corner of a sunlit space cluttered with legal files, bound registers of Zambian and British law, and scattered pages of case notes—the home of the legal department.

She took her seat and stared at her laptop. She had fifteen minutes to kill before Mwila left for the hospital. She thought of polishing the research memo she had been writing for Sarge but checked her email instead. The first message was from her brother, Trevor. The time stamp read 8:02 a.m.— 2:02 a.m. D.C. time. Trevor was an attorney with the K Street law firm representing A Brighter Tomorrow—the private political funding organization, or SuperPAC, supporting Jack Fleming's campaign. He never seemed to sleep.

Hey, sis, missing you. In case you didn't catch it on the Internet, Dad's coming your way in a few days. I don't expect you to care, but I thought you should know. Off to bed for a few hours at least. Ciao!

Below the message Trevor had copied a Web link to a story in the *Washington Post*. It read like a press release:

On Wednesday, after campaign stops in North Carolina and Virginia, Senator Jack Fleming, the current frontrunner in the presidential primary race, will travel to Africa with Senator Lindsey O'Toole to examine U.S. foreign assistance programs in the Democratic Republic of the Congo, Zambia, and Ethiopia. The Senators will also meet with embassy and government officials to discuss issues relating to the war on terror. A spokesperson for Senator Fleming reiterated the Senator's unwavering campaign commitment to fiscal responsibility. Due to security concerns, the full itinerary will not be released in advance.

* * *

Zoe tried to steady her breathing. A trip to the Congo and Ethiopia she could understand. But Zambia? He had to be coming for her. She scanned the remainder of her inbox. Sure enough, it was there— a message from her father. She glanced around the office, worried that someone might discover her secret. Other than Mariam and a few CILA executives in London, no one knew that she was Jack Fleming's daughter. After a moment, she realized how absurd she was being. No one was paying any attention to her. She steadied herself and opened the email.

Zoe, my dear, I hope this finds you well. I'm planning a last-minute trip to the continent and will be in Lusaka on Friday. Would you care to meet for dinner? I was thinking the other day how long it has been since we spent time together, just the two of us. What do you say?

Zoe read the message twice and then closed the mail application. Grabbing her backpack, she walked to the nearest exit, desperate for fresh air. She found a place in the sun beneath the red blooms of a lemon bottlebrush tree and closed her eyes.

The last time she had been alone with her father

was at her Yale Law School graduation. It had not gone well. After dinner at the Union League Café, they had taken a stroll across New Haven Green, and Trevor and Sylvia, her father's second wife, had lagged behind, locked in a discussion about social media in political campaigns. Zoe had tried to be civil toward her father, but the ground of their relationship was littered with landmines and he had stepped on one.

"Writing for the *Yale Law Journal*," he had said, "graduating near the top of your class, I'm proud of you, Zoe."

Pulling her sweater around her shoulders, she had glanced at him in the lamplight, daring to hope that his praise would be unadulterated. She was soon disappointed.

"You know, I spoke to Judge Anders," he went on. "One of his clerks backed out for health reasons and he's looking for a replacement. He'd love to have you."

The Honorable Jeremiah Anders was the Chief Judge of the Second Circuit Court of Appeals and one of the most respected jurists in the United States. Many considered him the next Supreme

Court nominee. Zoe, however, had already made up her mind. Her heart was in Africa.

"I'm going to Johannesburg," she said. "I gave Judge van der Merwe my word."

"In a year you could be clerking for the Supreme Court," he replied, as if he hadn't heard her. "After that, you can have your pick of any legal job in the world."

"It's an honor someone else can have. Judge van der Merwe is an international expert on human rights. He's never taken an American clerk before."

The Senator sighed in exasperation. "All doors open to you and you pick the Constitutional Court of South Africa. This country has never been big enough for you."

"I love America," she disagreed, stopping in front of Center Church, its great spire cloaked in night. "I just don't like being confined to it."

Zoe opened her eyes and saw Mwila standing in front of her, her face darkened by concern.

"Are you all right?" Mwila asked. "You were standing so still."

Zoe blinked, momentarily trapped by the past. She took a breath. "Are you ready?"

Mwila gestured toward a Toyota Prado idling in the driveway. "Maurice is waiting."

They climbed into the SUV, and the guard opened the steel gate. Maurice pulled out onto the street and accelerated to make the light at Church and Independence. The trip to the pediatric center was brief. When they approached the lobby doors, Zoe saw Joy Herald standing beside a pair of African women with notebooks—the Social Welfare contingent.

"We've taken care of the formalities," Joy said, greeting Zoe and Mwila, "but the girl has been a bit of a challenge this morning. I meant to bring my iPod, but one of my kids must have taken it out of my purse. I hope you have yours."

"I made her a mix this morning," Zoe said, following Joy into the outpatient center.

She heard the child before she saw her. The high-pitched sound—somewhere between a warble and a bleat—sliced through her. When she entered the admissions ward, she saw the girl rocking violently in her bed, a trio of nurses attempting to quiet her down.

"Where is Dr. Chulu?" Zoe asked. *He promised this wouldn't happen.*

"He's not on rotation this morning," Joy replied, picking up her pace. She quickly took charge of the nurses. "Give us a little space, please," she said.

When they stepped back, Zoe took out an iPod and put the headphones on the girl's ears. She selected the new playlist and stood back, watching as the music performed a feat that seemed almost magical. Like a lamp lit on a dark night, the soulful acoustic notes of John Denver's "Leaving on a Jet Plane" chased away the girl's turmoil. She placed her hands on the headphones, as if willing the song not to end.

Joy uncovered the girl's legs and swung them over the edge of the mattress. "Help me lift her," she said to Zoe.

The limpness of the girl's frame made her ungainly to carry, but together Joy and Zoe scooped her up and placed her feet solidly on the ground. When the girl stood on her own, she glanced around the room and blinked, looking disoriented. Joy knelt down in front of her and removed the headphones briefly.

"It's time to go now," she said in a soft voice. "I need you to walk with us."

Joy stood again and took the girl's hand, tugging her toward the door. The girl hesitated a moment longer and then followed in Joy's wake, clutching Dr. Chulu's monkey in her free hand. Her gait was slow and she walked with a slight limp, favoring her right leg. Zoe strolled beside her, holding the iPod and keeping the cable from tangling.

Eventually, they emerged into the sunshine. The Prado was waiting for them at the curb. Maurice opened the back door, and Joy and Zoe helped the girl onto the vinyl bench.

"I'll ride with you," Joy said. She slid in beside the girl, and Zoe climbed in after her.

The girl seemed to startle when the vehicle began to move. She looked around and let out a low moan. Joy took her hand again and squeezed. "I bet all of this is unfamiliar to her," Joy said. "Her family probably didn't take her outside much."

When Zoe frowned, Joy explained herself. "It's the stigma. Zambians think children with intellectual disabilities are cursed, so parents keep them locked up inside to avoid being judged. Sometimes the neighbors don't even know they're there."

★ ★ ★

The St. Francis Home for Children was located on a rocky plateau on the outskirts of Lusaka near the international airport. Every time she visited, Zoe was struck by the contrast between the arid expanse surrounding the home and the lushness of the property itself. The drive was rimmed with bougainvillea, and at its center was the largest poinsettia tree she had ever seen.

Maurice parked the Prado at the entrance, and the ladies from Social Welfare pulled in behind them. A gray-haired nun in a green and white habit stood in front of the low-slung building. She smiled when she saw Zoe.

"Sister Anica," Zoe said, taking the nun's hand.

"I'm so happy to see you again," the nun replied in a soft Slavic accent.

They turned toward the Prado and watched Joy help the girl out. Zoe could hear the faint strains of "Fields of Gold" emanating from her headphones. Joy knelt in front of the girl and uncovered her ears, placing the headphones and iPod in the girl's pocket.

"We're here," she said. "You're going to like

this place." Taking the girl's hand, she stood again and greeted Sister Anica. "She hasn't spoken yet, but she's quite fond of music."

The nun smiled at the girl and nodded to the ladies from Social Welfare. "Come, this way," she said, gesturing toward a pair of rosewood doors standing open to admit the breeze.

They followed Sister Anica down a hallway decorated with the drawings of children to a courtyard dominated by playground equipment and a majestic acacia thorn tree. There, Sister Anica introduced Zoe to a diminutive young nun with tropical blue eyes.

"Sister Irina will take you from here," she said. "The rest of us have paperwork to finish."

After Sister Anica departed with Joy and the social workers, Sister Irina knelt down before the girl. "I am Irina," she said. "Can I be your friend?" The girl hung her head shyly, and the nun smiled. "That's okay. We can talk about it later."

She led them down a breezeway to a brightly painted room with an array of toys. Two children with Down syndrome sat by the wall, playing with dolls. An older child with cerebral palsy sat in a special chair by the window, listening to a story read by an elderly nun.

Zoe saw an electric piano on the floor beside a stuffed bear. She found the power switch and hit one of the keys. The piano began to play "Fur Elise." A smile blossomed slowly on the girl's face, and she made a sound reminiscent of air being released from a balloon. She touched one of the keys, then another. While she was occupied, Sister Irina took Zoe aside.

"This is very unusual for us," she said. "All our children are orphans. If she has a family, we don't want her to get too attached."

"We're doing our best to locate them," Zoe assured her.

The nun looked toward the acacia tree, its limbs framed by the cobalt sky. "The things men do to children. Our rule teaches us to be merciful. But this . . . I tremble to say it, but I feel wrath. You must find the man who did this and put him in prison."

Zoe met her eyes. "We'll get him," she promised.

* * *

After returning to the CILA office, Zoe spent the afternoon pretending to research a point of British evidentiary law on which the Zambian courts had yet to rule. In fact she was thoroughly preoccupied by her father's email. She was trapped and she knew it. She could neither avoid a response nor deny his request—to do so would dissolve the goodwill she had succeeded in rebuilding when he and Sylvia had met her for dinner in South Africa at the end of her clerkship.

She sat by the window, pondering the contradictions in their relationship. Eleven years ago he had betrayed her with a kiss and she had run from him, until she realized she was a kite on a string, beholden to him still. Her charitable trust—a creation of her mother's will—was not yet hers, and the man who managed it was her father's puppet. Atticus Spelling, an octogenarian curmudgeon in New York, had vetoed many of her donations over the years, citing concerns about the fiscal discipline of the charities she favored. If not for her father's intervention, Spelling would have withheld funding from half a dozen small nonprofits doing life-saving work in southern Africa, including Special

Child Advocates and St. Francis. Zoe hated the subterfuge, but she was bound to it until her thirtieth birthday.

When five o'clock came, she finally sent an email accepting her father's invitation. Then she left the office and climbed into her Land Rover, sitting for a moment before starting the engine. She watched the lavender jacaranda blooms dance in the wind and tried not to think about Friday night. After a while, she started the SUV and pulled into traffic, taking Independence Avenue toward Kabulonga.

When she arrived at her apartment complex, she greeted the guard at the gate and parked beside a hedge of bird of paradise. Entering her apartment, she threw her backpack on the couch and went to her bedroom to change into her swimsuit. The air was cool in the falling light, and the pool would be frigid, but she didn't care. She had grown up swimming in the North Atlantic.

The gardens were deserted when she arrived. The pool had an emerald tint and its surface was dotted with wind-blown jacaranda blossoms. She set her iPhone on a lounge chair and took off her T-shirt and shorts. Putting on her goggles, she entered the water with a shallow dive. The cold enveloped her, hammering her nerves and stealing her breath, but she turned discomfort into speed, churning the water with a power that had qualified her to compete in the NCAA swim championships at Stanford.

After twenty laps, she pulled herself out and sat on the edge, drinking in the last golden drops of sunlight. A memory came to her from when she was fourteen: her mother on the beach at the Vineyard house, a blue and white scarf trailing in the stiff wind. Storm clouds blowing in from the south, turning the surface of Eel Pond into slate. Emerging from the water into the warm embrace of a towel. Running toward the house as the raindrops began to fall. Lightning searing the sky, thunder rumbling overhead. And her mother's laughter, like grace notes in the chorus. It was Catherine's last day on the Vineyard before she left for Somalia.

When the pool fell into shadow, Zoe dried herself off and walked back to her apartment, thinking about dinner. Her iPhone rang just inside the front door. It was Joseph.

"Mariam said to call you," he began. "A woman in Kabwata filed a report about a missing girl with mental problems. She identified herself as a friend of the girl's mother."

Zoe immediately forgot her hunger. "Are you going to talk to her?"

"I'm five minutes from your apartment."

"I'll meet you outside the gate."

The address given by the Kabwata police was on Chilimbulu Road, not far from East Point—a trendy discotheque known for turning up-and-coming Zambian bands into sensations. They parked outside a multi-story complex of flats and Joseph led Zoe to a ground-floor apartment. The door was slightly ajar, giving them a glimpse of the living area. A man about Zoe's age was lounging on a couch watching television, while two girls—one adolescent, one younger—and a woman in *chitenge* tended the stove in the kitchen. The air was thick with the aroma of cooking vegetables and *nshima*—Zambian maize.

The man came to the door when Joseph knocked. He glanced at Joseph and looked at Zoe. She put her thumbs in the pockets of her jeans and stared back at him.

"I'm Officer Kabuta," Joseph said in English. "I'm looking for Priscilla Kuwema."

"What do you want?" the man asked in a thick Bemba accent.

"I need to speak with her," Joseph replied.

"And the *muzungu*?"

"She's with me."

The man shrugged and called out to the woman before returning to the couch. The woman frowned and said something to the girls. Then she walked to the door, her face a mask.

"Are you Priscilla Kuwema?" Joseph asked.

The woman nodded slowly.

"You filed a missing-person report at the Kabwata Police Post?"

"Yes."

Joseph took out his camera and displayed the image of the girl. The woman stared at the photo, then turned her gaze to the floor. "Where is she?" she asked, looking ashamed.

"In a safe place."

"What happened to her?"

"Some people found her in Kanyama two nights ago."

The woman glanced at the man on the couch.

"Your husband?" Joseph asked.

"No, no," she said, flustered. "My husband is in Kitwe. He works the mines."

Joseph raised his eyebrows. "I need to ask you some questions. Can we sit down?"

The woman hesitated before nodding. She exchanged a few words with the man, her tone apologetic. The man reacted angrily, delivering her a sharp-tongued rebuke. The woman hung her head, and her reply sounded to Zoe like a plea. The man glared at her and stomped out of the apartment, bumping Zoe's shoulder.

"I'm sorry." The woman looked shaken. "He's my . . . cousin. He thinks he lives here."

She took a deep breath and gestured toward the couch, offering them water or beer.

"A Mosi would be nice," Joseph said. "I'll try to be brief."

"Water," Zoe said when the woman looked at her.

A minute later, she returned with a beer and a bottle of water, both chilled. She sat on the couch, folded her hands in her lap, and began to speak.

"I walked with my . . . cousin to the market.

Bright, my eldest, has a boyfriend who lives in the building. He was here with her. Gift, my youngest, was also here. Kuyeya—that is her name, this girl—was in the back room. Bright says she and her boyfriend were only gone a minute. I don't know if I believe them. They disappear sometimes. Gift told me she went down the street to play. I don't know why she didn't take Kuyeya. She usually does." The woman shrugged. "The door was open when I came home. Kuyeya must have left."

"What time was that?" Joseph asked.

"About nineteen hundred hours. It was after dinner."

"And after dark," Zoe clarified, scanning the apartment with her eyes. Beyond the living room and kitchen, she saw a hallway with three doors, all closed.

The woman nodded. "None of the neighbors saw her."

"Why does Kuyeya live with you?" Zoe asked.

The woman looked away. "Her mother died two years ago. She has no other family."

Zoe traded a glance with Joseph, concealing her frustration. "Where is her father?"

The woman shrugged. "I don't know."

"Kuyeya has light skin."

"So did Bella—Kuyeya's mother."

"How did Bella die?" Zoe inquired.

The woman fidgeted with her hands. "*Va banthu*. The illness came and never went away. I don't know." She glanced toward the kitchen. "Excuse me," she said, leaving to stir the *nshima*.

"She knows something she's not saying," Zoe whispered to Joseph.

"Probably a lot of things," he replied, "but we're getting off track. We're not here to talk about the girl's mother."

He waited until the woman sat down again and then took over the interview. "What did you do when you found out Kuyeya was gone?"

The woman blinked. "I talked to my daughters. I talked to people in the building."

"Did you look for her on the street?"

She nodded. "Of course."

"Where might she have been going?"

The woman shook her head. "Kuyeya is not like normal children. I don't understand her."

"Does she have friends down the street?"

"No. She usually stays in the back room."

"Your cousin," Zoe said, "does *he* have friends nearby?"

The woman narrowed her eyes. "He doesn't know anything."

By that you mean exactly the opposite. "What does he do for a living?"

"The better question," Joseph interjected, "is what sort of car does he drive?"

"He drives a jeep," the woman said. "A red Toyota."

"Do you know anyone who owns a silver SUV?"

The woman thought about this. "I don't think so."

At this point Joseph broke the news. "Kuyeya was raped. Do you have any idea who might have done it?"

The woman looked genuinely shocked. She stumbled over her words. "No, I . . . She never . . . How is she?"

"She's recovering."

The older of the woman's daughters—Bright—approached shyly and spoke to her mother in Nyanja. She glanced at Joseph and Zoe and then returned to the kitchen.

"Would you like to join us for dinner?" the woman asked.

"No," Joseph replied. "Will you be home tomorrow afternoon?"

She nodded.

"I'll come back then."

"She's lying about her cousin," Zoe said as soon as they were seated in Joseph's truck. She studied his face in the darkness, wondering whether he would give her a window into his thoughts.

"She *is* lying about the cousin," he said, putting the truck in gear and pulling onto Chilimbulu Road. "But not because he had anything to do with the rape. He's probably a live-in boyfriend. I'd guess she's also lying about her husband. I doubt she has one. She had no ring on her finger or pictures of a man around."

"How do you know the cousin wasn't involved?"

"I didn't tell her about the rape until the end of the conversation. She had no reason to lie when she said he went with her to the market. She also had no reason to lie about his vehicle. As it happens,

I saw a red jeep in the lot when we pulled in. It's more likely that the girl—Kuyeya—wandered out on the street like the woman said."

Zoe pursed her lips. "So we're no closer to a suspect than we were before."

Joseph glanced at her. "We'll find out more tomorrow."

"Can I come with you?" she asked eagerly.

He waited a beat before responding. "You have good instincts. And I need to talk to the neighbors. Perhaps you can ask Ms. Kuwema about the girl's mother."

"I thought she wasn't relevant," Zoe retorted with a grin.

He shrugged. "It would give you something to do."

"Other than bothering you?"

"Precisely."

Chapter 4

On Tuesday, Zoe left for work an hour early and took a circuitous route through Libala and Kabwata, following a hunch. She had slept poorly the night before, beset by dreams—half remembered, half imagined—of the young man in the bandana and his gang of hoodlums and of Priscilla Kuwema and the girl who had no family. When she woke again, she put the incident in Kanyama out of her mind and concentrated on the woman and the child. Something about the woman's demeanor, about the man she had called her cousin and the back room where Kuyeya stayed, whispered of secrets buried just below the surface.

She drove slowly down Chilimbulu Road and pulled to the shoulder. At seven thirty in the morning, the street was swarming with foot traffic—men sporting talktime dispensers, adolescent boys pushing carts overloaded with crates, children dressed in school uniforms heading to class, mothers in *chitenge* with infants strapped to their backs. A few hawkers tried to solicit her, but she ignored them, focusing on the apartment building where Priscilla Kuwema lived. She didn't know what she was looking for, but she had a feeling that morning might tell a different tale from evening.

A red jeep sat empty at the edge of the parking lot. She stored its license-plate number in her iPhone and began taking pictures. The four-story edifice was constructed of reinforced concrete with an open-air stairwell and balconies barely large enough to accommodate a clothesline. The windows were louvered and covered with grates, but Zoe could see movement behind a number of them. At the base of the stairwell, a group of men stood smoking.

After a minute, a young woman carrying a basket on her shoulder approached the men. One of the men gave her some money, and the girl handed him an oil-stained bag from her basket. *Fritas*, Zoe guessed. The girl then knocked on Priscilla Kuwema's door. Zoe switched from photo to video and maxed out the zoom, hoping the cousin would answer the door. Instead, a different man appeared, wearing rumpled trousers and a tank top. He squinted at the girl, scratching the stubble on his cheeks. A moment later, Priscilla Kuwema stood in the doorframe, dressed in a miniskirt and a tight-fitting shirt. She gave the girl a wad of bills, took six bags, and closed the door.

Zoe replayed the footage she had captured. The way the man was dressed suggested he had spent the night in the apartment. Was he sleeping with Priscilla Kuwema? If so, who was the cousin? And why had the man not paid for the *fritas*?

Fifteen minutes later, the man left the apartment looking more presentable. He climbed into a delivery truck and drove off. Before long the door opened again and the cousin appeared, a pretty girl in tow. He was dressed in a pink Oxford shirt and jeans, and the girl was heavily made-up and clad in a low-cut blouse and high heels. They kissed beside the red jeep. Then the man left and the girl flirted with the chain-smokers, trading smiles for *fritas*.

When a third man—older than the others—left the apartment with yet another scantily clad woman, Zoe knew that the riddle of Priscilla Kuwema had only two solutions: either she lived with roommates who had regular amorous visitors, or she was a *mahule*—a prostitute.

Zoe checked her watch. It was after eight. She had five minutes before she had to head to the office. She looked down the street and saw the *fritas* vendor soliciting a man on a motorcycle. She locked the Land Rover and waded into the sea of pedestrians. When the motorcyclist left, she approached the girl, money in hand.

"*Muli bwange,*" she said.

The girl smiled with her eyes. "*Ndili bwino. Kaya inu?*"

"*Ndili bwino,*" Zoe said. "Do you speak English?"

"Some."

"For fifty pin, I want a bag of your *fritas*, and I want to ask you a few questions."

"Okay," the girl said.

"Do you know Priscilla Kuwema?"

When the girl looked confused, Zoe pointed at the woman's apartment.

A shadow crossed the girl's face. She glanced down the street. "She not use that name."

Zoe remained impassive. "What name does she use?"

"Doris."

"Why doesn't she use her real name?"

The girl took a deep breath. "I don't know."

Zoe slid the money into her pocket. "If we are going to do business, I need the truth."

The girl hesitated. "The men," she said. "They call her Doris."

"Where is her husband?"

The girl studied the ground. "She not have husband."

"Who are the men?"

The girl looked scared. She handed Zoe a bag of *fritas*. "They come from the bars."

"Is Doris a *mahule*?"

The girl nodded. "Now I go. Please."

Zoe paid the girl and returned to the Land

Rover, her mind churning with possibilities. Had Kuyeya's mother also been a prostitute? Had she lived at the apartment with Priscilla Kuwema— Doris? How many of Doris's customers had seen Kuyeya? Could one of them be a pedophile? On the other hand, if Doris was a *mahule*, then why did she move so quickly to report Kuyeya's absence to the police? Joseph was right and wrong at the same time. Doris knew nothing of the rape, but Kuyeya's mother was hardly immaterial to the investigation.

Zoe arrived at the CILA office a few minutes before the all-staff meeting. She looked around for Joseph but didn't see him. She muddled through the meeting and the morning, conscious of her growing pile of work but consumed by the puzzle of Kuyeya's case. At noon Sarge asked for an update on her research into the laws of Britain. She extemporized on the fly, but even her near-perfect recall of case authorities didn't make up for her lack of progress.

Sarge raised an eyebrow. "I need something by the end of the day."

"I'll have it to you by four o'clock," she promised.

She sat down at her laptop and engaged her legal brain. She printed the report five minutes before four and set it on Sarge's desk, pointing at her watch. Sarge was on the phone, but he acknowledged her with a nod. She got a glass of water from the kitchen and returned to her desk, listening to him flip through the pages. She felt her iPhone vibrate in her pocket.

"It's Joseph," she told him. "I'm going to take it outside."

"Fine, fine," he said distractedly. "This is good . . ."

She took the call beside a trellis of flowering creepers.

"I'm almost at the office," Joseph said. "Are you free?"

"Perfect timing," she replied, walking to the gate. She crossed the road and climbed into his truck. "I have a surprise for you."

He peered over the rim of his sunglasses. "What would that be?"

"A little video I took this morning before work." She took out her iPhone and played him the footage. "The woman goes by the working name Doris. The men come from the bars. I spoke to a vendor of *fritas* on the street. Doris is her best customer."

"This changes things," Joseph said. "The perpetrator could be a client."

She nodded. "Doris has some explaining to do."

He put the truck in gear and entered the flow of traffic on Church Road. "You've made yourself useful. Well done."

"One other thing," she said, playing her advantage. "I'd like to talk to her alone."

Joseph navigated the double roundabout by the Zambia Supreme Court and sped east toward Nationalist Road. Zoe waited, allowing him to make the decision on his own.

"I suppose she might find it easier to talk to a woman," he said. Then he pointed at her phone. "Can you record the conversation?"

"With or without her consent?"

He laughed. "I don't want to make you a witness. I just want to hear what she says."

Ten minutes later, Joseph knocked on Doris's door. When she didn't answer, he knocked again, this time more insistently. An old woman peered down at them from a balcony on the third floor but withdrew as soon as Zoe noticed her. Joseph tapped his foot, growing impatient. Just then, Zoe saw two school-aged children—a boy and a girl—walking toward the stairwell.

"Excuse me," Zoe said to them, "do you know if Doris is home?"

The boy giggled. He turned to the girl and spoke a string of words in Nyanja.

"What's he saying?" Zoe asked Joseph.

"They're talking about an animal—what do you call it?—a genet. It hunts at night and sleeps during the day." He patted the boy on the head. "*Zikomo*," he said, and the children ran chattering toward the stairs.

They knocked again on Doris's door. After a while they heard the sound of shuffling feet, then the door opened a crack, revealing the face of Bright. The girl was dressed in pajama pants and a T-shirt. She stared at them fearfully. Joseph exchanged a few words with her in Nyanja.

"Her mother is taking a bath," he said to Zoe. "Why don't you wait for her? I'm going to walk around and ask some questions."

"*Muli bwange?*" Zoe said when Bright opened the door.

"I'm okay," the girl replied, gesturing toward the couch. "Wait here."

As soon as she disappeared, Zoe took a seat and studied the room around her. The furnishings were simple and clean. The couch had a matching chair. The floor was covered with woven rugs, and there were curtains on the windows. Beside the door was a bookshelf adorned with half-melted candles and carvings of game animals. The walls, however, were bare, save for an ebony ceremonial mask that hung over the door.

Eventually, Doris appeared and greeted Zoe with a plastic smile. Clad in a conservative *chitenge* gown, she barely resembled the seductress who had purchased six bags of *fritas* that morning. "Where is the officer?" she asked.

"He's outside talking to the neighbors. I wanted to speak with you alone."

Doris tilted her head. "Would you like tea?"

"Please," Zoe said.

Doris went to the stove and filled a kettle with water. "You are American?"

"I'm from New York," Zoe replied.

Zoe frowned. An *nganga* was a traditional healer. "Why didn't she go to a clinic?"

"She trusted the *ngangas*. They helped us with STDs."

"Did the men Bella brought here ever . . . touch Kuyeya?"

Doris looked horrified. "No. The child was not available."

Zoe took a breath. "We think her rapist may have been a client of yours or Bella's. Can you think of any man who showed an interest in her?"

Doris shook her head. "Kuyeya was like a shadow. A spirit. When Bella put her in the bathroom, she gave her medicine to sleep. The men left her alone."

Zoe sat back against the couch. Doris's lifestyle and Bella's history were interesting but irrelevant without a connection to a suspect. Then an idea came to her. It was bizarre, really—on the far side of remote. But she had no other cards to play.

"Did you ever keep a record of your clients? Did Bella?"

Doris narrowed her eyes and vanished into the hallway, returning moments later with a spiral-bound notebook. "Bella liked to write," she said, handing the book to Zoe. "I am not good at reading, but I kept it. Other than Kuyeya, it was her most precious possession."

Zoe studied the notebook. Its cover was worn, its pages dog-eared. On the inside cover, Bella had written in English: "Volume 3: April 2004 –"

"When did Bella die?" she asked Doris quietly.

"The winter of 2009. July, I think."

Zoe pointed at the inside cover. "This says 'Volume 3.' Are there other notebooks?"

"That's the only one I have seen."

"*Zikomo*," Zoe said. "I'm sorry to ask such difficult questions."

"Life is difficult," Doris replied. "Is the child well?"

"She's in good hands."

Doris nodded gratefully. "I owe Bella a debt I can never repay."

"What do you mean?"

"Ask her," Doris said, gesturing at the book. "I think she will tell you."

★ ★ ★

When Zoe emerged from the apartment, the sun hung low and molten above the horizon, and traffic on Chilimbulu Road was at a near standstill. She glanced at her watch and searched the crowded roadway for Joseph. It was almost 5:30 p.m. He was nowhere to be seen.

She leaned against the fender of his truck, waiting. She saw a group of boys knocking a soccer ball around. One of them gave the ball a swift kick—too swift for the intended recipient—and the ball rolled in Zoe's direction. She scooped it up and walked toward them, intending to ask about Joseph, when she saw him striding toward her, holding a stuffed doll and a pair of wire-framed eyeglasses.

"Where did you find those?" she asked, tossing the ball back to the boys.

"I could ask you the same thing," he said, eyeing the notebook in her hands.

"I asked first."

He grinned. "I'll show you."

She followed him down the road. When traffic began to move again, she caught sight of a pickup truck carrying a group of young Zambians in green T-shirts. She grabbed Joseph's arm, looking for the bandana-clad gang leader. It took her a second to realize that everything about the vehicle was different—the paint color, the model, the driver, the boys in the flatbed. Her dread quickly turned into irritation. *Get a grip! They're harmless.*

"Are you all right?" Joseph gave her a concerned look.

She nodded, starting to walk again. "I'll be glad when the election is over."

Joseph led her to the entrance of a walled alley separating two apartment blocks. The alley was rutted with tire tracks and littered with piles of trash and dog scat. "I found the doll here," he said, showing her a knee-high pile of cinderblocks. "The glasses were beside it."

"They could be anyone's," Zoe objected.

"It's possible. But I found a girl named Given who saw a silver SUV on Saturday at nineteen hundred. She said it was parked right here. I asked the neighbors to make sure, and no one claimed them. Where they were sitting, they could have gone days without being noticed."

Zoe gave him an intense look. "Did Given see the driver?"

"Only his back. She confirmed he was tall. I showed her the symbol that Dominic drew in the dirt. She recognized it, but she didn't know what it was."

"Did she see Kuyeya?"

"No. The man was climbing into the vehicle. The girl must have been inside already."

Zoe sighed. *Another witness who can be neutralized.*

They walked back to Joseph's truck, and he handed her the doll and glasses. "I hope you're not in a hurry to get home," he said, gesturing at the traffic crawling by.

She shook her head. "Nothing waiting for me but a swim and this notebook."

His eyes moved to the bound volume in her hands.

She smiled. "I'll tell you on the drive."

Forty-five minutes later, Zoe sat on a chair beside the pool, her skin tingling from an exhilarating cold-water swim. The sun was gone, leaving the garden in shadow, but the tall sky held the afterglow like the embers of a dying fire. She took long breaths, allowing the scented air to reach deep into her lungs. Overhead, in the jacaranda that shaded the pool, a Heuglin's Robin sang.

Zoe opened Bella's notebook and read the first page. It was a letter written in English.

Dear Jan,

Yesterday I argued with the girls again. They tell me I should pay more rent. They do not listen when I tell them I have no money. Kuyeya had a fever and the nganga charged one hundred pin for medicine. I paid him two hundred pin last week. The blisters were bad again, and I couldn't work. The girls stole my notebook and threw it in the toilet. It is ruined now. This is the second notebook I have lost. I should probably stop writing. But it is all I have, along with Kuyeya.

I need more money. The bars are too crowded. The men pay less than they used to. Girls make more on Addis Ababa. But some die, too. A girl told me about Johannesburg. She made videos and earned two million kwacha. But I am not as pretty as before. I am older and sick. Sometimes I dream that I am going to die. But if I die, what will happen to Kuyeya? I need to find another place to stay.

Zoe turned the page and found another letter:

Dear Jan,

Last night I went to Addis Ababa. Men stopped and talked to me. One was white. He sounded British. We did business in the car. He was rough, but he paid me a hundred pin. Later a colored man asked if I would come with him to the Intercontinental. He gave the guard money and took me in the back. There was another colored man in his room. They hurt me and only one of them paid.

I hate the street. But Kuyeya needs surgery. Her eyes are bad. I walked to the Pamodzi to find another customer. Some girls were there. They yelled at me and told me to go away. One of them hit me with a bag. I went to the Ndeke Hotel and an old man picked me up. He told me he was from Kinshasha. He was dirty, but at least he was kind.

On the following page, Zoe found a third letter addressed to "Jan." The letter read a lot like the first two—a lament of poverty, disease, and violence—but by now Bella was living with Doris. Kuyeya was ill again, this time with a rash on her face. A client had asked for unprotected sex, and

she had consented, but he had paid her the condom price and hit her when she protested. Another
client—one of her steadies—had stayed the night
with her and woken with a terrible hangover.
When he saw Kuyeya's rash, he screamed at her,
terrifying the child.

Zoe read until she could no longer see the
notebook. Every page contained an undated letter, and all were addressed to Jan. Each letter
carried the same matter-of-fact tone, the same
relentlessly depressing news. Bella used descriptions, not names, to refer to her clients. Among
them were the "truck driver from Nairobi," the
"man with the penguin suit," the "the AirTel
boy," the "man who paid double for all night,"
and "the minister who thinks he should be president." Jan himself remained a mystery. The only
revealing reference in the first ten letters was a
comment about *Mosi-oa-Tunya*—Victoria Falls.

She went inside and warmed up leftover *nshima*
and *ndiwo*—relish made of groundnuts, beans and
collard greens—from lunch the day before. Setting
the food on the dining room table, she uncorked a
bottle of South African pinotage and lit a candle.

Then she turned on some Johnny Cash and placed the notebook beside her. Somewhere buried in Bella's mordant recollections was a clue, Zoe was sure.

She would read until she found it.

Chapter 5

On Wednesday morning, Zoe drove to the office, feeling inspired. Her examination of Bella's notebook had revealed nothing about a suspect, but the handwritten letters had afforded her tantalizing glimpses into Bella's past. The more she had read, the more she had convinced herself that the missing pieces of the woman's story could shed light on the investigation.

At nine o'clock, the response team met in the conference room. Joseph laid the doll and glasses on the table, and Zoe placed the notebook beside them.

"It seems we've had developments," Mariam remarked. "Please fill us in."

Zoe traded a glance with Joseph, and he surprised her with a nod that said, *Go ahead*.

After collecting her thoughts, she offered the team a summary of their meetings with Doris, the discovery of the doll and glasses, and the appearance of a second eyewitness—Given. Joseph chimed in a few details but otherwise left the narrative in her hands.

At the end of her report, Zoe held up the notebook. "In the last five years of her life, Bella wrote one hundred and eighty-nine letters to a person named Jan. In them she describes the disintegration of her health, her desperate attempts to provide for Kuyeya, and her work as a prostitute. Joseph and I agree that Kuyeya's rape was likely premeditated. If that's true, the obvious suspects are customers. Unfortunately, Bella never named names. She referred to her clients in code. In addition, she never mentioned a client with an interest in her daughter."

She showed them the inside cover of the notebook. "That said, this is the third volume; the first volume, apparently, was lost and the second was destroyed. We know nothing about what Bella did before April of 2004. In the absence of a better approach, I propose that we fill in the gaps. I have a hunch that Bella will lead us to the man who raped her daughter."

After a pause Niza was the first to speak. "I'll admit I haven't read the letters, but Bella's past seems like an odd place to look for a suspect."

"Granted," Zoe said. "But even if I'm wrong, what I'm proposing should give us confirmation of Kuyeya's age."

Until now Sarge had been leaning back in his chair. At the mention of age, he perked up. In contrast to adult rape, defilement was a strict liability crime, meaning that consent was not an issue so long as the prosecution could establish that the victim was under the age of sixteen.

"Please explain," he said.

Zoe nodded. "Bella says surprisingly little about her childhood, but it's clear she grew up near Livingstone. She talks about Victoria Falls and her grandmother's village. She also dropped a hint that she studied nursing. There's a nursing school at the

Livingstone General Hospital. According to Doris, her parents are probably dead. But I bet we could find someone from her extended family who could establish Kuyeya's date of birth."

Niza shook her head. "Without a suspect in custody, evidence of age is meaningless. You could spend weeks tracking down her family and get us nowhere."

Zoe's eyes flashed. "We'll get nowhere sitting at our desks."

Mariam looked dubious. She turned to Joseph. "What's your opinion?"

"It's an intriguing theory," Joseph said. "But I suggest we wait on a trip to Livingstone."

Zoe frowned. "You have a better idea?"

"Not better," he replied. "More pressing." He fished in his pocket and removed his digital camera. "I took this on the way here," he said, handing it to her.

Zoe looked at the image in the frame. A black BMW sedan was parked beside a tall fence. In the background, slightly blurred, was the sign for the British High Commission.

"Look above the bumper," he said.

Zoe's heart lurched. Beside the license plate was a sky blue crest with an X at its center. Except the X was not a character of the alphabet. It was a pair of golf clubs crossed at the neck. The clubs were overlaid with three stenciled letters: LGC.

"The Lusaka Golf Club," she said softly.

"Let me see that," Niza said, taking the camera from her. She stared at the screen while Sarge and Mariam crowded around. "How can you be sure this is the right symbol?"

"I'll confirm it with our witnesses," Joseph replied.

"Are you going to stake out the golf club?" Zoe asked.

Joseph nodded.

"Can I come along?"

He smiled. "The more the happier."

She laughed. "Merrier, you mean."

He rolled his eyes. "Whatever."

Zoe was tempted to accompany Joseph to Kanyama to question Dominic about the bumper sticker, but the memory of the gang leader in the bandana dissuaded her. Until the election was over, she intended to stay out of the compounds. Agreeing to meet Joseph at noon, she climbed into her Land Rover and placed the doll and glasses on the seat beside her. If the objects were indeed Kuyeya's, she needed to give them back.

The drive to the children's home took half an hour. She parked in the scarlet shade of the poinsettia tree and found Sister Anica in the breezeway beside the courtyard. "We've made progress," she said, giving the nun an outline of their discoveries. "Her name is Kuyeya."

"So that's how you pronounce it," the nun replied. "Sister Irina said 'Kuwia.'"

Zoe was instantly curious. "She started to talk?"

"A little. Come, they're in the garden."

Zoe followed the nun through a trellis of bougainvillea to a cultivated field brimming with plants and herbs in the first stages of growth. She saw the girl rocking quietly on a bench, Sister Irina beside her.

"She spends hours here," Sister Anica said. "It's her favorite place."

Zoe recalled the fingernail marks in Doris's apartment. *You're learning to see the sun*, she thought. "How is she handling the pain?"

"She's taking her Tylenol," replied the nun, "but I doubt she'll run for a while."

They greeted Sister Irina, and Zoe sat beside Kuyeya on the bench. "Hi there," she said to the girl, wondering if she understood English. "Do you remember me?"

Kuyeya pressed her lips together and made the balloon sound.

"She does that when she's happy," Sister Irina explained.

"Hi, Zoe," Kuyeya said spontaneously, her tone flat and her speech slightly slurred.

"I taught her your name," Sister Irina explained. "She likes to say it."

Zoe laughed. "I have a present for you, Kuyeya. I bet you like presents."

The girl nodded, beginning to smile.

Zoe took out the glasses and tried them on her. They fit perfectly. The girl looked toward the trellis of bougainvillea in the distance. After a moment, she made the balloon sound again. This time it carried a faint chime of laughter. *She's nearsighted*, Zoe thought.

"I have another present for you," she said, handing over the doll.

The sight of the stuffed toy transformed Kuyeya. She snatched it away and began to rock back and forth, groaning softly under her breath. Suddenly, she spoke. "Baby is hurt. Baby is not bad. Baby is hurt."

Zoe felt a chill. "Who is the baby?" she asked, but Kuyeya didn't seem to hear her. Zoe looked at Sister Irina. "Has she talked about a baby before?"

The young nun shook her head.

"It might be a projection. She could be talking about herself." Zoe turned back to Kuyeya. "Who hurt the baby?" she asked slowly.

Instead of responding, the girl rocked faster.

Zoe tried again: "How is the baby hurt?"

Kuyeya crossed her eyes, then refocused. At last, she gave an answer: "The man hurt Baby. The man is bad. Baby is not bad."

At once, Zoe found herself acutely conscious of her surroundings. She heard the drone of an airplane overhead, the voices of children nearby, the whistle of the breeze in her ears.

"Who hurt the baby?" she probed. She willed Kuyeya to speak again, but the girl gave her nothing more. She gritted her teeth in frustration. *You saw his face. What is his name?*

She turned to Sister Irina. "It would be helpful to know what she says. Would you mind keeping notes?"

"I'd be happy to," the nun said.

Zoe touched Kuyeya's shoulder. "We need you to talk to us. Please talk to us."

Leaving St. Francis, Zoe dropped by her flat and made two brown-bag lunches. Then she drove to the golf club to meet Joseph. She parked at the edge of the lot beneath a jacaranda tree. The spot gave her a view of the gate and the clubhouse— a compact, single-story building with the familiar blue crest above the entrance. She scanned the lot and saw at least a dozen SUVs, including one that appeared to be silver sitting in the far corner.

Joseph arrived just after noon and parked in the space beside her. "Dominic confirmed it," he said, joining her in the Land Rover. "It's the symbol he saw."

Zoe nodded. "How do you want to do this?"

Joseph surveyed the lot. "I'm going to walk around. You stay here. Your face is too memorable."

"I'll take that as a compliment. There's a silver SUV on the far side."

"I noticed," he replied, and slipped out of the cabin.

Zoe watched as Joseph canvassed the ranks of parked vehicles, angling toward the silver SUV. He barely glanced at the vehicle before entering the clubhouse. A minute later, he returned to the lot with keys in hand, as if he had remembered something.

"It doesn't have a sticker," he said, climbing in again. "I only saw a couple of them in the lot. The lady in the club said they don't make them anymore."

"That'll make our suspect easier to find," Zoe replied. She reached into the back seat and handed him a brown bag. "I made you a sandwich."

His lips widened into a smile. "That's very kind of you."

The gift of food seemed to unlock something in Joseph. Suddenly, he became a conversationalist, engaging Zoe about everything from his childhood in the Southern Province to the issues at stake in the election. As the afternoon deepened and the sun traced out its westward arc, at least two dozen automobiles came and went. Zoe kept watch for another silver SUV but saw only rainbow colors in the parade.

Around four o'clock, their fortunes turned. A silver Lexus RX270 pulled into the lot and parked in their row. Two Zambian men—one tall and trim, the other shorter and muscular—collected golf clubs from the trunk and strolled toward the clubhouse.

"I'll check it out," Joseph said, leaving the cab. He wandered down the lane and continued into the clubhouse, emerging five minutes later with a troubled look in his eyes. He took out his camera and snapped a photo of the Lexus. Then he returned to the Land Rover.

"The crest is there, but it's on the wrong side," he said, showing her the photo and Dominic's sketch from his notebook. The boy had placed the crest to the left of the license plate. On the Lexus, the crest was to the right.

"Maybe he misremembered," she said. "It was dark."

Joseph frowned. "Right now his memory is the

best evidence we have. There's something else. I talked to the men. I asked if they'd played over the weekend. The tall one said he was in Johannesburg on business."

Zoe sighed, dejected. "We should confirm that. We also need to double-check Dominic's recollection."

Joseph nodded. "I'll run the plate."

Chapter 6

The Lexus, it turned out, belonged to the son of a bureaucrat at the Ministry of Finance who worked for Barclays bank. Joseph called his office and confirmed that he was, at least ostensibly, in South Africa on the night Kuyeya was raped. Dominic, too, seemed certain that the crest on the perpetrator's SUV had been situated to the left of the plate. The child even drew a sketch in Joseph's notepad. In a flash of insight, Joseph drew the emblems of the popular automobile manufacturers above the plate, and the boy circled the three-pointed star of Mercedes Benz. But of this fact he had been less certain.

Joseph returned to haunt the Lusaka Golf Club in search of another silver SUV. Zoe, meanwhile, spent her days at the office, whittling down the stack of legal work that had piled up. New case files had to be reviewed and status reports delivered to Mariam; two research memos she had written for Sarge and Niza required editing; and a brief Sarge had drafted for the Zambia Supreme Court needed footnotes with citations along with substantial grammatical polish. She checked her iPhone obsessively, hoping for a text from Joseph. But the time passed without incident and she found herself wishing that she had pushed Mariam to authorize the Livingstone trip despite Joseph's reluctance. Whatever the merits of her theory, searching for Kuyeya's family was far more interesting than being handcuffed to a desk.

On Thursday after work, Zoe vented her frustration, doing thirty laps in the pool without pause. Afterward, she sat on the edge and dangled her feet in the water, breathing steadily until her pulse—and her mind—stopped racing.

It was then that her iPhone chimed. She jumped to her feet, certain the text was from Joseph. She groaned when she saw it was from her father.

Zoe, I landed in Kinshasa last night. I'm really looking forward to our dinner tomorrow. Let's plan on seven o'clock at the Intercontinental. I'll book a table at the Savannah Grill. It will be a joy to see you again.

She walked the length of the pool, and then swam another ten laps for good measure. When she climbed out, the sun was gone and the garden had fallen into deep shadow. She dried off and walked home, slower this time, drinking in the twilight. She gave thought to calling Joseph but couldn't think of a legitimate excuse. Letting herself into her flat, she remembered something her father used to say: "*Patience is a necessary evil.*"

She smiled at the irony. *The apple doesn't fall far from the tree.*

The following evening, Zoe sat on the couch in her flat, staring at the clock and dreading the forced march of time. She crossed her legs, certain that the black dress and pearls she had selected were too formal. Although the Intercontinental was one of Zambia's premier hotels and her father would be wearing a suit—a Zegna, no doubt, with a crimson tie—Lusaka was worlds apart from Paris or New York. Still, it was the look he would be expecting, the Zoe Fleming who had dazzled the deans at Stanford and Yale Law, the daughter of elegant Catherine. She twisted her watch—a diamond-encrusted Charriol the Senator had given her as a graduation gift—and felt like a fraud.

When six thirty came, she collected her purse and left the apartment. The air was cool in the dwindling light, and a crescent moon hovered over the trees to the west. She drove to the Intercontinental in a daze, wishing she could have declined her father's invitation. It would have been easy to contrive an excuse—a critical business trip, a long-planned holiday with friends. But St. Francis had lost a third of its donors after the financial crisis, and SCA was struggling to stay afloat. They needed her support, as did the children they served, and she needed her father to run interference with Atticus

Spelling. For the thousandth time, Zoe wondered why her mother had named Spelling as her trustee. He was Catherine's antitype—calculating, institutionally minded, and instinctively bleak. It was a mystery that had baffled Zoe for a decade.

After parking in the hotel lot, she entered the lobby and made her way to the Savannah Grill. The restaurant was located on a covered terrace overlooking the pool. She saw her father at a candlelit table for two, studying the menu. She also saw his security detail—two men in suits, one by the grand savannah window and the other sitting by the pool, looking ridiculous.

The Senator stood when she appeared. "Zoe," he said, kissing her cheek, "I'm so glad you could come."

She touched his arm. "Hi, Dad."

He seated her formally and then returned to his place. Almost immediately, a uniformed waiter appeared, and Jack asked for a bottle of champagne.

She searched his face. "What are we celebrating?"

"That you're here, that I'm here. Do I need a better reason?"

She twisted her watch. "Why *are* you here, Dad?"

Something like annoyance flashed in his eyes.

"Is it such a crime for a man to want to take his daughter to dinner?"

"An interesting opening. I should think there are less contentious ways to begin a conversation between us."

He thought about what he'd said, and his eyes darkened. "Hardly intentional."

She shrugged. "You haven't answered my question."

He grimaced. "I'm in Africa to—"

"I know why you're in Africa," she said, cutting him off. "You're here to satisfy your constituents that the cuts you're proposing to the foreign-aid budget don't stand a chance of making the Dark Continent any brighter. So what difference does it make if a few hundred thousand AIDS patients die an early death?"

He looked wounded. "You accuse me of heartlessness. You know as well as I do that I voted *for* PEPFAR, not against it. I'm not suggesting that it be eliminated, just reined in a bit."

"That's not what your campaign is saying," she retorted.

He gave her a calculating look. "That's just politics."

"Precisely," she said.

He took a sharp breath. "It's been eleven years. I thought by now you would have . . ."

The anger in her eyes seemed to interrupt his train of thought.

Would have what, Dad? she almost said. *Gotten over it? Are you really that naive?*

She allowed him to stew in discomfort until the waiter appeared with the champagne. The Senator took his glass and looked out over the gardens. Zoe left hers on the table untouched. When the waiter asked if they wished to order, she shook her head.

"Give us a few more minutes, please," she said kindly.

She stared at her father, wondering how this was going to play out. She had hoped she might find a way to socialize with him with her emotions chained in the basement. Obviously, she had miscalculated. The problem was she needed his support.

"So how is the campaign?" she asked, attempting to make conversation. "The BBC says you're up in the polls."

He turned back to her. "The Brits tend to understate things. We're well ahead."

"Which makes it doubly odd that you're here," she said, unable to help herself. "You don't need to win any austerity points."

"I'm on the African Affairs Subcommittee," he said.

She smiled. "I'm your daughter. Your DNA is better than a lie detector."

He tensed. "What do you want me to say?"

"Why don't we start with the truth?"

Her father just stared at her.

"Okay, let me guess. Sylvia wants you to make sure I keep quiet. Am I getting warm?"

The Senator blanched. It was no secret how little Zoe cared for his second wife. Yet he never seemed to grasp how well she could read Sylvia Martinelli's mind.

"I thought we had an . . . understanding," he said slowly.

"You mean the suggestion you gave me when I was seventeen? That doesn't count."

The waiter reappeared, looking gun-shy. This

time the Senator waved him away. "You would talk about it in public? Why?"

"What I might contemplate and what I intend to do are not necessarily the same."

He frowned. "This isn't a law class. You don't get points for being coy."

"True, Dad, but it's so much fun."

He looked away and sipped his champagne. To her surprise, he dropped his guard. "You're right, Sylvia wanted me to come. But it was a good excuse to get away. I wanted to see you. I thought we turned a corner in Cape Town."

She steadied her breathing. "In a way we did. You stood up to her."

He shrugged. "The trust is almost yours, and Atticus is a bit of a Scrooge."

"So you'll talk to him again this year?"

"Only if you finish the meal with me and leave the old grudges out of it. I want to hear about you. Talk to me like you did when you cared what I thought."

He made the statement so baldly, so unsentimentally, that Zoe almost missed the emotional charge beneath it. Then the words registered, and she felt like she had been punched in the gut. Even after all he had done, had she ever stopped loving him? It was a question too painful to examine, let alone to answer with conviction.

"All right," she agreed. "Just pleasantries and platitudes."

"And a good old-fashioned African braai," he said with a smile.

The meal passed without incident. Zoe filled up on tenderloin while her father regaled her with scuttlebutt from the campaign trail—the media snoops digging for dirt; the rows with the other candidates; the hanky-panky between interns; even a self-effacing gaffe or two. She couldn't help but wonder at the political animal he had become. He was born brilliant and charismatic, a lord among leaders. But since his departure from the boardroom, he had added polish to his innate sense of timing and delivery. At moments, Zoe found herself mesmerized by him.

They finished off the meal with espressos, and then the Senator walked her to the parking lot, his security detail in tow. He nodded at the Land Rover. "I'm glad old Atticus isn't stingy with your living expenses."

In spite of herself, Zoe smiled. "It's the only time he's not." She hesitated, then gave him a kiss on the cheek. "Goodnight, Dad. Thanks for the invitation."

He looked into her eyes. "I wish I could change the way things are between us."

"Please don't. I was almost beginning to enjoy myself."

The pain in his eyes was sincere. "Be safe," he said, seeing her into the SUV.

She watched him walk back to the hotel, flanked by bodyguards, and then keyed the ignition. She flipped on her headlights and started to pull out when she recognized something in her peripheral vision. She peered into the shadows, searching for an explanation. At once her mind processed what she was seeing—a black Jaguar sedan with the blue crest of the Lusaka Golf Club on its bumper.

She scanned the lot, noting the silhouettes of at least twenty SUVs. *What if the rapist is here?* she thought with a shudder. She got out of the Land Rover and walked slowly down the row, her heels clicking on the tarmac. She passed two silver SUVs, but neither bore the familiar crest. At the end of the row, she caught sight of another candidate in the corner of the lot. She glanced around, taking in her surroundings. The darkened lot was eerily quiet. She walked through the last row of cars and approached the SUV.

Something moved at the edge of her vision.

She froze, her senses on high alert. She stared into the shadows. Something was not quite right, but she couldn't tell what it was. A memory came to her suddenly: Johannesburg, 2010. The night she had stayed late at work; the long walk to the car; the gang that had appeared out of nowhere; the guns they had pointed at her face; the thought that she was about to die.

Suppressing her nervousness, she looked toward the silver SUV, now fifteen feet away. For some reason, the driver had backed into the space. To see the trunk, she would have to walk around the vehicle. She focused on the hood and traced out the emblem in the dark. It was the three-pointed star of Mercedes Benz. Her heart soared. *Dominic saw a Mercedes.*

She stepped around the SUV. The shadows here were nearly complete. She reached into her purse, thinking to use the flashlight app on her iPhone, when she heard scratches on asphalt. She swiveled around and saw two men crouching behind the next car. One of them was holding an object in his hand. The fear came upon Zoe in an instant.

She was sure the object was a gun.

Kicking off her heels, she took off barefoot across the lot. She heard a muffled shout and poured on the speed. She didn't have enough of a lead to use the cars as a screen. Her only option was to reach the hotel. She ran through the rows of vehicles, bypassing the Land Rover and sprinting toward the brightly lit entrance.

Two hundred feet. One hundred.

At once she realized something—the only footsteps she could hear were her own. She glanced over her shoulder and saw no one behind her. Suddenly, an engine roared and a yellow sports car careened across the lot, heading in her direction. For a second she stood transfixed. Then she jumped out of the way.

The truth dawned on her slowly. *They aren't muggers; they're car thieves.*

"Are you all right, miss?" said a male voice, as the sports car sped out of the lot and vanished into the night.

She turned around, feeling an extraordinary sense of relief. The man was older—perhaps sixty—and slightly heavyset, though his girth was concealed by an elegant three-piece suit. Beside him stood a gaunt young man in a pink dress shirt and expensive jeans.

She nodded. "I think they just stole that car."

The older man followed her eyes. "I'm glad you were not injured."

"I should call the police," she said.

"You could, but they would not be helpful. The owner of the hotel is a friend. I will alert him about the incident. Insurance will replace the car."

Zoe frowned, thinking of Joseph, but decided to take the man's advice. She hadn't seen the faces of the thieves, and she had no information about the car beyond its color. The man offered to escort her to her vehicle, and she agreed. She chatted with him briefly, but he didn't offer his name or that of his companion. The younger man didn't speak at all.

Zoe locked herself in the Land Rover and sighed, letting the residue of fear flood out of her. She watched through the windshield as the men shook hands and parted. The older man angled toward the black Jaguar she had seen earlier, and the younger man disappeared down the lane. At once Zoe remembered her lost shoes and the Mercedes SUV. With the thieves gone and the lot no longer deserted, she decided to take another look.

She pulled out of the space and drove down the lane, retracing the path she had taken on foot. At the end of the row, she looked toward the last rank of cars. Her jaw dropped when she saw the empty parking space. Seconds later, the silver Mercedes passed her in the lane, the young man in the pink shirt behind the wheel. She craned her head around but couldn't see his bumper in the gloom. The thought struck her with sudden force: *He matches the profile exactly.*

She made a swift U-turn and followed the SUV. The man made a left on Haile Selassie Avenue and then a right on Los Angeles Boulevard. When traffic opened up, Zoe pressed down on the accelerator and gained on the SUV. She pulled to within two car lengths of the vehicle and studied its bumper. Staring back at her across the African night was the Lusaka Golf Club crest, positioned to the left of the plate and below the emblem of Mercedes Benz.

She took out her iPhone and opened the camera, zooming in until the license plate and the crest stood in opposite corners of the frame. The plate was slightly blurred but the characters were legible. She took a few pictures and then called Joseph and told him everything.

He whistled. "Don't get too close. I'll meet you at the Kabulonga roundabout."

"Hurry!" She dropped back and changed lanes. "We'll be there in three minutes."

The suspect kept a leisurely pace through the suburbs and took Kabulonga Road off the roundabout. Zoe glanced in her mirror and saw a new pair of headlights behind her. *That was fast*, she thought. Two turns later, the suspect stopped outside an iron gate manned by a guard. Zoe drove past the gate and saw the upper story of a European-style villa over the electrified walls. *He's a member of the elite*, she thought, *and he lives in my neighborhood.*

She checked her mirror and saw the outline of Joseph's face in the glow of her brake lights. At the end of the road, she reversed course and drove slowly back toward the gate. Turning off her headlamps, she pulled to the grassy shoulder fifty yards from the driveway. She saw the guard standing in a puddle of light cast by wall-mounted security torches. He glanced her way and then ambled back to his chair.

Zoe used her iPhone to download a satellite image of her location. She zoomed in until she could see the layout of the property beyond the gate. The grounds had the appearance of a park with grass and trees surrounding the house and two outbuildings, one of which looked like a garage. Beside the house was a swimming pool.

Joseph pulled up behind her and turned off his engine. Before long, another vehicle turned into the driveway. It was the black Jaguar from the hotel. The guard opened the gate, allowing the sedan to enter the property. Zoe conjured the older man in her memory—the piercing black eyes, the flared nose and strong jaw, the expanding waistline and bespoke suit—and compared him to the thin man. *Father and son*, she guessed.

She heard her phone ring. "How did you find him?" Joseph asked when she picked up.

She told him the story, omitting only the detail about her father.

He was silent for a moment. "You didn't get a picture of him, did you?"

"Why would I have done that?"

Joseph grunted. "We need something to show the witnesses. I'm going to stick around."

"He might not leave until morning."

"It won't be the first time I've sat up all night."

"Do you want me to stay with you?"

"No, your truck's too visible. Did you get the license number of the SUV?"

She found the image on her iPhone and recited the number for him.

"Thanks. I'll call my friend at the Department of Road Transport in the morning."

"Tomorrow is Saturday."

"He owes me a favor."

She studied the guard sitting beside the ornate gate. Instead of slouching with his legs crossed, he sat erect with his hands resting on his knees. "There's something peculiar about that guard," she said. "He looks ex-military."

Joseph murmured his agreement. "He's also sitting outside the walls after dark, not inside in the guard shack. Obviously, they want him to be seen."

Zoe scanned the walls again and noticed a tubular device mounted on a stand at the corner of the property. "They have cameras, too. Maybe his father is a government minister."

"Or an industrialist. He's obviously worried about a break-in."

"Robberies aren't common in Kabulonga," she objected.

"But when they do happen, people often end up dead." He took a breath and let it out. "Go home and get some sleep."

"Promise me you'll keep me in the loop."

He laughed drily. "I'll call you if anything interesting happens."

Chapter 7

At nine fifteen on Saturday morning, Zoe sat in the CILA conference room tapping her fingers on the table, waiting on Joseph. At her request, Mariam had summoned the response team for an emergency meeting. All but Niza had arrived in casual attire, and Zoe had briefed them on the events of the night before. Joseph, however, had yet to show up. She had left two messages on his mobile, but he had not returned her calls.

By nine thirty even Mariam was showing signs of irritation. "This isn't like him," she said, checking her watch. "I'll send an SMS."

Suddenly, Zoe heard a horn and saw the nose of Joseph's truck pull into the drive. A minute later, he sauntered in with an insouciance that belied the tension in the room.

"Sorry to leave you in the dark," he said, "but I was busy, as you'll see." He found an empty chair and smiled at them. "The suspect's name is Darious Nyambo, son of Frederick Nyambo, founder of Nyambo Energy Company, Ltd. Darious is thirty-one and a television producer at ZNBC. Frederick was Minister of Energy and Water Development under President Mwanawasa. I had breakfast with a friend who works at the Department of Energy, and he gave me the scoop on the Nyambos. Frederick is the leading private investor in the coal and hydroelectric sectors on both sides of the Zambia–Zimbabwe border. His holdings and government connections make him one of the most powerful men in Zambia."

"Any relation to Patricia Nyambo?" Mariam asked.

"She's his wife."

Zoe leaned forward in her chair. "You mean the High Court judge?"

"Exactly." Mariam's voice was grave.

Zoe's eyes went wide. "Why have I never heard of Frederick?"

"He keeps a low profile," Joseph replied. "You saw the security at his house. According to my friend, he's a businessman, not a politician. He peddles influence quietly."

"All of that makes for delicious gossip," Niza broke in, "but what proof do you have that he's the assailant?"

Joseph nodded. "I took photos of him and his SUV and showed them to our witnesses. Dominic and Given both recognized the SUV, and Dominic felt strongly that Darious is the man he saw. Given wasn't quite as certain, but she agreed that they look a lot alike."

"That's enough for probable cause," Zoe said, glancing at Mariam.

Niza held out her hands, as if trying to stop a runaway train. "Darious might have picked the child up and dropped her off, but what do we have linking him to the rape itself? For all we know, he took her somewhere and another man raped her."

"We have Dr. Chulu," Zoe disagreed. "And we have DNA."

Niza rolled her eyes. "You act as if that's a simple proposition."

"You act as if it's impossible," Zoe shot back.

Mariam spoke up: "Sarge, what do you think?"

"The child witnesses are a problem," he said calmly, "and we don't have firm evidence of age. I would say we stand a fifty percent chance of getting assigned a magistrate who won't consider DNA in a case involving the son of Patricia Nyambo." He looked at Mariam. "That said, we should talk to the Director of Public Prosecution. If he agrees, we should co-prosecute."

"What?" Niza exclaimed. "You just shot holes in the airplane, and now you're telling us to take off. We need something more, a lot more."

Sarge nodded. "I agree. But that doesn't mean Joseph can't make the arrest. We have time to develop our evidence before trial."

"You know as well as I do how dirty they're going to fight," Niza persisted. "They'll hire Benson Luchembe and his band of con artists. They'll tie the magistrate's head in knots and line his pockets with enough kwacha to give his wife and children visions of grandeur. And that doesn't take into account the pressure the Nyambos will exert behind the scenes."

Sarge stared at Niza. "Since when have you run from a fight?"

Anger flared in her eyes. "Are you calling me a coward?"

Sarge shook his head. "I'm saying that all of us are here because we believe in the possibility of justice. When a child is raped in this city, we're the ones who stand up to her abuser. Skeptics have no seat at this table. If you aren't a believer, I need to know."

Niza stomped out of the room, ignoring Mariam who tried to wave her back to the table.

Sarge looked around. "Sorry to do that. I'm sure she'll get over it."

Mariam cleared her throat. "I'll contact the DPP at home and walk him through the evidence." She stood, clutching her notebook. "Any more issues we need to discuss?" No one spoke. "Good. Joseph, Sarge, I need you on the call with me. And Niza, if you can find her."

"I'll get her," Sarge said.

Joseph motioned to Zoe, and she followed him to the kitchen.

"Impressive work," she said.

He shrugged. "Darious was your discovery. Listen, I'm not sure it's relevant, but he didn't stay at his father's place last night. He went to Alpha Bar and left with a couple of *mahules*. He stayed at a flat in Northmead. Early this morning he drove back to Kabulonga."

"If he's consorting with prostitutes—"

"Then he could have been a client of Bella's. I think it might be beneficial to have another talk with Doris. Show her the pictures I took; see if she remembers him."

She looked at him carefully. "You're going to let me do it?"

He nodded. "She trusts you."

Zoe smiled. "Send me the photos and I'll stop by her place when I leave."

A few minutes after ten o'clock, Mariam called Zoe into her office. Joseph, Sarge, and a chastened-looking Niza were already there. For the past fifteen minutes they had been on a conference call with Leviticus Makungu, the Director of Public Prosecution. It was a call Zoe had asked to join, but Mariam had excluded her on account of her expat status. The DPP was sensitive about foreign interference in the justice system.

Zoe sat down. "How did it go?"

Mariam took a breath. "Levy expressed curiosity and caution. In light of the suspect's identity, he's concerned about evidence. He wants to see our reports."

"Any favors we can call in?" Zoe asked.

"I used them all to keep him on the phone. He wasn't thrilled about being bothered on a Saturday. The best I could get was the promise of a quick decision."

"So we're going to wait on the arrest?"

"I think it's wise to get DPP approval," Mariam said. "Darious isn't going anywhere." She folded her hands. "I'll tell you what I told the others. Certain elements of this case don't add up. Why would a man from such a prominent family rape a girl like Kuyeya? Joseph told us about Darious's activities last night. It's clear he has access to women. It doesn't make sense, unless . . ."

"Sex wasn't the only motive," Zoe finished for her.

"Precisely." Mariam met her eyes. "If Darious is the rapist, he must have assaulted Kuyeya for a reason. If we can find it, we might stand a better chance of persuading the Court to take this case seriously." She took a breath. "You wanted to investigate Bella's past. I'm giving you permission. Joseph told me you're going to talk to Doris?"

Zoe nodded. "As soon as I leave."

"Fine. But I want a full report on Monday."

Twenty minutes later, Zoe stood outside Doris's flat in Kabwata. The apartment complex was noisy with the sounds of weekend recreation— the voices of television newscasters wafting out of windows, the shouts of boys playing soccer in the parking lot. She knocked on Doris's door. Silence. She knocked louder. Eventually, Bright appeared, wearing sweatpants and a scowl.

"What do you want?" the girl asked.

"I need to talk to your mother again."

"She's asleep. Come back later."

Zoe didn't budge. "It's important. It's about Kuyeya."

The girl wavered in indecision. Then she disappeared into the hallway beyond the living room. Zoe heard a door open, then a bump and a groan, and finally the sound of loud whispering.

Bright returned and shook her head. "She isn't available. Come back in a couple of days."

Zoe felt compassion for the girl. "Did something happen?"

Bright blinked and Zoe saw moisture in her eyes. "Is she all right?" Zoe persisted.

The girl stood stiffly, unsure of herself.

"Where is Gift?" Zoe inquired, remembering Bright's younger sister.

"She's with him," Bright murmured.

"Who?"

"Her father."

"Is he here?"

Bright shook her head. "He took her away."

Suddenly, Doris appeared, stooping like an old woman. She sat down on the couch and stared at the floor. Zoe was taken aback. Her lip was split, and she had bruises on her face.

"Who did this to you?" Zoe demanded, as Bright slipped by and vanished.

Doris rubbed her palms together. "It doesn't matter. What do you wish to ask about Kuyeya?"

Zoe took a seat on the chair. "It *does* matter. The officer I work with is a member of the Victim Support Unit. He can file a report."

"It wouldn't do any good. Ask me your questions."

Zoe eyed Doris sadly. In all likelihood, the woman was correct: involving the police was a fool's errand in a culture in which men considered it a privilege, even an obligation, to abuse women.

"Okay," she conceded. She showed Doris an image of Darious Nyambo that Joseph had taken. "Do you recognize this man?"

Doris tensed. "I know him."

"How?" Zoe asked.

"He was a client."

"When did you last see him?"

"A few weeks ago."

"Where was that?"

Doris gestured toward the door. "He was sitting in a truck on the street."

Zoe's heart rate increased. "Was he watching your apartment?"

Doris shrugged. "I don't know. I went inside quickly."

"You didn't want him to see you."

Doris touched her bruised cheek. "I didn't want to work for him again."

"Why not?"

"He was mean to me. And he was sick."

Zoe raised her eyebrows. "How was he sick?"

"He had sores in his mouth and on his . . ." She pointed between her legs. "Also, he lost weight. He used to be bigger."

"Before a few weeks ago, when was the last time you saw him?"

Doris hesitated. "It was two years ago. Not long after Bella died."

"Was Darious a client of Bella's, too?"

Doris nodded. "They were close. But then things changed and he stopped coming."

Zoe felt a surge of gratification. "When were they close?"

"A long time ago. I don't know. It was after she moved in with me."

"Why did they have a falling out?"

"She didn't tell me."

"When you say 'close,' what do you mean?"

Doris shifted in her seat and winced. "He took her out to the bars and bought her talktime. He gave her gifts. He was kind to her."

Zoe softened her tone. "But he wasn't kind to you."

Doris closed her eyes and began to rock. When the silence lingered, Zoe considered her next move. Doris's candor was the product of a fragile trust. It might not survive a misstep.

"You don't have to tell me what he did to you," Zoe said. "But it might help Kuyeya."

After a moment, Doris opened her eyes again. She gave Zoe a haunted look. "The last time I saw him as a client, he beat me. Then he . . ." Her voice trailed off, and she began to cry.

"What did he do?" Zoe probed.

At last Doris choked out, "He raped Bright."

The confession took Zoe's breath away. She sat back against the chair, her gut churning with a strangely personal anguish. Bright was probably seventeen; two years ago she would have been around fifteen.

"I'm so sorry," Zoe said after a long time. "Did you report it to the police?"

Doris collected herself. "They do not listen to women like me."

Waiting a beat, Zoe asked, "Did he ever show an interest in Kuyeya?"

Doris shook her head. "He ignored her. It was as if she didn't exist."

Suddenly, Zoe had an idea. "Did Bella call him something other than his name?"

The question appeared to perplex Doris. "His name is Darious."

"Never mind," Zoe said. She slid to the edge of her chair, thinking of Bella's journal resting on the coffee table in her flat.

She had to get back to it.

Chapter 8

It was noon by the time Zoe returned to her flat. She called Joseph and left a voicemail: "We were right about the client connection. But there's more to it. Darious raped Doris's daughter two years ago. It's also possible he has AIDS. I don't know if you're up to it, but you might find a girl at Alpha Bar who would talk about him. I want to know how sick he is."

Hanging up, she fixed herself a sandwich and ate it in the dining room. Afterward, she changed into her swimsuit and walked to the pool, carrying her backpack and Bella's journal.

The garden was resplendent in the sunlight, festooned with the colors of spring—spade-tongued coleus, sprawling blue plumbago bushes, clusters of fern-like cycads, and bulb-rich rose bushes. She saw her neighbor, Kelly Summers, reading a novel on a lounge chair. The child of white Zimbabwean farmers, Kelly was married to Patrick Summers, a British-born World Bank consultant. Zoe spread out her towel beside Kelly and took a seat.

"Another pristine day," she said, beginning to apply sunblock to her fair skin.

"Couldn't be lovelier," Kelly agreed, setting down her book.

Patrick emerged from the water and gave his wife a dripping kiss. "Hi, Zoe."

"Many thanks, love," Kelly replied, pushing him away. She smiled at Zoe. "We were thinking of having a braai at our place tonight. Save you the trouble, hey?"

The invitation took Zoe by surprise. She blinked behind her sunglasses, astonished that she had forgotten her own tradition. "You don't need to do that," she said, disguising her relief.

"Our pleasure," Kelly said, as Patrick dived into

the pool again. "We've noticed you've been busy. A new case? Or a boyfriend, perhaps?"

"A new case," she replied.

"That's a shame. A boyfriend would have been fun." Kelly pointed at Bella's journal. "What's that?"

Zoe looked down at the notebook. "Something from work. It's a long story."

"And confidential, no doubt." Kelly smiled. "Listen, there's a new analyst at the World Bank office. His name is Clay Whitaker. He's very smart—a Yale graduate, like you—and he's been all over southern Africa. He's going to be at the braai tonight."

At that moment, Zoe found herself grateful for the veil afforded by her sunglasses. "That's kind of you," she said, forcing herself to smile, "but I'm not looking."

She stared at the moving water, feeling suddenly nauseous. *It's only a name, a random string of four letters. Get over it.* But she couldn't. Over and over the name played in her mind, like a record stuck on a discordant note. *Clay . . . Clay . . . Clay.* At once she felt the sun on every inch of exposed flesh. She steeled her mind against the memories: a picnic at East Beach in late summer; the Vineyard air heated to a blaze; the calls of the gulls competing with the pounding of the surf; the boy whose mouth carried the taste of sea stones; the lines of verse he read; the rhapsody of infatuation, desire tempered by nerves; the line she drew, the "no" she spoke, and the moment he overpowered her and his love became a lie.

She felt the weight of Bella's journal in her hands and focused all her mental energy on the present. But it wasn't enough. Abandoning the chair, she broke the surface of the pool with a dive and went limp, allowing herself to hang in suspension, buoyed by the air in her lungs. The raw shock of cold on her hot skin cleansed her mind, leaving behind only the immediacy of the moment. She floated through the haze until she could no longer hold her breath. She found her footing and stood, blinking away the reflected light.

"Everything all right?" Patrick asked, treading water. "You were under a long time."

"I'm fine," Zoe said.

She returned to her chair and dried off, feeling more composed. Opening Bella's journal, she worked out a strategy. If Bella had a relationship with Darious after she met Doris, then it was likely she had mentioned him in the first half of the journal. The problem was she had concealed his name in code. The clues Doris offered were threadbare: they went out to the bars and he gave her gifts. But Zoe understood the power of gestalt—the truth spoken by the whole, not simply by the particulars.

She read for two hours, pausing only to reapply sunblock. She found a number of repeat clients in the pages. One Bella called "Levi's man," but he met her on the street and never spent the night with her. Another she called "Mr. Niceguy." In addition to sex, he took her dancing at the bars. A third she called "Godzilla." He paid double her rate but often left her with bruises. Finally, there was "Siluwe." He was complex, educated, a conversationalist. But she didn't seem to trust him. Indeed, her descriptions suggested that she had feared him.

Zoe ruled out the Levi's man and Godzilla and weighed Mr. Niceguy against Siluwe. According to Doris, Darious had given Bella gifts. Mr. Niceguy always paid with cash. Siluwe, by contrast, was a regular Santa Claus. *Siluwe is Darious Nyambo*, she decided.

They had met at Alpha Bar. He had bought her drinks and lavished her with such affection that she had forgotten to charge him the next morning. He reappeared in four subsequent letters. Each time Bella described his gifts—an expensive meal, a mobile phone—but her sentiments were guarded. Then without warning he disappeared from the journal.

She heard her iPhone chirp in her bag, and saw a text message from Joseph: "*Good idea about Alpha. Are you hosting a braai tonight?*"

She typed back: "*Friends next door are cooking. Let Sarge and Niza know.*"

A few seconds later she received his response: "*Will do. I'll be there around 1800.*"

Then Zoe had a thought. "*Does the name Siluwe mean anything to you?*"

He replied: "*Siluwe means leopard in Tonga. Why?*"

Zoe felt a chill. "*I'll tell you over dinner.*"

★ ★ ★

That evening, Zoe put on her favorite jeans and a black top and walked across the parking lot to the house rented by Patrick and Kelly Summers. She tossed a greeting to Patrick at the grill and went looking for Kelly. She found her in the kitchen assembling a cheese tray with the help of a thirty-something blond man in khakis and a button-down shirt.

"You must be Zoe," the man said, smiling at her in an easy way. "I'm—"

"Clay," she said. "The expat community is like a fraternity. New pledges make waves." She leaned against the countertop. "So what's your angle? Are you coming to the Bank as a supporter or critic of the development program?"

"Both, I suppose," he said. "But I've been with the Bank for seven years."

"Then you can't be too much of a critic."

He shrugged. "I'm only critical of projects that don't work."

"Ah. So here's a project guaranteed to succeed. Build a DNA lab in Lusaka. Show the world that reforming the African justice system is as important as infrastructure and investment."

He scratched his chin. "An intriguing proposition. But I work in the energy sector."

"Right. Not your problem." She looked at Kelly. "What can I do to help?"

Her friend handed her a chopping knife and pointed to a cluster of vegetables. "Slice and dice," she replied, watching Clay carry the cheese tray out to the porch. "And try to be nice."

At six fifteen, the guests arrived in a rush. They were a diverse bunch—development types and foreign servants, along with a British academic and a Peace Corps volunteer leader in from the hinterlands. With unconscious precision, they sorted into gender-defined cliques—the men by the grill, sipping beers and swapping war stories, and the women on the porch, chatting over glasses of wine. Only Clay broke the barrier. All of the ladies seemed taken by him except Zoe who found herself looking toward the gate, watching for Joseph.

When at last he arrived, Patrick was dishing out burgers and chicken. "Just in time," she quipped, handing him a paper plate.

He smiled at her. "Nice to see you, too."

"Are the others coming?"

"Sarge had family obligations, and Niza wasn't in the mood."

After filling their plates, the guests ate together on the lamp-lit porch; the few who couldn't find chairs sat on the ground. In between bites of hamburger, Zoe filled Joseph in on her conversation with Doris and her discovery of Siluwe, the leopard, in Bella's journal.

"Do you think you can convince Doris to testify?" he asked.

"I'm not sure. She hates him, but she's also afraid of him."

"Siluwe. It's a fascinating name. The leopard hunts in the dark."

Zoe was about to respond when the voice of Clay Whitaker interrupted her thoughts.

"The power station at Batoka Gorge might actually get off the ground," he was saying to a doe-eyed girl from USAID. "It's an extraordinary thing, really, for a private company to guarantee the debt of a sovereign."

"Isn't that what the Bank and the IMF do all the time?" Zoe said, joining in. "They loan money to governments."

"True." Clay replied. "But the funds come from nation states, not private investors."

"Who's the investor in the Batoka project?"

"Ever heard of Nyambo Energy?" he inquired.

She stared at him. "What's Nyambo's interest in the Batoka Gorge?"

"I don't know the precise terms of the deal. But I have a theory."

Zoe leaned forward intently. "Okay, let's hear it."

"You know the story of Batoka, I take it?" he began. "Zimbabwe and Zambia are in crisis mode; there isn't enough electricity to power the grid. The Zambezi River is the obvious savior, but Zambia won't invest in another hydroelectric project until Zimbabwe pays off its Rhodesia debt. Zimbabwe threatens to go forward alone, but nobody believes Mugabe has the money to make it happen. In comes Frederick Nyambo with an offer to cover the debt and start construction. Everyone thinks he's crazy. Why invest in a floundering state like Zimbabwe?"

"Unless the floundering state offers you something you can't refuse," she said. "Like a kickback from the sale of power."

Whitaker looked at her closely. "Or a stake in the power company itself. Zimbabwe is considering privatizing its public utility. If Nyambo were to acquire a majority stake—"

"Then he would be entitled to a large portion of the profits."

"Exactly. It's a gambit fifteen years in the making."

Zoe narrowed her eyes. "What do you mean?"

Whitaker folded his hands. "Zimbabwe commissioned its first private power project in 1996. Nyambo Energy was the contractor. When the Batoka project ran into the debt roadblock and privatization stalled, Frederick Nyambo directed the commercialization of Zambia's public utility as Minister of Energy. The way I see it, he's been playing both sides of the fence, lobbying the Zambian and Zim governments to divest ownership of the utilities while positioning himself as the heir apparent."

Zoe was astonished. Frederick Nyambo was either a financial daredevil or one of the shrewdest entrepreneurial visionaries in Africa—or both.

"Anyone need another drink?" Kelly asked, over the din of intersecting conversations.

The Garden of Burning Sand

Whitaker held up his glass. "I'll take some more red."

Zoe met Joseph's eyes. "Will you walk with me?"

They left the yard by the front gate and took the path that led to the pool. The gardens were empty and the dark water still.

"Batoka is near Victoria Falls," she said. "I wonder if there's a connection to Bella."

Joseph shook his head. "I'm sure it's a coincidence. Frederick's interest in building a hydro plant on the Zambezi has no relation to his son's appetite for prostitutes."

"Can I ask you a question? I want an honest answer."

"Of course."

"Will the courts give us a fair trial?"

He met her eyes. "Nyambo isn't invincible. Every adversary has a weakness."

She stared at him, wondering at the uncanny symmetry between his words and her father's so long ago. "Someone once told me the same thing. He called it the Rule of Achilles."

Joseph smiled. "Whoever he was, he was right."

PART TWO

A clear conscience fears no accusation.
—*African proverb*

Bella

Lusaka, Zambia
July, 2004

The air in the bar was warmer than the night itself. So many bodies pressed together on the dance floor, it felt like a pocket of summer in the middle of winter. She was dancing near the center of the crowd, as she did when she was looking for clients. Everyone could see her here. She was wearing red—her favorite color. Her dress was a slinky thing, poorly suited to the cold but a magnet for attention. The song they were playing was new to her, but it had the sort of thumping beat that infused her with courage.

Bella knew everyone at Alpha: the bartenders, the regular customers, and the girls. On Saturday nights, there was at least one girl for every man in the place. The competition was cutthroat, and Bella trusted no one but Doris. The price of a transaction was influenced by many factors: the duration of the encounter, the presence or absence of a condom, the need for a hotel room, and the visible means of the client. To Bella, the client mattered more than anything. She charged foreigners more than Zambians, coloreds more than blacks, Zambians with nice watches more than those without, and so on. The system worked because demand for her services was high. Even at twenty-seven, she was still one of the prettiest girls in the room.

After the song ended, she slipped to the bar and took a bottle of Castle lager from the bartender, purposely avoiding the eyes of the men on either side of her. She was an expert at the game. The men who had money wanted the illusion of conquest—a girlfriend experience. They wanted to believe that the attraction was a shared phenomenon. She put on her bored face and took a small swig of beer, waiting while another pulse-pounding song turned the dance floor into a hive of sweat and motion.

It didn't take long for a young man to approach her. He was dressed casually, but she could tell he had money from the cut of his leather jacket, the shine of his shoes, and the gold watch he wore on his wrist.

"Hey, honey," he said in Nyanja, "let me buy your beer."

Bella had heard the line countless times over the years. When she was younger and still thought the world could change, she had despised it. She had loathed the bars and the men, the exchange of intimacy for kwacha. That part of her—the girl who believed in the future—had eventually died, leaving behind only numbness and need. The come-on meant nothing to her now. It was business, the job that kept Kuyeya and her alive.

"That's nice of you," she replied, clearing a space for him.

The man put some kwacha on the counter and leaned toward her, speaking over the music. "A girl as pretty as you, why haven't we met before?"

She studied him carefully. She guessed he was in his early twenties and a young professional—a lawyer or a businessman. There was something vaguely familiar about his face, but she couldn't place it.

She gave him a flirty smile and ignored his question. "What's your name?"

"What's yours?" he asked.

"Bella," she answered, playing along.

"I like that. Tell me, Bella, what's a girl like you doing in a place like this?" He swept his arm across the room. "These men have no refinement, no class."

His contempt surprised her. Alpha was one of the hippest bars in Lusaka. She touched his arm. "If you don't like it, we can go somewhere else."

"But you just started your beer." He signaled the bartender to bring him a bottle of Mosi, then placed his hand on hers. "I knew another girl named Bella. She was from a village in Tuscany. Do you know where that is?"

"Italy," she replied swiftly. She wasn't a simpleton.

He laughed. "How far did you go in school?"

"I got my diploma," she said, the lie more alluring than the truth. "How about you?"

"I went to university in London." He gestured with his hand. "Why don't we sit down?"

She allowed him to take her arm and lead her to a table by the door. The air was colder here, and goose bumps quickly formed on her skin. He surprised her again by wrapping his jacket around her shoulders.

"You didn't tell me your name," she said.

He gave her a sly smile. "If it matters so much, why don't you guess?"

"There are an infinite number of names in the world," she objected.

"Ah," he said, "now I know you don't belong here."

She feigned a flattered laugh and searched his eyes,

trying to figure out his agenda. She was not used to this, the client being in control. She waited until the silence became awkward and then took a guess. "Is it Richard?"

He shook his head. "But you're close. It's the name of a king."

"George," she guessed.

"Not a mere monarch. A king of kings."

"Alexander, I don't know."

His eyes glinted in the light. "Most girls bore me. It's rare to find one who does not."

She gave him a blank look, suddenly weary of the contest. If he didn't want to tell her his name, she would give him one: Siluwe. He had the cunning of a cat.

"I have a flat close by," he said, touching her fingers with his. "I promise you'll like it."

She hesitated. As a rule, a girl never went home with a new client. Sex could be had in a hotel, a bathroom, a car. In a private residence, the risk of violence was too great.

"Name your price," he said, sensing her reticence.

She folded her hands and felt the absence of the ring. She had left it with Kuyeya as she always did when she went out. She looked toward the dance floor, doing a calculation in her mind. She had doctor bills to pay. Kuyeya needed medicine for her heart. There was danger in taking the man's offer, but danger was nothing new. Any client could turn into a monster.

"A million kwacha," she said. "For an hour, no more."

He stared at her for a long moment, and she had the thought again that he looked familiar. Something about his eyes, his self-assurance, what was it? She couldn't figure it out.

At last he gave her a lopsided smile. "Darious. My name is Darious."

Chapter 9

Lusaka, Zambia
August, 2011

The response team congregated again on Monday morning. Zoe sat across from Joseph, anxious to hear his report. She had left him a voicemail on Sunday asking about his nocturnal adventures at Alpha Bar, but his response had been a cryptic text: "*Good things come to those who wait.*"

She had replied: "*They better be good. I hate waiting.*"

When everyone assembled, Mariam looked at Zoe. "I talked to the DPP about Darious's history with Bella and the incident with Bright. He was guarded, of course, but he's going to review the case today." She turned to Joseph. "Zoe tells me you have an update?"

He nodded. "I went to Alpha Bar on Saturday night. I spent time with a couple of girls."

"I hope you wore protection," Niza said wryly.

He laughed. "Condoms don't fit over my ears." He placed his hands on the table. "The girls go by the street names Candy and Love. They know Darious. He's a fixture at Alpha. But they don't go with him anymore. They think he has HIV."

"Is he on medication?" Zoe inquired.

"They didn't know, but I don't think so. I watched him for a while. He has lesions on his skin, and he's thinner than he should be. He went to the bathroom four times in an hour. He was drinking, but so was everyone else. I'd guess it was diarrhea. If I'm right, he's pretty far along."

"How would you know that?" asked Niza.

Joseph was silent for a long moment. "My little sister died of AIDS."

Even Niza seemed shocked by his admission. "I'm sorry," she whispered.

Zoe looked at Joseph with newfound understanding. It explained, in part, why he was so devoted to his work.

Mariam spoke up. "I'm very sorry to hear about your sister, Joseph. But I'm curious about your theory. If Darious has AIDS, why wouldn't he be on ARVs? This isn't the 1990s. The drugs are everywhere now, and they're free."

"The myths still have power," Zoe responded.

"As does the stigma," Sarge agreed.

Zoe nodded. "If a man as enlightened as Thabo Mbeki can question whether HIV causes AIDS, then anyone can question it," she said, referring to the controversy fueled by Nelson Mandela's successor in South Africa.

"But Mbeki lost that debate," Mariam objected.

"You and I know he was wrong," Sarge said. "But a lot of people still agree with him. The suspicion of Western motives runs deep."

"Sarge is right," Joseph said. "Darious may or may not question the science, but I'm certain he's afraid of what his family will think. My sister was. She didn't tell me until she was too sick to stand. Even then, she swore me to secrecy. My father thinks she died of pneumonia."

At that moment, Zoe had an idea. "Wait a minute," she said. "Kuyeya is a disabled child. The obvious assumption is that she's a virgin. What about the old myth that sex with a virgin can cure HIV? Darious knew where she was living. Doris saw him a few weeks ago. What if he was lying in wait?"

"Of all the fanciful scenarios," Niza rejoined. "Darious is too smart to believe in fairy tales. He might be apprehensive about disclosing his status. But to rape a disabled girl in an attempt to cure himself? It's hard to believe."

Zoe looked at Niza in frustration. "Bright is proof that Darious has no concern about raping a child. And desperate men are gullible. The other day on the street I got a flyer from an *nganga* advertising therapy for bad luck, witchcraft, relationship problems, penile enlargement, and AIDS. The flyer was printed in English. It was aimed at the literate. People like Darious."

"Zoe has a point," Sarge said.

"It's frightening, but believable," Joseph agreed.

"Am I the only level-headed person in the room?" Niza said. "Even if by some vast stretch of the imagination all of you are right, how in the world are we going to prove it?"

The silence descended so quickly it was as if a curtain had been dropped. Everyone stared at Niza until she held up her hands defensively. "It's a fair question."

"Granted," Sarge said. "But we have a way to go before we need to worry about proof."

"I'll start asking around," Joseph offered. "There are a lot of *nganga*s in Lusaka, but there can't be many that Darious would trust. If he went to one, I should find out about it eventually."

Mariam looked at the clock on the wall. "It's nine thirty. Zoe and Niza, help Sarge prepare the paperwork for co-prosecution. Joseph, put your findings in a report. I'll get Mwila to contact Dr. Chulu. He should know that Darious may have the virus. I'll inform you as soon as I hear from the DPP. Let's hope for a green light."

The call from the Director of Public Prosecution came a few minutes before three in the afternoon. This time Mariam invited Zoe into her office on the condition she remain quiet.

"This case is very troubling," said the DPP. "Has the child seen a psychiatrist?"

"Not yet," Mariam said, "but we're working to schedule an examination."

"And her family? No one knows when she was born?"

"We have her physical appearance, and we have Doris who she lived with—"

"Yes, yes," he interjected. "But the woman's testimony is pure conjecture. I'm not trying to be difficult, but I'm a lawyer. The weakness is obvious enough."

"We have other leads," Mariam said. "We'll find someone who can tell us her age."

The DPP sighed. "Mariam, I have great respect for your team. Sarge and Niza are two of the best attorneys in Lusaka. But this isn't some illiterate criminal you're talking about. This is Darious Nyambo. His father is a former cabinet minister. His mother sits on the High Court."

"Look, Levy," Mariam said, "I know it's a risk for you. I don't want to be embarrassed by this either. But we're in a dilemma. Our case isn't airtight without DNA, but we can't get a blood sample without a court order. To get a court order you have to let us prosecute."

The pause that followed was pregnant with the DPP's unspoken doubts. "Why didn't Doris report her daughter's rape? It could have prevented all of this."

The question was rhetorical, and Mariam didn't respond.

"You promise me the samples haven't been tampered with?" he said at last.

Mariam nodded. "Dr. Chulu is preserving them at the hospital."

The DPP cleared his throat. "The law is ambiguous, but it needs to change. Rape is far too common in this country. The only way we can create a lasting deterrent is to use DNA. Mariam, if you are willing to stake your reputation on the guilt of Darious Nyambo, then I'm going to let you. But if you fail, it could undermine everything you've worked for."

When the DPP granted his consent, Zoe's heart soared, but her eagerness was not reflected in the faces around the table. Mariam and Sarge were grave, and Niza looked ashen.

"Why don't you think about it and let me know," the DPP said, and ended the call.

For a long moment, no one in the room moved or spoke. Zoe held her breath, waiting for someone to break the ice.

"Sarge?" Mariam said at last.

Sarge tented his hands, returning her gaze. "A crime is a crime. I believe the evidence. I'm ready to move forward."

Mariam turned to Niza. For once the young attorney had nothing to say.

"Niza, look at me," Sarge said in a quiet voice, waiting until she did before continuing. "This is our chance to do what the politicians only talk about. We can change a life. We can change the system itself. But we need your help. I need your help."

Finally, Niza spoke. "You know how much my father sacrificed for standing on principle?" she asked in an anguished voice. "He tried to convince Robert Mugabe to end the land-reform program. Mugabe might have had him killed if we hadn't fled to Zambia."

"Your father had courage," Sarge replied. "He couldn't ignore his conscience."

As Zoe watched, something changed in Niza's face. Her eyes narrowed and her jaw tensed with sudden resolve. "Nyambo will treat this as an act of war," she said, smiling grimly. "If we want to stand any chance of winning, we have to do the same."

Mariam picked up the phone and held the handset in the air. "Shall I make the call then?"

Niza answered for all of them. "Make the call."

At six o'clock that evening, Joseph arrested Darious outside his father's house in Kabulonga. It was an event Zoe wished she could have witnessed, just to see the look on Darious's face when Joseph put him in handcuffs. But she couldn't be there; she was an American, a woman, and an attorney. There were protocols to follow. And there was the matter of her safety.

Joseph conducted the interrogation at the police post in Woodlands. Zoe heard from him after he had placed Darious in the lockup.

"He denies all of it, of course," Joseph said. "He claims he was with his father on the night Kuyeya was raped. We searched the SUV and didn't find anything. Bella was right in naming him Siluwe. He's extremely calculating."

"You sound like you're enjoying yourself," she replied, sitting on the couch in her flat.

"I've been waiting a long time for a case like this. Listen, I have to write the report. I'm going to deliver the docket to the police prosecutor's office in the morning. I have a friend who'll make sure it's indicted and sent to the Principal Resident Magistrate right away. We should get an initial hearing by the end of the week."

"I take it Darious will get out on bond?"

"It's already been arranged."

"Did he hire Benson Luchembe?"

Joseph chuckled. "Of course. He's coming down here in a few minutes."

"So this is the beginning."

"Yes," he said, "but don't get too excited. We have a long road ahead."

Joseph was right. The wait for an initial hearing lasted only three days. On Thursday morning, Zoe climbed into Maurice's Prado for the short trip to the Subordinate Court. Niza joined her in the back seat and Sarge settled in up front.

The magistrate's court complex, built in 2005 at the behest of President Mwanawasa, a former lawyer, was a thing of uncommon beauty in a city dominated by drab, Soviet-style architecture. The stately brick edifice had a vaulted lobby with glass block windows and a dozen courtrooms that were reached by way of a covered arcade.

They entered the lobby and met David Soso, the police prosecutor assigned to the case. Clad in a chalk-stripe suit and purple tie, he looked more banker than lawyer. "Hi, Sergeant," he said, shaking Sarge's hand. "We're in Courtroom 9. Magistrate Thoko Kaunda."

"The judge, who is he?" Zoe asked Niza, walking behind Sarge and David.

"He's young," Niza replied. "He was hired straight out of school."

Zoe shook her head. "Excellent. A new member of the bar deciding the fate of Darious Nyambo. Cue the puppet show."

They strolled down the arcade between patches of grass and open-air skylights. Zoe saw a group of young attorneys waiting outside the court-room along with two men who looked like elder statesmen. The first was Benson Luchembe. Tall and corpulent with a mane of white hair, the lawyer carried himself like a village chief at a political rally—a figurehead who persuaded with pageantry. The second was Frederick Nyambo. He was taller than Zoe recalled from their brief interaction at the Intercontinental, but his face was unmistakable. In contrast to Luchembe, he had the aloof look of a monarch who ruled by divine right.

Luchembe tilted his head, and Frederick turned to watch them pass. Zoe met his eyes and smiled wryly. *We remember each other, but you can see I'm not impressed.*

Sarge led the way into the courtroom and set down his briefcase. Niza and David Soso sat next to him at counsel table, and Zoe took a seat in the front row of the gallery. Designed in the British style, the courtroom had high ceilings, wood trim and benches, and a dock cordoned off by a railing. Zoe doodled on a legal pad until the defense team sauntered in. Cocking her head, she saw Frederick Nyambo take a seat at the back of the courtroom alongside a handsome woman in a jade *chitenge*. *That must be Patricia*, she thought.

Joseph slid in beside her and whispered, "The jackals have gathered."

"Along with the lion and lioness," she replied, gesturing with her head toward the Nyambos.

He nodded. "Must be expecting a feast."

Suddenly, the door to chambers opened and Thoko Kaunda climbed the steps to the elevated bench, lugging a raft of binders. He took a seat and placed the binders in piles like a student arranging pencils at an exam. He was no older than thirty-five, with a high forehead and wireframe glasses. Zoe felt a churning in her stomach. *Unless you are tougher than you look, Luchembe is going to eat you for lunch.*

Kaunda waited until everyone was seated and then read the docket so quietly that Zoe strained to hear. He waved a hand toward the courtroom deputy who summoned Darious from a holding room. Darious was thinner than Zoe remembered. She looked at him closely and saw the blemishes on his skin. He took his place in the dock, staring at the magistrate with feline eyes. Like his father, he had the insouciant bearing of a superior being.

After dispensing with a preliminary matter, Kaunda called their case. He held up the charge sheet so that it obscured the bottom half of his face and read the statutory description of defilement in a monotone. Then he looked at Darious and raised his eyebrows almost apologetically.

"Do you admit or deny the charges?" he asked.

"I deny them," said Darious without a flicker of concern.

The magistrate turned to the lawyers seated at counsel table. "In light of the defendant's plea, we must schedule a trial date."

Sarge and Luchembe stood at the same time. Kaunda motioned to the defense attorney, giving him the first word.

"Your Worship," Luchembe began, choosing the honorific usually reserved for appellate judges, "I must apologize to the Court. My trial calendar is booked until December of next year."

Sarge shook his head. "Your Worship, this case involves the testimony of children. Their memories diminish rapidly over time. We don't need more than five or six months to complete our preparations. There is no excuse to delay this case beyond April of next year."

Kaunda shuffled his papers, then opened a notebook. "If you can try the case in one day, I have dates in June. If you need more time, I will give you a date in December. It is your choice."

As Luchembe gloated, Sarge conferred with Niza. "If the Court will allow us to bring witnesses into the evening," he said, "we can try this case in one day."

The magistrate frowned. "The Court will adjourn no later than seventeen hundred hours."

Sarge looked deflated. "Then we ask for two days in December."

Kaunda nodded and wrote something in his notebook. "This case will be set down for trial on the twelfth and thirteenth of December, 2012," he intoned. "Do we have any other matters to deal with at the present time?"

"The defense is satisfied," Luchembe replied.

"There is another issue," Sarge replied, handing Luchembe a stapled document. "We wish to test the biological evidence acquired by Dr. Chulu on the night of the incident against a sample of the defendant's DNA. We have prepared an application for an order requiring the defendant to provide a blood sample. I respectfully suggest that the matter be brought for mention immediately."

Luchembe scanned the document and puffed out his chest. "Your Worship, this application intrudes upon my client's constitutional rights. There is no precedent for this request in Zambia—"

"There is, indeed, Your Worship," Sarge interjected. "Such samples are routinely ordered in paternity cases where the accused wishes to prove that he did not father a child. In addition, the courts of Britain and many other countries permit this sort of testing in rape cases. We agree that it is a matter of first impression in Zambia, but we submit that the question has a straightforward answer."

This exchange seemed to paralyze Kaunda. He sat motionless on the bench, and then flipped through paperwork. "The samples from the victim," he said at last, glancing at Darious, "have they been preserved according to protocol?"

"Yes, Your Worship," Sarge replied.

"Where are they currently?"

"In Dr. Chulu's possession."

At this point, Luchembe made a last ditch appeal. "Your Worship, my client is a man of considerable reputation in Lusaka. This prosecution is a farce perpetrated by a British organization that doesn't believe Zambians have the ability to enforce our own laws. This Court adjudicates defilement cases all the time. There is no need for DNA."

Kaunda looked at Luchembe over his wireframe glasses. "If an application is before me, I have no choice but to hear it. Even if it has disturbing constitutional implications." He studied his notebook again. "The election is scheduled for the twentieth. I believe this matter can be resolved before then. Does counsel object to a hearing on the fifteenth?"

"No, Your Worship," Sarge said.

Luchembe's eyes smoldered. "The defense objects to this whole proceeding."

"Duly noted," Kaunda said. "I am placing the case on the docket for the fifteenth of September at ten o'clock. This matter is adjourned."

As the lawyers gathered their briefcases, Zoe turned to Joseph and managed a hesitant smile. Out of the corner of her eye, she saw Frederick Nyambo speaking to Patricia in a whisper. Zoe shuddered. *They didn't have a chance to corrupt him before now. But they see how easy he will be to manipulate.*

As if intuiting her thoughts, Joseph said, "I'm worried about the judge."

"That makes two of us," she replied. "He's out of his depth."

When she glanced toward the Nyambos again, they were gone.

Chapter 10

The next week passed in a blur. In five business days, Luchembe's legal team produced a rebuttal memorandum attacking the constitutionality, rationality, and morality of DNA testing in a rape case. Ignoring the weight of foreign authority in favor of DNA, Luchembe cherry-picked and misconstrued a South African decision questioning the efficacy of profiling where only small samples were used. Worse, Luchembe referred to Kuyeya as a "mentally disturbed child," playing upon the

African suspicion of people with intellectual disabilities. The memorandum was a masterpiece of misdirection and prejudice—just the sort of charade that could fool Thoko Kaunda into ruling against them.

After reading the brief, Sarge looked as angry as Zoe had ever seen him. "The only way to fight this *warped* rhetoric is to give Kaunda something enticing, something to feed his ego."

Niza's eyes lit up. "Why don't we dress him up as a freedom fighter? I bet he's spent most of his life wishing he were related to Kenneth Kaunda, hero of Zambian independence. Let's turn DNA into a weapon of reform."

Zoe laughed. "Brilliant."

Sarge tossed the memorandum on his desk. "I have no idea if it will work, but I like it."

Two days before the hearing, Zoe drove out to St. Francis for Kuyeya's psychiatric evaluation. Dr. Mbao met her at the entrance to the children's home. A garrulous middle-aged woman with a megawatt smile, she pumped Zoe's hand as if they were dear friends. They found Kuyeya sitting under the giant acacia tree, watching Sister Irina put on a puppet show.

"Hi, Kuyeya," Zoe said, sitting down beside her. "How are you today?"

Kuyeya made the balloon sound. "Hi, Zoe. I like your music."

Sister Irina grinned. "Especially your collection of Johnny Cash."

"Johnny plays the guitar," Kuyeya said.

Zoe laughed. "You have good taste."

Throughout this exchange, Dr. Mbao stood in the background. Now she stepped forward. "I'm Margie," she said cheerfully, sitting on the bare earth beside Kuyeya. "I'm so happy to meet you." She pointed at the toy monkey. "Does your friend have a name?"

"He's Monkey," the girl replied, holding him against her chest.

The psychiatrist looked at Sister Irina. "Zoe says you've been keeping a journal of her words. Have you detected any themes?"

"She talks a lot about noise," the nun said. "When the children are playing, she sometimes says things like: 'The children are loud. The children are not happy.' Or: 'The children should be quiet. I like quiet.'"

"Does she mention her mother at all?" the psychiatrist asked.

The nun nodded. "When I give her medicine, she says, 'Medicine is good. Mommy gives me medicine.' But when I ask her about her mother, she shuts down."

"What about her pain? Does she talk about it?"

Sister Irina shook her head. "The other day she stumbled over a rock and started to cry. I could tell she was hurting by the way she pressed down on her inner thighs. But when I asked her about it, she didn't talk. She made a sound—a bit like a groan—over and over again."

"Mmm," the doctor said. "I'd like to see your notebook. But before that, I need to spend some time alone with her."

Sister Irina stood and walked with Zoe to the breezeway. "Sister Anica says you made an arrest," she said. "What kind of man is he?"

"He's from a very powerful family," Zoe replied.

Sister Irina looked across the courtyard. "Is he sick?"

"He might be. We're not sure."

Tears came to the nun's eyes. "I'm praying she will be well. When will the trial be held?"

Zoe grimaced. "Next December. The defense attorney succeeded in delaying things."

"I think she will talk by then," Sister Irina said. "I think she will tell her story."

"According to Joy Herald, Dr. Mbao is the best. Perhaps you're right."

The morning of September 15, five days before the national election, Maurice drove Zoe, Sarge, and Niza back to the Subordinate Court. The streets of Lusaka were thronged with political demonstrators, waving banners and flags. Green-clad supporters of the Patriotic Front yelled angry slogans, denouncing President Banda, while blue-clad devotees of the incumbent MMD shouted, "*Boma ni boma!*"—"Government is government!"—and sang raucous songs.

Zoe searched the sea of green T-shirts for a sign of the young man in the bandana but didn't see him. It had been three and a half weeks since the confrontation in Kanyama. Her shock after the incident had sublimated into a perpetual unease hovering at the periphery of her consciousness. Most of the time she thought nothing of it, but occasionally when she saw a PF cadre cruising the streets, she felt the fear again.

When they entered the courthouse lobby, Zoe saw Joseph talking with David Soso, the police prosecutor. She hadn't seen Joseph in over a week. Mariam had told her he was tied up in meetings at police headquarters, but Zoe had texted him and received no reply.

"Hey, stranger," she said, touching his arm. "What've you been up to?"

Joseph shook his head almost imperceptibly. "Sorry I didn't make it to the braai on Saturday. I heard it was fun."

"We missed you," she replied giving him a curious look. "The impala was a hit."

They walked down the arcade to Courtroom 9. As before, Benson Luchembe and his retinue stood in a huddle outside the entrance, but this time Frederick Nyambo was absent. Luchembe frowned at Joseph when he and Zoe passed by.

"What was that about?" Zoe asked after they entered the courtroom.

"Darious isn't the first of his clients I've put in jail," he replied.

They sat together in the gallery and watched Sarge and Niza unpack their briefcases at counsel table. The CILA attorneys were as serious as Zoe had ever seen them. The hearing was critical, and even the unflappable Sarge looked tense.

Magistrate Kaunda appeared a few minutes after ten o'clock. He made himself comfortable on the bench and gave the lawyers a thoughtful look. Zoe glanced around and realized that the Nyambos were not in the courtroom.

"I've read your application," the magistrate said to Sarge. "And your submission in opposition," he said, turning to Luchembe. "And I'm prepared to hear argument. I plan to take the matter under advisement and issue a written decision. I will hear from the applicant first."

Sarge stood and held out his hands. "Your Worship," he began, "DNA is not a Western phenomenon. The science of genetics is not only valid in lands where people's skin is white. DNA is here is Africa, in this courtroom. And in it dwells the truth. The truth offered by DNA is more credible than the testimony of eyewitnesses who can misunderstand and forget. The truth of DNA is more compelling than the testimony of the most competent investigating officer. It is a truth that exists apart from passion and faction, a truth that respects nothing but itself. And in a court of law, where truth and impartiality are paramount, DNA deserves an audience."

He fixed Kaunda with a righteous stare. "Today, fifty years after our country gained its independence, girls in our cities are not free. They live in fear. They are afraid because they are targets, because some men consider sex with the girl of their choosing to be a moral right. It is up to us— lawyers, judges, keepers of the law—to liberate our children from fear."

As Sarge took a theatrical pause, Zoe regarded him in admiration. He spoke as if inspired.

"It would be one thing," he went on, "if the weight of authority stood against the use of DNA in the context of rape. But exactly the opposite is true. Courts in many nations have embraced DNA, and rapists have been sent to jail. The same will be true in Zambia. It would be one thing if the laws of Zambia *prohibited* the taking of a blood sample from an accused. But they do not. The only thing that separates children like Kuyeya from justice— and freedom from fear—is indecision."

Sarge raised his voice in emphasis. "Mark my words. One day a decision *will* be made. One day in this very courtroom DNA will be used to convict the rapist of a child. The only question before this Court is whether today is the day."

Sarge returned to his seat in the silence of a spellbound courtroom. Benson Luchembe took his time standing up, and his tone, when he began to speak, was unsteady.

"Your Worship, I'm reminded of an old saying. If something is not broken, there is no need to fix it. The crime of defilement has existed in Zambia for decades. The law offers this Court many tools to prosecute it. DNA is not one of them. Our system may differ from the rest of the world, but it is *our* system. And the system is not broken. There is no need to fix it."

Over the next ten minutes, Luchembe rehearsed

the high points from his memorandum: that Zambia's Constitution protects a person against unlawful search; that while a court may order a criminal defendant to submit to a medical examination to ascertain any matter material to the proceedings, the word "examination" should not be interpreted to include a blood sample; and that a court-ordered DNA test would not only violate Darious Nyambo's constitutional rights but would also pave the way for the rights of all defendants in rape cases to be infringed.

The defense attorney's performance was remarkably lackluster, and Zoe found herself nursing a fleeting hope that Kaunda would grant their application. She looked at Sarge, expecting him to deliver a point-by-point rebuttal, but his reply, when it came, was spare.

"Your Worship," he said, "the choice before you is not an abstraction; it is a child. Kuyeya deserves justice. This Court has the power to deliver it. I trust you will do so."

The magistrate nodded. "I thank counsel for your words. As promised, I will take this matter under advisement. Let's hope the election in a few days is peaceful."

When Kaunda disappeared into chambers, Benson Luchembe stomped out of the courtroom, prompting a scramble among his staff.

Zoe stood and moved toward Sarge to congratulate him. "That was an argument worthy of the Supreme Court," she said.

Sarge glanced at the bench. "Somewhere along the way, this case became personal."

Zoe smiled. "Let's hope young Thoko feels the same."

Chapter 11

The magistrate's opinion arrived by email the next morning. Zoe had never heard Sarge curse before, and the sound of it shocked her. He jerked away from his desk. "Kaunda had it written before the hearing," he exclaimed. "He only pretended to listen to me."

He stood up quickly and disappeared into Mariam's office. Minutes later, Mariam called the response team to a meeting. Zoe walked to the conference room with Niza and found Joseph already there. He glanced at her but didn't speak, his eyes fraught with anger.

After everyone was seated, Mariam said, "The ruling is a setback. We need to decide what to do about it. Joseph, do you have any evidence that Kaunda was corrupted?"

Joseph blinked as if coming out of a trance. "I followed him everywhere. He didn't meet with anyone from the Nyambo family or Luchembe's firm. But that doesn't prove anything. They could have spoken on the phone or by email."

That's why I didn't see you for days, Zoe thought. *You were shadowing the magistrate.*

"In light of that, we have two options," Mariam went on. "First, we take the DNA issue to the High Court. Second, we proceed to trial without DNA."

"An appeal will take months and give Luchembe an excuse to delay the trial further," said Niza. "There's no chance that a High Court judge will make an example of Patricia Nyambo's son. They'll find a way to rule against us on a technicality."

Sarge shook his head. "The magistrate has to be compromised. You don't write an entire opinion on a subject so significant before you hear oral argument."

"He could have written it last night," Mariam suggested.

"It's the longest decision I've ever gotten from him. Ten pages of careful reasoning. He knows we stand little chance on appeal. He wants us to try this case in front of him without DNA. We have to find a way around him."

"The only way around him is to get him recused," Mariam said. "But without evidence of bias or corruption, we can't go to the Principal Resident Magistrate."

Joseph leaned forward in his chair. "I have a thought. It's been bothering me since the beginning. Did any of you see the way Kaunda looked at Darious at the initial hearing? He was apologetic. What if they know each other?"

"Now that I think about it," Zoe said, "I saw the same thing."

Sarge furrowed his brow. "It's an intriguing idea. But they would have to have a substantial relationship to create a conflict of interest. The Principal Resident Magistrate will never intervene if they're just acquaintances."

"It's worth a look," Mariam said to Joseph. "Let us know what you find. In the meantime, does anyone vote for an appeal?"

All heads shook in unison.

"Okay," she said. "That means we have to proceed on the assumption that the burden of proof must be met without DNA. We need more evidence. We need an adult eyewitness. We need someone who can tell us definitively when Kuyeya was born. And if there was a personal motive, we need to figure out what it was."

"I'm working on the virgin rape angle," Joseph said. "I'll go back to Kanyama and Kabwata and beat the bushes. Perhaps I'll find someone I didn't talk to before."

"And I'll keep digging into the past," Zoe said. "I think a trip to Livingstone is in order."

"I agree," Mariam said. She looked at Joseph. "If you can spare a couple of days, I'd like you to go along. We'll cover your expenses."

He gave Zoe a hint of a grin. "The falls are nice this time of year."

* * *

Zoe returned to her desk and powered up her laptop, barely containing her enthusiasm. Victoria Falls was one of her favorite places on earth. She purchased a pair of round-trip tickets to Livingstone, reserved a rental car, and booked two rooms at the Zambezi Safari Lodge. At noon, she drove home to pack. She threw some clothes into a duffel bag and placed her MacBook and Bella's diary in her backpack. Then she cobbled together a lunch of grapes and cheese and ate it on the deck while studying a map of Livingstone.

Just after one, Joseph met her at the gate in his truck, wearing a short-sleeve shirt, cargo shorts, and sandals. She tossed her duffel into the flatbed and climbed in, wedging her backpack between her knees. He smiled and gunned the engine, throwing her against her seat.

"Are you excited or something?" she asked.

"I haven't been on an airplane in years," he said with a laugh.

"What is it with men and mechanical things?" She rolled her eyes. "My brother is like a kid every time he's at an airport."

Twenty minutes later, they parked in the lot at

the Lusaka International Airport and entered the terminal, joining the queue of passengers waiting to pay the departure tax. Before long, Zoe's eyes began to wander. The airport reminded her of the Park Street bus station in Johannesburg—a modernist cavern with wide-open floors and a confusing array of gates.

Suddenly, she frowned. Thirty feet away, a man was leaning against a wall, staring at them. Dressed in a floral-print shirt and black sunglasses, he had the build of a bull—large head, no neck, and a body sculpted out of muscle. She stared back at him until he turned away, searching her memory for his face. She couldn't place him. He was holding a duffel bag. He was probably just another passenger.

When their flight was called, they boarded the twin-engine propeller plane and took seats at the rear—Zoe by the window, Joseph by the aisle. The last passenger to board the aircraft was the man in sunglasses. He looked toward them briefly and then sat down in the second row. Zoe studied the back of his head, feeling a vague flutter of concern. She considered pointing him out to Joseph, but she didn't want to seem paranoid.

The plane took off and banked to the south-west, climbing into the spotless sky. Zoe watched Lusaka recede into the distance and then vanish altogether, like a mirage in the highland bush. She took out Bella's notebook and began to reread pages she had marked with sticky notes. Halfway through the volume, she reached the only letter Bella hadn't written in English. She had meant to ask Joseph about it some time ago.

"Is this Nyanja?" she asked.

"It's Tonga," he said, scanning the letter. His eyes darkened.

"What?"

"Didn't Doris tell you she owed Bella a debt?"

Zoe nodded. "What does it say?"

He translated the letter in paraphrase. It was summer—the year was unclear. Bella had been working the streets with Doris and a girl named Loveness. One evening a man in a Jaguar flashed a wad of cash and asked if they wanted to party. He took them to a bungalow where they found a group of seven men, all snorting white powder. It wasn't long before the men turned violent. They held Loveness down, forced her to swallow a pill of some kind, and raped her repeatedly. Two of the men dragged Bella into another room, waved knives around, and joked about circumcising her. Fearing for her life, she kicked one of the men in the groin and plunged his knife into the other man. She fled the room and found Doris spreadeagled on the floor, crying. Loveness was nowhere to be seen. At this point, Bella did something with the knife that resulted in a great deal of blood—her description in Tonga was threadbare. Then she and Doris ran naked into the night. They wandered for a while, hiding in bushes when cars passed. At the edge of Kalingalinga, they found an old woman who took pity on them and gave them clothes. They never saw Loveness again.

When Joseph finished, Zoe didn't speak for a long time. Her senses felt raw from the reading. "Doris took care of Kuyeya because Bella saved her life," she said at last.

"It appears that way." He stared at the notebook. "Do you know how Bella died?"

Zoe nodded. "Let me show you." She flipped to the end of the notebook and watched over his shoulder as he read the words of Bella's last entry.

Dear Jan,

I have AIDS. It is very advanced. My CD4 count is 42. That is why I have been sick so much. I have been coughing for months, sometimes with blood. I have fevers and sweats at night. I see terrible things in my sleep. The woman who tested me told me what I already knew. It is TB. She said I need treatment right away. I went to the hospital, but there were no doctors or nurses. Something happened in the government. They told me to come back in a week or two. I don't know if I will be able to make the trip.

I took my last client in May. I don't have strength to do it anymore. I am running out of money. If not for Doris, I would not have food for Kuyeya. I am very worried about her. Who will take her when I die? She is not like other children. She needs special care. Her heart is weak. She has bad eyesight. Who will pay for her medicine and get her new glasses? People do not understand her. They say she is cursed. I am afraid she will be abused. I trust Doris, but I don't trust the other girls or the men who come here.

I don't know why I keep writing. What do these words matter? There is nothing here but pain. And now death is coming. I will give what I have left to Kuyeya. I must go. She is having a nightmare.

Zoe stared at the period at the end of the last sentence and felt the sorrow afresh. Bella's final letter was like her life—cut off prematurely, bereft of resolution.

"She was prescient about the men," she said. "But she underestimated Doris. The irony is Doris was the reason she waited so long to get tested. Doris was suspicious of ARVs. She thought AIDS was invented by the West to kill Africans. Bella went to the *ngangas* to placate her. Then when she finally asked for help, the nurses were on strike."

"The Ministry of Health scandal," Joseph said softly.

Zoe nodded. The story was infamous in Zambia. In the winter of 2009, tens of millions of dollars had disappeared from the Ministry of Health, prompting international donors to suspend aid payments and health-care workers to abandon their posts in protest.

"I'm sure the kleptocrats who took the money never thought anyone would die," she said. "They just wanted Ferraris and Swiss bank accounts."

Joseph tensed when she said this. He looked as if he was about to reply, but the words never quite materialized. After a moment, he reclined his seat and closed his eyes, bringing an abrupt end to the conversation.

Zoe watched him carefully, puzzling over his reaction. It wasn't Bella's battle with AIDS that set him on edge. That would make sense, given his sister's death. It was the embezzlement at the Ministry of Health. But why? Why did he seem to take the scandal personally? Finding no answer, she took out the inflight magazine and read until the pilot announced their final descent into Livingstone.

When the plane parked outside the terminal, the man in sunglasses was the first to disembark. He hefted his duffel bag and left the aircraft without a glance in their direction. By the time Zoe stepped onto the tarmac, he was halfway to the terminal. Seeing the purpose in his stride, she set aside her earlier suspicions. *He's just another passenger in transit.*

She led the way into the terminal and finalized the rental of a Toyota pickup, ignoring Joseph, who had yet to speak. The attendant escorted them to the lot and gave her the keys.

"You drive," Zoe said, handing them to Joseph.

"Where are we going?" he asked in a surly tone.

"Livingstone General Hospital," she said, stifling the urge to ask what was wrong. "I bet the nursing school is still open."

On the drive into town, Zoe stared out the window at the bush, its scrub-like blanket a stark contrast to the cerulean sky. She waited for Joseph's mood to improve, but he just gazed out the windshield, lost in his own world. When they reached the city limits, he turned right on Mosi-oa-Tunya Road and headed toward downtown.

"I think we turn here," she said, remembering the road from the map she had studied.

He tossed her a glance. "I was under the impression you wanted me to drive." She studied his face and saw with great relief that the storm clouds had passed.

"You're cheering up, thank God."

He didn't respond, but the corners of his mouth turned upward.

A few minutes later, they parked in the hospital lot. At once antiquated and austere, Livingstone

General had the look of a nineteenth-century sanitarium transplanted in African soil. Its bricks were the color of riverine clay, and its louvered windows, darkened by dust, were open to admit fresh air.

They went to the reception desk and greeted an officious-looking matron. When they asked for the registrar of the nursing school, the woman shook her head.

"Her office close seventeen hundred."

Joseph repeated the question, noting that they had ten minutes left before five o'clock. Reluctantly, the woman directed them toward a hall on the far side of the lobby. Skirting a filing cabinet brimming with paperwork, they entered the admissions office of the nursing school. Behind a wooden desk sat a heavyset Zambian woman clad in a pantsuit that clung a little too tightly to her frame. The woman shook their hands.

"I am Kombe," she said in accented English. "I am Dean of Admissions."

Joseph made the introductions and then deferred to Zoe, who gave the woman a sanitized version of their interest in Bella—Charity Mizinga.

"We believe she was a student here sometime before 2004," Zoe said.

The dean typed on her keyboard. "All students enrolled after 2001 are on our computer system. She is not listed."

"What about students admitted before 2001?" Joseph asked.

"We have a paper registry," the dean replied. She disappeared through another door and returned a minute later with a dust-coated book. She dropped the book on her desk and waved away the particles that flew up. "It is organized by year and surname. If you start at the back, you'll see the roll for 2000, 1999, 1998—you understand."

"What we're really looking for is information about her family," Zoe said. "Is there anyone who might remember her? A professor or a doctor, perhaps?"

The dean ushered them to the door. "Dr. Mumbi has been here more than twenty years. I don't know if he is on rotation today." She pointed. "There are chairs down the hall that you can use. Leave the registry with the receptionist. If you have additional questions, I will be in the office tomorrow."

They took seats on folding chairs, and Joseph cracked the musty book. It wasn't long before they found Charity's name in the 1995 term. An asterisk had been placed beside her name, together with a date: April 15, 1996. Returning to the front of the book, Joseph found an explanation for the asterisk. It referred to a student who left the program before the conclusion of the term. He flipped to the 1994 term, and they found Charity's name again.

He furrowed his brow. "She dropped out in her second year."

"Something serious must have happened," she said.

He nodded. "Let's find Dr. Mumbi."

They returned to the lobby and waited for the receptionist to finish a phone conversation.

The woman arched her eyebrows, staring at the registry in Joseph's hands. "You back?"

"*Inga ndayanda kwambaula chitonga. Ino yebo?*" he said. "I prefer to speak Tonga. Don't you?"

Hearing her native language, the receptionist's face transformed.

They chatted briefly and then Joseph turned to Zoe. "Dr. Mumbi is here today. He usually walks the wards, but he just stepped outside to take a call. He hasn't come back yet."

While Joseph thanked the receptionist, Zoe walked out the door and saw a man in a white lab coat talking on his mobile phone. He was wiry and bespectacled with a shock of white hair. When he ended the call, he moved toward the entrance, lost in thought.

"Dr. Mumbi?" Zoe said.

The man looked startled. "I'm sorry. Do I know you?"

Zoe introduced herself and Joseph who had just joined her. "We're looking for the family of a girl who studied nursing here in 1996. We understand you've been here twenty years."

"1996 is a long time ago," the doctor replied. "What's the name of the student?"

"Charity Mizinga," Zoe answered.

Dr. Mumbi thought out loud. "Charity Mizinga in 1996. That was the year we were wrapping up the pediatric AIDS study. Yes, now that I think about it, I remember her. She was a gifted student, but she left the school without graduating. A shame."

"Do you have a few minutes to talk?" Zoe asked. "It's very important."

Dr. Mumbi checked his watch. "I need to get back to the wards, but I can spare a minute or two." He gestured toward the door. "Come. We'll find a more comfortable place."

He led them through a maze of hallways and up two flights of stairs to a tiny conference room furnished with a table and chairs. Though drab in every respect, the room was blessed with a window that admitted the late afternoon sunlight.

Dr. Mumbi took a seat and pointed at the book in Joseph's hands. "That is the student registry. May I see it?" When Joseph handed it over, he scanned the pages. "I don't know why, but I remember Charity quite well. She was one of those students you love to teach: intelligent, motivated, she seemed to absorb everything."

"Do you know why she dropped out?" Zoe asked.

Dr. Mumbi stared at the ceiling. "I recall only that it was abrupt. I don't think she ever gave me an explanation."

"Do you know where she lived when she was in school?"

He nodded. "She stayed with an uncle in Dambwa North. I think his name was Field."

"Where in Dambwa North?" Joseph asked.

Dr. Mumbi closed his eyes. "I don't remember the street, but I have a vague recollection that there was a large tree in the yard—a mopane, perhaps. I gave her a ride home a few times."

Zoe traded a glance with Joseph. "Let's go talk to Field."

They found Charity's uncle with minimal effort. Every person in Dambwa North seemed to know about the house with the giant candelabra-shaped tree in the front yard. A man was sitting outside the door, eyes closed and arms hanging limply at his sides. Zoe saw half a dozen packets of *tu jili-jili*—the cheapest alcohol in Zambia—crumpled up beneath his chair.

"They should ban that stuff," she said, walking toward him. "It's worse than moonshine."

"If Prohibition didn't work in America," Joseph replied, "here it would be a joke."

He shook the man's shoulder. "Field," he said.

The man stirred and drool escaped from the corner of his lips. Joseph shook him harder. The man finally opened his bloodshot eyes. He scrunched his face and mumbled something, then closed his eyes again. Joseph shook his head and knocked on the door. After a moment, a woman peered out. She and Joseph exchanged words in Tonga, and she opened the door wider, glancing at Field.

"Ugh," she said, switching to halting English. "*Tu jilijili* very bad."

She ushered them into a sparsely furnished sitting room. A Zambian news program was on the television, but the sound was muffled. Zoe and Joseph took seats on a couch while the woman fetched a bowl of tubers from the kitchen.

"*Chinaka,*" she said, gesturing at the bowl. "Tea?"

Joseph took a tuber and politely declined the beverage. When Zoe followed suit, the woman sat down on a sagging chair beside the television and fidgeted nervously with her hands.

"Are you Field's wife?" Joseph asked in English.

She nodded. "He from my village. Not so drunk then."

"Perhaps it would be easier if we spoke Tonga," he said.

While Joseph questioned the woman, Zoe studied her body language. Neither pretty nor plain, she had the open manner of a village girl, yet her face was lined and timeworn. As soon as Joseph mentioned Charity, the woman tensed. She stared at her hands and twisted her wedding ring. Her pain appeared in the cadence of her words.

"What is she saying?" Zoe whispered.

"Be patient," Joseph replied.

The exchange continued until the sky outside lost the last of its light. Zoe chewed the *chinaka* and listened to the muted voices of the television newscasters discussing the presidential campaign. President Banda had accused the Patriotic Front of inciting violence in the rural areas. Michael Sata had lashed back, accusing Banda of ineptitude and corruption. *Politics is the same everywhere*, she thought. *It's just that the West is more practiced at hiding the ugliness*.

After a while, Joseph stood and said, "Let's talk outside."

Zoe followed him to the truck. Looking up, she saw the constellation of Scorpio stretched out across the night sky and Sagittarius, the archer, locked in pursuit. She had never been superstitious, but the celestial clash felt like a portent of things to come.

"Field is Charity's uncle," Joseph said when she slid into the passenger seat. "Apart from two cousins, everyone in her family is dead—parents, aunts, siblings. Her grandmother was the last in line. She died about five years ago."

"Was it AIDS?"

Joseph navigated the truck onto the street. "Agatha—that's the woman's name—said it was TB, pneumonia, and cerebral malaria, but the pattern suggests HIV for everyone but the grandmother. Charity's father drove a truck between Tanzania and Johannesburg. He was the first to go. She had two younger brothers who died before the age of five. When her mother died, she went to stay with her grandmother. Two cousins came to stay with them later."

"I've read about families being wiped out by AIDS, but I've never met one."

"Charity lived here in nursing school," he went on. "Agatha didn't like it."

Zoe remembered the way the woman had tensed. "Why not?"

"She thinks Charity's family is bewitched."

"Because of all the death?"

"She said Field didn't drink much before Charity came. She's convinced the girl brought a curse upon her home. She tried to get her to leave, but Field didn't want her to."

I wonder why, Zoe thought. "Does she know why Charity dropped out of school?"

"Her grandmother had a stroke. Charity had to get a job to provide for her cousins."

"Did Agatha say anything about how Charity became Bella?"

"That's the hole in the story. When she moved to Lusaka, she never made contact with them again. Agatha didn't know about Kuyeya. She didn't know about Charity's death."

"Where are her cousins? They're the last link to her past."

Joseph glanced at her. "The older one, Cynthia, lives with her husband. Her brother, Godfrey, stays in the Copperbelt. The other is in Mukuni Village."

"Where Charity's grandmother lived," Zoe replied, recalling a passage from her journal.

He nodded. "I thought we would go there tomorrow."

Zoe closed her eyes, undone by Charity's story. *It was trauma enough to lose my mother. I can't imagine what it would be like to lose my entire family.* She touched Catherine's ring and the memories flooded back. New Canaan, Connecticut—August 6, 1996. The ringing phone had woken her just after three in the morning. Clouded by sleep, her mind had attributed the sound to the burglar alarm. She had listened for her father's footsteps, but she had heard his voice instead. His words were a murmur in the still August night: "*Hello? Yes, this is Jack Fleming.*" Then came the crash. She ran down the hall and found him on his knees, the phone broken beside him.

It was the only time in her life she had seen him cry.

Chapter 12

Livingstone, Zambia
September, 2011

The next morning after breakfast, Zoe and Joseph drove south toward Victoria Falls. Traffic on the main road was sparse, and Joseph pushed the truck well beyond the speed limit. On the outskirts of town, they came across a herd of elephants crossing the tarmac. The bull elephant, a regal beast with yellowed tusks, stood sentinel as cows and calves passed over, leaving behind a forest littered with broken trees.

Just before the entrance to the falls, they turned left onto a dirt road that led into rural pastureland dotted with homesteads. Apart from a majestic baobab tree just off the road, the rolling landscape was mostly bare of vegetation. The village appeared suddenly, its collection of rondavels and modern buildings sprinkled across a hillside taller than the rest. The roads were active with foot traffic, but few vehicles were about.

They drove into the village center and parked next to a sprawling acacia tree. Zoe was about to ask how Joseph intended to find Godfrey when a handsome Zambian woman wearing *chitenge* made her way toward them, her dress billowing in the wind. Joseph rolled down the window and greeted her.

"I am Margaret," she said in fluent English, "the village guide. Are you here for a tour?"

When Joseph explained that they were looking for Godfrey, she looked disappointed. "He works at the falls. He usually leaves just after sunrise."

"What does he do there?" Zoe asked.

Margaret scrutinized her. "He sells tickets. Why are you looking for him?"

Thinking quickly, Zoe replied, "We have news from his cousin, Charity."

"You know her?" Margaret looked surprised.

Zoe nodded. "In a manner of speaking."

Margaret brightened. "I knew their grandmother, Vivian, well. She was a good and wise woman. While you're here, would you like to see where Godfrey stays?"

Zoe traded a glanced with Joseph. "Why not?"

They climbed out of the truck, and Joseph handed Margaret twenty thousand kwacha. "For everything you know about Godfrey's family."

The woman smiled broadly, flashing her large white teeth. "This way," she replied.

They walked some distance into the village. Eventually, Margaret stopped outside a collection of huts and pointed. "Vivian used to stay there. Godfrey stays in the one next to it. He is the last of his family in the village."

"When did Charity leave?" Zoe asked.

"She shifted to Livingstone for secondary school," Margaret replied.

"Do you know why she moved to Lusaka?"

Margaret pursed her lips. "Vivian got sick and couldn't make her baskets anymore. She told me a man offered Charity a good job."

Zoe was instantly curious. "What man?"

Margaret shrugged. "Ask Godfrey. All I know is that he was wealthy."

"Does the name Jan mean anything to you?"

Margaret looked puzzled. "I remember it, but I don't know why. Sometimes we have white doctors who help in the clinic."

"Do you know how long Charity kept the job in Lusaka?"

The tour guide shrugged. "She sent money until three years ago. That's when Godfrey obtained his twelfth-grade certificate. Other than that I can't say."

So no word of Charity's life as a prostitute ever reached the village, Zoe thought. "Did you know she had a daughter named Kuyeya?"

"A child? No! How old is she?"

Zoe shook her head. "We're not sure."

"What do you mean? Why don't you ask . . . ?" Suddenly, Margaret understood. "Is Charity dead?"

Zoe nodded. "She died a couple of years ago."

Margaret looked confused. "You said you had news from her."

234

Zoe glanced at Joseph. "The news is about Ku-yeya," she said. "A few weeks ago, she was raped. We're prosecuting the man who did it."

When the words sank in, Margaret's expression turned bleak. She looked out over the rooftops of the village and then spoke again. "There was once a medicine man who lived near Vivian. After her husband died, the *nganga* raped her. She told the chief, but the chief sided with the *nganga*. When Vivian's children died young, people said the *nganga* had cursed her family. Now only Godfrey and Cynthia are left."

Zoe noticed that Margaret's words had unsettled Joseph. "Do you really believe that?" she asked. "That the deaths could be linked to witchcraft?"

Margaret responded indirectly. "I am a Christian. I do not visit the *nganga*s. But there is a proverb I have heard. 'A riddle made by God has no solution.' I think that about Vivian." She paused. "Godfrey is a good boy. I pray that God will let him live a long life."

Zoe shivered in the breeze. "So do I."

★ ★ ★

They drove to the falls in silence, the only sounds in the cab generated by the truck and the wind. As they approached the river, the air lost its restlessness, becalmed by the dense thicket of forest surrounding the cataracts. Joseph parked in the lot beside a line of stalls offering everything from woodcarvings of rhinos, elephants, and giraffes to malachite jewelry and tribal drums. They made their way to the ticket office and joined a line of tourists waiting for admission to the park.

"I came here when I was a boy," Joseph said. "My father wanted us to take pride in Zambia's wonder of the world."

"I was ten when I came the first time," Zoe replied. "My mother brought me. We stayed on the Zimbabwe side."

Five minutes later, they stepped into the ticket office and saw two Zambian men and a woman dispensing tickets and guidebooks. Zoe moved toward the younger man. "Are you Godfrey?" she asked.

He glanced nervously at the older man. "Yes."

She placed a pair of fifty-pin bills on the counter, more than enough to cover the cost of tickets.

"I know you're busy, but I need to talk to you about your cousin, Charity."

His eyes widened. "Do you know how she is? We haven't heard from her in two years."

She nodded, keeping her expression neutral. "When can we meet?"

"I take a break at ten o'clock," he said, handing her tickets and maps. "I'll find you at Knife Edge Point." Then he turned to a Chinese couple standing behind them and acted as if the conversation had not happened.

After browsing in the merchant stalls, Zoe and Joseph followed the signs to the Knife Edge trail. Before long, the thick tangle of forest gave way to loamy grass, and Zoe caught sight of the Eastern Cataract across the chasm. The majesty of so much water roaring over the edge of basaltic rock and plunging into the Zambezi far below took her breath away.

She followed Joseph along the edge of the cliff, taking care not to slip. The only protection against a deadly fall was a thin wooden railing. They crossed the Knife Edge Bridge in single file, Joseph in front and Zoe behind. The bridge spanned a deep cleft in the gorge. The drop was at least three hundred feet. On the far side, they scaled a long stretch of rock steps to the top of a knoll and then descended the hill to the windy perch that was Knife Edge Point.

Not seeing Godfrey, Zoe walked to the railing and looked down the gorge toward the cloud of mist that obscured the main falls. She remembered the first time her mother had brought her here—Catherine's exuberance in the rainforest across the river, the way she had skipped beneath the dripping trees and squeezed Zoe's hand when they saw a rainbow arching over the falls. Zoe had been cool toward her mother at first, resentful of her frequent absences and constant traveling. But Catherine's joy had softened her heart and left an impression that Zoe could still feel after twenty years. It was on that trip—in this place—that she had fallen in love with Africa.

She turned around and watched the path for Godfrey. Joseph stood beside her, leaning against the railing. Tourists milled around them, chattering in different languages. Suddenly, Zoe narrowed her eyes. A man was looking toward them from the crest separating Knife Edge Point from the bridge.

It was the man in sunglasses.

"Do you see that guy at the top of the hill?" she asked Joseph. "He was on our flight yesterday. I saw him watching us at the Lusaka airport."

"I've seen him before," Joseph said. "He's been following me around ever since I arrested Darious."

"*What?*" she exclaimed. "Who is he?"

"I don't know. I sent a picture of him to Interpol. I haven't heard back yet."

"And you didn't tell me?" she demanded.

"He hasn't done anything. I didn't think it was important."

She shook her head. "I don't like it when people hide things from me."

He gave her an inscrutable look. "I'll keep that in mind." He pointed. "There's Godfrey."

Zoe turned and watched as Charity's cousin slipped by the man in sunglasses and walked down the path. When he reached the railing, he regarded them carefully. "Who are you?"

Shelving her apprehension, Zoe made introductions.

"How do you know Charity?" he asked.

"I know her daughter. We're trying to help her."

His eyes went wide. "She told us she didn't have a child."

Zoe's heart sank. *Even Kuyeya she kept hidden from her family.*

"How is she?" Godfrey went on. "It's been years since we talked."

Zoe spoke frankly. "She died in 2009. I'm very sorry."

He stood motionless for a moment. "Was it TB?"

"How did you know?"

"She coughed a lot on her last call. Why didn't anyone contact us?"

Zoe returned his gaze. "We didn't know her then."

Now it was Godfrey's turn to be puzzled. "What do you mean?"

Zoe gave him an overview of the investigation, including their visit to Mukuni Village. When she finished, he gripped the railing and looked toward the falls.

"My family has endured so much," he said with sudden bitterness. "They say we are bewitched, did you know that? All because my grandmother accused an *nganga* to the chief."

Instead of responding, Zoe offered him a tether to the present. "You can help us. You know more about Charity than anyone else."

"My sister, Cynthia, knows more," he said. "But I can tell you she didn't have a daughter when she left for Lusaka. That was in 1996. Kuyeya has to be younger than fifteen."

Zoe studied him. "How do you know?"

"She couldn't have hidden a child from my grandmother. A pregnancy, maybe, but not a baby."

"Do you think she was pregnant?" Zoe asked.

He shrugged. "My grandmother did. She was certain the man who took her to Lusaka was the father. She could think of no other reason why Charity left nursing school."

Zoe was incredulous. "I thought she went to Lusaka because she needed a job."

"That was her excuse, but my grandmother didn't believe it. Charity's mother had a good job in Livingstone before she died. She left behind a savings account that paid for Charity's schooling. It's true my grandmother had a stroke. But we could have survived."

"Do you know the name of the man who took her to Lusaka?"

He shook his head. "I was only seven. All I remember is that he was a big man and wore a suit. Cynthia might know his name. She's the one who told me all of this."

"Do you know anyone named Jan? Margaret thought he might have been a white doctor who worked at the village clinic."

Godfrey gave her an inquisitive look. "I remember a white doctor. But he worked at the hospital, not the clinic. He treated me for cerebral malaria. It was severe, and I almost died. He had light hair and blue eyes, like you do. I thought he was an angel."

"What year was that?"

"It was before Charity left. She was the one who brought him to the village." He glanced at her watch. "What time is it?"

"Almost ten thirty," she replied, wishing she could ask him a dozen more questions.

He spoke in a rush. "I have to get back. Talk to Cynthia. Charity sent her letters."

"Letters?" Zoe inquired.

He nodded. "Her husband is Mwela Chansa. He works at the Nkana Mine in Kitwe."

"What's your number?" Zoe asked, fishing in her backpack for her iPhone.

He recited the digits and hastened up the path toward the bridge. When he reached the top of the hill, Zoe noticed that something was missing from the scene.

The man in sunglasses was gone.

Unnerved again, she turned to watch the Zambezi race through the rocky teeth of the escarpment, frothing and tumbling to the base of the gorge. "I'm sorry I didn't let you ask any questions," she said to Joseph.

"I'm getting used to it," he said with a dry laugh.

"We need to talk to Cynthia about the letters."

He hesitated. "You can call her if you want, but I don't have time for a trip to Kitwe. I need to focus on connecting the magistrate to Darious."

Zoe nodded, trying not to show her disappointment. "So we go home."

Joseph smiled enigmatically. "Our flight isn't until the morning."

She looked at him in puzzlement. "What are you thinking?"

His eyes twinkled. "A swim might be nice. Followed by a cruise on the river. I haven't done that since I was a kid."

After an afternoon relaxing by the pool, they changed clothes and drove to the Zambezi Waterfront, arriving a few minutes shy of four o'clock. They followed the steps down to the wharf and crossed the gangplank to the *MV Makumbi*. The riverboat was an elegant antique, its handsome wood trim showing the wear of years. They climbed stairs to the upper deck and took seats at the rear of the boat behind a group of chattering international students.

Zoe closed her eyes to the sun, enjoying the way the light suffused her eyelids. The wind blowing off the river lifted her hair and played with the fringes of her skirt. She opened her eyes again and saw Joseph staring at her.

"You could almost pass for an African," he said, as the riverboat got underway.

Zoe was taken aback. She touched the small mole above her eyebrow, remembering how many times her mother had said that the finest people she knew were Africans.

"When it gets in your blood there's no reversing it," she replied.

"What do you mean?"

"Once you live here, it's hard to leave."

"But this isn't your home."

"I'm not sure I have a home," she admitted, surprised by her own candor.

He frowned. "Your family must miss you."

She looked toward the far bank of the river. "I suppose," she said, hoping he would let the subject drop. But her hesitation only seemed to intrigue him.

"What does your father do?"

"It's not important."

He tilted his head. "You asked me the same question a while ago."

She took a breath. "He's in government."

After a moment he asked, "You're father isn't *Jack* Fleming, is he?"

Damn, she thought. *That's why I didn't want to*

answer the question. "I really don't want to talk about him. Do you mind?"

"That's fine," he said. He gestured toward the bow of the boat where the host, a middle-aged Zambian in a shirt and vest, was opening a bottle of wine. "Would you like—"

His voice trailed off, and Zoe followed his gaze. A large man had just climbed the ladder from below decks. Her heart skipped a beat when she saw the floral-print shirt and sunglasses.

"How did he get on the boat?" she hissed.

"I don't know," Joseph replied. "I wasn't paying attention."

"How did he even know we were here?"

"Good question."

Zoe watched as the man got a glass of wine from the host and took a place at the railing. He didn't look at them, but she was certain he could see them in his peripheral vision. Her fright turned quickly into anger.

"I'm going to talk to him," she said, starting out across the deck.

Joseph put his hand on her arm. "There's no need to bother him."

"I thought you said he's harmless." she retorted.

She marched toward the man, her heels clicking on the wooden planks. When she was ten feet away, he glanced at her and turned back to the river. His indifference fueled her antagonism.

"Hey," she said. "Why are you following us?"

The man took a sip of his wine, ignoring her.

"Who do you work for?"

When he failed to respond, she raised her voice: "You want me to make a scene? Why are you *here*? Did the Nyambos send you?"

At last he faced her and spoke, his voice hard. "I would be careful who you offend." Then he shouldered past her and walked toward the stairs.

She watched him until he disappeared below decks, her heart hammering in her chest. She realized that everyone was staring at her—the host, the international students, the other guests. She turned toward the railing to conceal her embarrassment. Joseph joined her a minute later, holding a beer bottle and a glass of red wine.

"It looks like you could use a drink," he said softly.

She accepted the wine without a word and

watched the river move in the wind. Near the bulrushes on the opposite bank, a hippopotamus stretched its jaws. In a tree not far away, a heron took flight.

"My mother used to say that light turns water into music," she said, trying to salvage the moment. "I always liked the metaphor."

Joseph was quiet for a while. "My mother died when I was five. I barely remember her."

His spontaneous confession surprised Zoe. "I was fourteen," she said. "She was on a humanitarian mission to Somalia."

He studied her thoughtfully. "Then Africa owes you a debt."

"No. She told me Africa saved her."

"Do you know what she meant?"

"The way she told it, she grew up in a glass house," Zoe said. "Her father was a shipping magnate. She almost never saw him. Her mother was from an old Boston family. She spent money and had affairs. It was a shallow life. After college, she traveled for a while and then went to Kenya with the Peace Corps. She said it was like being reborn. She might never have come home if her parents hadn't died in a boating accident." She paused. "I take it you've heard of the Catherine Sorenson Foundation?"

He nodded. "That's her?"

"She liquidated the entire fortune. She kept two things: a house on Martha's Vineyard and this ring." Zoe held up her hand to the sun, allowing the diamonds to catch the light. "It's funny—almost all of my memories of her have something to do with Africa. She wasn't much of a homemaker. Trevor and I spent a lot of our childhood with nannies. But when I got old enough, she brought me with her. Her passion for this place rubbed off on me."

Joseph regarded her without speaking.

"What are you looking at?" she asked, feeling self-conscious.

"My grandmother once told me that the souls of the seers are like the grass of the savannah. They only appear to die. Then the rains come and they return. When I look at you, I wonder if I'm looking at her."

His words pierced Zoe like a surgeon's blade. All her life men had praised her, but their words had been insubstantial things, and she had never believed them. With a single insight Joseph had redeemed the very notion of a compliment. She faced the river again, trying to hide the blush on her skin.

"You have a law degree," she said. "Will you practice?"

He shook his head. "I want to be Inspector General of Police."

She whistled. The IG was the top law-enforcement official in Zambia.

"The system rarely works for the poor," he explained. "I intend to change it."

"That's a tall order," she said. "Why do you think you'll succeed?"

"Because I made a promise."

"To whom?"

He looked suddenly reflective. "I think I will tell you someday. But not yet."

She turned her gaze toward the sun, sinking into the haze above the horizon, and thought of Darious sitting smugly in the dock, of Frederick Nyambo pulling strings and Magistrate Kaunda dancing like a marionette, of the threat delivered by the man in sunglasses.

"To justice," she said, holding up her wine glass, "no matter what it takes."

He touched his bottle against her glass. "I'll drink to that."

Chapter 13

Lusaka, Zambia
September, 2011

On Election Day, Zoe awoke in a sweat-stained tangle of sheets. She had spent the night—indeed the past three nights—slipping in and out of dreams. It was as if probing the mysteries of Charity's past had unlocked a hidden vent in her subconscious, releasing a torrent of memories. One moment she was on her father's yacht helping Trevor hoist the mainsail; the next moment she was walking the streets of Johannesburg, fearful of a mugging; after that, she was in Joseph's truck in Kanyama, gang members pounding on the roof.

The coup de grâce—and the thought still lurking in her mind—was Clay Randall's hands pressing her into the hot Vineyard sand.

She threw aside the mosquito net and stumbled into the bathroom. *Don't go there*, she thought, staring at her reflection in the mirror. She showered and put on shorts and a linen shirt over her swimsuit. In honor of the election, Mariam had given everyone the day off. She ate a bowl of cereal and then called Joseph. She had seen him only once since their return from Livingstone. When he didn't answer, she left him a message.

"Hey, it's Zoe. I'd love an update about the magistrate. Give me a call."

She dialed a second number and listened to the ring. *Come on, Godfrey, pick up.* But there was no answer. She left a voicemail—the third in as many days—and sent him a text message, asking for Cynthia's phone number. Then she ran a Google search for Nkana Mine. She called the main number and learned that the personnel manager was not in the office. She left a recording, requesting contact information for Mwela Chansa, Cynthia's husband.

Unable to sit still, she went for a swim. She did ten laps at a leisurely pace, allowing her brain to rest. When she finished, she treaded water in the deep end. It was then that the thought came to her. She had forgotten something—something critical. She pulled herself out of the pool and dried her hands on her towel. Picking up her iPhone, she conducted another Google search and called the number for Livingstone General Hospital.

"Is Dr. Mumbi doing rounds today?" she asked the receptionist.

"He on the ward," the woman said curtly. "You talk to me, please."

"It's urgent that I reach him today. Can you give me his mobile number?"

"Not possible."

"I spoke with him recently about a child I'm trying to help," Zoe protested, wishing she could hand the phone to Joseph to converse in Tonga. "Can you at least give him a message?"

There was silence on the line. Zoe heard the woman put the phone down and engage in a muffled conversation. Soon, her voice returned with a crackle of static.

"Tell name and number. I pass along."

She recited the information and hung up, at once berating her forgetfulness and blessing the cold water for helping her to remember. His name was on almost every page of Bella's journal—Jan. Like the narrator in a nineteenth century novel, his presence lurked behind every thought Bella had written. The whole sordid story of her exploitation had been written to him.

Minutes later, her phone rang. "Hello?" she said.

"Ms. Fleming?" replied a polished African voice.

Dr. Mumbi! "Yes, doctor, thank you so much for calling me back."

"Pleasure. You are looking for information about a child?"

"No, I'm helping one. I need to know if a doctor named Jan worked at the hospital in 1996, when Charity Mizinga was a student."

"Yes, Dr. Jan Kruger. He was with us for two years doing a study on HIV and childhood illness. He's now one of the leading authorities on AIDS in Africa."

Zoe's heart raced with the thrill of discovery. "Would Dr. Kruger have known Charity?"

"Of course. She was one of his assistants in the study."

My God, Zoe thought. "Where is he now?"

Dr. Mumbi took a breath. "After he left us, he went to the University of Cape Town. He was involved in the Khayelitsha study."

"You mean with Médecins Sans Frontières?" she asked, remembering an article she had read about MSF's pioneering research into ARV distribution in Cape Town's largest slum.

"Correct. I believe he is still at the university."

"Is he South African?"

"He is from Zimbabwe. But I believe he has family near Cape Town."

"Thank you. I can't tell you how helpful this is."

The doctor paused. "Did you ever find Charity's family?"

"Yes," she replied, avoiding the trap of a more complex response.

"I'm glad. If you talk to Dr. Kruger, please give him my best."

Zoe thanked him and hung up. She tapped in a query for HIV research at the University of Cape

Town and placed a call to the Desmond Tutu HIV Centre.

"Dr. Kruger, yes," said the woman who answered the phone, her voice carrying the brogue-like notes of Afrikaans. "He is on the faculty of the Institute for Infectious Disease and Molecular Medicine. But he is currently participating in a multi-national study on HIV/AIDS at the University of the Witwatersrand in Johannesburg."

"Is there a way I can reach him? It's very important."

The woman put her on hold and came back a minute later. "Dr. Johannè Luyt is the director of HIV research at Wits. I'm sure she can put you in touch with Dr. Kruger."

Zoe walked around the pool, wrestling with how to approach Dr. Luyt. From what Dr. Mumbi had said, Jan Kruger was an epidemiologist of renown. And Bella's journal was a catalogue of horrors. Their connection was forged fifteen years ago, when she was still Charity Mizinga, a promising nursing student. The fact of her degradation and death wasn't the kind of thing to spring on him without warning. Or was it?

She heard her phone ringing again. She rounded the corner of the pool and lifted it off the chair. She smiled when she saw Joseph's name on the screen.

"Thanks for calling me back," she said. "Where are you?"

"The Lusaka Golf Club," he replied.

She heard voices in the background. "This isn't a good time, is it?"

"Not really. What are you doing for dinner?"

"I hadn't given it much thought."

"I would say let's meet at Arcades, but nothing will be open on Election Day."

"You could come over here," she said, feeling a little flutter in her stomach.

"You mean to your flat?"

"Yes. As you know, I'm a good cook."

He hesitated. "What time?"

Her smile broadened. "How about eighteen hundred?"

"Good. I'll be there."

Zoe put down the phone again and resumed her pacing, struggling not only with the dilemma of Jan Kruger but also with her feelings about Joseph. She probed her heart, wondering whether, and when, her respect for him had become attraction. Finding no answers, she stood motionless in the sunlight, enjoying the prickle of grass between her toes and contemplating how to tell Dr. Kruger about the way Charity's life ended. She stared at the surface of the water, an idea taking shape in her mind.

I need another airline ticket.

Joseph arrived at Zoe's flat at dusk. She met him at the door in an apron and led him to the kitchen. Looking at him, dressed casually in a polo shirt and khakis, she was glad she had selected capris and a cardigan instead of a sundress.

"I hope you like Indian food," she said. "I didn't make it to the store before the election, but I had the fixings for curried chicken and rice."

"That's wonderful," he replied.

"Do you want beer or wine?"

He grinned. "I'll have whatever you're having."

She stirred the chicken a final time and turned off the burner, placing her apron on the counter. "We're eating on the deck. I'll bring everything out."

When he left, she fixed two plates and set them on a tray, together with a basket of flatbread and two glasses of chardonnay. She took the tray onto the terrace and found him looking out over the gardens. She distributed the food and wine and lit a few candles. They took seats across from one another and Zoe said, "Bon appétit!"

"This is really good," he said, eating with gusto.

She smiled. "Did you find anything at the golf club?"

He shook his head. "The magistrate isn't a member. I went to the University of Zambia, too, thinking maybe he and Darious were classmates. But Darious didn't study there."

She took a bite of chicken, enjoying the spice of the curry. "What about their childhood? Perhaps they were friends in primary school."

"Or secondary school. They could have been neighbors; their families may know each other; Darious might have dated Kaunda's sister, if he has a sister. Lots of possibilities."

She took a sip of wine. "I've been trying to reach Godfrey to get Cynthia's phone number. I haven't heard from him."

"Ah." Doris sounded almost wistful. "Lusaka is small to you?"

Zoe shrugged. "You can see the stars at night."

They continued to make small talk until the tea finished steeping. Doris handed Zoe a mug and took a seat on the chair. Zoe reached into the pocket of her suit jacket and touched her iPhone, commencing the recording.

"Ms. Kuwema," she began, "I want you to know that I'm not here to investigate you. I'm here because of what happened to Kuyeya. I need your help to find the man who raped her."

Doris nodded, looking nervous.

"I know how you make a living," Zoe said, speaking softly to lessen the blow. "I know you go by the street name Doris. I know that the man who was here last night is not your cousin. I saw the men who were with you this morning, and the other women."

Doris stared at her.

"I don't want to make problems for you," Zoe continued. "But I need you to answer my questions exactly as I ask them, leaving nothing out. Will you do that, for Kuyeya's sake?"

The silence between them extended until it became awkward. Zoe was about to restate her plea when Doris spoke, her tone low and even. "I will tell you what I know."

Zoe let out the breath she was holding. "Good. How old is Kuyeya?"

Doris shrugged. "I think she is thirteen or fourteen. But I'm not sure."

"When did you meet Bella?"

Doris looked at the ceiling. "It was winter, the year Chiluba was arrested."

Zoe processed this. Frederick Chiluba, the first Zambian president in the multi-party era, had been charged with corruption by his successor, Levy Mwanawasa, and subjected to public prosecution—an event that had shaken Zambia's patronage system to the core. She searched her memory for the year. "That was 2004?"

"Yes."

"Where did you meet her?"

Doris placed her hands in her lap. "On Addis Ababa Drive, near the Pamodzi hotel."

"You were streetwalking?"

Doris nodded. "She was new. The other girls were unkind because she was pretty and they didn't want to lose business. I took pity on her. She reminded me of my sister."

"Where was she staying at the time?"

"I don't know. I think it was a flat in Northmead."

Zoe took another sip of tea. "Did she move in with you?"

"Yes. Soon after we met. She helped with rent."

"Was Bella her street name?"

Doris nodded again. "Her real name was Charity Mizinga."

"She never mentioned anything about Kuyeya's age?"

Doris thought about this. "I think she was born in January. I do not know what year."

"Where was Bella from?"

"She came from Southern Province. Her mother was Tonga."

Zoe felt a twinge of hope. "Are her parents still alive?"

Doris shook her head. "I think they are dead."

"And her extended family?"

"I don't know. She never talked about them."

Zoe took the conversation in a different direction. "When Bella brought men here, what did she do with Kuyeya?"

Doris stood. "I will show you."

Zoe followed her down the hallway to the door on the right. The room beyond was bare except for a mattress and a chest of drawers.

"This was her place," Doris said. "Now I rent it to other girls. When Bella did business here, she put Kuyeya in the bathroom. When she went out, she left Kuyeya in this room."

On the far wall, Zoe saw thin marks in pairs and triplets. She knelt down and examined them carefully. From their spacing, she guessed they had been made by fingernails. She pictured the girl scoring the wall, and remembered Joy Herald's explanation of the stigma of disability. The indignation she felt was tempered by sorrow.

"Bella was popular with the men," Doris said when they returned to the living room. "But she never had enough money. She was always giving it to *ngangas* for Kuyeya's medicine."

Joseph shrugged. "That doesn't surprise me."

"You think he's afraid?"

"Wouldn't you be if your family was dead and your village thought you were cursed?" He put down his fork. "There's also a chance the guy who's been following us had a talk with him. He wasn't on our flight back."

She grimaced. After the riverboat had docked, the man in sunglasses had vanished. She had almost managed to forget about him. "I called Nkana Mine, looking for Cynthia's husband. No one was there on Election Day."

"I doubt she'll help us," he said. "I'm sure Godfrey talked to her."

Zoe pursed her lips, then said, "I'm going to Johannesburg tomorrow."

He frowned. "Why?"

"I found Jan, the man in Bella's journal," she said, relishing his look of disbelief. "He's an epidemiologist at the University of Cape Town, but he's doing a study at Wits in Jo'burg."

Joseph sat back in his chair. "How did you—"

"Some luck and a little detective work."

After she told him the story, he shook his head.

"Impressive deduction, I admit. But how do you know Jan isn't someone she met in Lusaka?"

She smiled. "I had the same thought. This afternoon I skimmed the journal again. I realized how much medical detail she included in her descriptions. You could argue that her language was a holdover from her nursing school days. But I don't think so. I think she was writing words that he would understand, even if she never believed he would read them."

He examined her carefully. "That's a fascinating insight."

She turned away, not knowing what to say.

After a while, he asked, "Why did you invite me to dinner?"

She felt herself begin to blush. "As you recall, you were about to invite me."

"But your home is different from a restaurant."

She looked at his eyes in the candlelight. "I enjoy your company."

A smile played across his face. "Then our reasons are the same."

Chapter 14

Just after dawn the next morning, Joseph drove Zoe to the airport. In the aftermath of Election Day, the streets of Lusaka were eerily calm. The vendors that normally crowded the roadways were absent, and foot traffic was astonishingly light. The winner of the election had yet to be announced, and the media had begun to recycle bland polling-station footage to fill the void.

"I'm worried about PF if Banda wins," Zoe said. "They'll never accept that it's fair."

Joseph frowned. "If MMD stays in power, PF

might resort to violence. But I doubt it would spread beyond the compounds. Zambians are peaceful people."

"Everyone said that about Kenya," she rejoined. "Then the whole country blew up."

They reached the airport as the sun rose above the plains. Joseph pulled into the drop-off lane and stopped beside the curb. He regarded her silently, and she realized that he was at a loss for words. Something had changed in their relationship the night before. She felt more comfortable in his presence, but at the same time she felt vulnerable, as if in giving voice to her attraction she had shed a layer of psychological clothing. From the look in Joseph's eyes, she knew the feeling was mutual.

"I'll call you when I buy my return ticket," she said. She hesitated and then kissed him lightly on the cheek before climbing out of the truck.

After passing through security, she took a seat in the departure lounge. At some point, her eyes were drawn to a television monitor hanging from the ceiling. A newscaster from the BBC was giving an update on the primary race in the United States. In advance of the debate in Orlando, her father's lead had tightened from fifteen points to eight, and a new challenger—the Governor of Kansas—had surged on a wave of anti-establishment rhetoric. The telecast showed the Senator waving to a cheering crowd, while the announcer, in voiceover commentary, questioned whether he could hold on to his advantage. Zoe shook her head. It was surreal to see her father surrounded by such adulation and controversy.

The flight to Johannesburg lasted a brief two hours, and she dozed through most of it. When the plane began its descent, she watched the city take shape through the skein of brownish haze. She saw the great flat-topped mine dumps of the Witwatersrand in the distance, and smiled. During her year in the judicial trenches with Judge van der Merwe, she had explored the many dimensions of the city— the gritty urban core, the not quite desegregated townships, the leafy suburbs and lush parklands— and had developed a deep fondness for it. While in many ways crass and dangerous, Johannesburg was the birthplace of the Soweto uprising against apartheid and the repository of the continent's greatest legal treasure—the South African Constitution.

The plane touched down at OR Tambo International Airport at half past nine. An hour later, she left the airport driving a sporty Volkswagen coupé. She navigated toward the N12 and placed a call to Dr. Johannè Luyt. At first, the epidemiologist was skeptical of her request, but she warmed when Zoe told her about Dr. Kruger's role in saving Godfrey's life. She took Zoe's number and promised to call her back.

Traffic heading into the city center was a bumper-to-bumper mess of flashing lights and honking horns. Zoe's iPhone rang in the midst of the gridlock.

"I spoke with Dr. Kruger," said Dr. Luyt. "Can you come to Wits?"

"Of course. Where shall I meet you?"

"How about the steps of the Great Hall?"

"I'll be there in half an hour."

Zoe arrived at East Campus of the University of the Witwatersrand a few minutes ahead of schedule. After obtaining a visitor's pass, she parked in the lot at the top of the hill and followed a path to the terraced lawns of the quad. The campus was alive with activity—students hurrying to class, professors engaging in conversation, and rugby enthusiasts grappling with one another in the grass. She walked toward the imposing edifice of the Great Hall. A thin middle-aged woman in a white lab coat was standing on the steps.

Zoe waved. "Dr. Luyt," she said, holding out her hand, "I'm Zoe Fleming."

The doctor returned her handshake curtly. "Dr. Kruger is in the field today."

"Will he be available tomorrow?" Zoe asked.

Dr. Luyt looked at her carefully. "I might be able to arrange a meeting, but I wanted to speak to you first. The findings of our recent study have generated an avalanche of interest. We have had to be cautious with our time."

Zoe concealed her puzzlement with a fib. "I know of the study but not the findings."

Dr. Luyt's voice grew passionate. "We worked with HIV-discordant couples—that is, one positive partner and one negative partner—and introduced antiretrovirals early, as prevention rather than treatment. We had only one new infection in the study period—an astonishing result. We now believe that with early ARV treatment and prenatal treatment of HIV-positive mothers it may be possible to eliminate the transmission of the virus over the next generation."

"Eliminate?" Zoe was astounded. "You're talking about a future without AIDS?"

"It would take time, but yes. The only question is whether the politicians will give us the funding." She began to walk down the path beneath flowering trees. "Tell me more about the young man Dr. Kruger saved."

Keeping pace with her, Zoe filled in the details of Godfrey's story. When she concluded, Dr. Luyt took out her mobile phone. "That's what he told me. I'm sure he will meet with you."

The telephone conversation was brief. Afterward, Dr Luyt regarded Zoe again. "There is a coffee shop called Sun Garden outside Cosmo City. He will meet you there." She shook Zoe's hand. "I am sorry for delaying you."

Zoe nodded. "I hope you get your funding. It could change the face of Africa."

Dr. Luyt looked suddenly wistful. "It could, indeed."

* * *

Zoe found the coffee shop inside a plant nursery in one of Johannesburg's northwestern suburbs. She left her car in the gravel lot and walked through the showroom, taking a seat on a bench beneath a shaded trellis of vines. At eleven in the morning, the place was mostly empty. A waitress approached her, and Zoe ordered a cappuccino.

On the drive, she had worked out a strategy for her talk with Dr. Kruger, but she was not excited about it. In fact, she felt a strong sense of guilt. She thought of Kuyeya, and the guilt became sorrow. If only Charity had finished her nursing degree, if only she had never met Darious, if only she had sought treatment in time, Dr. Kruger could have been left in peace.

She reached into her backpack and extracted Bella's journal, placing it at the center of the table. The waitress brought her coffee, and she sipped it, looking toward the entrance. A few minutes later she saw him. He was as Godfrey recalled—fair-haired and blue-eyed. He caught sight of her and walked briskly to her table.

"Ms. Fleming," he said, glancing at the journal. "Pleasure to meet you."

"Dr. Kruger," she said, "thank you for your time."

He sat down across from her. "How is Godfrey these days?" he asked, his pronunciation that of an educated Rhodesian.

"He's trying to make a life for himself," she replied. "Most of his family is dead."

A shadow darkened the doctor's face. "I'm sorry to hear that. How did they . . . ?"

"AIDS, mostly."

He shook his head. "We have so far to go."

She took a breath to calm her racing heart. "I'd like talk to you about Charity Mizinga."

In the silence that followed, she studied his face, searching for traces of pain or remorse, but she saw none. *Either you are an excellent actor, or you came prepared for this.*

"Charity," he said eventually. "She was a talented student."

"I've heard that before." Zoe pointed at the journal. "She left you a gift."

Dr. Kruger's eyes narrowed, but he recovered quickly. "What do you mean?"

She gestured at the book. "See for yourself."

He stared at her, ignoring the journal. "You asked me here on the pretense that you wished to speak about Godfrey. I don't like being deceived."

Zoe struggled to control her frustration. "Would you rather I'd told you that the student you regarded so highly spent the last years of her life as a prostitute in Lusaka? Would you have preferred me to say that she wrote hundreds of letters describing her debasement? Every single one of them is addressed to you. I want to know why."

He turned his eyes toward the journal, wavering. Finally, he opened the cover. He scanned a number of pages and then set the book down again. "I don't know why she wrote these," he said quietly.

"When did you last see her?"

He fingered the journal. "She dropped out of school in her second year. I can't recall which month. It came as a shock to all of us."

"She didn't give you a reason?"

"She didn't even say goodbye."

"Yet she wrote you hundreds of letters."

He shrugged. "Sometimes students have infatuations. You understand that, I'm sure."

Zoe looked at him skeptically. "Did you ever get the sense that she had feelings for you?"

The doctor shook his head. "Our relationship was strictly platonic."

"How friendly were you?"

"We saw each other almost every day. She was very dedicated to the research. When Godfrey contracted malaria, she helped me save his life. I knew her fairly well."

"Did you know she had a daughter?"

"What?" He appeared genuinely shocked. "She had a daughter in Livingstone?"

"You tell me."

He shook his head. "When I knew her, she never talked about a child."

"So her daughter was born after she dropped out of school?"

"I have no idea. How old is the girl?"

Zoe paused, meeting his eyes. "That's what I'm trying to find out."

He sat back in his chair, his expression thick with mistrust. "Who *are* you?"

"Charity's daughter was raped in Lusaka," she replied, laying all of her cards on the table. "We believe the perpetrator is a young man named Darious Nyambo, son of Frederick Nyambo, the industrialist. I'm one of the attorneys working on the case."

As soon as Zoe spoke these words, she knew she had lost him.

He stood up angrily. "You not only deceived me, you deceived Dr. Luyt. What happened to this girl is a terrible thing. But it has nothing to do with me."

Gritting her teeth, Zoe threw her calculation to the wind. "Did you have an affair with Charity Mizinga? Is that why she wrote you all these letters?"

His eyes flashed. "How dare you come here and accuse me of such a thing? Please give Godfrey my best. But do not contact me again."

With that, he turned around and left.

Zoe took the expressway back to OR Tambo and bought a ticket on the mid-afternoon flight to Lusaka. When the plane landed, she met Joseph at the curb and slid into the passenger seat, preempting the question in his eyes.

"The trip was an abysmal failure. There, I said it."

He stayed silent until they left the airport complex. "Did you learn *anything*?"

"I learned that sometimes I need to keep my mouth shut. Oh, and I learned that a bunch of epidemiologists have proven that we could end the AIDS epidemic in a generation, but that the politicians might scuttle it by gutting foreign aid."

He laughed under his breath. "You do speak your mind. What did you learn about *Jan*?"

She calmed down. "I think he's hiding something. He explained the journal by suggesting that Charity had some sort of schoolgirl crush. I think something happened between them, but I have no proof." She looked at him. "You think all this is crazy, don't you? You don't think it relates to the case."

He shook his head. "When you have a hunch, you have to follow it. I can't tell you how many cases I've broken that way."

She took a breath, grateful for his vote of confidence. "So what did you do today?"

He glanced at her. "I found a link between the magistrate and the Nyambos."

"You're kidding!"

He smiled. "I had lunch with my friend at the Department of Energy. When I mentioned Thoko Kaunda, he told me that Kaunda's father is high-level official in the Department of Water Affairs. He was hired by a certain Minister of Energy."

Her eyes lit up. "Frederick Nyambo," she said. Then she had another thought. "With Nyambo's interest in Batoka Gorge, I wonder if they still have a relationship."

"It's possible. The link isn't as direct as a personal friendship, but it raises doubt about the magistrate's impartiality. Mariam is going to take it to the DPP tomorrow."

Zoe looked out the window and saw that traffic was unusually light. "Have they announced the election results?"

"Sata is ahead, but it's too close to call. PF is making a lot of noise about fraud."

"If anything happens in Woodlands, you can stay over at my place. Kabulonga will be safer than anywhere else." She regarded him and saw the weariness in his eyes. "You look tired. Are you getting enough sleep?"

"Probably not."

"Is it the case?"

He tightened his grip on the steering wheel. "I have dreams. They keep me awake."

"About what?"

"My sister." He blinked as if trying to shake off the memories. "It's too long a story."

"Not if we get dinner. I bet Arcades is open tonight."

He shook his head. "I really don't want to talk about it." Then he surprised her with a grin. "But I wouldn't mind dinner. What about Plates?"

She laughed. "You're on."

Chapter 15

The following morning, Zoe took a seat at the table in Mariam's office. Joseph, Sarge, and Niza were already there. Mariam dialed the DPP's number on the speakerphone, and Levy Makungu answered after three rings. His tone made obvious his displeasure.

"I heard about the decision on DNA. I presume you plan to appeal?"

"Not exactly," Mariam replied. "We believe the magistrate has an undisclosed conflict of interest.

His family has a relationship with the family of the accused."

The DPP took a breath. "I'm not sure I want to hear this."

Mariam forged ahead. "We could file an application for recusal, but we're certain he won't remove himself without persuasion."

"Just a minute," Makungu said, and put the phone down. Seconds later, Zoe heard the sound of a door being closed. The DPP came back on the line. "Unless you have concrete evidence of bias, I'm going to hang up and forget you called."

"Our VSU officer is in the room. Joseph, will you tell Levy what you found?"

Joseph rolled his chair closer to the phone and shared his findings and his source.

Makungu grunted. "I'm going to need confirmation."

"I can give you his number," Joseph said. "He'll talk to you."

The DPP took his time replying. "Mariam, what do you propose I do about this?"

Mariam shifted in her seat. "Give the information

to the Principal Resident Magistrate. He'll know how to handle it."

"I have great respect for Flexon Mubita, but he assigned Kaunda to the case. What if he already knows about this?"

"I trust him more than anyone on the bench. But you're right. It's a risk we have to take."

Makungu cleared his throat. "If the officer's story checks out, I'll talk to Flexon."

Mariam looked relieved. "Thank you, Levy. I owe you one."

"More than one," he replied, and hung up.

Zoe spent the remainder of her morning polishing a brief she had written in another child-rape case. The client this time was an eleven-year-old girl from the Ng'ombe Compound whose great-uncle had molested her for years before she finally confessed to her mother and her mother went to the police. After threatening the child, the uncle had hired an attorney, and the attorney had threatened the mother. At Niza's request, Zoe had drafted an application for contempt, but she expected the magistrate to overrule it. The accused and his attorney had denied making the threats, and the child's mother was a poor widow standing on nothing but her word.

At lunchtime, Joseph announced that he was in the mood for *nshima*, and Zoe smiled at him, taking the hint. They drove down the street to Pamela's, a favorite haunt of attorneys in the government quarter, and strolled across the grass to the outdoor buffet. A Zambian matron took their orders and spooned *nshima*, chicken, groundnut relish, and collard greens onto plates. After paying for the food, they sat at a table on the mostly empty lawn.

"Where is everyone?" Zoe asked, looking around.

"There were riots in Ndola. I heard it on the radio. PF thinks MMD is rigging the election in favor of Banda. I imagine a lot of people stayed home today."

"Has there been violence in Lusaka?"

Joseph shook his head. "The compounds are restless, but nothing yet."

"They need to declare a winner," she said in exasperation.

They ate for a while, enjoying the sunshine

and silence. Eventually, Zoe asked, "What are you going to do until we hear from the DPP?"

He finished off a bite of *nshima*, and then said, "I'm going to talk to some *ngangas* about HIV. I'm also going to talk to people in Kanyama outside Abigail's neighborhood. I think Darious knew his way around the compound. Otherwise, he would have left Kuyeya closer to Los Angeles Road. He's got a flashy car. If I'm right, I'll find someone else who saw it."

She frowned, only partly in jest. "Your job is far sexier than mine."

He grinned. "An interesting choice of words."

"I didn't mean it like that."

His expression turned serious. "If you want something to do, I have an idea. I handled a case a few years back. Two adolescent boys lured a girl into their house and raped her while their parents were away. After they finished, they threatened her and let her go. She was brave, and she was lucky. Her family took the case to the police, and the post commander gave it to me."

The tale turned Zoe's stomach. "Did you get a conviction?"

"We did. A neighbor saw the girl go into the house. Her testimony convinced the magistrate. I've been wondering what Darious did with Kuyeya between the time he picked her up in Kabwata and the time he dropped her off in Kanyama. Five hours is a lot of time."

"You think he took her somewhere."

Joseph nodded. "I'm wondering if he took her home."

She gave him a dubious look. "He did a near-perfect job of covering his tracks. Why would he commit a crime on his own property?"

"Because it's the one place he can completely control. I haven't been inside the walls, but I would guess he has a separate house or a wing to himself. What if his parents were gone? What if he took her home and did the deed and then drove her into Kanyama? The neighbors and the guards wouldn't have seen anything. There's only one person who might have seen something."

"Who?"

Joseph smiled. "Their housekeeper."

"How do you know . . . ? I mean, I'm sure they have one, but it's a monumental guess."

He shrugged. "You may be right. But you handled Doris so well I thought you might be interested in talking to her."

"How do you propose I do that?"

"Wait outside the house until she leaves. I'm sure she takes a regular trip to the market. Someone drives her, but I'd be willing to bet she shops alone."

At once Zoe felt fear. "Why would she talk to me?"

"She might not. But you could get lucky."

After a moment, Zoe nodded. "I'll talk to Mariam."

When they returned to the CILA office, they found it deserted, except for Sarge who was sitting in the conference room typing on his laptop. He looked up at them and said, "There was violence in the Copperbelt. The office is closed until the election is announced."

"Why are you still here?" Zoe asked, feeling anxious again.

"I have a hearing in the High Court next week. I have to finish the brief."

Leaving Sarge to his computer, Zoe followed Joseph outside. At once she realized how quiet it was. Situated near the center of one of Lusaka's busiest districts, the office was usually awash in street noise. This afternoon it was as serene as a botanical garden.

"Well," she said, "I can't offer you a river cruise, but I do have a pool."

"A swim sounds nice," Joseph replied. "As long as you have a radio."

They returned to Zoe's flat and spent the afternoon lounging by the pool along with half of the residents of the complex, all on temporary leave. When the shadows grew long on the grass and the sun disappeared into the trees, Zoe invited Joseph to a makeshift dinner of ham sandwiches and apples—all she had left in her refrigerator. Afterward, they retired to the living room to watch movies, keeping Zoe's iPhone tuned to the ZNBC news broadcast.

The hours marched on without an announcement. When the credits began to roll at the end of *District 9*—an alien invasion film set in Johannesburg—Zoe yawned and checked her watch. It was past midnight. She was about to make a trip to the bathroom when she heard the voice of Chief

Justice Ernest Sakala of Zambia's Supreme Court come on the radio. She turned off the TV and increased the volume on her iPhone, holding her breath as Sakala began to recite the vote count.

"Michael C. Sata of the Patriot Front: 1,170,966 votes. Rupiah B. Banda of the Movement for Multiparty Democracy: 987,866 votes. Hichilema Hakainde of the United Party for National Development: 506,763 votes . . ."

Zoe turned to Joseph and heaved a great sigh of relief. "It's over, thank God. And PF has nothing to complain about."

Joseph gave her an enigmatic look. "The people wanted change. But they chose another old man to lead them. I wonder what they will say about Sata in four years."

Zoe imagined President Banda sitting in his palace, contemplating the end of two decades of MMD rule. How many of his friends had benefited from his patronage? How many in his government now feared for their livelihoods? She had a terrifying thought. He still had the military at his disposal. In Africa votes were paper things, no match for men with guns.

"Will Banda concede?" she asked. "What if he uses the army to force a recount?"

Joseph looked at her quizzically. "What is this worry? You are usually so confident."

"I don't know," she admitted, feeling strangely vulnerable.

He shrugged. "Who knows what will happen? But life will go on. The President doesn't make the world turn."

This simple reassurance found deep purchase in Zoe's heart. Her pulse increased, and she scooted closer to him. She couldn't remember the last time she had responded this way to a man. All of her previous relationships had been transient things, inspired more by passing attraction than by compatibility or genuine passion. Watching her girlfriends receive rings and walk down the aisle, she had often thought that something inside her was broken. Every time she pictured herself in their place, she felt Clay Randall's hands driving her into the sand. With Joseph, however, she felt safe. His dark eyes were only kind.

She placed a hand on his chest and leaned toward him. He grazed her cheek, and his touch made her shiver. Just before their lips met, she closed her eyes, wondering what it would be like to take him to her bed.

Suddenly, she felt fingers on her lips. "Not yet," he said softly.

She opened her eyes. "Why?" she whispered.

He searched her face. "Good things should not be rushed."

She didn't know what it was that restrained her, but the anger she felt passed as quickly as it came. *If he wants to wait, I can wait*, she thought, nuzzling into him.

After a while she led him to the door and kissed him chastely. "Be safe tonight."

"This was a good day," he replied, and turned toward the stairs.

That night Zoe had one of the most vivid dreams of her life. She was standing on Los Angeles Road in Kanyama watching the gang leader in the green bandana and a hundred other kids celebrate PF's victory when a convoy of trucks rumbled to a standstill, carrying soldiers with AK-47s. Shouts were exchanged and then the army opened fire on the revelers. As the street filled with bodies, the gang leader leered at her and said, "The fun is only beginning."

In the morning, Zoe awoke with a sense of dread. She opened her MacBook and checked ZNBC, certain that the night had been consumed with violence. What she found astonished her. Rupiah Banda had called a press conference and was expected to deliver a concession speech. She read the story in disbelief, marveling that such a bitter contest could end without bloodshed.

After breakfast, she called Mariam and learned that the CILA office would reopen at noon. Remembering Joseph's suggestion the day before, she pitched Mariam about approaching the Nyambos' housekeeper. Mariam hesitated at first but eventually agreed.

"Please be careful," she said. "If anything happens, phone Joseph right away."

Zoe dressed quickly in jeans and a pullover, drew her blond hair into a ponytail, and put on her sunglasses and a baseball cap. She looked at herself in the mirror and shook her head. The glasses hid her blue eyes, but otherwise her Caucasian features were impossible to miss. She grabbed her backpack off the floor and stuffed it with enough reading material to occupy her for a few hours. Then she locked her flat and drove her Land Rover out of the gate.

It took her barely a minute to reach her destination. As she had done before, she pulled to the shoulder as far from the house as she could without limiting her view of the gate. She studied the guard sitting outside the wall. He had the same muscular physique as the night guard, but he didn't seem as intent on his duties. He was leaning back in his chair, absorbed in a newspaper.

She took out her iPhone and pulled up another satellite image of the property. She had given little thought to the outbuildings before, but now she studied them carefully. The larger one sat beside the driveway and resembled a garage; the smaller one stood beside the outer wall in the shade of a tree—probably the housekeeper's cottage. The cottage faced the rear of the house and had a direct line of sight across the pool to the larger outbuilding.

She sent Joseph a text, letting him know where she was.

His reply came swiftly: *"Watch the guard. If he gets suspicious, leave. Call if you need backup."*

She looked down the street. The guard had not budged from his seat. She switched on the radio and lowered the volume. She wanted to hear Banda's press conference but none of the commentary. She took out her copy of *Swann's Way* and immersed herself in Proust.

Around nine o'clock, President Banda came on the radio. Zoe listened as he addressed the nation. There was an undercurrent of sorrow in his voice, but his words were generous and conciliatory. He spoke with deep feeling about the country that had elected his archrival to replace him, and he prevailed upon all Zambians to ensure a peaceful transition.

When he concluded, Zoe had tears in her eyes. Never before had she heard an African politician concede defeat with such dignity. Names flashed through her mind: Idi Amin, Joseph Mobutu, Charles Taylor, Muammar Al-Gaddafi, Robert Mugabe—the self-appointed dictator kings of Africa. The list was long and littered with the dead. By presiding over an orderly transfer of power, Banda had not only prevented carnage in the compounds, but he had also refuted the cynic's song that Africa was an irredeemable land.

Zoe was so enthralled by the moment that she almost missed the Toyota sedan leaving the Nyambos' property. She blinked in the bright sunlight and realized what she was seeing. Two people were in the vehicle: a man in the driver's seat and an older woman in the back, dressed in *chitenge*. The sedan turned left out of the gate and headed in the direction of Bishop's Road. She keyed the ignition and fixed her eyes on the guard, fearing the sound of the engine would attract his attention. But he seemed oblivious to her.

She accelerated up the lane and kept pace with the sedan as it meandered through the central suburbs. Ten minutes later, the Toyota turned into the Manda Hill shopping center, an ultra-modern Mecca of African consumerism. The driver nosed to the curb in front of Shoprite, and the old woman left the car with a handbag. Zoe pulled into a parking space and watched the driver puff away on a cigarette. She shook her head, marveling at Joseph's prescience.

Grabbing her backpack, Zoe entered the store and found the old woman pushing a cart through the produce section. She studied the woman while pretending to examine papayas. Her face was lined with wrinkles, and she walked with a stoop, but her stride was strong.

Zoe moved toward the wall, looking for an opening. Eventually, the woman wheeled her cart toward a case stocked with milk and cheese. The closest shopper was twenty feet away. *Now*, Zoe thought and crossed the floor, stopping beside the woman.

"You work for Frederick and Patricia Nyambo," she said quietly.

The woman stiffened. "Who are you?" she asked.

Zoe picked up a liter of milk. "I'm an attorney. I'm helping a girl who was raped."

The woman looked confused. "How does that relate to me?"

Zoe met her eyes. "We believe Darious Nyambo was the perpetrator."

The woman glared at her. "I don't know anything

about it." She placed two liters of milk in her cart and moved toward a table piled high with loaves of bread.

"The girl is young," Zoe persisted. "She needs your help."

"I don't know this girl," the woman said, placing a bag of bread in her cart, then a package of beef from the meat counter. She turned away and angled toward the front of the store.

Zoe delivered a last-ditch plea. "She could be your granddaughter."

The woman paused and pain shot through her eyes. "I do not have a granddaughter."

Zoe watched her walk away, feeling sympathy and mistrust. Given her age and occupation, she was likely a widow and the Nyambos' employment her sole source of income. In a country without a social safety net, a job was often a widow's only alternative to destitution. Yet Kuyeya was a child. What woman turned her back on a child?

"Wait," she said, catching up to the woman. She pulled out a ten-thousand-kwacha note along with a pen and wrote her mobile number on the money. "You can reach me at that number." Then, almost as an afterthought she added, "The girl's name is Kuyeya."

The housekeeper stared at Zoe as if stricken. Her fingers went limp, and she dropped the money on the floor. She bent over to retrieve it and fumbled with the zipper of her handbag. Her mouth opened as though she was about to speak. Then she looked away and pushed her cart toward the checkout line.

Zoe returned to the Land Rover, her thoughts a blur. She had seen something in the woman's eyes when she spoke Kuyeya's name, something mercurial and arresting—a glimpse of recognition. She called Joseph and he picked up immediately.

"I talked to the housekeeper," she said. "I got nowhere when I confronted her about Darious. But when I mentioned Kuyeya, she looked shocked. I don't understand. Is Kuyeya a common name?"

"Not at all. I've heard it once or twice, but only in Southern Province."

"Do you think Darious took Bella home with him?"

"Not to his parents' house. He might have treated her like a girlfriend at the bars, but he never would have introduced her to his family."

Something nagged at the edge of Zoe's consciousness. "What if the housekeeper knew Bella some other way?"

"Outside of her employment?"

Zoe shook her head. "Not necessarily. What if Bella had some sort of connection to the Nyambo family, not just to Darious? We still don't know what she did when she got to Lusaka. She came in 1996. The journal Doris gave me starts in 2004. That's a gap of eight years."

"It's possible, I suppose. But where does that get us?"

Zoe let out a sigh. "I have no idea."

"Look, you did a great job. I'm impressed. Are you coming into the office?"

"Yeah," she responded, starting the engine. "I'll see you later."

She left Manda Hill and drove toward the government quarter. She tried to put the housekeeper out of her mind, but she couldn't shake the sense that she was missing something. In the early stages of the investigation, her curiosity about Bella's history had been prompted by instinct. But the more she had dredged, the more links she had discovered between Bella and Darious. It was no longer reasonable to consider the past irrelevant. But what did any of it *prove*?

She ran into traffic south of the Addis Ababa roundabout and took out her phone. She placed a call to the Nkana Mine and asked for the manager of personnel.

A man picked up. "How can I be of assistance?" he asked, sounding bored.

Zoe introduced herself and explained her business. "I'm trying to reach Mwela Chansa. He works at one of your mines. It's a family matter."

The man typed on his keyboard. "I can give you his mobile number."

She memorized the digits and dialed them. After three rings the line connected and a recorded voice said: "You've reached Mwela Chansa. Leave a message."

"Mr. Chansa," she said, suppressing her frustration, "this is Zoe Fleming. I met Cynthia's brother, Godfrey, in Livingstone. I'd like to talk to Cynthia about her cousin, Charity Mizinga. Charity's daughter is in need of help. I'd be very grateful if Cynthia would give me a call."

She left her number and hung up. It was another barrier, another waiting game. Why was it that almost everyone who touched the case seemed to have secrets? Bella. Doris. Godfrey. Cynthia. Jan Kruger. Magistrate Kaunda. The housekeeper. The Nyambos. Even Joseph. In a moment of reflection, she realized she had left a name off the list.

Her own.

PART THREE

The love of power is the demon of men.
—*Friedrich Nietzsche*

Bella

Lusaka, Zambia
January, 2006

*S*he saw Darious for a year and a half, whenever he had the fancy or the need. Sometimes they went to his flat, other times to a hotel. Once in a while, he went home with her, and she put Kuyeya to sleep in the bathroom. He treated the matter of payment as if it were a gift. He gave her talktime and designer clothes, perfume and jewelry, and occasionally wads of kwacha. He didn't ask what she did when they were not together; he never inquired about the other men she saw. He was predictable—he wanted sex and then he wanted to talk.

The talking was what made her fear him. He spoke

of abstract things, like a philosopher. Many of the names he mentioned were unknown to her, but sometimes she recognized one—Nietzsche, for instance, Lenin, Mussolini, Mugabe. He admired their power and their disdain for anyone who exercised borrowed authority. He loathed democracy, the messy elections, the way officials kowtowed to constituents. But he loved Western media. "Television is a god," he said. "Those who rule the mind rule the world."

He also talked about mukwala—*African medicine—and the influence of the spirit world on the world of men. He wore an amulet on his neck and was obsessed with hexes. He knew many* ngangas *and consulted them often. He despised the influence of modern medicine in Africa—he called it "neocolonialism"—and he had contempt for the Westerners who put so much stock in it.* Mukwala *and people who understood it were the things he missed most during his studies in London. In his mind,* mukwala *was the truest form of power.*

On a rainy night in January, he called her on her mobile and asked to meet at Alpha, as they always did. She heard something peculiar in his voice, a tension that belied his usual calm, but she agreed without hesitation.

Kuyeya's myopia was getting worse, and the ngangas were demanding payment for the herbs she took to treat her rashes. She hitched a ride with a friend—she never seemed to make enough money to buy a car—and arrived just before midnight. He greeted her with a kiss, but she saw agitation in his eyes.

"Something wrong?" she asked in Nyanja.

"Nothing you can't cure," he said enigmatically. "Let's get out of here."

"You don't want a drink?" He had never broken their ritual before.

Instead of answering, he took her arm and escorted her to his SUV. She hesitated at the door, trying to work out what could be bothering him. She felt a twinge of apprehension, an intuition that she shouldn't go with him tonight, but she suppressed it. She was getting older and sicker, and she needed his money.

The drive to his flat was brief. She walked beside him up the steps, ignoring his too-tight grip on her bicep. A light was on in the kitchen, but the rest of the flat was dark. He keyed the door and pushed her into the hallway.

"What's going on?" she asked, alarmed. She searched his face in the shadows, but she could see only the whites of his eyes. "Something's wrong."

"You deceived me," he said after a pause. "Charity Mizinga."

A bolt of fear shot through her. She had never told him her real name.

"You didn't really get your nursing diploma, did you?" he said, advancing on her.

She backed down the hallway. "How did you . . . ?"

It was then that he hit her—a painful blow to the cheek. Through a burst of stars, she saw him clearly for the first time: the anger submerged beneath the polished surface of his personality, the hidden capacity for violence. She turned and ran into the kitchen, looking for the block of knives beside the stove. He caught her before she reached the counter and wrapped his arm around her neck. She twisted from side to side as he dragged her into the living room, but the harder she fought, the harder she found it to breathe.

"You're going to pay for what you did," he hissed, grabbing her hair and shoving her face into the rug. "You're going to feel what I felt."

She didn't know how long he spent raping her. It might have been a minute or half an hour. The pain was all consuming, as was the terror that flooded her mind. Afterward, he sat back on the couch and stared at her silently.

She curled into the fetal position and wept, wondering if he was going to kill her. When he made no move to stand, she collected herself enough to stumble toward the door. She was barefoot and her dress was torn, but she didn't care. She wanted only to escape.

As she struggled with the heavy deadbolt in the darkness, he came up behind her and held it fast. The touch of his fingers sent a shockwave through her body.

"Look at me," he commanded.

She gave up fighting and swiveled around, pressing her back against the door. He turned on the light and she saw his face above her, his cat-like eyes. Siluwe. She had been right to call him that.

"You still don't understand," he sneered. "Let me give you a hint. Livingstone General Hospital. 1996."

At once she realized the truth she had been missing all along. She couldn't believe it, but it was right there in front of her, written in the shape of his nose, the way his lips hung open after he spoke, the frankness with which he appraised her. So many other things were different, but these were the same.

As soon as she said his name—his full name—he took his hand off the deadbolt and let her go. She turned the door handle quickly and slipped out of his flat into a drizzle of night rain. *Running down the steps, she fled into the dark streets, thinking only of Kuyeya.*

The ghosts of the past had come for her, but she had survived.

Chapter 16

Lusaka, Zambia
October, 2011

September turned into October, and the warmth of the late dry season became the blistering heat that always presaged the arrival of the rains. Zoe checked her iPhone regularly, but neither the Nyambos' housekeeper nor Cynthia attempted to contact her. The transition of governments from MMD to PF took place with few partisan skirmishes, and people began to talk as if Zambia had blazed a new trail for sub-Saharan Africa. The mood in Zoe's circle was less sanguine—everyone expressed relief at the absence of violence but felt that Sata had much to prove.

On the fifth of October, Zoe was sitting at her desk in the legal department when the receptionist handed a stack of letters to Sarge. She glanced up from her laptop as he flipped through them and then looked back at the screen. Her concentration lasted only a few seconds. Suddenly, Sarge leapt to his feet, his face shining beneath a sheen of sweat.

"He did it!" he exulted, waving a document around. "Kaunda transferred Kuyeya's case!"

Zoe rushed to his side, barely beating Niza, who knocked a stack of files off her desk.

"Go ahead," Zoe said.

"You first," Niza replied with a smile.

Zoe read the order in wonderment. It was a technical document, devoid of detail, but it accomplished something almost miraculous—the reallocation of judicial power in a pending criminal prosecution. Using vague statutory language, Magistrate Kaunda recused himself for administrative reasons and submitted the case to the Principal Resident Magistrate for reassignment. In addition, he scheduled a status hearing for the following Monday.

Zoe handed the order to Niza and laughed like a giddy child. "This changes everything. We should ask the new magistrate to reconsider the DNA issue."

Sarge nodded. "It's worth a try. We might get lucky."

She gave him a hopeful look. "Do you mind if I draft the memo?"

He smiled. "You're welcome to it."

It took Zoe two days to produce an application that satisfied everyone. Persuasive writing was one of her passions, and she had honed her craft for more than a decade, writing columns for the *Stanford Daily*, notes for the *Yale Law Journal*, and briefs and opinions for Judge van der Merwe. She had even published an article in *Harpers* magazine on human rights in post-apartheid South Africa. She wrote like she swam, with single-minded intensity, tuning out all distraction until the last word was on the page.

She approached the memorandum like an appellate brief, highlighting the legal aspects of the DNA question and mentioning its social significance only in passing. She wanted the new judge to understand that using DNA in a rape case was not only de rigueur in courts around the world, but that Zambia was ready for it, that the law permitted it, and that justice demanded it.

Sarge filed the application on Friday, and Zoe spent the weekend in a state of agitation. Joseph, who joined her for a swim on Saturday, took delight in ribbing her.

"You're like a tiger in a cage," he said. "Pacing doesn't change the fence."

"It helps me forget about it, though," she replied.

That evening, Zoe hosted a braai, and Joseph took charge of the grill, churning out buffalo burgers and chicken breasts for a dozen guests—CILA staff, neighbors, and expat friends. When conversation began to ebb, Zoe suggested dancing at Hot Tropic. Sarge groaned and complained about the heat, but Niza batted her eyes and elbowed him into submission.

They drove to Kalingalinga in three vehicles and piled into the club, which was already packed with young Zambians, drinking, chatting, and moving to the beat. After a few beers and a bit of prodding, Zoe convinced Joseph to dance with her.

They carved out a space between tables and picked up the rhythm of a disco track. The combination of alcohol, sweat, and bass-heavy music drove Zoe into Joseph's arms. She looked into his eyes and felt the stirring of desire.

"Let's go back to my place," she said.

"The time isn't right," he whispered into her ear.

"When then?" she demanded, feeling tipsy.

"Patience," he said, leading her back to the table and the stability of her chair.

But patience was the furthest thing from Zoe's mind. *You're clearly attracted to me. What's holding you back?*

At last, Monday arrived and with it the hearing at the magistrate's court. Maurice chauffeured the legal team to the courthouse where they met David Soso, the police prosecutor.

"I can't understand it," David said, looking at Sarge with wide eyes. "Do you know why Magistrate Kaunda transferred the case?"

Sarge shrugged nonchalantly. "Any news of a replacement?"

David shook his head. "The docket entry is blank."

"I'm sure everything will sort itself out," Sarge replied. He guided David through the lobby, and Zoe and Niza followed them, stifling grins.

The air in the arcade was oppressively hot, but the breeze afforded some relief. Zoe saw Benson Luchembe and his flock of defense lawyers in their usual huddle, this time outside Courtroom 10. Instead of standing with them, Frederick Nyambo was resting nearby on a bench, dabbing his forehead with a handkerchief. He appeared less imposing off his feet. The hubris was there in his steel-gray eyes, but he looked like a man contemplating the limits of his power.

Zoe entered the courtroom and found Joseph waiting for her on the front bench. She smiled and sat beside him. The defense team filed in just before ten o'clock. Ever the professional, Luchembe took a seat at counsel table, his expression neutral.

Soon, the door to the judge's chambers opened. The middle-aged man who ascended to the bench was a study in contrasts. He had the imposing frame of a linebacker and the avuncular visage of

James Earl Jones. At first Zoe didn't understand the significance of his presence, but when she heard his name spoken by one of the defense lawyers, her heart skipped a beat.

Flexon Mubita. The Principal Resident Magistrate himself.

Mubita sat down and took off his round spectacles, wiping his nose bridge. "Hello, Sarge, Benson," he said in greeting, his rich, resonant voice echoing in the courtroom.

At that moment, another door opened, and the courtroom deputy led Darious into the dock. Zoe had not seen him in the month since the initial hearing. His eyes were still bright, but his frame looked more skeletal than gaunt and his face and neck were marked with lesions.

"I summoned the accused," said the judge, "because I was not the one who read the charges at the initial hearing. He should know the magistrate who will decide his case."

When the words hit Zoe's ears, she felt a thrill unlike anything she had experienced in an African courtroom. Mubita had not only removed the case from Thoko Kaunda's hands, he had taken it upon himself to see that justice was served. She glanced around at the ashen faces of the defense lawyers and could not help but smirk. The reversal of fortunes was monumental.

Benson Luchembe stood slowly. "The defense is delighted to have such an august judge handling this case. But might I ask what prompted Your Worship's *personal* interest?"

"I assign cases by lottery," Mubita responded simply. "My name was chosen."

Luchembe hesitated, then sat down in a huff, shuffling papers.

The judge folded his hands. "I have reviewed the status of this case and the orders entered thus far. I have also reviewed the prosecution's application to reconsider the question of DNA. I believe the matter is weighty enough to merit reconsideration, and I will do so on the briefs. You should receive my decision within a week."

Luchembe leaped to his feet again. "Your Worship, with all due respect, Magistrate Kaunda heard argument from counsel and wrote a very thoughtful opinion, taking into account the weight of

Zambian and foreign authorities. There is no need to review the issue."

Mubita raised his eyebrows. "I will give proper deference to Magistrate Kaunda's decision, but I will be trying this case. I intend to decide all issues that bear upon the trial."

Zoe clutched Joseph's arm, barely able to contain her excitement.

The judge, however, was not finished. "There is also the matter ovf the trial date. I'm disturbed to see that the trial is not scheduled until next December. With child witnesses, this is unacceptable. The Court has dates in March and early April. What is counsel's preference?"

Luchembe could not contain himself. "Your Worship, I explained to Magistrate Kaunda that my calendar is booked until next summer."

Mubita narrowed his eyes. "You have a first-rate staff. I'm sure you can manage."

Luchembe glanced at the floor, looking trapped. After a pause, he opened his calendar. A brief negotiation ensued, and the judge set the trial for April fifth and sixth.

Mubita then turned to Darious. "Does the accused need clarification before we proceed?"

Darious gave the judge an insolent look, and their eyes locked like horns in a bullfight. The silence dragged on, save for the ticking of the clock on the wall. All at once, Darious lost his composure and looked at the floor.

"Since everyone is satisfied," Mubita said, a trace of amusement in his voice, "this Court is adjourned."

When the judge disappeared into chambers, Benson Luchembe traded a shell-shocked glance with Darious and strode out of the courtroom, his defense team in tow. Zoe grinned at Joseph, incapable of hiding her elation. There was so much she wanted to say, but she couldn't say it until the defendant left the dock. She waited, watching Darious as he stared at the door to chambers. His look sent a chill up her spine. His eyes were full of loathing.

In time, he turned toward the rear of the courtroom, searching for something. For a moment his confidence seemed to waver, then the hatred returned. Zoe followed his gaze and saw the empty bench.

Frederick Nyambo was gone.

* * *

The judge's opinion on the matter of DNA arrived by email on Friday morning. Sarge printed it off and read it silently, then reclined in his chair, his lips curling into a smile of vindication. He waved the decision at Zoe and Niza, who read it together.

After examining the Constitution and statutes of Zambia, Mubita found no prohibition against a court-ordered blood sample in a defilement case and waxed eloquent about the benefits DNA would accord the justice system. He wrote:

Crimes of sexual violence assault the very fabric of Zambia's communal society, and no prosecutor or court should be deprived of a constitutionally sound tool to identify the perpetrators of such crimes. If DNA changes the face of criminal justice in our country, so be it. The time has come to bring an end to the horrific acts of defilement and rape that leave our wives, daughters, mothers, and grandmothers afraid of walking the streets alone.

★ ★ ★

Mubita ordered Darious to submit a blood sample to Dr. Chulu at UTH by Monday afternoon and directed that the defendant's blood and the samples taken from Kuyeya on the night of the rape be submitted to the DNA lab in Johannesburg for analysis.

Zoe gave Sarge a triumphant look. "We should have it framed," she said.

He shook his head in wonderment. "This is going to change the way we practice law. Can you imagine it? A genuine deterrent against child sexual assault." He stood up suddenly. "Wait until Mariam hears about this."

That afternoon, when the last of the staff left the office, Zoe tidied up her workstation and found Joseph waiting for her at the gate. She touched his arm. "Interested in a drive? I haven't seen Kuyeya in a couple of weeks."

He pondered this. "I was going to check on the samples at UTH."

"It's up to you," she said, giving him a playful nudge.

He shrugged. "I'll come with you."

They drove through the city and took Great East Road toward the airport. The tarmac shimmered in the heat, and the sky was the color of mustard, clogged with wind-driven dust. When they reached the spur road, Zoe rolled up the windows to keep out the grit. The six-month absence of rain had turned the highland plain into a sandy desert.

At St. Francis, they parked beside a bougainvillea bush and left the air-conditioned comfort of the Land Rover. Much to their surprise, they found Dr. Chulu in the breezeway talking to Sister Anica and Joy Herald. The physician so dwarfed the nun and the SCA director that their exchange looked almost cartoonish.

"Zoe!" Sister Anica said. "You chose a good day to visit. The doctor is about to test Kuyeya again."

"Has it been six weeks already?" Zoe asked, waving at Joy.

"Almost to the day," Dr. Chulu replied, shaking her hand and Joseph's.

Sister Anica led them through the breezeway and across the sunbaked courtyard to the garden. In the distance, Zoe saw Sister Irina kneeling on a patch of turned earth with children in a circle around her. Kuyeya had the privileged position on the nun's left, but she seemed as much a part of the group as the other children.

"I was telling Joy and Dr. Chulu that she started running again last week," Sister Anica said. "Her injuries appear to have healed. And she's making good progress with Dr. Mbao. She's started to talk about her mother."

"What does she say?" Zoe asked.

"Her mother told her stories. That's what she seems to remember most. Stories about animals and village people."

"Has she said anything more about the incident?"

Sister Anica shook her head. "Dr. Mbao says she needs more time."

They approached Sister Irina and the group of children. Zoe sat in the dirt beside Kuyeya, deciding not to worry about her office clothes. Joy took a seat on the other side.

Kuyeya looked at Zoe and made the balloon sound. "Hi, Zoe," she said.

Zoe smiled. "How are you today?"

"Good," the girl replied. "I like your music." She began to hum rhythmically.

Listening, Zoe discerned a familiar tune. "'I Walk the Line,'" she said, nudging Kuyeya's shoulder. "That's one of my favorites."

"I like Johnny," Kuyeya said.

Dr. Chulu knelt down next to Zoe. "Hi, Kuyeya. I'm Manny, your doctor."

At the sound of his voice, Kuyeya clutched her monkey. She turned away from the doctor and began to rock back and forth, her eyes on her lap.

"Why don't we get the clinic ready?" Sister Anica said, looking at Dr. Chulu and then at Joy and Joseph. "Zoe can bring her in a minute."

"Good idea," replied the doctor with obvious relief.

As soon as they left, Zoe sang the chorus to 'I Walk the Line,' and Kuyeya began to hum again. Then she spoke the last line. "'Because you're mine, I walk the line.'"

Zoe laughed and regarded Sister Irina. "Where is the iPod?"

"In the playroom," said the nun.

Zoe touched Kuyeya's hand. "Let's go get some music."

She helped Kuyeya to her feet and led her out of the garden at a leisurely pace. Kuyeya's stride was much stronger now, and her limp was barely detectable. She accompanied Zoe easily, swinging her monkey by the arm.

After collecting the iPod, they entered the clinic. Zoe put the earphones over Kuyeya's ears and led her to a chair beside the sink. The girl sat obediently, paying no attention to Dr. Chulu or the others. She kept her eyes on the floor and rocked in time with the music.

"Sister Anica is a nurse," Dr. Chulu said quietly. "She's going to take the sample."

The nun took Kuyeya's left hand and cleaned her middle finger. Squeezing the fingertip, she pricked the skin with a lancet and collected a sample of blood in a vial. Kuyeya moaned in protest and pressed down on the headphones with her free hand. Dr. Chulu took the vial and ran the rapid test. Zoe looked over the doctor's shoulder and held her breath.

"Non-reactive," he said, showing her the result window.

The relief Zoe felt was overwhelming. She watched as Sister Anica bandaged the girl's finger and gave her a sweet. Kuyeya held her injured hand and savored the confection. Joy asked the nun a question about Kuyeya's relationship to the other children, and they began to chat. Dr. Chulu motioned for Zoe and Joseph to join him outside.

"I heard about Flexon Mubita's decision," he said, standing in the breezeway. "He's an honorable man."

"How long will it take the DNA lab to do the analysis?" she asked.

"A few weeks. They're very careful."

"Will they need to send an expert to testify at trial?"

The doctor shook his head. "I'm qualified to do it. All I need is the report."

"How secure are the samples?" Joseph inquired.

"They're locked in a cabinet in the library. I check it every evening before I leave."

"How many keys are there to the cabinet?"

The doctor frowned. "I have the only one."

Joseph nodded. "As soon as you get Darious's blood, I'll take the samples to Jo'burg myself. I don't want to take any chances."

Chapter 17

On the drive into the city, Zoe asked Joseph if he wanted to go out for dinner, but he declined, citing an obligation to a cousin. She gave him a hard time about it until she realized that he was serious. The cousin had traveled from Southern Province for a job interview and needed a ride home. Joseph was the nearest family member with an automobile.

"Will you stay the night in Choma?" she asked.

He shook his head. "I'll be back by midnight."

You could come over then, she almost said. "Will you be at the braai tomorrow?"

He smiled. "I wouldn't miss it."

She dropped him off at the CILA office beside his truck. The road was empty except for a blue sedan parked some distance away.

She took her usual route home: Independence to Nyerere Road, past the homes of ministers and ambassadors to Los Angeles Boulevard, and along the Lusaka Golf Club into Kabulonga. When she negotiated the roundabout at Chila Road, she checked her mirror and saw a blue sedan three car-lengths back. She recognized it with a start: it was the one she had seen near the office. She focused on the driver's face and felt a sharp pang of dread.

It was the man in sunglasses.

Gripping the steering wheel, she intentionally missed the turn to her apartment and drove around the military airport. When she approached Kalingalinga, pedestrians began to crowd the roadway, and she had to slow to avoid an old woman who crossed the street without looking. She turned into the compound and made a random series of turns, skirting smoldering piles of trash and children scampering through the streets. The sedan followed her unerringly.

She navigated toward the exit onto Kamloops Road, keeping an eye on the car in her side mirror. *I have to find a way to lose him. I don't want him to know where I live.* An idea came to her, but it would require a bit of luck to work. She glanced down the side lanes, watching for an opportunity. Just then, a flatbed delivery truck nosed into the lane behind her, forming a barricade between her Land Rover and the blue sedan. It was the opening she needed.

She floored the accelerator and sped toward the intersection at Kamloops Road, praying she wouldn't hit anyone. Rounding a bend, she saw two women walking in the middle of the lane, carrying baskets on their heads. She honked loudly and the women leapt to the side in fright, sending papayas rolling across the road.

"Sorry!" she exclaimed, as the Land Rover rolled over the fruit.

She peered into the cloud of dust behind her. She saw the nose of the delivery truck, but no blue sedan. She took the turn onto Kamloops Road without slowing. The top-heavy Land Rover canted to the side, but its tires never lost traction. She raced along the tarmac, weaving around slower-moving cars. Then, without warning, she threw a hard right onto a rutted lane that led back into the warren of Kalingalinga.

She made two quick turns and braked to a stop, her heart pulsing with adrenaline. Around her people gestured and stared. Children knocked on her window and opened their palms. Ignoring them, she conjured the face of her pursuer. *Why is he following me?*

After a few minutes had passed without sign of the blue sedan, she started to breathe again. She drove east toward Mutendere, her eyes glued to her mirrors. It took her ten minutes to escape the compound and another five to reach Kabulonga. She turned onto Sable Road and focused on her apartment complex. She felt a stab of fear.

The blue sedan was parked a short distance from the gate.

She accelerated up the street, her mind struggling to process the implications. She squealed to a halt outside her complex and honked urgently. For a distressing moment, the gate didn't move. Then it opened with a creak, and the guard let her in.

She parked outside her flat and scanned the ten-foot walls that surrounded the property, taking comfort in the shards of glass and quintuple strands of electrified wire. She found her iPhone and called Joseph. He answered on the first ring.

"Are you still in Lusaka?" she asked, a bit breathless.

"I'm on the road. What happened?"

"The guy with the sunglasses followed me home."

Joseph took a measured breath. "I was afraid this might happen."

"What do you mean?"

"The DNA decision. They're escalating the threat."

"But I didn't have anything to do with that."

Joseph was silent for a long moment.

"What?" she asked. "What are you not telling me?"

He sighed. "We got an identity from Interpol. His name is Dunstan Sisilu."

Zoe heard the gravity in his voice. "Who is he?"

"He's from Johannesburg. He was one of the ringleaders of the Pan Africanist Congress in the early nineties. The apartheid regime suspected him in a number of deadly attacks, but nothing was ever proven. When Mandela took office, he went underground. There were rumors he joined one of the Jo'burg gangs, but he's never been linked with organized crime. Nobody knows what he's been doing since then."

Her stomach began to churn. "Do you think you can tie him to the Nyambos?"

"I doubt it. He's clearly a professional."

She glanced at the walls again. "What do you want me to do?"

"Tell the guard not to let him in. And don't go out tonight. I'll be there in the morning."

"Please come as soon as you can."

She went to the guardhouse and made her request, giving the guard a fifty-pin tip. Then she entered her flat and walked through each room, checking the locks on all doors and windows. Afterward, she ate a sandwich in the dining room, thinking about Dunstan Sisilu. *He killed people in a war*, she consoled herself. *Even Mandela tolerated violence*.

When evening came, she watched a documentary on the financial collapse of 2008—an event her father had predicted four years before—and then immersed herself in *Swann's Way* until she began to drift off. She checked the locks a second time and got ready for bed. After taking out her contact lenses, she turned off the light and slid under the covers, imagining what it would be like to wake up beside Joseph.

Soon, she thought. *Very soon*.

Sometime in the early hours of morning, she awoke with a start. She looked around the pitch-black room but saw nothing. She held her breath and listened instead, straining to hear the sound that had disturbed her sleep—a sharp crunch.

Something moved in the doorway.

She tried desperately to make out the shape in the dark. It was a lump at floor level, but the haze in her vision blurred its features. She heard quiet footsteps retreating down the hall, then the crunch again. Fear and adrenaline shot through her like an electrical surge.

She threw off the mosquito net and found her glasses in the drawer at her bedside. She switched on the light and looked toward the doorway. The lump was a burlap sack, and it was moving. She shuddered. She had seen a sack like it before—in a snake charmer's booth in Mombasa.

Suddenly, a head emerged from the sack. *What is it?* she thought in terror. *A puff adder? A viper? A cobra?* Then she saw it—the grey color of the snake—and she knew.

It was a black mamba.

She watched, mesmerized, as the long snake uncoiled on the cement floor. At first it looked like it might head down the hallway, but then it tensed and raised its head, looking in her direction. It let out a long, low hiss. She stared at it, not daring to move a muscle. She had two choices: remain on the bed in hope that the snake would find a distraction, or find a way around it and out of the apartment—but not the way the intruder had gone. The dilemma was paralyzing. A black mamba was the fastest serpent on earth. It was also a natural climber.

With glacial steadiness she reached out and retrieved her iPhone from the bedside table. The clock on the screen read 3:12 a.m. She called Joseph, praying he hadn't silenced his mobile before turning in. He picked up on the third ring.

"Zoe, what's happening?" he asked groggily.

She watched as the snake lowered its head and began to slither along the wall. "Someone broke into my flat," she whispered urgently. "They left a black mamba in my room."

He cursed under his breath. "Are they still in your apartment?"

She listened closely and heard nothing beyond the eerie susurration of the snake sliding across the floor. "I don't know, but I don't think so."

"Where is the snake?"

"It's moving toward my laundry basket."

He inhaled sharply. "It's probably looking for warmth. The cement is cold. If it coils up, it will stay put. I don't want you to leave the room until I'm at your door. Do you understand?"

"What if it doesn't coil up?"

"Use your best judgment. Give me ten minutes." He hung up the phone.

She curled her legs beneath her and focused on the snake. It was nearly six feet long and an inch and a half in diameter. It probed the wicker cords of the laundry basket with its coffin-shaped head, its tongue spearing the air like a switchblade, before moving hesitantly into the pocket of air behind the basket. She let out the breath she was holding and glanced toward the doorway, training her ears on the apartment beyond.

She heard nothing.

The next ten minutes were the longest in Zoe's life. The snake, once comfortable in the corner, did not stir again. Nor did she hear any sound of movement from the apartment. The mamba was clearly a warning, as was the break-in. They—whoever *they* were—meant to terrify her. But what did they hope to achieve? She was involved in the investigation of Darious, but she wasn't the face of the prosecution. She was just an expat intern.

She heard the trill of an incoming text and looked at the screen.

"*Outside,*" Joseph wrote. "*Guard with me. No cars outside gate. Intruder?*"

"*No,*" she typed back. "*Snake is quiet, too.*"

"*Can you get to front door?*"

"*Going now. Send guard back. Come alone.*"

Taking a deep breath, she slipped her feet onto the chilly floor and glided stealthily to the doorway, watching the snake out of the corner of her eye. It didn't budge. She pulled the door shut and turned to the darkened hallway, listening. She switched on the light and moved toward the entrance to the living room. She paused just beyond the threshold, wishing she had a weapon.

At last she mustered the courage to round the corner. Her eyes darted around the living area, searching the shadows for a human silhouette. Her heart hammered in her chest, but she saw only the shapes of furniture. She looked toward the kitchen and saw a reflection, actually many reflections, in the moonlight on the floor. *Shattered glass*, she thought.

At once she understood how the intruder had gotten in. The window over the sink had been replaced the week before, and its bars had been removed to aid the workmen. Her landlord had promised to replace them, but she hadn't seen him in days.

She turned on the light and unlocked the front door. Joseph was waiting on the porch, holding his rifle. He entered the flat with barely a glance at her and began to search the apartment. She followed him from room to room. The look in his eyes left no doubt: he was prepared to shoot.

It took him less than a minute to satisfy himself that they were alone, but in that short span a fountain of emotion opened up in Zoe. The protection Joseph offered her was more than the product of his oath as a police officer. It was personal. When he placed his gun on the couch, she went to him and lost herself in his arms.

In time, he stepped back, his face betraying his anger. "How did they deliver the snake?"

"In a sack. It's in the hallway."

He went to the kitchen and returned with a wooden spoon. "I need you to get the sack."

He led her down the hallway to the bedroom and opened the door slowly. The mamba was still curled up in the corner. He moved toward the laundry basket on the soles of his feet, making no sound. He slowly pulled the basket away from the snake and set it aside. As the serpent began to move, he used the shaft of the spoon to draw its coiled body away from its head. The mamba displayed signs of alarm, but Joseph was prepared. With a flick of his wrist, he lifted the tail high off the ground and used the spoon to pin the snake's head to the floor. The mamba writhed in his arms, and Zoe was afraid he would lose his grip. But Joseph held the serpent fast. Suddenly, he let go of the spoon and grasped the snake behind the head, lifting it off the ground.

"The bag," he said. "Hold it open at my feet."

Heart pounding, Zoe did as he asked.

Joseph maneuvered the mamba into the bag until only the head and tail were outside. The snake thrashed about, but it couldn't escape the burlap. Joseph dropped the serpent's tail into the opening and wrapped his free hand around the neck of the bag like a vise, sliding it up until he was gripping the snake's neck and the bag together. He took the cinch cord with his other hand and in a single motion dropped the bag and cinched it closed, swinging it around and around and twisting the cord until the serpent had no chance of escape.

He regarded her with amusement. "All that and you could have charmed it with a dance."

She laughed, remembering that she was in her underwear. "Are you going to kill it?"

"I don't kill animals unless I have to. I'm going to take it on a drive."

"I'm coming with you," she said. "I can't stay here alone."

* * *

They drove north into the plains and deposited the snake on a rocky swale beneath a sky awash with stars. They returned to Zoe's flat a few minutes before five in the morning. As they approached the gate, Joseph pointed out where the security fence had been breached. Along a four-foot section of wall glass shards had been cleared and the bottom strand of electrified wire had been severed.

"The bottom wire leads to ground," Joseph said. "It's the only wire that could be cut without triggering the alarm. They probably bundled the other wires with a towel so they could slip through. I would guess there were three of them. The guard told me he didn't see anything, but I bet he took a bribe. They knew exactly what they were doing."

"And where they were going," she deduced. "The window they broke in the kitchen was repaired last week. That's why the bars were gone."

"Did you see the repairmen?" he asked, parking outside her flat.

"They looked like ordinary Zambians."

"No doubt they were. They finished the job

and took home a few hundred pin for leaving the window unbarred." He took a breath. "The people who came tonight were professionals. Did you notice the way they broke the glass?"

She shook her head.

"They weakened it with a cutter of some kind. The hole they made was a neat circle and no larger than a hand. Just enough to reach inside and undo the latch."

She remembered the sound of shattering glass that woke her from sleep. "It took time to plan this," she said, thinking of Dunstan Sisilu parked outside her gate. "It wasn't just about the DNA decision."

She looked out the window and interrogated herself, wishing she weren't so tired. How had she distinguished herself in the investigation? What had she done to make them afraid?

Then it came to her.

"I talked to the housekeeper," she said. "They must have seen me. Or maybe they caught my Land Rover on camera when I was staking out the house. That was over three weeks ago."

He nodded slowly. "That makes sense. She

must have seen something on the night of the rape. Or they think she saw something. We have to find a way to reach her."

"No," Zoe disagreed. "Approaching her again would only endanger her. All we need to nail Darious is DNA."

He studied her. "You should get some sleep."

She looked at her building and felt the terror again. "Stay with me tonight. Please."

"Of course," he replied. He got out of the truck and led her up the stairs to the flat. "I'll sleep here," he said, pointing at the couch.

She shook her head and took his hand, drawing him toward the guest room because her bedroom was a haunted place. She climbed into bed with her clothes on and cast aside the covers. He put the gun on the floor and slid in beside her. She pressed her back against his chest and closed her eyes, trying hard to block out the memory of the intruder and the snake.

"I feel safe now," she whispered, and realized that she meant it.

Chapter 18

Zoe slept until ten o'clock and woke to an empty bed. She blinked her eyes against the sunlight pouring through the open window shades and remembered she was in the guest room. She put on her glasses and went to the bathroom to freshen up. A few minutes later, she walked to the kitchen and found Joseph drinking a glass of water.

"Morning," she said. "Hungry?"

He set the glass down in the sink. "Famished."

She whipped up a breakfast of coffee, scrambled eggs, and toast with jam, and they ate on the deck.

After a few bites she asked, "Should we file a report about last night?"

"Ordinarily, I'd say yes," he replied. "But this is the Nyambos' neighborhood, too. If they have friends at the police post, I don't want them nosing into our investigation." He gave her a somber look. "You're not going to like this, but I don't think you should stay here for a while."

She shook her head. "This is my home. I'll get the landlord to replace the bars and install a security system."

"You're a brave woman. I admire that. But all the precautions in the world don't matter if you can't trust the people around you."

She wrestled with her emotions. She had never run from a fight. She had been robbed at gunpoint in Johannesburg, but she hadn't stopped walking the streets of Hillbrow. She was partial to her flat and the freedom it afforded her. Hotels were a nuisance, as was guest status in someone else's home. But she couldn't protect herself in her sleep.

"Where do you suggest I go?" she asked.

He looked relieved. "You need a place that's secure. You have friends at the Embassy?"

She nodded. "I know Tom Prentice, the director of the CDC office. His wife was a close friend of my mother's."

"You should talk to her. The home of an American diplomat is one of the safest places in Zambia. The Embassy has its own security company."

As much as Zoe hated to admit it, the idea made sense. "They have an extra wing," she said eventually. "And a live-in housekeeper. It probably wouldn't be an inconvenience."

Joseph looked into her eyes. "Please, Zoe. I don't want to worry about you."

"I'll think about it," she sighed, knowing the decision had already been made.

Zoe called Carol Prentice after cleaning the dishes. A twenty-year veteran of the Foreign Service, Carol was fearless and formidable, a champion of the cocktail party circuit and her husband's greatest political ally. Zoe's story, however, left her at a loss for words.

"My God," she said at last, "you expect that sort of thing in Lagos or Kinshasha, not Lusaka. Of course you can stay with us."

"You sure it's no trouble?" Zoe asked.

Carol laughed. "Honey, your mother was one of my dearest friends. You can have the guest suite for as long as you like."

Zoe hung up and went to her bedroom to pack. She laid two suitcases on the floor and stuffed them with clothing and personal items. Afterward, she took a shower and pulled her hair back in a ponytail. A few minutes before noon, she met Joseph in the parking lot and threw her bags in the Land Rover. They drove to the Prentices' separately— Zoe in the lead and Joseph behind. She watched her mirrors for the blue sedan but saw nothing.

The Prentices lived in a sprawling bungalow in nearby Sunningdale. The house was a model of colonial charm, its solid block construction, white stucco, terracotta roof, and plant-covered terraces reminiscent of a bygone era.

Carol greeted them at the door and gave Zoe a hug. "I'm so sorry about what happened," she said. "I phoned Tom right away and he *insisted* you stay with us. The house needs a little spunk. It feels like a museum since the kids left."

She held out her hand and escorted them to

the guest suite. Inside, the bungalow had the feel of a safari lodge, with breezy living spaces, wood ceilings, and animal carvings in every corner. The guest suite was in a different wing from the Prentices' sleeping quarters and had its own sitting room and bathroom.

Carol handed Zoe a set of keys. "You can come and go at your leisure and have visitors any time." She winked at Joseph. "You're not a guest; you're at home. We eat dinner at six. If you're here, you can join us. If not, we'll eat without you. No expectations either way."

Zoe touched her arm. "It's very kind of you."

"Think nothing of it," she said. "Well, I'll leave you to it." She tossed a "Ciao!" over her shoulder and left the room.

Joseph was impressed. "I like this place. It's built like a bunker."

"You'll have to get to know it then," she replied, taking his hand and drawing him toward her until their faces were inches apart. She searched his dark eyes and waited, feeling shivers along her spine. He smiled and leaned in to kiss her. At that moment his phone rang.

"Let them leave a message," she urged. "It's Saturday."

He grunted. "My job never ends." He took the phone out of his pocket and frowned. "It's Mariam." He took the call and listened intently. The muscles in his jaw tightened. "Tell him to stay where he is. I'm on my way."

"What happened?" Zoe asked.

"The samples at UTH. They're gone."

They found Dr. Chulu pacing in the hallway outside the hospital's library. When he saw them, he led them to the cabinet without a word. The library was a clinical cube, outfitted with a conference table, computer benches, and two rows of cabinets. The cabinet in the corner was missing a door—it had been carefully removed and placed on the floor.

"They took out the hinges," Dr. Chulu said hoarsely. "I don't know how they got into the room. We always keep it locked."

Joseph walked to the open cabinet and examined the frame. "When did this happen?"

"I don't know. No one has been in here since last night."

"Are you the one who found it?"

Dr. Chulu nodded. "I've already talked to my staff. No one saw anything."

"Who knew the samples were here?"

"I keep all evidence in this cabinet. My assistants knew about it."

Joseph's eyes blazed. "I want to talk to them. And I want to talk to anyone who was in this wing after you left last night."

Dr. Chulu scratched his chin. "It's going to take a while to round them up."

"I'll wait."

When the doctor left the room, Zoe sat down at the conference table and buried her face in her hands. After all they had achieved, after all Kuyeya had suffered, after Flexon Mubita had commandeered the bench and set the prosecution of Darious Nyambo on an historic course, the evidence that carried the truth about a little girl's horror had just disappeared. She felt too deflated for anger, too enervated to rebuke the voice of despair.

A memory came to mind, a patchwork of words

her father had spoken to her mother before she left for Somalia. "They've been killing each other for centuries," he had said, standing by the bay window at the Vineyard house. "Nothing you do is going to change that."

"Damn it, Jack," Catherine had retorted, "their children are starving; their daughters are being assaulted; their sons are being slaughtered. They see our planes, our doctors, our supplies, and they remember how to hope."

Jack had shaken his head wearily. "After centuries of rape and murder, hope is the smile stamped on the face of a fool. Achebe said it, not me."

It was the only time Zoe remembered her mother wavering in her resolve. A week later she was dead.

Joseph's voice interrupted her thoughts. "Mariam," he said into his phone, "all of the samples are gone. And last night someone broke into Zoe's flat and left a snake." He paused, listening. "She's fine. She's here with me. I want you to call Benson Luchembe and tell him that his client is obstructing justice. Tell him I've made it my mission to bring Darious down."

Zoe borrowed strength from his words.

"How soon can you arrange another hearing?" Joseph asked Mariam. "I want Sarge to put me on the stand and let me tell Mubita why he should hold the defense in contempt." He listened for a moment and then said, "Good. Arrange it."

He put the phone away and regarded Zoe in silence.

"I needed to hear that," she said. "Thank you."

"Words are cheap. The payoff is all that matters." He turned toward the window and searched the sky beyond. "You once asked me why I'm doing this. It's because of moments like this, when the powerful take advantage of the weak."

"You told me you made a promise," she ventured, recalling their cruise on the Zambezi. "It didn't seem cheap to me."

He hesitated. "I made that promise to my sister."

"What did you tell her?"

"That her death wouldn't be in vain."

Zoe was perplexed. "I thought she died of AIDS."

"The virus was the bullet," he said. "My uncle pulled the trigger."

She processed this in an instant. "He . . . ?"

Joseph nodded. "When she was nine. I caught him in the act, but I couldn't stop him. I was twelve. He threatened to kill us if we talked. We never spoke of it again. We had no choice. He was Deputy Commissioner of Police."

Zoe shuddered. "Where is he now?"

"He died four years before Elaine. Of course, they didn't call it AIDS. They called in pneumonia. But when she died, too, I knew."

Zoe took his hand and squeezed. "I'm so sorry, Joseph," she said, understanding everything at once—why he waited to go to college, why he was obsessed with his work, why he wanted to be Inspector General of Police.

She heard footsteps in the hallway outside the library. The door opened and Dr. Chulu led a group of people into the room.

"All of them were here last night," the doctor said. He pointed to two young women. "These are my assistants. You've already met Nurse Mbelo."

Joseph nodded. "I'll talk to her first. The rest of you wait in the hallway."

The interviews lasted over an hour. Joseph drilled down deep, probing every inconsistency, watching faces and mannerisms for anything that might signal guilt, but neither the night staff nor Dr. Chulu's assistants yielded anything of value. When he dismissed the last of them, he looked at Zoe in frustration.

"Where you're from, a forensics team would take fingerprints, hair samples, skin samples, and check them against an electronic database. In Zambia, we have trained technicians but nothing to do with the evidence without a suspect. What do you call it? A Catch-22."

She nodded. "And even if you did find a suspect, you wouldn't be able to connect him to the Nyambos. We need to talk to the judge. Then we need to go back to the drawing board."

"The *ngangas*," he said.

"The housekeeper," she added. "And Cynthia in Kitwe."

He shook his head. "We could have set a precedent with this case."

She smiled, her old confidence beginning to return. "Perhaps we still will."

* * *

Thanks to Sarge's efforts, the case was scheduled for a hearing the following Tuesday. After everyone assembled in Courtroom 10, the judge climbed the bench and waved to the deputy who swiftly cleansed the chamber of all spectators, including Frederick Nyambo. The deputy nodded to the judge and stepped outside, closing the door behind him.

Mubita gave Benson Luchembe an icy stare. "This Court will not tolerate threats to members of the prosecution or the theft of critical evidence."

Luchembe stood, affecting a look of surprise. "Your Worship," he said deferentially, "my client insists he had nothing to do with the break-ins. He submitted a blood sample yesterday, pursuant to your order."

Anger flared in the judge's eyes. "Evidence disappeared from a locked room barely twenty-four hours after I ordered it to be tested. Who benefited other than the accused?"

Luchembe held out his hands. "I don't know, Your Worship."

Mubita shook his head and turned to Sarge. "I realize you have witnesses who would like to testify, but unless they can prove the involvement of the accused, I can't do anything with it."

Sarge nodded reluctantly. "It appears the perpetrators left without a trace."

The judge leaned forward, looking at Luchembe. "While I have no grounds for contempt, the loss of evidence prejudices the prosecution. With DNA, we would have known your client's guilt or innocence in a matter of weeks. Without DNA, we must try this case the old-fashioned way. I want you to know that I'm going to give the prosecution wide latitude to present its evidence at trial. I'll take this incident into account to the extent I'm permitted by the rules."

Mubita's eyes swept the courtroom, confronting every lawyer with equal intensity. "I have not prejudged this case. The accused is innocent until proven guilty. But I will not allow any man or woman to tilt the scales of justice. This Court is adjourned."

As soon as the magistrate left the bench, the defense team piled out of the courtroom. Zoe conferred with Joseph in a whisper while Sarge and Niza packed their briefcases.

"I've been thinking about how to get the house-keeper alone again," she said.

"If your interest in her triggered the attack on your flat," he replied, "they're going to watch her carefully."

"They can't live without food. I'm going to hang out at Shoprite."

"That won't work if you're being followed."

She pictured Dunstan Sisilu. "I haven't seen him since the attack."

"Neither have I, but that doesn't mean he isn't there."

She met his eyes. "It's a risk I have to take."

Chapter 19

Every other day for the next three weeks, Zoe patrolled the aisles of the Shoprite at Manda Hill. She conducted her surveillance between eight thirty and ten in the morning, bracketing the time she had last seen the housekeeper there. She kept watch for Dunstan Sisilu but never saw him. Inside the supermarket, she played the role of the indecisive shopper, meandering through the store and occasionally placing things in her cart. She waited for a glimpse of the old woman's wrinkled face, but each time she was disappointed.

"Maybe your timing is wrong," Joseph suggested one evening.

"Or she's shopping somewhere else, or someone is shopping for her," she said. "The possibilities are endless. I've been thinking about staking out the house again."

He shook his head. "It's too dangerous."

"I could take Carol's Prado. I could dye my hair."

"You can't color your skin."

Exasperated, she said, "I'll keep trying."

When October turned to November, tall clouds started to gather in the late afternoons. For days the rains only threatened, but then, at last, the sky opened up and poured out such a torrent that the streets swam with mud and refuse. The advent of the rainy season had a paradoxical effect, darkening the sun but brightening faces—including Zoe's—that had grown weary of the sweltering air. Overnight, the parched plains broke into bloom. It was Zoe's favorite time in Africa, when all things tired and worn became new again.

She settled easily into the routine of living with the Prentices. They treated her more like a neighbor than a guest, yet every evening she found her laundry cleaned and her bed made. Their housekeeper, Rosa, was exacting, scrupulous, and a genius in the kitchen. Carol Prentice sang her praises and trusted her implicitly. On workdays, Joseph escorted Zoe home to ensure she wasn't followed. Often he stayed for dinner, and the Prentices grew fond of him.

On Sunday afternoons, Zoe visited Kuyeya. Her affection for the girl deepened with each meeting. Though slow at first, Kuyeya's therapy with Dr. Mbao began to bear fruit. The psychiatrist probed the girl's memory for stories she learned from her mother and used them to piece together details about her past. Kuyeya's favorite tale involved a bee-eater who made friends with a hippopotamus. Whenever she said "bee-eater," she burst into a fit of laughter.

In the middle of November, Zoe at last conceded that her strategy to flush out the housekeeper had been an abysmal failure. She considered staking out the residence without telling Joseph, but the memory of Dunstan Sisilu and the black mamba tempered her enthusiasm. One morning when she sat down to breakfast, she heard Rosa washing dishes in the kitchen, and an idea came to her. She couldn't believe she hadn't thought of it before.

"Do you have a minute?" she asked Rosa.

"Of course," the woman replied, drying her hands on a towel.

Zoe gave her a sketch of the case and told her about the search for the Nyambos' housekeeper. "If you were trying to find her, what would you do?"

Rosa thought for a moment. "Does her mistress wear *chitenge* or Western clothes?"

Zoe searched her memory for details about Patricia Nyambo. She had only seen her once—at the Subordinate Court on the day of the arraignment. Had she been wearing a business suit? In a flash Zoe remembered. She had been wearing a dress made of green *chitenge*.

When she told Rosa this, the woman asked, "Is the cloth expensive? Is the color rich and the pattern fine?"

"I think so," Zoe guessed, figuring Patricia Nyambo would settle for nothing less.

Rosa nodded. "There is a woman at the City

Market who sells the finest *chitenge* in Lusaka. She keeps a stall on Saturday only. My last mistress often sent me there. I saw many other women like me."

"It's worth a shot," Zoe said, and asked Rosa how to find the stall.

Early on Saturday morning, Joseph and Zoe drove downtown. The largest of Lusaka's markets, the City Market, sat on a parcel of land wedged between the Cairo Road commercial center and the more pedestrian Soweto Market. The nicest stalls were housed in an enclosed arcade with tributaries branching off the main hall like side streets in an urban grid. Zoe had visited the market only once in her year in Lusaka, but most Zambians she knew were frequent customers.

On any given day, downtown Lusaka was a bustling place. On Saturdays, however, the commercial district had a festival atmosphere. The streets were jammed with traffic, and the sidewalks were crawling with shoppers hungry for a deal. They parked beside a *salaula* stand brimming with secondhand clothing from the West. Joseph took Zoe's hand and navigated the labyrinth, side-stepping moving bodies and merchandise laid out along the roadside.

They slipped into the covered arcade and joined the stream of customers shuffling through the main hall. The diversity of goods on display beggared imagination – shoes, boots, leather, bags, textiles, *chitenge* fabric, rugs, woodcarvings, jewelry and clothing. All around customers haggled with vendors. The noise and commotion made Zoe's head spin.

"Rosa said the stall is on a side aisle halfway down," she said. "The woman's name is Chiwoyu. She said we should expect a crowd."

They found the stall exactly as Rosa had described. The fabrics were beautiful and the queue extended down the aisle. Most of the customers were Zambian women over fifty—many no doubt employees of the elite. Zoe searched their faces but didn't see the housekeeper.

"Where should we wait?" Zoe asked.

Joseph led her toward a stall stuffed with racks of men's shoes. Outside the stall was a folding chair. "Sit here," he said. "Pretend you're pregnant."

Zoe took a seat and watched Chiwoyu dispense bolts of fabric while Joseph struck up a conversation with the shoe vendor. Eventually, her back started to hurt. She stood up and walked toward the exit, stretching her muscles. As she neared the end of the aisle, an old woman entered from the outside. The woman glanced at Zoe and stopped in her tracks.

It was the housekeeper.

"We met before," Zoe said quietly, making no move toward the woman.

The housekeeper's eyes darted around, as if seeking a way out.

"I understand why you don't want to talk to me, but I need your help. Kuyeya needs your help. Can I show you a picture of her?"

Zoe took out her iPhone and found an image of Kuyeya at St. Francis. The woman stared at the screen and tears came to her eyes. Still, she didn't speak.

"I think you know her," Zoe said. "Or maybe you knew her mother. Her name was Charity Mizinga, but she also went by Bella. She died two years ago."

At last the old woman found her voice. "There is nothing I can do for you. Even God cannot change the past."

You do know her! Zoe thought. "Perhaps," she said, keeping her excitement in check. "But the truth is easier to come by."

The housekeeper regarded her sadly. "What would you do with the truth?"

Zoe steadied her breathing, certain she was close to a breakthrough. "I would tell it to the judge and let justice take its course."

The old woman shook her head slowly. "Your justice would change nothing."

"It would change everything," Zoe countered. "Darious raped a girl before."

The housekeeper's eyes filled with fear. "I need to go."

"Please. We can offer you protection."

"You don't know what you're asking," the old woman replied.

She clutched her handbag and headed toward Chiwoyu's stall. For excruciating seconds, Zoe held out hope that the woman might reconsider. But the housekeeper took her place at the rear of the queue and acted as though the exchange had never happened.

"What did she say?" Joseph asked, meeting Zoe in the aisle.

"She knows something, but she doesn't want to talk about it."

He angled his head thoughtfully. "I'm not sure you're right."

"What do you mean?"

"I watched her face. She listened to you, but she's afraid. She has your number, right?"

Zoe nodded. "I gave it to her at Shoprite."

"Give her time. She may come around."

As the days passed, Zoe checked her iPhone regularly for a message from the housekeeper, but nothing came. She distracted herself with half a dozen new case referrals from Dr. Chulu. All were horrifying—the youngest victim was six years old—but the perpetrators were family members or neighbors, and the process of compiling evidence was fairly straightforward.

She tried several times to reach Cynthia Chansa

by phone. She left her husband a number of voice-mails—each time dropping a bit of information about Kuyeya and the obstacles faced by the prosecution—but she received no response. After three calls a disembodied voice informed her that the mailbox was full. She tried Godfrey again, but he didn't answer.

One morning in December, Zoe was sitting in the office editing an appellate brief for the High Court when Maurice appeared in the doorway to the legal department. He crossed the floor to her desk and stood silently until she looked up at him.

"Can I help you?" she asked.

He nodded. "There's a woman at the gate look-ing for you."

She felt burst of excitement. "Who is it?"

"I don't know."

The housekeeper! She walked through the office and steadied her breathing. *Be cool*, she told herself. *Don't frighten her.*

She left the bungalow and headed down the lane toward the gate. She nodded to the guard, and he beckoned to someone standing on the far side of the barrier. A woman in a pale pink suit and high heels stepped through the opening, and Zoe stopped in shock.

She was not Zambian. She was American.

"Hello, Zoe," said Sylvia Martinelli, surveying the landscape around the CILA office. "Is everything in Lusaka so lovely?"

Zoe stared at her, paralyzed by the unexpected collision of worlds. She hadn't seen or spoken to Sylvia since the dinner they had shared in Cape Town at the conclusion of her clerkship. The détente she had forged with her father over the disbursal of funds from her charitable trust had not extended to his second wife. If ever the conditions had been right to build a bridge between them, that had been the moment. But Sylvia had squandered it by defending Atticus Spelling.

"Why are you here?" Zoe finally managed.

Sylvia smiled. "It's almost noon. Let me take you to lunch. The concierge at the Intercontinental told me about Rhapsody's. It sounded very nice."

"It is. But you haven't answered my question."

Sylvia glanced at the guard. "This isn't the best place."

Zoe felt suddenly anxious. "Is something wrong with my father?"

Sylvia laughed. "No. He's as indefatigable as ever. But my visit does relate to him. Please, Zoe. I know we've had our disagreements. I'm only asking for an hour of your time."

Zoe was ambivalent, but she didn't have it in her to be cruel. "Okay."

She grabbed her backpack from inside the office and followed Sylvia to a waiting SUV. A Zambian driver opened the door for them and they climbed in. Ten minutes later, they entered Rhapsody's, a trendy South African import with electric-blue mood lighting. The hostess greeted them and showed them to a table.

"Is the steak good?" Sylvia inquired, scanning the menu.

"Yes," Zoe replied evenly. "But I want an answer to my question."

Sylvia gave her an inscrutable look. "Will there ever be peace between us?"

Zoe met her eyes. "Peace without reconciliation is a lie."

"Okay, then tell me about reconciliation."

"It starts with the truth."

Sylvia looked puzzled. "What truth are you talking about?"

"You were raised Catholic," Zoe said, keeping her expression neutral. "You remember the thirty pieces of silver."

Sylvia frowned. "Come now. Must you be so melodramatic?"

A dozen responses came to Zoe's mind, but she held her tongue, staring at Sylvia until the silence became uncomfortable.

At last Sylvia spoke again. "You know how committed Jack is to winning the election. He's the right man for the job. Our country desperately needs his leadership."

Zoe nodded. "I'm well aware of his ambitions. And yours."

Sylvia softened her tone. "It doesn't matter what you think of me. I never tried to fill your mother's shoes. I couldn't have, anyway." She gave a little laugh. "But Jack loves you. He's your father. He's made mistakes and he regrets them. He'd really like your support."

Zoe shook her head. "I can't support him. His

solution to the budget crisis is to gut the programs that benefit the people I work with every day."

"That's hardly true. You know better than I do how much Jack cares about the poor. He gives generously to your mother's foundation. In times of crisis, everyone has to cut back."

Zoe's eyes flashed. "You take a billion or two from the Pentagon, and people will complain, but they'll get over it. You take that money from AIDS relief and thousands of Africans will die. There's a difference between cutting and killing."

Sylvia put up her hands. "Look, I didn't come here to talk about policy. I came because Jack is going to win the New Hampshire primary. It would mean the world to him to have you on stage with Trevor when he gives his victory speech."

Zoe considered this, knowing Sylvia was right. In the end, however, her conscience wielded an absolute veto. "I can't do it. Tell him I'm very sorry."

Sylvia raised her eyebrows. "Even if it means he won't make the call to Atticus?"

Zoe felt as if she had been sucker-punched. "He gave me his word."

Sylvia shrugged, allowing the silence to inspire doubt.

Zoe stood up. "I have nothing more to say to you."

"Wait," Sylvia protested. "Please don't go."

But it was too late for rapprochement. Zoe walked out of the restaurant, ignoring the waiter who was bringing them bread. She thought of her father as he was before her mother died—the Harvard-educated child of a Midwestern insurance salesman; the savant who ascended to the pinnacle of Wall Street but never lost the middle-class chip on his shoulder; the sailor who taught her how to hoist the jib on his yacht and rescued her from drowning when she fell overboard in a squall; the husband whose love for Catherine Sorensen-Fleming sent him into clinical depression when she died. *Why didn't you find another woman like her, Dad? Why did you have to marry Sylvia?*

She placed a call to Joseph and asked for a ride. Then she took a seat in a small plaza and listened to the bubbling fountain behind her. The sky was mostly clear, and the sun was hot upon her skin. Distracted by unwanted memories, she barely noticed when a group of businesspeople approached the hostess at Rhapsody's. It was the voice that caught her attention, the booming basso profundo that carried such gravity in the courtroom.

She looked across the plaza and saw him—Flexon Mubita. With him were two Zambians, a tall man in a dark suit and a handsome woman in *chitenge*. The man she didn't recognize. But she remembered the woman well. Her stomach clenched involuntarily.

It was Patricia Nyambo.

Zoe took a few hasty photographs with her iPhone and then sat back against the bench, trying to make sense of what she had seen. Mariam trusted Mubita more than anyone on the bench; Dr. Chulu considered him an honorable man. His behavior in Kuyeya's case had been unimpeachable. He had ruled in their favor on DNA and given Benson Luchembe a tongue-lashing over the theft of evidence. He and Patricia were both judges; they surely knew one another. It could just be a friendly lunch meeting.

The more Zoe thought about it, however, the less likely that seemed. Mubita was presiding over the trial of Patricia's son. She sat on the High

Court, which would hear any appeal in the case. What was it Judge van der Merwe had told her? *"Judging is one of the loneliest jobs in the world because relationships are always secondary. A judge can't tolerate even a hint of impropriety."* Perhaps judicial ethics were looser in Zambia, but conflicts of interest were the same everywhere. Besides, the Nyambos had proven their guile. Evidence had gone missing; someone had broken into her flat; Thoko Kaunda had been influenced. The thought struck Zoe with sudden force: what if the same thing happened to Mubita?

When Joseph pulled up to the curb, she jumped into the passenger seat. "Look who's having lunch together," she said, showing him the photos.

His eyes darkened. "They're in there now?"

She nodded. "Who's the tall guy?"

"The Deputy Minister of Justice."

She shook her head. The involvement of a powerful politician—a deputy cabinet minister, no less—only accentuated her concerns. "What are we going to do?"

"If she compromises him, I doubt there's anything we *can* do. But we don't know what they're talking about." He looked at the pictures again. "Mariam's husband has political connections. Maybe he can make a few inquiries."

Zoe struggled to compose herself. *First Sylvia. Now this.* "Please take me home. I can't go back to the office right now."

Joseph nodded and pulled out onto Great East Road, heading toward Kabulonga. After a while, he asked, "What were you doing at Arcades?"

"It's a long story."

He glanced at her. "I don't have anywhere else to be at the moment."

Out of habit she almost deflected his inquiry, but something in her counseled the benefits of disclosure. She was tired of policing her words, tired of subjugating her feelings and hiding her scars.

"Okay," she said, surprised by the lightness she felt in saying something so simple. "If you want to hear it, I'll tell you."

When they reached the Prentice bungalow, they found the carport empty. Zoe unlocked the front door and called out to Rosa, but she heard nothing beyond a marbled echo. She led Joseph to the terrace, and they took seats on wicker chairs facing the pool. She looked across the water and felt a tremor of apprehension. For an instant, she reconsidered her decision, but she knew she had to do it. The burden needed to be shared.

"My dad and I have a . . . *complex* relationship," she began. "We're very different, but I grew up respecting him. We had a lot of fun together, and he loved my mom more than anything." She let out a chuckle. "Except making money, perhaps. He took it really hard when she died. Trevor and I had to figure things out on our own. It was a difficult time."

She listened to the birds singing in the *msasa* trees. "A year later, he met a woman named Sylvia Martinelli at a charity function. She was a celebrity publicist—essentially an image consultant. She was beautiful and he was lonely. I didn't like her, but it wasn't her fault, at least not at first. After they got married, Dad started to change. His ambitions grew. He'd built a hugely successful fund on Wall Street, but it wasn't enough. Suddenly, he wanted to be President of the United

States. I don't know if it was Sylvia's idea, or she just encouraged it, but his decision to run for office changed everything."

She took a nervous breath. "His first race was for the U.S. Senate in 2000. He asked his investment partner—one of his best friends—to run the campaign. His name was Harry Randall. Our families were close. Every summer, the Randalls spent two weeks with us on Martha's Vineyard. That year, Dad and Harry were too busy with the campaign, but the rest of us went. Harry had a son named Clay. I had a crush on him. He was affectionate, and I was seventeen and naive. It was all very juvenile, but I was foolish enough to believe he loved me."

She glanced at Joseph and saw a far-off look in his eyes. "Am I boring you?"

He shook his head. "No. I'm starting to understand you."

"All right, I'm going to get this out," she said, feeling a tear break loose. "My brother left after the first week to get ready for Harvard. As soon as he wasn't around, Clay got more physical. He asked me to sleep with him. I told him I wasn't ready. On our last day on the island, we went to the beach together. He started kissing me, and I played along. We'd done it before. But he wanted more. I said no. He didn't accept that."

Her tears were flowing freely now. "I didn't expect this to make me a mess."

"Take your time," Joseph encouraged.

She laughed. "You're never in a hurry."

He shrugged but didn't respond.

"I didn't know what to do," she went on. "Trevor was in Massachusetts. Dad was on the campaign trail. I finally broke down in front of Sylvia. She called my dad, and he came home. When I told him, I saw his fear. I sat in the living room while he and Sylvia talked. After that, he started asking questions. How far had I gone with Clay before? How far with other boys? It was clear what he was suggesting. I asked him what he planned to do, and he said there was nothing he could do. It was just a misunderstanding. I needed to forget about it."

Anger gleamed in Joseph's eyes. "Have you ever told anyone about this?"

She shook her head, feeling depleted. "I wanted to tell Trevor, but every time I talked to him he was busy with his studies. Then Dad won the election, and I dived into my senior year. I guess I never found the right moment."

He placed a hand on hers. "I'm so sorry, Zoe. It wasn't your fault."

She nodded. "I know that now. Men take what they want and women get the blame. It's happening today all over the world."

He thought about this. "What were you doing at Arcades?"

"Having lunch with Sylvia."

"Ah, now I understand."

She looked into the sky and saw clouds forming. By mid-afternoon it would storm. "We should go back to the office."

He looked into her eyes. "Are you sure you're ready?"

She nodded, wiping away the last of her tears. "You need to talk to Mariam."

Chapter 20

Lusaka, Zambia
December, 2011

A few days later, Mariam summoned the response team to a morning meeting. Since the samples had been stolen from UTH, the legal team had retooled its approach to prosecuting Darious, focusing on the development of new evidence, and Joseph had spent two months beating the bushes in Kabwata and Kanyama, searching for an eyewitness he had missed. In the past week, he had also been working with Mariam to investigate Flexon Mubita. When he sat down at the conference table wearing a satisfied look, Zoe knew that he'd discovered something.

"I have good news and bad news," Mariam began. "I'll start with the bad news. As you know, my husband works for the Ministry of Home Affairs. At my request, he made some inquiries about the Principal Resident Magistrate. His official slate is clean. He's a sharp, experienced, fair-minded judge. Unofficially, he's been in the running for a seat on the High Court for years, and he's always been passed over. Apparently, he hasn't made the right friends."

She placed her hands on the table. "It's possible he met with Patricia Nyambo and the Deputy Minister of Justice for entirely proper reasons. I'd love to believe this, but I have serious doubts. A vote from the Ministry of Justice could guarantee him the next opening on the High Court. If I were in Mubita's shoes, I would never agree to meet with them, not when I'm presiding over Darious's trial. It raises too many questions. My guess is the Nyambos are courting him. With the parties involved, we have no way to stop that. If he turns against us, the best we can do is try the case and hope for an appealable issue."

Niza looked skeptical. "Doesn't a lunch meeting in public suggest they don't have anything to hide? Rhapsody's is an odd place to do a backroom deal."

Sarge shook his head. "A restaurant gives them a legitimate excuse. Location isn't the issue. It's the meeting itself. I agree with Mariam. A careful judge would never agree to it, not under these circumstances. That he did agree to it suggests he's thinking about something other than his reputation."

Zoe looked at Mariam. "You know him. How likely is it that he'll be corrupted?"

Mariam shrugged. "It depends on how much he wants what they're offering. He's always been fair to us. But that doesn't mean he can't change."

Niza pursed her lips. "So what you're saying is that this case could turn out to be a complete waste of time. What's the good news?"

Mariam turned to Joseph. "Why don't you tell everyone what you found?"

He leaned forward in his chair. "A while ago we had a discussion about whether the virgin rape myth played a role in Kuyeya's assault. It was a wild theory, but I've been pursuing it. I now have evidence that the theory may be right."

"You found an *nganga*," Zoe said in amazement.

When he nodded, Niza asked, "How did you manage that?"

He smiled, enjoying the moment. "About a month ago I found an old woman in Kanyama who recognized Darious's SUV. She said she'd seen it outside the house of an *nganga* by the name of Amos. I visited Amos and told him a story about being HIV-positive. I went back a couple of times, claiming the herbs he gave me didn't work. Yesterday, I demanded a cure. I offered him a million kwacha. Guess what he prescribed?"

"You're kidding," Niza said. "He actually told you to have sex with a virgin."

"Worse," Joseph said. "He said a child would do the trick."

"Did you record him?" Zoe asked.

"I did. I showed it to him afterward and offered him two options. Either I'd throw him in jail on felony charges or he'd talk about Darious Nyambo. He made a bit of a fuss—"

"Just a bit?" Niza interjected.

Joseph held out his hands. "He was enraged, but

he wasn't stupid. He agreed to talk so long as he had a lawyer present."

"Who's his lawyer?" Sarge asked.

"Bob Wangwe."

Niza laughed. "Lawyers get the clients they deserve."

"Who's Wangwe?" Zoe inquired.

Sarge answered. "He's a shady character who represents other shady characters."

"When are you meeting them?" Zoe asked.

"This afternoon," Joseph responded, "as long as we get the DPP on board. Amos said Wangwe wouldn't let him talk without a promise of immunity."

"What does Amos have on Darious?" said Niza.

"He wouldn't tell me. I threatened to arrest him, and he stood firm."

"You should have a witness," Sarge said. "In case he contests it later."

"I'll go," Zoe volunteered, trying not to sound too eager.

"Is that all right with you?" Mariam asked Joseph.

He nodded. "We make a good team."

* * *

Just before two o'clock, Joseph and Zoe drove to Kanyama in his truck. Somewhere in the traffic snarl southwest of Cairo Road, she put into words the question at the forefront of her mind: "Why didn't you tell me about Amos?"

"I didn't know if it would work."

"Are you sure he's going to cooperate?"

"You mean is he going to run? I doubt it. He's been in Kanyama for a decade."

A few minutes later, Zoe saw a sign that read: "Dr. Mwenya Amos, Herbalist and Traditional Healer." They turned before the sign and drove down a dirt lane to a white house flanked by shade trees. Unlike the shambling residences around it, the *nganga*'s house had embroidered curtains, an herb garden, and a door painted bright red. Two cars were parked outside—a dingy yellow sedan and a white Prado SUV.

"See the door?" Joseph said. "Red is a symbol of spiritual power."

"So he's repugnant *and* delusional."

He shrugged. "His clients obviously don't think so."

382

A bespectacled Zambian in a pinstripe suit met them in the yard. He coughed once, covering his mouth with his hand, and then offered the hand to Joseph. "Officer Kabuta, I'm Bob Wangwe, Dr. Amos's attorney."

Joseph ignored the handshake. "Is your client ready?"

Wangwe cleared his throat. "He'll be out shortly. He has to purify the space."

Zoe rolled her eyes. "How long is this going to take?"

"Who are you?" Wangwe asked with a frown.

"An attorney for the prosecution," she said.

The lawyer grunted. "Does the DPP offer my client full immunity?"

"Your client is guilty of a felony," Joseph replied matter-of-factly. "We'll see what he has to say. If it's helpful, we'll give him immunity. If not, he goes to jail."

Wangwe glanced at his watch—a shiny gilded piece that looked to Zoe like a Rolex knock-off— and turned toward the house. Before long, another man appeared on the threshold, wearing trousers and a loose white shirt. He walked to the garden and knelt down, harvesting a handful of herbs. He handed a herb to Wangwe, another to Joseph and a third to Zoe.

"Chew it and spit it out," he said. "It will cleanse you of the spirits of the dead."

Zoe's impulse was to say no, but Joseph silenced her with a look. He placed the herb in his mouth, ground it with his teeth, and spat it onto the earth. Reluctantly, Zoe followed suit. The herb left her mouth tasting bitter.

"Come," said Dr. Amos, leading them into the house.

The first thing Zoe noticed about the *nganga*'s residence was the pungent odor. The living room was cluttered with tables displaying the articles of his trade—incense, herbs, feathers, bones, and remnants of animals. Bottles of all sizes were strewn about. Some contained powder, some herbs; the rest were empty. At the center of one of the tables lay the mutilated carcass of a bird encircled by a halo of dried blood. Zoe felt nauseous. She braced herself against the wall, controlling her breathing.

The *nganga* pointed to a shadowy bedroom. "This way."

The bedroom was half the size of the living room and empty of furniture. With heavy curtains veiling the windows, the room had the atmosphere of a cave. Two rugs were on the floor, one white and the other red. Between them was a pile of partially burnt sticks. Dr. Amos sat cross-legged on the red rug and gestured for Joseph and Zoe to sit on the white one. The lawyer, Wangwe, looked around before squatting awkwardly on the cement slab.

Joseph threw aside the curtains, admitting wide shafts of sunlight. "We're not here for a consultation," he said, disregarding the *nganga*'s smoldering stare. "I want to see your eyes."

When everyone was situated, Wangwe was the first to speak. "I am advising my client not to answer questions until you agree to offer him full immunity."

Joseph stared the lawyer down. "He'll answer my questions now, or I'll conduct the interrogation at the Woodlands Police Post."

"That will not be necessary," Amos replied hastily.

"I thought so." Joseph took a digital recording device out of his pocket and placed it on the floor. "I'm going to record our conversation."

"And I'm going to make a backup," Zoe said, taking out her iPhone.

Wangwe shifted uncomfortably but didn't object.

Joseph began with an introduction, stating the names and offices of everyone in the room, the date and time, the voluntary nature of the interrogation, the fact of recording, and the terms of immunity being offered. When Amos and Wangwe affirmed their agreement, he turned to the matter at hand.

"We're interested in the services you provided to a man named Darious Nyambo," he began. "Darious is the defendant in a pending defilement prosecution. When did you meet him?"

"He came to me last year when the rains ended," Amos said. "He thought he had AIDS."

"Had he gone for testing?"

Amos shook his head. "He didn't want a diagnosis from Western doctors."

"Why not?"

"Western medicine is for the weak. His father is a prominent man."

"How do you know Frederick?" Joseph asked.

Amos chose his words carefully. "He consults a friend."

"Is Frederick sick, too?"

The *nganga* shook his head. "He is a man of *mukwala*. He has medicine."

"Meaning he practices witchcraft?" Zoe inquired.

Irritation showed in Amos's eyes. "That is a word used by *muzungus* to describe what they do not understand. Mr. Nyambo has knowledge of the spirits."

Something clicked in Zoe's mind. *Darious was afraid he had AIDS, but he was even more afraid of his father's medicine. So he avoided testing and ARVs and came to Amos.*

Joseph picked up the questioning again. "How did Darious find you?"

Amos shrugged. "Most of my patients are referred by someone. I didn't ask who."

"Did he tell you who he was?"

The *nganga* shook his head. "Not initially. But after a few visits he opened up."

"What do you mean?"

Amos took a breath. "Officer Kabuta, I am not like white doctors who dispense pills and send their patients home. I encourage my patients to think of me as a friend. In the course of treatment, many tell me their stories. Darious was no exception."

"What story did he tell you?"

The *nganga* frowned in puzzlement. "He told me many things."

Joseph regrouped. "I'm interested in what he thought about his sickness."

"He believed a *mahule* had given it to him."

"Who was the *mahule*?" Joseph asked, trading a glance with Zoe.

The *nganga* opened his hands. "He didn't tell me her name. But he thought she was a witch. He believed she had put a hex on him and stolen his health."

"Why would he think that? Did she practice magic?"

"I know only what Darious told me. He said she had bewitched his family."

"Did he say what he meant?"

The *nganga* gave him a grave look. "He said the *mahule* had brought a curse upon his parents. She was the cause of great strife and pain."

Zoe was astounded. *Was Frederick also a customer of Bella's? Did Patricia find out and confront him about her?*

"Did he tell you anything else about his parents?" Joseph asked.

The *nganga* held out his hands. "That is all I know. But Darious hated the *mahule* deeply. The damage must have been great."

"If he hated her so much, why did he sleep with her?" Zoe asked.

"He said he didn't know who she was until it was too late."

The gears of Zoe's deduction ground to a halt. How could he not have known? Had she hidden her identity from him?

"The curse upon his family, when did that happen?" Joseph asked.

"Darious was a young man," replied the *nganga*. "Sixteen years old, I think he said."

Zoe stared at Amos. "Darious is thirty now, isn't he?"

He nodded. "A terrible shame for one so young to be so sick."

She sat back, beginning to understand. *Whatever happened between Charity and the Nyambos happened soon after she arrived in Lusaka. But Darious didn't meet her then. When he met her at Alpha Bar years later, he thought she was just a prostitute.* Suddenly, she had questions the *nganga* couldn't answer. She made a mental note to talk to Clay Whitaker at the World Bank.

She had one last thought: "How did he find out who she was?"

The *nganga* searched his memory. "I don't know," he said at last.

Joseph cast a questioning glance at her, and she gestured for him to proceed. He took the conversation in a new direction. "When Darious came to you with his fears—about AIDS, about the *mahule*'s curse—what sort of medicine did you prescribe?"

"I gave him the same herbs I gave you," said Amos. "One for TB, one for diarrhea, one for headaches. My own triple combination therapy."

"How long was it before he asked for something more potent?"

"It was about two weeks. He said the herbs helped with the diarrhea, but he needed something for his skin. He had lesions on his face and neck. He also had a rash in his crotch."

"What did you give him then?"

"I gave him a powerful herb that—how do you say it in English?—*detoxifies* the body, including the skin. I also gave him some medicine for STDs. It seemed to help."

"But he came to you again."

"A few months later."

"When precisely?"

The *nganga* looked out the window and Zoe saw beads of perspiration on his brow. "I think it was in July. It was very cold."

"What did he tell you?"

"He said the herbs weren't working. He was very afraid of the hex on him. He wanted to fight it with strong *mukwala*."

Joseph leaned forward. "How did you respond?"

For the first time the *nganga* showed signs of apprehension. "I told him I could help him with that. My grandfather was a great *nganga*, and he was adept at healing spells."

"Did you perform a spell for him?"

Amos shifted on the rug. "No. He wasn't interested in them. He wanted revenge against the *mahule*. He wanted to hurt her the way she had hurt him. I told him *mukwala* didn't work that way. He didn't want to listen to me."

Joseph gave the *nganga* a forceful look. "If you

lie to me, even one time, you lose any chance of immunity. Is that clear?"

Amos swallowed hard and sweat began to run down his cheeks.

"Go on," said Joseph.

The *nganga* glanced at his attorney and his hands began to tremble. "I tried to reason with him, but he wanted a cure. He told me he'd heard a story from a friend—that a man could sleep with a virgin and the poison would pass to her. He asked me what I thought of that. I told him I'd heard the same thing. It's true. There are many *ngangas* who believe that."

Joseph waited a beat and then asked, "Did he say anything else?"

Amos's eyes shifted to the floor. "He asked me how he could tell if a girl was a virgin."

"What advice did you give him?"

The *nganga* sighed and seemed to shrink. "I said he would see blood."

At this admission, Zoe nearly flung herself at Amos. For a moment she fantasized about choking him to death. Joseph placed a hand on her knee and squeezed gently.

"How did Darious respond?" he asked the *nganga*.

"He smiled," Amos said. "I remember it well. He said was going to bewitch the witch."

"Those were his exact words?"

Amos nodded. "It is not the sort of thing a person forgets."

"Did he say anything else, anything about a child?"

The *nganga* shook his head. "He paid me and left. I never saw him again."

When Joseph concluded the interview, Bob Wangwe reiterated his client's demand for immunity and threatened to file a complaint with the Commissioner of Police if Joseph didn't grant it. The lawyer's smugness so infuriated Zoe that she stood abruptly and stomped out of the house, leaving Joseph to negotiate the terms of the deal.

She skirted the edge of the herb garden and set off up the ramshackle lane toward Los Angeles Road, her pace just short of a run. She knew the evidence offered by the *nganga* could put Darious behind bars, but suddenly winning the case wasn't enough. Thousands of girls like Kuyeya were suffering across southern Africa. Until the authorities put the fear of God into men like Amos and Darious, the sorority of victims would only increase.

She didn't notice the gray Toyota Prado in the lane behind her until she reached the intersection at Los Angeles Road. She stopped beside the *nganga*'s sign and harbored a fleeting fantasy of whittling it down with a chainsaw. It was then that she saw the SUV and the man behind the wheel. She stared at him in shock.

It was Dunstan Sisilu.

With a roar the Prado leaped forward, screeching to a halt only inches from her. She felt an overwhelming instinct to flee, but her legs didn't translate the message from her brain quickly enough. Sisilu jumped out of the vehicle, brandishing a huge, silver-plated revolver.

"Get in the car," he commanded, as her iPhone began to vibrate in her pocket.

Joseph! she thought, staring at the gun. *Where are you?*

Sisilu pressed the revolver against her ribs and shoved her roughly into the passenger seat. He threw the Prado into reverse and stomped on the accelerator, catapulting them backward down the dirt lane. After a short distance, he made a jarring turn into an alley strung with clotheslines and slammed on the brakes. When the SUV came to rest, Zoe could barely see the lane through the curtains of hanging garments. She felt her iPhone vibrating again—

Without warning Sisilu put the barrel of the gun against her head. Her heart stopped, then nearly jumped out of her chest. The odor of his breath turned her stomach.

"You do not listen very well," he said, pulling the hammer back until it clicked.

She closed her eyes, certain this was the end.

Then the moment passed and he went on: "You think you can hide behind your boyfriend and his badge. You think your Embassy friends can protect you. You think your father, the Senator, can protect you. You are wrong. This is Africa. There is no place I can't reach you. If you continue to meddle in matters that don't concern you, someone will die."

He drove the butt of the revolver hard into her temple, and stars exploded in her vision even as darkness swept over her. Something thumped, then a hand pushed her, and she felt like she was falling. She saw another meteoric shower of stars.

Then everything went black.

The first thing she heard was an echo. The sound repeated and she realized it was her name. She jolted in fear, then recognized the voice—it was Joseph. She groaned. Her head felt as if a spike had been driven into it. Her senses slowly returned. She was lying on her side in the dirt. Something colorful was fluttering above her—a bolt of *chitenge*. She saw Joseph's face hovering over her. He was saying something. The words echoed in her brain. At once she understood.

"What happened? Who did this to you?"

She groaned again and sat up. The splitting pain in her head intensified. She opened her eyes wider and saw that the alley was empty, except for Joseph's truck. She massaged her face and looked at him. His dark eyes were fraught with anxiety.

"Dunstan Sisilu," she said at last.

"*What?*" Joseph hissed. "I watched for a tail."

"He was driving a gray Prado."

"Can you stand?" he said with sudden urgency. "We need to get out of here."

She gave him her arm and lurched to her feet. "He knows everything," she said, leaning on him until she got to the truck. "You, the Prentices, my father. He put a gun to my head and told me if I didn't leave this alone, someone would end up dead."

He helped her into the vehicle and then said, "Just a minute. I need to check something."

She sat heavily in the passenger seat and closed her eyes. He was gone a few seconds, then he climbed in and placed something on her lap. She looked down and saw a compact piece of black plastic about the size of a mobile phone.

"What is it?" she asked, not understanding.

"A GPS tracking unit. It was under the bumper." Joseph started the engine and pulled out into the lane. "You remember when we were in Livingstone? Sisilu seemed to know everywhere we were. I figured I must not have been paying attention. I was paying attention today. "I should have thought of this sooner."

"You're saying he put one of these things on our rental car?"

"It would have been easy to do."

She felt a sliver of dread. "Do you think he put one on my Land Rover?"

"I'm certain of it. It explains why you couldn't find the housekeeper at Shoprite."

"What should we do?" she asked, fingering the device.

"I think we leave the units alone. Let him think we don't know. Unless we want to disguise our movements. Then we leave them at home."

She had a terrifying thought. "He knows everything. All our witnesses . . ."

He glanced at her, his expression grave. "From now on, we need to be very careful."

"It must have been a good job to take her away from nursing school."

When Cynthia didn't reply, Zoe thought the call had disconnected. "Are you still there?"

"How long is this going to take?" Cynthia said, sounding wary again.

"Not much longer. Did the man have a relationship with Charity?"

Cynthia sighed. "How would I know? I was only a child at the time."

"Your grandmother thought she was pregnant—"

Cynthia interrupted her. "My grandmother had her own ideas."

"She sent you letters, didn't she?" Zoe asked. "Did she ever mention a relationship?"

Cynthia's reply was curt. "What about the letters?"

At this point Zoe laid all her cards on the table. "Look, I know this is awkward. I know your family has suffered. But I've found no one who knows about Charity's life in Lusaka before 2004. If she sent you letters, they might help us put the man who raped Kuyeya in prison."

Suddenly, Cynthia shut down. "You know nothing about what we have suffered. My husband told me not to talk to you. I should have listened."

The line went dead. Zoe stared at the phone angrily and her headache flared up again. She breathed deeply, trying to quell her frustration. Then she placed the third call.

"Clay Whitaker, please," she said to the World Bank receptionist. "It's Zoe Fleming."

A few seconds later, Whitaker picked up. "Zoe. This is a nice surprise."

"Thanks, Clay. Listen, I have a favor to ask. I need to know what Frederick Nyambo and his company were up to in 1996."

"Is this for a case? Because I can't testify in court."

"It's for a case. But I'll let you off the hook as soon as you answer my question."

Whitaker laughed. "Are you always this friendly?" When Zoe didn't reply, he said, "Okay, 1996. That was the year Nyambo Energy won the contract for Zimbabwe's first private power project. It was a step in the direction of privatization, though it didn't pan out as Frederick hoped. We talked about that before."

"How did the private power project come about? Did Nyambo go to Zimbabwe?"

"I imagine he did. Why?"

Zoe weighed her options and decided to trust him. "I need to know if he made a trip to Livingstone or Victoria Falls in March or April of that year."

"I doubt the project would have taken him there. The Zimbabwean government does most of its dealings in Harare. But Batoka Gorge was on everyone's mind at the time. It's possible he went to Vic Falls for that reason. When do you need this?"

"Soon."

"Let me make a couple of calls. I'll get back to you quickly."

"Thanks," Zoe said and hung up.

She wandered back to her desk and frittered away the next hour on menial tasks. When her iPhone vibrated, she walked out to the driveway again.

"Your hunch was right," Whitaker told her. "I called a friend at the southern African Power Pool. He told me there was a meeting of dignitaries in Victoria Falls in April of 1996. My friend wasn't there, but he seemed pretty certain that Frederick Nyambo was."

"Would he have stopped in Livingstone?"

"I don't know. Any interest in telling me what this is about? You've gotten me curious."

"Not really. But thanks for the favor."

"Maybe now you'll be nice to me," he quipped.

She ended the call and took a long, slow breath, listening to the jacaranda leaves fluttering in the wind. *Sometimes I feel like I know you, Charity Mizinga. Like we're sisters, like Kuyeya is family. But I still don't understand. How did you meet him? Why did you drop out of school? What was it that Frederick promised you? And what happened when you got to Lusaka? What drove you onto the street and into the beds of strangers?*

She saw dark clouds building on the horizon. The storms would come early today. She entered the office again and found Joseph filling a water glass at the kitchen sink.

"I'm making you a special dinner tonight," she said. "Tom and Carol are away."

"Are you sure you're up to it?" he asked.

She nodded. "The best way to forget pain is to drown it with celebration."

"What are we celebrating?"

"Christmas. It came early this year."

★ ★ ★

Late that afternoon, a powerful thunderstorm swept through Lusaka, pelting the city with hail-stones and flooding the streets with brackish water. Zoe shut down her workstation and went to the window to watch the storm. Lightning speared the sky and thunder shook the ground. The wind whipped violently through the trees and rain drummed on the roof, drowning out all conversation. Soon Zoe's colleagues abandoned their duties to watch the spectacle.

In time the storm began to relent and the great clouds trundled off over the plain to the south. Lightning continued to flash, but the roll of thunder was muted by distance. When the staff dispersed to wrap up business for the day, Zoe collected her backpack and looked at Joseph.

"Do I need to change?" he asked.

"Not unless you want to," she said. "You're welcome to come over now."

He smiled. "In that case . . ."

They drove to the Prentice bungalow in separate vehicles. Zoe watched her mirrors but saw no sign of Dunstan Sisilu. They entered the gate and parked together on the drive. The grounds of the bungalow were sodden after the storm and carpeted with flower blossoms.

Zoe inhaled the moist air and grinned when the sun broke free of the clouds. "It seems the gods have given us a royal greeting."

Joseph looked up, shielding his eyes. "'Earth perfumed in dewdrop fragrance wakes.'"

"Achebe," Zoe said, taking his hand and drawing him toward the door. "I'm impressed."

"Occasionally, we Africans read our own poets."

When they entered the foyer, he asked, "So what's for dinner?"

"I have some steaks from the commissary," she said, heading toward the kitchen. "I also have some of the best wine in Zambia. Hungry?"

He smiled. "Ravenous. I'll turn on the grill."

When the steaks were done, she served them on two of Carol's fine china plates alongside mounds of mashed potatoes and green beans fresh from the garden. She handed the plates to Joseph and followed him to the patio, carrying a tray with bread and butter and two glasses of red wine. They took places across from one another, and Zoe lit candles.

For a while they ate in silence, savoring the food and the serenity of the gardens. The sky fluoresced around the setting sun and then began to darken. A gusty breeze left behind by the storm made the candle flames dance.

"I talked to Cynthia," she said. "She wasn't very helpful."

Joseph's eyes widened. "You didn't tell me?"

"I'm telling you now. She's hiding something. I'm certain it relates to Charity's move to Lusaka. I don't really blame her. I just wish she would rise above her fear." She paused. "I also talked to Clay Whitaker at the World Bank. He told me that Frederick Nyambo was in Victoria Falls in April of 1996. The timing is intriguing, to say the least. That's the same month Charity left nursing school, the same month a wealthy businessman from Lusaka offered her a job."

Joseph frowned. "Are you suggesting Frederick might be the businessman?"

She smiled. "The thought had crossed my mind."

He looked skeptical. "It's a fascinating theory, but it's a leap."

"True, but remember what Amos told us. He said that whatever happened between Charity and the Nyambos happened not long after her arrival in Lusaka. Look, it's perfectly possible that they met here and that all of this is just coincidence. But what if the dots are connected? You have to admit it fills in a lot of gaps."

He regarded her in the flickering candlelight.

"What?" she asked. "You don't agree?"

"I wasn't thinking about that," he said.

She fingered her napkin, suddenly self-conscious. "What were you thinking?"

He met her eyes. "I was thinking how beautiful you are."

Zoe sat back in her chair, surprised by how much his words moved her. Suddenly, she lost all interest in conversation. She wanted him more than she had ever wanted anything in her life. She sipped her wine impatiently and watched him clean his plate. She had the leftover half of a chocolate cake Carol had baked in the refrigerator, but she decided not to mention it.

"I have a surprise for you," she said, standing up.

"What is it?"

"You'll see," she said.

She led him through the darkened house to her bedroom, her skin tingling with anticipation. She threw aside the mosquito net and took his hand, drawing him onto the bed. He lay beside her and their lips met. She pushed him onto his back and straddled him, beginning to unbutton the sweater she had put on before dinner. Suddenly, she felt his hand on her arm.

"Wait," he whispered, his eyes as dark as slate. "There's something you should know." He tried to sit up. "Please, I have to tell you."

She moved off him slowly, her desire merging with apprehension and anger. "*Damn it!* You can't keep doing this to me."

"I'm sorry," he said, crossing his legs on the bed. He looked at her in the shadows and spoke a truth she never could have imagined. "I'm HIV-positive."

In the silence that followed, the grandfather clock chimed the hour.

"*Why?*" she said at last. "Why didn't you *tell* me?"

She sprang from the bed and fled into the living room. She looked out the window and saw the Southern Cross lying on its side above the tree line. A memory came to her of her mother standing on the night-shrouded plains of Kenya's Maasailand. "*When the world gets you down*," she had said, "*don't forget to look up*." Zoe closed her eyes. *Not tonight, Mom.*

Joseph broke into her thoughts. "Please, Zoe, listen to me. I didn't know this would happen. I never expected that you would be so fantastic. And then when I saw what was happening, I didn't want it to end. I should have told you earlier, but I didn't know how."

"I didn't ask for this either," she replied, tears gathering in her eyes. She sat down heavily on the couch. "How long ago were you tested?"

"The summer of 2009. My CD4 count was 710. I haven't been back since."

She twisted her mother's ring. "What are you going to do?"

He was silent for a long moment. "What should I do?"

"I think you should get tested again. If they let you, you should start on ARVs."

He went to the window and looked out at the dark sky. "My grandmother once told me that *muzungus* are intelligent but weak-willed. That's why the colonists left Africa—they had no stamina. She made me promise I would never love a white woman. You've broken all the rules, Zoe. As far as I'm concerned, you're the only one I want."

Her tears began to flow again. "I need you to give me time. I need to think."

He nodded. "I'm sorry to ruin your surprise."

She didn't know where the laugh came from. "By God, you *did* ruin it. I've been looking forward to this."

"That makes two of us."

Chapter 22

For Zoe, the last days of 2011 passed excruciatingly slowly. Joseph's revelation had the effect of an emotional tourniquet, at once throttling the natural flow of her feelings and accentuating her sensitivity to every disturbance. To distract herself, she learned everything she could about HIV—the stages of disease progression, the treatment guidelines from the World Health Organization, the effectiveness and side effects of antiretroviral therapy, the risks associated with sex between

HIV-discordant couples, the methods of protection and their failure rates.

She read a summary of findings from the study conducted by Drs. Kruger and Luyt in Johannesburg. Where HIV-positive individuals began ARV treatment early—at a CD4 count between 350 and 550, not the original WHO trigger of 200—the rate of new infections decreased by 96%. Zoe took solace from the data, but it didn't answer the deeper question: did she want a relationship in which every act of intimacy entailed risk, however slight?

CILA closed for the holidays on December 23 and didn't reopen until January 2. Zoe spent Christmas weekend with the Prentices. Initially, she was thankful for the diversion, but by Monday she felt suffocated and restless. Desperate for a change of scenery, she bought a plane ticket to Namibia, rented a car at the Windhoek airport, and drove west across the Namib Desert to the sea. Her destination was a beach hotel in Henties Bay.

In all her travels, she had never made it to the Skeleton Coast. Wild, wind-whipped, and littered with shipwrecks, the stretch of ocean along the northern coast of Namibia was named "The Land God Made in Anger" by the Bushmen of the interior. At the height of the summer, its drama was unparalleled. For four days, Zoe submerged her pain in the thunder of driving surf, combing the beach for rocks and shells as she had on the Vineyard when she was a girl, savoring glasses of wine on the patio as the setting sun turned the sky into a rose garden, and leaving behind all reminders of time. She didn't just want to be off the grid; she wanted to disappear.

When she boarded a plane again on New Year's Eve, she felt refreshed but no less perplexed than when she left Lusaka. Love bound her to Joseph like a cord. It might stretch but it would not break, unless, of course, she severed it. And that was a step she could not take without denying everything she believed about the world.

The flight from Windhoek landed in Lusaka at noon. Zoe checked her phone, thinking Joseph might have sent her a message, but her inbox was empty. She had asked for patience, and he seemed willing to grant it. She threw her bags into her Land Rover and drove to Sunningdale.

The guard let her onto the Prentice grounds, and Carol greeted her in the foyer. "Was Namibia as dreamy as I remember it?" she asked, giving Zoe a hug.

"Like no place else," Zoe replied. "Has Joseph called?"

Carol looked at her closely. "He hasn't. Did something happen between you?"

Zoe shrugged. "It's a long story."

"Well, I'm all ears if you want to talk about it. We're having a little soiree tonight with some friends from the Embassy in case you're looking for a distraction."

Zoe forced herself to smile. "It wouldn't be New Year's Eve without a party."

"Oh, I almost forgot. A parcel arrived from the States. It came from a law firm."

Zoe's smile turned genuine. "It's from my brother. My birthday is the second."

"You didn't tell me! What year is this?"

"Twenty-nine."

"You're so *young*! What I wouldn't give to be twenty-nine again." Carol laughed. "The box is on your bed. Oh, and don't worry. I'll make sure you have a proper cake."

Zoe dropped her bags in her room and took the parcel onto the terrace. The box was squat and heavy, about ten inches by twelve. She opened it carefully and found the contents encased in bubble wrap. Atop the padding was a card with a photo of a pig cavorting in the mud. She giggled at the caption: "Some people find pleasure in the strangest places."

Inside, Trevor had written:

Happy 29th, sis. I love you lots. I keep telling myself I'm going to get on a plane and come visit you, but the damn job never relents. I suppose I have Dad to blame for that. One of these days I'm going to go MIA and show up on your doorstep. Enjoy the goodies!

Beneath the bubble wrap were four bags of gourmet candies, a pint of Vermont maple syrup, a set of iPhone earbuds, a bound photo book of Trevor and his girlfriend, Jenna, on the Vineyard, and a pewter sea turtle with an engraving on its belly: "*The race is not to the swift or the strong but to the persistent.*" It was one of Catherine's aphorisms, adapted from a verse in Ecclesiastes.

Zoe placed the turtle carefully in the box and paged through the photo book. Across the bottom of the last picture—an image of Jenna on the beach at sunset, tossing a smile over her shoulder—her brother had written: "*Think she's the one? I'm starting to believe it.*"

Tears came to Zoe's eyes. She had traveled to the edge of the world, but she could no more escape her history than she could alter her genetics. And there was the rub. She had never intended to leave it all behind. Not forever, at least. She wanted what her mother had—one foot in Africa and one foot in the West. *How does Joseph fit into that picture?* she wondered. *How am I supposed to make sense of this?*

On her birthday, Zoe woke at sunrise, took a hot shower, and opened her MacBook. She started Skype and checked her watch. Trevor had promised to call her at 6:15 a.m.—just after midnight D.C. time. It was a tradition in their relationship. No matter where they were, no birthday could pass without a conversation.

Right on time, Zoe heard the electronic trill of an incoming call. "Hey, Trev," she said, watching the video screen and smiling when his face appeared.

"Happy birthday, sis," Trevor replied, his voice slightly distorted by interference. "Sorry to wake you with the birds."

She laughed. "Sorry to keep you up so late."

"Ha! I just got off work. Midnight is the new six o'clock."

"How many cups of coffee have you had today?"

"Enough to make me consider exchanging my salary for Starbucks stock." He sighed. "It's crazy. The primaries haven't even started yet."

"That's what you get for sleeping with ABT." It was a longstanding point of contention between them that Trevor's firm represented the legal interests of A Brighter Tomorrow, the SuperPAC that supported Jack Fleming's campaign.

"Hey, she's fancy and she's got loads of money. Seriously, how are you? It's been ages since I got anything but emails from you."

"I could say the same for you."

He grunted. "Busyness is a narcotic. It's hard to break the habit."

"I'm okay," she said, dropping the banter. "Thanks for the package. I love the turtle."

"So what do you think about my question?" he asked with a smile.

"You mean about Jenna?"

He nodded. "Think she's the one?"

"You look happy, and she's a great girl. What more can I say?"

"I bought a ring," he confessed, displaying a hint of nervousness.

"That's wonderful!" She tried to sound chipper, but the thought of Joseph injected a false note. "When are you going to propose?"

"We're going to St. Kitts next month. I'm going to do it there." He frowned, studying her image on his screen. "Something's the matter. I can hear it in your voice."

She hesitated. "It's complicated."

"It's a guy, isn't it? Is he African?"

He knows me so well we could be twins. "I really don't want to talk about it," she replied.

He shrugged. "Fair enough."

"The Iowa caucuses are tomorrow," she said, taking the conversation in a different direction.

"From what I hear, Dad's numbers are sliding in the heartland."

Trevor grimaced. "It's primary season. They'll support him after the nomination."

"But will they be *motivated*? It's hard to unseat a sitting president."

"The economy will drive the general election. Dad's a businessman. He knows how to get the country back on track."

"Sounds like you've been drinking the Kool-Aid."

Trevor laughed. "I believe in what he's doing."

"How is it that we're so alike and yet so different?"

For a moment he looked nonplussed. Then he changed gears. "I'm sorry you won't be with us in New Hampshire. I was hoping to see you."

She shook her head. "I can't, Trev. I can't support his position on austerity."

"A lot of that is posturing. You know his convictions."

"Do I? I knew Mom's. I know Sylvia's. But Dad is a chameleon."

"I thought you hated single-issue voters."

"This isn't about voting. It's about endorsement."

"It's not, though. It's about *family*."

His words knocked the wind out of her and transported her at the same time. Suddenly, she was eight years old again, worshiping the ground her father walked on. She had thought him incorruptible. But chance and choice had proven her wrong.

"I'm sorry," she said in time. "I don't expect you to understand."

"I don't need to. You're my sister." At once he brightened. "Hey, it's your birthday. What are you going to do today?"

She forced herself to smile. "I'm going to sit out by the pool and do absolutely nothing."

He applauded. "Good for you. Wish I could join you."

"Come visit," she said, feeling a resurgence of her fondness for him.

He winked at her. "You never know. I might just do that."

The following day, Zoe returned to work, her conscience tangled in knots. At the all-staff meeting, she found herself glancing surreptitiously at Joseph, wondering what he was thinking. She spent that day and the next three weeks in turmoil. Workdays were tolerable because of their activity. Cases required prosecution, evidence had to be gathered, witnesses needed to be interviewed, and briefs required polishing. Evenings and weekends, however, were insufferable. To escape thoughts of the past and the future, she immersed herself in the present.

She increased the frequency of her visits to St. Francis and spent time with Kuyeya. The girl was particularly fond of gardening. She loved to watch Sister Irina and Zoe harvest vegetables and herbs from the earth. But observing wasn't enough— she liked to touch everything. As she rummaged through the pickings, Zoe encouraged her to talk.

"What's that?" Zoe asked one Sunday, pointing at the object in Kuyeya's hands.

"Potato," Kuyeya said. "Mommy says potato is good with *nshima*."

Zoe held up a large leaf. "What's this?"

"Pumpkin," said the girl, dropping the potato. "I like pumpkin with groundnuts."

She put the leaf beneath her nose to smell it. Then she remembered the potato. She picked it up again and put it back in the basket. Her scrupulousness endeared her to Zoe. Regardless of what was happening around her, Kuyeya insisted that her world make sense.

When Zoe had downtime at home, she devoured everything she could find on the Internet about her father's presidential campaign. Her allegiances were capricious. Some moments, she pilloried him for his policies; other moments, she found herself defending him against personal attacks. As the Iowa caucus voted and the debates and stump speeches accelerated on the road to New Hampshire, his rhetoric became increasingly strident. On everything from immigration to health care to education and defense, he preached a message calibrated to appeal to the fringe. On foreign assistance, he called for substantial retrenchment from all non-defense-related largesse. She remembered his excuse over dinner: "*That's just politics.*" And Trevor's: "*A lot of that is posturing.*" But Zoe wasn't sure. In turning his ambitions from finance to politics, Jack had submitted his convictions to focus groups and advisors. He had lost his moral clarity.

After watching the New Hampshire debate, Zoe channeled her agitation into action and began to write. Initially, the essay was a vague pastiche of impressions, related but not fused. As she poured her thoughts onto the page, however, an article began to take shape. It was her mother's story and it was her story, a story of charity and justice, of ideals in action. It was the story of America, the America Catherine had taught her to believe in—the country that had rebuilt Europe after the Second World War, founded the United Nations and the Peace Corps, funded the World Bank and PEPFAR, and transformed the world with not-so-random acts of kindness. It was also her father's story—the middle-class kid whose ticket into the world of influence was a full scholarship to Harvard. She depicted him kindly, describing him as an ardent supporter of her mother's work. Writing about him offered Zoe an unexpected gift. It allowed her to resurrect the Jack Fleming she had loved as a child—the man, not the partisan. At four thousand words, the piece was at once a deeply personal memoir and a passionate argument against parsimony—a call for governments and citizens to rise above debt crises and economic woes and provide for the poor and oppressed. *Mom*, she thought, *this one's for you.*

She sent the article to Dr. Samantha Wu, her favorite law professor and the closest thing to a mentor in her life. An expert on international human rights, Dr. Wu had taken Zoe under her wing, advising her on the *Yale Law Journal*, steering her toward a clerkship with Judge van der Merwe, and encouraging her to write. Zoe's article on justice in post-apartheid South Africa had been her idea, and she had brokered the connection at *Harpers* to get it published. After that success, she had made Zoe a standing offer: "*If you write it and it's good, I'll find a home for it.*"

Dr. Wu responded promptly:

Zoe, I have to admit I was a bit skeptical about this. But you won me over. It's fresh, it's timely, it's meaningful and controversial. Given your father's platform and your publishing history, I shouldn't have any trouble placing it. I'd love to see it in Time, *but I think it's a stretch. I'm going to give it to Naomi Potter at the* New Yorker *and Brent Lyle at the* Atlantic. *I know both of them well. I'll get back to you soon!*

★ ★ ★

In the latter part of January, something shifted in Zoe's heart. She knew she could no longer keep Joseph at arm's length. He had been impossibly tolerant, treating her with kindness when work required collaboration but making no move to close the intimacy gap. It was she who had grown impatient. The situation required resolution. He deserved the dignity of a choice.

The next morning at work, Zoe received a call from St. Francis.

"Kuyeya had an accident," said Sister Anica. "She seems to be all right, except for some pain in her neck. I'm taking her to see Dr. Chulu. Sister Irina asked me to call you."

"What happened?" Zoe asked.

"No one knows. She just fell down."

"You're coming to UTH?"

"Yes. The doctor agreed to see her at fourteen hundred."

"I'll meet you there."

She turned around and saw Joseph watching her. "Is it Kuyeya?"

When she relayed the news, he looked pensive, like he wanted to say something. She felt the pressure building in her chest. At last, her mouth formed the words her heart had already chosen. "Why don't you come along?"

He looked uncertain. "You want me to?"

She saw the query for what it was—a plea for acceptance. "I've missed you," she replied, answering his question and her own.

They met Sister Anica and Kuyeya on the terrace outside the pediatric center at UTH. Kuyeya was holding her monkey by the arm and shifting her weight between her feet. Her eyes lit up when she saw Zoe, and her grimace quickly turned into a grin.

"Hi, Kuyeya," Zoe said.

The girl made the balloon sound. "Hi, Zoe. Do you have your music?"

Zoe smiled. "I do. What kind would you like?"

"Can we play Johnny?" She hummed for a moment, and Zoe tried to make out the tune. Suddenly, Kuyeya said, "'The one on the right was on the left.'"

Zoe laughed. It was the name of the song and also the first line of the chorus. She recited the next line: "'And the one in the middle is on the right.'"

Dr. Chulu emerged from the lobby and greeted them. "One of the intake rooms is available. Shall we?"

At the sound of the doctor's voice, Kuyeya stopped humming and began to moan softly. Sister Anica took her by the hand and led her into the waiting area, and Zoe followed. Nurse Mbelo stood beside an open door, holding a clipboard.

Dr. Chulu pointed at a chair beside the bed. "I need her to sit while I look at her neck."

"I have your iPod," Sister Anica replied, handing Zoe a canvas bag.

As soon as Kuyeya sat in the chair, Zoe placed the earphones over her ears.

"Can we play Johnny?" the girl said again.

"Of course," Zoe said, selecting "Ballad of a Teenage Queen".

When Kuyeya began to rock to the rhythm, Zoe joined Joseph by the door and watched Dr. Chulu perform the examination. He placed one hand on the girl's forehead and used the other to probe the

Chapter 21

The next morning, Joseph gave the response team a report on the interrogation of Dr. Amos and its violent aftermath, including the discovery of the GPS tracking unit on his truck and a second unit on Zoe's Land Rover. Zoe sat beside him at the table, nursing a headache that no amount of Tylenol could alleviate. Mariam had insisted she take the day off, but she had no interest in sympathy. In spite of the discomfort, she was determined to enjoy the moment. The *nganga*'s story had not only lent credence to her theory about Bella's past, it had given shape to a story that once had seemed incomprehensible.

"Unless I'm missing something," Mariam said, "we have a case again. But we need to take precautions. The Nyambos are going to do everything they can to hurt us."

Sarge nodded. "You should talk to the security company about posting a night guard."

"I'll do that today," Mariam replied, making a note to herself. "And the rest of us should check our vehicles. If we're being watched, we need to know about it."

"This is all well and good," Niza said, "but I don't think the evidence is there yet. Amos didn't identify the prostitute. Nor did he know about Kuyeya. We have to make the link."

Zoe shook her head painfully. "Doris can testify about Bella and Darious."

Niza spoke in a measured tone. "That's helpful. But Luchembe will trot out all of the other *mahules* Darious knew. We have to answer the question, 'Why Bella?'"

"She had a history with the Nyambos," Zoe retorted. "And she had a disabled daughter."

"Look," Niza said, "I think Bella *is* the prostitute. But I don't think we can prove it yet."

As much as Zoe hated to admit it, Niza had a point. They needed to explain the past.

As soon as the meeting ended, Zoe placed three calls from the driveway. The first was to Godfrey. When he didn't answer, she left him an imploring message, highlighting the critical stage of the investigation and Kuyeya's desperate need for family assistance. Her second call was to Mwela Chansa, Cynthia's husband. To her astonishment, he answered on the third ring.

"*Moni?*" he said in Nyanja.

Zoe was so shocked to hear his voice that her mind went blank. "*Sindimalankhula chinyanja,*" she said after a pause. "Do you speak English?"

"Who is this?" he asked hesitantly.

"My name is Zoe Fleming. I'm trying to reach Cynthia about her cousin, Charity."

She heard static on the line and then a woman said, "Hello?"

Zoe's heart clutched in her chest. "Are you Cynthia?"

"Yes," she responded, sounding wary.

Zoe introduced herself. "I met with Godfrey in Livingstone. We talked about your cousin, Charity, and her daughter, Kuyeya."

Cynthia took an audible breath. "He told me. Why are you calling?"

"He thought you might remember the name of the man who took Charity to Lusaka."

"Why do you want to know?"

"Did Godfrey tell you what happened to Kuyeya?"

"It's a terrible story," Cynthia said quietly.

Zoe planted the hook. "Charity had a history with the man who raped Kuyeya. I'm trying to find out what that history was. I need to know why she came to Lusaka."

After a while, Cynthia said, "I don't know his name. We met him only once."

Zoe didn't allow her dejection to show. "Can you tell me about that meeting?"

"He bought us lunch in Livingstone. He told us he'd offered Charity a job."

"What kind of job?"

"I didn't pay attention."

region between her hairline and collar. He asked Sister Anica a series of questions about the fall and Kuyeya's discomfort, and then he observed her standing still and walking.

Eventually, he shook his head. "Her muscles are underdeveloped, but that's common in children with Down syndrome. She shows no sign of imbalance, nor does she seem to be in obvious pain. The fall gave her a jolt, but I think she's all right."

Zoe wondered about an X-ray, but she knew the answer she would get. In state hospitals, technology was a luxury reserved for acute cases.

Afterward, Dr. Chulu walked with them to the parking lot. Zoe held Kuyeya's hand until Sister Anica pulled the St. Francis van up to the curb.

"It's time for you to go home," Zoe said, removing the headphones and looking into the girl's eyes. "I'll come visit you soon."

"Home is where the bee-eater lives," Kuyeya said, swinging her monkey.

The Zambezi, Zoe thought. *Charity left you with her happy memories.* "Would you like to see a bee-eater someday?" she asked.

"Yes. And a hippo."

After helping Kuyeya into the van, Zoe tucked the iPod into her seat and slid the door closed. She stepped back and waved as Sister Anica drove the van toward the street.

"Are you sure she's okay?" she asked Dr. Chulu.

"Kids get bumps and bruises," he replied. "You don't need to worry. What's the status of her case? Have you found any new evidence?"

Joseph glanced at Zoe and said, "We found a new witness. It's complicated."

Dr. Chulu shook his head. "I still can't believe we lost the DNA. My staff . . . I can't believe one of them . . ." He clenched his fists. "Put me on the stand at trial and I'll make Flexon Mubita so angry at Darious that he won't be able to sleep at night."

Zoe pictured Mubita with Patricia Nyambo and thought: *I hope you're right.*

"I should be going," the doctor said. "Call me if she starts to have pain again."

Zoe walked with Joseph to the Land Rover. In the privacy of the cab, she asked him the question she had been suppressing for a month. "Did you get tested again?"

He nodded. "My CD4 count was 330. I started on ARVs."

She exhaled, both anxious and relieved. "How are you doing?"

"I had some vomiting at first. I'm hungrier than I used to be. Otherwise, I'm okay." He stared out the window. "The good news is the drugs seem to be working. I went back two days ago and my CD4 count was 625. My viral load was almost undetectable."

God, the jargon is dehumanizing, she thought, taking a left onto Independence and merging into the thick of afternoon traffic. *Once a person, now a lab rat.*

A wave of doubt washed over her. *This is his life now—drugs twice a day, side effects and opportunistic infections. Being with him won't be easy. The virus will overshadow everything.* Almost immediately, she felt a backlash of guilt. *How can you think like that? You adore him; you want to be with him. The ARVs will let him live a reasonably normal life. If you let him go, you'll never find another like him.*

Suddenly, she remembered something from the past, something her mother had told her at an Ethiopian orphanage surrounded by malnourished children wearing irrepressible grins: "*Life is a broken thing. It's what we do with the pieces that defines us.*"

"Look, Zoe," Joseph said, "I won't blame you if you're having second thoughts."

"I don't regret loving you," she said, struggling to hold back her tears.

He studied her intently. "Does that mean . . . ?"

She nodded. "I don't know how to do this, but I'm willing to try."

PART FOUR

An angel rides in the whirlwind.

—*John Page*

Darious

*S*he was there, he knew she was, closeted away in the back of the flat. Doris had kept her after Bella's death. He had confirmed it with the girls at Alpha. But he hadn't seen her on the street. Doris came and went, as did her girlfriends and her daughters and the men who paid her for sex. But Kuyeya remained out of sight. The thought of her made Darious seethe with hatred. Memory, her name meant. The keeper of all wrongs.

He made regular passes by Doris's flat, scouting the area and hoping Kuyeya would appear. Most of the time he stayed in his SUV, staking out the building from a spot

437

across the road. Occasionally, however, he struck up conversations with the street vendors or shared a smoke with men from Doris's complex. He asked about their families, and about the children who lived in the building. He waited for one of them to mention Kuyeya, but none of them did. It was as if she were a ghost. To them she didn't exist.

As the weeks passed, he grew irritable. There were thousands of girls in Lusaka, but only one was the daughter of Charity Mizinga. That worthless nganga, Amos, didn't have the brains to appreciate the medicinal power of symmetry. Fire needed to be fought with fire, a hex with another hex. There was danger in that, of course. If the original curse was supported by stronger mukwala, the whole plan could backfire. But Darious had no choice. The alternative was a shame he could not bear—his father's rejection.

One day near the end of July, he parked in his customary spot and watched Doris's flat. Traffic was heavy at the end of the workday, which reassured him. Chilimbulu Road was a commercial thoroughfare. But the neighborhood was working class, and a Mercedes was an uncommon sight. Eventually, people would start to talk. And if they talked, they were more likely to remember. He didn't want to give the police an unnecessary lead.

He focused on Doris's flat. The smokers were in their

usual place. An old woman on the third floor was hanging clothes out to dry. Doris herself was probably still asleep, but her daughters were no doubt awake. The older one might be out with her boyfriend. She was a pretty girl. Before long, she would end up at Alpha, making more money than her mother.

After a while, Darious grew tired of sitting still. He left the SUV and approached a girl selling fritas. His skin itched as he walked. He was tired of the sickness, tired of being exhausted, tired of the runs and the weight loss and the cough. He had to find a way to get Kuyeya out of the flat. Everything after that would be simple.

He took a bag of fritas from the vendor and chatted with her about her family. He invented a story about three sisters and two brothers and their many children. After a few minutes, he mentioned his sister's "difficult" child. He described the girl—the round face and flat nose, the eyes set wide apart, the limited speech.

The vendor began to nod. "My cousin has a child like that. It is very hard."

"My sister doesn't know what to do with her," Darious replied. "She keeps her in the back room, out of sight. I tell her to take her outside, but she's afraid of what people will think."

"*My cousin is the same. People say the child is bewitched, but I don't think so. She is just like other children. She likes to play and laugh and sing.*" Suddenly, the vendor pointed at Doris's building. "*There is a girl like that who lives there. She sometimes comes to play at my building. You should talk to the woman who takes care of her. Her name is Doris.*"

"*She comes outside sometimes?*" Darious asked, hiding his satisfaction.

"*After dinner. Doris sends her with her younger daughter, Gift.*"

Darious returned to the Mercedes and touched the amulet on his chest. In winter, dinner ended after sunset. It was the perfect opportunity.

He cast a parting glance at Doris's building and his heart skipped a beat. A woman was staring at him across the distance. Her dress was more conservative than the outfits she wore to the bars, but he recognized her immediately. It was Doris. He clutched the steering wheel and watched her scamper into her flat. She was afraid of him for good reason, given the lesson he had taught her. But there could be no doubt.

She had seen him.

Chapter 23

Lusaka, Zambia
January, 2012

As soon as Zoe made the decision to embrace her feelings for Joseph, he took her out for a celebratory dinner at the Intercontinental, ignoring her protest that it was too expensive. He insisted that she dress for the occasion, and he did the same, showing up at the Prentices' in a gray suit and blue tie that complemented his dark skin and eyes. When she met him on the porch, he looked her up and down and grinned at her red shift dress and heels.

"You're gorgeous," he said. "Why don't we skip dinner?"

"You made me wear this," she rejoined. "Now you're going to have to wait."

At the restaurant, they sat at a table by the grand savannah window and reconnected over oysters, tenderloin, and a bottle of French champagne. They talked about everything and nothing, bridging the gap of lost time with banter and laughter and stories. Beneath the good cheer of reunion, however, the current of desire ran strong. Studying him in the candlelight, Zoe realized again that she loved him. He was from a different world, but he was more attractive for it. He was steady but not boring, brave in the face of fear, and unafraid to talk about his feelings. She couldn't predict the future, but she trusted him with her life. It was more than enough for now.

After the meal, he drove her home in a silence alive with satisfaction and expectation. She took his hand without a word and looked out the window at the darkened streets. The summer stars twinkled high above and the quarter moon hung like a lantern in the sky. When they parked in the driveway, she looked deep into his eyes and said, "Come."

He followed her into the house and down the lamp-lit hallway to her quarters. Kicking off her heels, she took him to her bed and kissed his lips. He pushed her back and cradled her face in his hands, saying with his eyes what she already knew in her heart. The pleasure that followed belied all of her deepest fears. She didn't think about the virus, she thought only of Joseph, and afterward, she felt a deep measure of contentment.

She laid her head against his chest and listened to the beating of his heart.

"When I first met you," he said after a while, "I thought you were arrogant. Now I realize that it's passion that drives you, not pride."

She laughed softly. "When I first met you, I thought you didn't know how to smile."

He stroked her hair and murmured, "Understanding takes time."

"Stay with me," she said, lifting her head and facing him.

"Of course."

"I don't mean just tonight."

The next day, the universe seemed to smile on Zoe. In the morning, she received an email from Samantha Wu.

Zoe, it gives me great pleasure to inform you that Naomi Potter at the New Yorker *loved your article. She told me that your mother once wrote a piece for them. They're going to run it in April, and Naomi is going to edit it, which in my experience means a lot of red ink. She'll push you harder than I ever did, but she'll bring out the shine. She thinks it's going to be big. Congratulations! In case you're wondering,* Time *passed on the article but opened the door for an interview. Let me know if you're ever interested.*

Zoe fired back an exclamatory email, then found Joseph in the kitchen and told him the news. Her enthusiasm proved infectious. Before long, they were wearing matching grins.

That afternoon, Zoe was sitting at her desk when a call came through. She didn't recognize the number and allowed it to go to voicemail. A minute later, her iPhone vibrated. Curious, she picked up the phone and played the voicemail.

"Ms. Fleming, this is Cynthia Chansa. I apologize for being rude when we spoke. Charity's death has been very hard for me to accept. I want to help Kuyeya. I don't know if what I remember will matter, but I've put it all in writing. I'd like to send it to you, along with Charity's letters. Text me your address, and I'll put them in the post."

Zoe sent the text with warm words of gratitude and then tried—but failed—to concentrate on the police medical report she was reading.

That evening, Joseph joined her for dinner at the Prentices', and Tom and Carol went out of their way to give them privacy. Over chicken and couscous, Zoe gave Joseph a crash course on her father's campaign. After winning the New Hampshire primary, he had lost South Carolina to the Governor of Kansas, igniting a debate among the pundits about his chances in the general election. Some claimed that he was too moderate, others that he wasn't comfortable talking about religion, still others that his wealth put him out of touch with the American people. To make up ground, the Senator and his SuperPAC fired a fusillade of attack ads at the Kansas governor. The polls responded favorably, but doubts persisted about Jack Fleming's electability in November.

"All of this must be so strange for you," Joseph said when she finished her summary. "Seeing your father's every move analyzed and criticized, his whole life under scrutiny."

She laughed. "Sometimes I think I'm going to wake up and find myself in the headlines. I've gotten a few queries from reporters, but nothing intrusive. Somehow his people have kept our relationship out of the press."

His eyes became pensive. "Can I ask you a question? From a purely objective standpoint, what kind of president would he make?"

She hesitated, but opted for candor. "The Jack Fleming I grew up with would be a star in the Oval Office. He's brilliant and charismatic; he has an even temper; he's a collaborator, not a dictator; he's an idea guy; he cares about people. But the Jack Fleming I've seen on television looks like a different person. He used to hate polemics. Now every time I listen to him he's slinging mud at the President. It's like he's speaking with someone else's voice."

A few days later, Cynthia's parcel arrived at the office. Zoe took it into the conference room and opened it carefully. Out of the manila envelope fell a stack of folded pages. The first was a letter from Cynthia herself.

Dear Zoe,

This is what I remember. I hope it helps you. Godfrey and I came to stay with my grandmother in the village when I was seven. Godfrey was just a baby. Charity stayed in Livingstone with an aunt who lived near her school. After she received her twelfth-grade certificate, she entered nursing school. At that time she stayed with her uncle, Field, and his wife. I do not think it was a good situation, but she was close enough to walk to the hospital.

She visited us in the village many times. She also sent us money every month from an account her mother left when she died. Godfrey and I loved Charity more than anyone but our grandmother. Sometimes she took us into town to eat ice cream and see movies. She was beautiful and all the boys loved her, but she was only interested in her studies. She wanted to be a nurse. She talked about her brothers all the time. Their names were Jacob and Augustus. They died before I was born.

Something happened in Charity's second year of nursing school. We didn't see her as much. Her mind was

somewhere else. During the rainy season, my grandmother had a stroke. Then Godfrey got sick with malaria.
Charity came to the village with a white doctor and they
took Godfrey away with them. I was scared he would die,
but he lived. Not long after that, Charity came to visit us
and said that she was leaving school. She said a man had
offered her a good job in Lusaka. She said she would make
a lot of money.

I was very sad. I was only eleven and didn't understand. It was not until I was older that my grandmother
told me what she believed about Charity's decision. My
grandmother was certain she was in love with a man but
that the man did not love her. She didn't know the man's
name, but she believed he was at the nursing school. She
was also afraid that her uncle, Field, was hurting her.
My grandmother tried to convince Charity to find a new
place, but Charity was afraid of Field. My grandmother
believed that Charity was pregnant. She asked Charity
about these things before she left for Lusaka, but Charity
denied them.

I do not know if my grandmother was right. It is possible that Charity had a love relationship with a man. It is
possible that Field was hurting her. It is also possible that
she was pregnant. In my own thoughts, however, I think

the job was the reason she left. At that time, it was difficult for a woman to find a good job, even with a nursing degree. It is still the same today. The man who offered her a job was someone important. I have tried to remember his name, but it was long ago.

She never told us she had a child. You will see from her letters that she told us nothing about what she was doing in Lusaka. All I know is that she sent us money until Godfrey graduated from secondary school. Without her we would not have had food to eat, and we would not have been able to pay our school fees. She was like a mother to us.

Zoe set the letter on the table, struck by the convergence of her own suspicions and those of Charity's grandmother. She thought back to her visit with Field and Agatha in Livingstone—the packets of *tu jilijili* on the floor, Field's incoherence on the porch, Agatha's agitation, and Joseph's words in the darkened truck. "*Agatha didn't want her. She thinks Charity's family is bewitched.*" Another memory came to her: the way Agatha had fingered her wedding ring. Cynthia's use of the word "hurt" was almost certainly a euphemism for "rape." It made perfect sense. Agatha had tried to get Charity to move out, but Field had intervened to prevent it.

Then there was the matter of Charity's "love relationship with a man." Charity's grandmother, Vivian, had suspected a man at the nursing school. Had she seen Charity's journal, she would have been more specific. Charity was in love with a doctor—Jan Kruger. But what had prompted Vivian to ascertain that she was with child? Who did Vivian think was the father?

Charity's letters did not tell her much. In them, she wrote about the past and encouraged Cynthia and Godfrey to take care of their grandmother. What references she made to Lusaka were devoid of detail. The only useful insight offered by the letters was a glimpse into Charity's psyche. When she left Livingstone in 1996, she still had a capacity for delight. In this respect, the letters contrasted dramatically with the third volume of her journal. The penmanship was the same, but by April of 2004 her joy had died.

Zoe stuffed the letters back in the envelope and walked to Joseph's desk. For all that Cynthia had disclosed, she still couldn't explain the genesis of

Darious Nyambo's hatred. Joseph took one look at her face and set aside the report he was reviewing. He read Cynthia's letter, reserving comment until the end.

"This is interesting," he said, "but it leaves gaps. We still don't know what happened when she got to Lusaka."

"Precisely. We need the housekeeper."

Joseph nodded. "Tomorrow's Saturday."

"I've been thinking about updating my wardrobe."

He laughed. "I like the thought of you in *chitenge*."

Early the next morning, they drove to the City Market in Zoe's Land Rover. Before leaving the Prentice property, Joseph removed the GPS unit from beneath her bumper and put it with its twin in his truck. If Dunstan Sisilu was paying attention to their movements, he would think they were enjoying a Saturday morning at home. Nevertheless, Joseph took an indirect route and made two stops to ensure they were not followed.

They entered the market by the main gate and walked slowly toward Chiwoyu's stall.

"I'll meet you there," Joseph said suddenly, ducking down an aisle.

Zoe shuffled along and watched the crowd, trying to suppress her nervousness. She passed Chiwoyu's aisle and didn't see the housekeeper. She turned down the next aisle and stopped beside a display of bags, looking toward the entrance to the market. She saw a flash of black sunglasses, and her heart jumped into her throat. But the man wearing them was rail-thin and had a mane of silver hair.

She took a breath and walked the length of the aisle. She met Joseph on the other side.

"If he's here, he's invisible," he said.

Zoe nodded. "It looks like the shoe vendor could use some company."

As before, she took a seat on the vacant chair and watched the aisle. This time they didn't have long to wait. At twenty past nine, a slightly hunched figured emerged from the exit. Zoe immediately recognized the housekeeper. She stood quickly and moved in the old woman's direction. The housekeeper saw her when they were twenty feet apart. She lowered her head and tried to get past, but Zoe stepped into her path.

"Please listen to me," Zoe said, knowing her time was limited. "Darious raped Kuyeya because he has AIDS and she was a virgin. His crime was not random. He hated her mother and he feared her. He was certain she'd cursed his family. The mystery is why. What happened between Frederick and Charity fifteen years ago?"

The housekeeper didn't speak, so Zoe went on. "I'm convinced Frederick met her in Livingstone and offered her a job. I know she left nursing school and came to Lusaka. I know something painful happened. But I don't know what it was. Somehow Charity ended up on the street as a prostitute. Somehow a girl who had all the promise in the world died of AIDS."

To Zoe's astonishment, the housekeeper began to cry. "What you say is true," she said. "But I am old and have no one to protect me."

"I can protect you," Zoe said quickly. "I have friends in the diplomatic community. I can get you a new job."

The housekeeper hesitated. "I must think about this."

Zoe pulled a fifty-pin note out of her wallet,

along with a pen. As she had done at Shoprite, she wrote her mobile number on the margin of the bill. "You can call me or send a text. The trial is the first week of April. We need the information soon."

The housekeeper stuffed the money in her bag and headed toward the *chitenge* stall. Zoe watched her walk away. *Would I take the risk?* she asked herself honestly. *Would I defy the Nyambos and trust a stranger to keep me safe?*

Seeing Joseph approach, Zoe said, "She knows the whole story. But she's still afraid."

"I can't say I blame her," he replied.

"Neither do I."

Chapter 24

Lusaka, Zambia
February, 2012

In the middle of February, the legal team began in earnest to prepare for the trial of Darious Nyambo. Zoe collaborated with Sarge and Niza in compiling a witness list and assembling signed statements and affidavits, and she worked with Joseph to confirm the willingness of each witness to testify at trial. Soon, Sarge convened a meeting to discuss the evidence.

They went through the preliminary witnesses chronologically—the teenage girl, Given, who saw the silver SUV in Kabwata, not far from

Doris's house; the adolescent, Wisdom, who saw the SUV heading down the lane at midnight; the boy, Dominic, who saw Darious and Kuyeya outside Agnes's house; Agnes, who heard the sound of an engine and doors closing; Abigail, who found Kuyeya on the street; and Dr. Chulu, who examined her at the hospital.

When they got to the subject of Joseph's testimony, Sarge sat back in his chair. "We'll run through your investigation, the arrest, and your conclusions about Darious's health. We'll wrap up with your discovery of the *nganga*, Amos."

"Is the good doctor still in Lusaka?" Niza interjected.

Joseph nodded. "I saw him a week ago. He's still there."

"That brings us to Doris," Sarge said. "She can talk about Bella's history with Darious."

"*If* she agrees to testify," Zoe said. "The last time I talked to her she was undecided."

"I have confidence you'll convince her," Sarge replied. "After Doris is Amos. He'll develop Darious's motive. If he strays from his prior testimony, we can use the recordings against him. When was the last time you spoke to Bob Wangwe?" he asked Joseph.

"I talked to him a few days ago. He'll be there with his client."

"Very good," said Sarge. "The last witness on my list is Kuyeya."

"I don't think the judge will let her testify," Niza countered. "Dr. Mbao said—"

Sarge interrupted her. "Mwila told me yesterday that Dr. Mbao has revised her assessment. Kuyeya can answer simple questions."

Niza frowned. "It's a gamble. We don't know how she'll react in Darious's presence."

"That's why we'll prepare her," Sarge said. "What's the worst that could happen? She doesn't speak. She starts to cry. Other kids have done that, and it hasn't stopped us from putting child victims on the stand. I hate the thought of traumatizing her again. But we don't have DNA. Without her testimony, we could lose the case."

Zoe glanced at Joseph. "I'm still hoping the housekeeper will come through."

"Do you honestly believe she would testify?" Niza asked.

Zoe took a breath. "I don't know."

Sarge surveyed the faces around him. "There is one other matter we need to discuss—the media. If word gets out about the trial, we could have a lot of attention. The *Post* would love to cover this, and if the *Post* covers it, so will the *Times*."

Zoe shook her head emphatically. "A leak would be devastating. Doris would never testify, to say nothing of the housekeeper."

"I don't see it happening," Niza chimed in. "The Nyambos don't want press any more than we do. Darious's reputation is expendable, but Frederick's and Patricia's are not."

"Regardless," Sarge went on, "if someone from the media contacts you, send it to me. We need to handle it delicately. We want the press on our side in case Nyambo appeals."

A week later, Zoe drove to Kabwata to visit Doris. She left the GPS tracking unit at the office and took a roundabout route, reversing course several times and keeping watch for a tail. She hadn't seen Dunstan Sisilu since the day he put a gun to her head, but the memory of his revolver and ominous words replayed often in her mind. When she satisfied herself that nothing was out of the ordinary, she parked in the lot outside Doris's apartment and knocked on the door.

Bright appeared in a T-shirt and jeans. "What do you want?"

Zoe didn't blink. "I need to speak to your mother."

"I'll talk to her," Bright conceded.

Zoe sat on the couch and studied the ancestral mask above the door.

Eventually, Doris entered the room and sat down. "Why do you keep bothering me?" she asked. "I told you I have not decided."

"Kuyeya needs you to decide," Zoe said frankly. "The trial is in a month."

Doris stared at the floor.

"I know you're afraid. But you owe it to Bella."

Doris looked up sharply.

"It's in her journal, what she did for you. She could have run, but she saved your life."

Doris closed her eyes. "Darious is dangerous. He could hurt my children."

He already did, Zoe thought, empathizing with the woman. "I know it's a risk, but the judge needs to hear about the relationship he had with Bella."

Doris rubbed her hands together nervously. "You asked me once whether she called him something other than his given name. I thought of it the other night. It was a Tonga word."

"*Siluwe*," Zoe said softly.

Doris froze. "How do you know?"

"She used it in her journal," Zoe replied, struggling to contain her excitement. Suddenly, Bella's diary was not only relevant but also admissible as evidence. "Do you know why?"

Doris shook her head. "If I come to court, can I tell the judge about Bright?"

"I wish you could, but it might derail the prosecution."

Doris stared at the floor for a long moment, then met Zoe's eyes again. "I suppose it would be enough to see him put in prison."

Kuyeya fell again during a visit with Dr. Mbao. Sister Irina called Zoe in a state of bewilderment.

The circumstances of the fall made no sense. They had been walking to the garden, as they always did, when Kuyeya collapsed. She sat up on her own, but she seemed disoriented and began to groan from deep in her throat. She didn't speak and didn't respond to questions. Even Zoe's music didn't seem to bring her peace.

"Dr. Chulu is on rotation," Sister Irina said. "He's going to examine her again."

"Are they en route now?" Zoe asked.

"They left twenty minutes ago," the nun replied.

"I'll meet them there."

Zoe parked on the street outside the pediatric unit and waited for the arrival of the St. Francis van. When it pulled to the curb, she greeted Sister Anica and opened the sliding door. Kuyeya gazed back at her through glassy eyes.

"Hi there," Zoe said, taken aback. "I'll help you out." She reached for the girl's shoulder and noticed that she was scratching the bump behind her right ear. "Was she doing that before?" Zoe asked, pointing at Kuyeya's hand.

Sister Anica frowned. "I don't know."

Zoe slid her arm around Kuyeya and helped her to the ground. "Does your head hurt?" she asked, removing her headphones.

"Buzz goes the bee-eater; sting goes the bee," Kuyeya replied.

"Is your head buzzing? Does it feel like a bee sting?"

Kuyeya nodded, scratching behind her ear again.

"Okay, we're going to get you help." She led Kuyeya into the waiting room and saw Dr. Chulu chatting with Nurse Mbelo.

"I think she's in pain," Zoe told the doctor. "She's rubbing a spot behind her ear."

The doctor gestured toward an examination room. "Let's take a look."

Thirty minutes later, he took a seat by the bed while Kuyeya listened to Johnny Cash.

"Her discomfort is clear," he said. "What I don't know is whether it is a cause or consequence of the fall." He eyed Sister Anica. "Has she showed signs of fatigue or irritability?"

The nun pondered this. "No more than usual."

"What about incontinence?"

"I don't know. Sister Irina is in charge of her ward."

Dr. Chulu glanced at Nurse Mbelo. "I think it's time to get a full set of cervical X-rays."

The nurse left the room and returned a minute later, looking troubled. She conferred with Dr. Chulu in a whisper, and the doctor's expression darkened.

"It seems our chief radiologist is on leave," he said with a trace of irritation.

"What does that mean?" Zoe asked.

"It means I'll read the films myself."

Zoe checked her watch and looked at Dr. Chulu. "I have to go. I have a hearing in half an hour. Will you call me with an update?"

He nodded. "As soon as I review the films."

The call came the following afternoon, just before the end of the workday.

"Do you know what's wrong with her?" Zoe asked, leaving the office to stand in the sun.

"Not exactly. I didn't see anything amiss in her spine, but I'm not the chief radiologist. Until he returns, the best we have is guesswork."

"Isn't there someone at the hospital who could offer a second opinion?"

Dr. Chulu cleared his throat. "I sent the films to orthopedics, and I'm going to monitor the situation with Sister Anica. If Kuyeya's condition worsens, I'll order an MRI."

"Why not do one now?" Zoe asked, feeling frustrated and anxious at the same time.

"I understand your concern, but our resources are limited. An MRI is a last resort."

Zoe took a deep breath and released it slowly. *It's not his fault*, she thought, redirecting her anger. *He's doing the best he can.*

With less than a month to go before the trial, Zoe devoted every spare minute at work to Kuyeya's case. As the legal team fleshed out the order of proof, she joined Sarge and Niza in developing strategies for examination and cross-examination. She had never seen her colleagues prepare so zealously for a trial before. They were ruthless in pointing out weaknesses in the evidence, and creative in inventing solutions. They were determined to find a way to win.

In the evenings when she wasn't spending time with Joseph, Zoe wrestled with her *New Yorker* article. As Samantha Wu had predicted, Naomi Potter had marked up the pages with so many suggestions and annotations that Zoe saw more red ink than black. Never had she been so heavily edited, and she found the experience irritating and humbling. Naomi was particular about everything—narrative flow, logical clarity, word choice, syntax—but her greatest concern was the impression the article would leave with the reader.

"*We have to finesse this,*" she said in an email when she sensed Zoe's frustration. "*You're placing your family—indeed, your father himself—at the heart of an argument that isn't consistent with his campaign message. There's no margin for error. We have to get this right.*"

On Sunday afternoons, Zoe visited Kuyeya, sometimes alone, sometimes with Joseph. The girl recovered quickly from her second fall. There were times when she seemed to fumble things with her hands, other times when she favored her neck. But the episodes were brief and her overall disposition positive. Dr. Chulu continued to monitor her, but he was sanguine about her prognosis. Whatever

465

orthopedics thought of the girl's X-rays, Zoe never learned.

Six days before the trial, Zoe stayed at the office after hours, working on her examination notes for Sarge. A few minutes after six o'clock, she shut down her computer and looked at Joseph who was finishing up a report in another case.

"Sometimes I drive myself crazy," she said with a sigh.

He put down his pen. "That's what gives you an edge."

Suddenly, Zoe heard her iPhone vibrate. She picked it up and froze. On the screen was a text message from an unrecognized number. "*Meet me at market tomorrow. Bring protection.*"

Zoe showed the message to Joseph.

He whistled. "The housekeeper."

Zoe nodded. "She wants a way out."

They arrived at Chiwoyu's aisle at eight forty-five the following morning. As before, they cased the market for a sign of Dunstan Sisilu, then hovered around the shoe vendor's stall, watching for the housekeeper's silhouette. Zoe had a vague premonition of danger, which she attributed to nerves. The step they were about to take—offering protection to a critical witness—was unprecedented in CILA's history. No one knew how the Nyambos would respond.

The housekeeper emerged from the sunlight just after nine o'clock, holding only her shoulder bag. She walked briskly up the aisle, keeping her head down. Zoe didn't move until the housekeeper acknowledged her. Immediately, she saw the depth of the woman's fear.

"Did you do as I asked?" the housekeeper asked.

"There's an Embassy couple in Ibex Hill that needs help," Zoe replied, struggling to steady her nerves. "We can take you there now."

Joseph joined them. "Where is the man who brought you here?"

"In the taxi lot. He will come if I don't return by nine thirty."

Joseph looked at Zoe. "Stay with her. I'll get the Land Rover."

Zoe led the housekeeper to the end of the aisle and watched as Joseph skirted the edge of the market and disappeared. "What is your name?" she asked.

The woman blinked. "I am Anna."

Zoe was about to ask another question when something registered in her peripheral vision. She squinted against the slanting light of the sun, searching for anything recognizable. Vendors were pushing carts of goods, shoppers were carrying bags and baskets, and children of all ages were scurrying about, laughing and chattering. Watching carefully, Zoe saw a shape duck into an aisle thirty feet away. Her sense of foreboding turned into fear.

"What does your driver look like?" Zoe asked.

Anna glanced at her. "He is big and always wears sunglasses."

Zoe put her arm around the woman's waist. "We have to go now," she said, shuttling the startled housekeeper up the lane away from the taxi lot. She glanced over her shoulder and saw Dunstan Sisilu emerge from the shadow of the market, moving in their direction. "We need to run," she urged, scanning the lane for Joseph.

Anna was spry for an older woman, but she was

not fast, and Sisilu steadily gained ground. Zoe slipped her hands under Anna's armpits and half-dragged her up the lane, her legs burning from the exertion. At last she saw the Land Rover make the turn. Joseph lurched to a stop in front of them, and Zoe piled Anna into the back seat.

"Step on it!" she shouted, jumping in. "He's *here*!"

Joseph jammed the transmission into reverse and accelerated up the lane. Almost instantly, a horn blared, and he hit the brakes hard, barely avoiding a Coca-Cola delivery truck that had blocked their path. He threw the Land Rover into drive and headed toward Sisilu again. Zoe watched terror-struck as Sisilu pulled out his revolver. She pushed Anna's head toward the floor, listening for the sound of a gunshot, but none came. Then they were past. She glanced out the back window and saw Sisilu running after them.

"*Stay down!*" Joseph yelled, giving the Land Rover gas.

They surged toward a cluster of buses parked in front of a warehouse. Suddenly, Joseph yanked the wheel to the left and sent them down an alley flanking a dense network of shanty stalls. Zoe lost sight of Sisilu and felt a rush of relief. Then a boy wandered into the alley pushing a cart loaded with textiles. Joseph slammed on the brakes and laid on the horn, scattering people in every direction. The boy, however, struggled to move the cart out of the way.

Zoe looked back and saw Sisilu sprinting up the alley. For a man so large, he was surprisingly agile on his feet.

"*Go!*" she cried.

At last the lane cleared, and Joseph punched the accelerator. The alley closed in on them, and time seemed to liquefy in Zoe's mind, reducing the world to a jumble of impressions: the shouts of shoppers; the hard line of Joseph's jaw; the glint of sunlight on Sisilu's gun; Anna, hunched over, head in her lap.

Seconds later, they reached the end of the alley and Joseph made a hard right turn, sending them careening across an empty lot toward Lumumba Road. They shot through a gap in traffic and headed east toward the commercial center. Out the back window, Zoe saw Sisilu pull up short and watch them go. Then a tractor-trailer lumbered by and he was gone.

Zoe gripped Anna's hand as they sped away from the market. "We made it," she said softly, beginning to breathe again.

Joseph took a series of random turns, keeping his eyes on the rearview mirror. After a while, he turned onto Great East Road and drove toward the suburbs. Zoe looked at Anna, a thousand questions rattling around in her mind. The housekeeper was staring at her hands, and she decided to ask only one of them.

"How long has he worked for Frederick?"

"Many years," Anna said. "He is in charge of security."

After passing the Chainama Hills Golf Club, Joseph turned south toward Kabulonga. In time, Zoe sighted the monolithic fortress of the American Embassy towering over Ibex Hill. Their destination was an upscale bungalow situated in a forested grove well back from the main road. They were greeted at the gate by an armed guard.

"Are you certain you were not followed?" he asked in careful English, checking Joseph's identification.

"As certain as I can be," Joseph replied.

The guard spoke tersely into a handheld radio

and admitted them to the property. They parked beneath the boughs of a jacaranda tree.

"The Thompsons have excellent security," Zoe told Anna, "and Bernie is as tough as they come. He was in the Special Forces back home. As long as you stay behind these walls, you'll be protected. Out there," she said, waving at the gate, "is another story."

She climbed out and greeted a blonde woman wearing a blouse and scarf and a muscular man in a golf shirt and chinos. "Carter, Bernie!" Zoe said, embracing them and introducing Anna. Like Carol Prentice, Carter Thompson knew how to make a person feel welcome. She took Anna's hand and led her toward the house, chatting happily as if they were old friends.

"Eventful morning?" Bernie said, looking at Zoe and then at Joseph.

"You could say that," Zoe replied and told him the story.

They waited for Anna on the Thompsons' covered porch surrounded by flowering plants. Zoe sat in a wicker chair overlooking a grassy lawn, and Joseph took a seat beside her. Bernie served them mango juice in tumblers and then left them alone. Zoe saw the tension in Joseph's face. He was scratching the stubble on his chin—a habit he took up when he was preoccupied.

"He's not going to leave us alone, is he?" she asked quietly.

Joseph shook his head.

"Is there any way you can arrest him, put him in jail until the trial is over?"

He gave her a sideways glance. "What would I charge him with?"

"He assaulted me."

Joseph shrugged. "He'd be out on bail in two days. You could press, but I doubt he'd ever be prosecuted. Not with the Nyambos behind him."

They lapsed into silence. Zoe watched the Thompsons' seven-year-old daughter, Emma, scamper across the lawn with a Labrador puppy. The innocence of the scene did little to ease her disquiet. She heard Sisilu's voice like an echo in her brain: "*If you continue to meddle in matters that don't concern you, someone will die.*"

When Carter and Anna returned from their tour, Zoe took the housekeeper aside. "I have so many questions. The trial starts in five days."

Anna nodded and sat down across from them. "How is Kuyeya?" she asked. "She was only a baby when I saw her last."

Zoe stared her in amazement. "Do you know when she was born?"

"It was January, 1997," Anna said. "An *nganga* was there and I was there. It was a hard birth, but Charity was strong. When Kuyeya came, I knew something was different. The *nganga* saw it, too. She said the child was cursed."

Zoe traded a look with Joseph. "Tell me about Charity. How did she come to Lusaka?"

"Frederick went to Zimbabwe for a meeting," Anna explained. "He got very sick. He heard about a white doctor in Livingstone, so he went there. Charity was at the hospital, and she nursed him." Anna sighed. "I have thought many times about what would have happened if he'd had a different nurse. It would have been better if none of us had met her."

"He fell in love with her?" Zoe asked, putting the pieces together.

"It was not love. It was obsession."

"He offered her a job?"

"She came to Lusaka as his personal assistant. He paid for a nice flat and gave her a driver. I didn't know about any of this at first. He kept it hidden. But when she got pregnant, he knew she would need help. He took me to meet her a month before Kuyeya was born."

"Is Frederick the father?"

Anna shook her head slowly. "He thought he was. I did, too. But he was not. I don't know who the father is."

Zoe frowned, wondering at Anna's certainty. "How do you know?"

Anna looked out at the yard. "It was Patricia who found out. Frederick had many girlfriends. Patricia knew this, but she tolerated his follies. Things changed when he met Charity. He began to treat Patricia badly. She is a proud woman from the family of a chief. She told me she knew about my trips to Woodlands. She demanded to know about Charity."

Anna closed her eyes. "I took her there—to the flat. Kuyeya was two months old and very small. I have never seen Patricia so angry. She threatened Charity. She told her that she would ruin her if she didn't leave Frederick alone. Charity was terrified. She didn't know about Frederick's family. Patricia took a book from her. I was nearby when she showed it to Frederick. She told him that Kuyeya was not his daughter."

"The book," Zoe asked in fascination, "what happened to it?"

Anna reached into her bag and removed a spiral-bound notebook. As soon as Zoe saw it, her heart began to race. She took the notebook and opened it. Unlike the journal Doris had given her, the inside cover was blank. But the salutation on the first page was the same: "Dear Jan . . ."

"This is the original volume," Zoe said, showing it to Joseph. "How did you get this?" she asked Anna.

"Patricia kept it in the closet. I saw it every time I brought her laundry."

"Did you read it?"

Anna looked ashamed. "I cannot read. I only completed the sixth standard."

"But your English is so good."

"Patricia hired a tutor to work with me. They spoke only English in the house."

Zoe folded her hands. "I assume Frederick cut Charity off and left her with the baby."

"Patricia threatened him with divorce. I never saw Charity again."

"Did you know she had a relationship with Darious?"

Anna looked at her sharply. "When?"

"Sometime after 2004."

Anna's eyes lit up. "That is how he knew about Kuyeya." She explained herself before Zoe could ask. "When I heard about the rape, I didn't understand. He didn't meet Charity when he was a boy. But I knew the crime could not be a coincidence."

"Did he know about the book?" Zoe asked.

"Yes," Anna said. "I once saw him with it in his parents' bedroom."

Suddenly, another piece of the puzzle fell into place. Darious had learned about his father's affair with Charity as a teenager, but when he met her in the flesh, years later, he knew her as Bella. She never told him her real name, and he probably never asked. However, the question remained unanswered: how did he make the connection?

She refocused on Anna. "Did you see anything on the night of the rape?"

Anna gave her a look tinged with remorse. "Frederick and Patricia were gone. He went away for a while in his truck. Then he came back and parked in the garage. I saw him walking around in the dark, behaving strangely. I didn't know what he was doing."

Zoe conjoured the layout of the property and recalled that the housekeeper's cottage offered a direct line of sight to the garage. "Did he see you watching him?"

Anna began to fidget with her hands. "I don't know."

Zoe waited a beat, then asked the most delicate question of all: "Will you testify?"

Anna regarded her gravely. "If I do not disappear, they will kill me." She gestured at the notebook. "The truth is there. Show it to the judge."

* * *

Half an hour later, Zoe and Joseph returned to the Prentice bungalow. They greeted Carol, who was reading in the living room, and walked to the terrace, taking seats in the sunlight by the pool. Zoe removed Charity's notebook from her backpack.

"Read it out loud," Joseph said.

She nodded and opened to the first letter.

Dear Jan,

When I came to Lusaka, I thought I would find a way to forget you. But I think there is no way. Not now. You are in South Africa, as you wanted to be. You have a long life to live. You are a gifted doctor. I was foolish to think that I could be with you after nursing school. But you will always be with me. I sometimes dream that I will wake up and find you beside me again. I am still a foolish girl. But I know what it is to love. You may forget me, but I will not forget you.

"You were right," Joseph said. "They had a relationship."

Zoe nodded and turned the page. She read the next letter, and the one after that, and then ten more letters scattered through the volume. Some shed light on the web of deceit and chaos that had defined Charity's first year in Lusaka—Frederick's temper, his sexual demands, and her confusion about it all. A few were touching explorations of motherhood. The rest, however, were letters to Jan inked in the pain of unrequited love.

After a while, Zoe found that she could stomach no more. She stared into the pool, knowing what she had to do. When she told Joseph, he regarded her thoughtfully.

"How long will you be gone?"

"I'll be back by Wednesday, one way or another."

Joseph nodded, his eyes catching the flame of the sun. "I'll take you to the airport."

Chapter 25

Cape Town, South Africa
April, 2012

Zoe landed in Cape Town just before eleven in the evening. She rented a Kia crossover and drove into the night, heading west in the direction of Table Bay. She had packed her suitcase expecting autumn rain, but the Cape air was dry and cloudless, cleansed by a stiff wind blowing in from the sea. *The Southeaster*, Zoe thought, sighting the Southern Cross above the lights of the city. *If it holds, I'm in for a spectacular visit.*

And she was. The next morning, she awoke to sunlight streaming into her room at the Table

Bay Hotel. She went to the window and looked across the harbor at the flat-topped massif of Table Mountain rising from the expanse of the city bowl. She remembered the first time her mother brought her here—to the cape Sir Francis Drake had called the fairest in the whole circumference of the earth. "*Drink it in, Zoe,*" Catherine had said. "*You will never feel more alive than in Cape Town.*"

After a quick breakfast, Zoe drove east through the clutch of metropolitan traffic and took the N2 across the coastal plain. Exiting onto the R102, she headed north across the fertile greenbelt of the *veld* to Stellenbosch. Bounded by the towering Hottentots Holland Mountains to the east and the rocky peak of the Simonsberg to the north, the winelands of the Western Cape had splendor to spare. Her destination was the Kruger Estate, a boutique winery on the slopes of the Simonsberg dating back to the late nineteenth-century.

Zoe parked in the dirt lot at the entrance to the estate and walked down the forested path, following hand-carved signs to the wine shop. She entered the shop through a heavy wooden door. The tasting room had the cozy feel of a cellar, with flagstone floors, hardwood furniture, stone pillars and directional lighting. Since it was still fairly early, the shop was empty except for an old man behind the counter and a young couple flirting in a corner booth.

Zoe took a seat at one of the tables and examined the menu. The old man greeted her hospitably, his English inflected with a trace of Bavaria. Zoe noticed the resemblance immediately. *This is going to be easier than I imagined*, she thought.

"I'll try the reds," she said.

The old man retrieved a bottle of Merlot from the counter and poured a sample into her glass, describing the bouquet of flavors and their mineral origins like a master sommelier. After the Merlot, he brought her a Pinotage, then a Shiraz and a Cabernet Sauvignon, and finally a blend called the "Grand Reserve." Zoe chatted with the winemaker about his vintages and paid the bill. Only then did she broach the reason for her visit.

"You are Hendrik Kruger," she said. "I know your son."

The old man's face brightened. "Ah, why did you not mention it before? I would have given you the tasting for free."

She smiled. "No need. I'd be grateful for a favor, though."

"For a friend of Jan, anything," replied Hendrik.

"I need to find him. I spoke to the people at the University of Cape Town. They said you might know where he is."

Hendrik's expression turned opaque. "What is the concern?"

Zoe gave him a shaded version of the truth. "A friend of ours—a woman Jan was close to—died recently. She left something for him."

The old man took a moment to make his decision. "There is a place near Hermanus," he said. "It is called Vrede. People go there when they are seeking consolation. I'm not certain, but I think you may find him there."

"Consolation?" she inquired.

"Peace," Hendrik clarified. "You'll see."

He rummaged in a drawer for a piece of paper and wrote out directions.

Although the N2 over Sir Lowry's Pass would have been faster, Zoe decided to take the coastal road to the seaside town of Hermanus. Like California's Pacific Coast Highway, the route from Gordon's Bay to Kleinmond was a stretch of tarmac that could turn anyone into a poet. Winding along precipitous cliffs and through picturesque beach communities, the R44 hugged the ragged edge of land that joined the Hottentots Holland Mountains with the eternal blue of the ocean.

Zoe reached Hermanus by early afternoon. Following Hendrik Kruger's directions, she turned off the main road just before the town center and drove inland through the Hemel en Aarde Valley. The mountains of the Overberg rose up on all sides, blotting out the sky, but the slopes adjacent to the roadway were dotted with vineyards and Cape Dutch homesteads.

After a few miles, Zoe saw the sign for Vrede Retreat Center. The access road was bumpy and lined with tangled shrubs. Soon, however, the hilly terrain gave way to a vast meadow tucked in between rocky cliffs. Zoe parked in a gravel lot beside a white cinderblock building with a hanging sign that read: "Office." She left the SUV unlocked and greeted a lanky silver-haired man sitting on a deckchair. The man stood and shook her hand.

"Welcome to Vrede," he said in a polished voice. "I'm Robert Vorster."

"Zoe Fleming," she replied, looking around. "It's beautiful here."

"Heaven on earth," he replied with a grin, and then explained himself. "*Hemel en Aarde*. It's Afrikaans." He gave her a thoughtful look. "I don't believe we were expecting you."

She shook her head. "I'm looking for someone—Dr. Jan Kruger. His father sent me."

Vorster hesitated. "Do you have business with him?"

She chose her words carefully. "I suppose 'business' is an appropriate description."

Vorster gestured toward a path that led into the trees. "Will you walk with me?"

Zoe nodded. *Another gatekeeper. Jan certainly knows how to protect himself.*

They strolled up the path beneath the boughs of evergreens and came upon a clearing at the foot of an old chapel. Beside the chapel was a fishpond surrounded by vegetation, and beyond the pond on the hillside was a cluster of whitewashed homes.

Vorster took a seat on a carved stone bench. "Have you been to Vrede before?"

"No," she replied, sitting beside him.

"Many would say this is a holy place. We've hosted opponents of apartheid, members of the Truth and Reconciliation Commission, politicians, clergy, and cultural leaders, along with visitors from around the world. At Vrede everyone is the same. We are all people searching for peace in troubled times. There is only one rule: do no harm." Vorster gave Zoe a direct look. "Does your 'business' with Dr. Kruger meet that standard?"

Zoe watched a leaf tumble through the air and land in the pond. She knew she had to tell the truth. "I'm a lawyer," she said. "I'm helping a child in Lusaka who was raped. The trial of her abuser starts in four days. Jan has information critical to the case. I need to talk to him."

Vorster was silent for so long that Zoe thought she had lost him. Then, suddenly, he stood and faced her. "After lunch, he went on a walk. I suspect you will find him at the falls. The trail begins at the bridge across the meadow."

"Thank you," she said, offering her hand, which Vorster took.

"Jan is a good man," he said. "I urge you to remember that."

Zoe found the trailhead on the far side of a foot-bridge that spanned a highland stream. She took a slow breath, listening to the music of water dancing upon round stones, and then began to walk. Before long, the meadow gave way to more rugged terrain, dominated by shrub-like vegetation. Zoe followed the serpentine course of the stream, traversing groves of towering oaks and slowly trading distance for elevation.

Eventually, she reached a fork in the trail. The main path led through a tangle of trees, and a second path—much narrower—led upward along a rocky defile toward the crest of the mountain. She could hear the sound of falling water nearby, but she couldn't see it. She ventured into the thicket, pushing branches out of the way and stepping around exposed roots. Soon, she emerged on a patch of grass at the edge of a muddy pool. She saw the waterfall and the bench at the same time. A man turned and looked at her.

It was Jan Kruger.

If he was shocked to see her, he didn't show it. Instead—paradoxically—he looked almost relieved. After a while, she sat down beside him and stared at the waterfall.

"Why are you here?" she asked at last.

He looked at her curiously. "If you don't know, I should ask you the same question."

"Is this some sort of penance?"

He angled his head thoughtfully. "Penance and peace are related but not the same."

"Peace without reconciliation is a lie," she rejoined, repeating the words she had delivered to Sylvia months ago. "You seem fond of lies."

He waited a beat before responding: "I could say that we're even."

"You could say, '*Voetsak*,'" she replied, pronouncing the expletive like an Afrikaner. "But we're not even."

Jan gave a short laugh. "A curious expression,

hey? You're right. Your lie to Dr. Luyt was selfless; mine the height of selfishness." He scratched his chin. "How did you discover it?"

Zoe retrieved the first volume of Charity's journal from her backpack. "She wrote about you," she said, handing the notebook to him. "She loved you."

He turned the journal over in his hands. "This isn't the one you showed me before."

"That was the third volume, written much later. This is the original one. She wrote her first letter soon after she left Livingstone."

He played with the cover but didn't open it. "What does she say?"

"That you were lovers. That you made love in your office late at night; that you were gifted, the most gifted doctor she had ever met; and that she wanted more than anything to be your wife. There was a time when she believed that was possible."

He winced. "I suppose I let her believe that."

She narrowed her eyes. "You suppose? She was your student. She had lost most of her family to disease. She was in school so she could get a good job and take care of her grandmother and her cousins. I know Zambian women. They don't make the first move."

Jan examined the waterfall. "It was an intense year," he said eventually. "My research in Livingstone was meaningful but not essential. I had applied for a position in Cape Town, but I didn't know if they would offer it to me. Charity was . . . I don't know. She had a glow about her, a gift of insight and intelligence that I found irresistible."

He glanced up at a bird flying overhead. "When Godfrey got sick, we were with him all night. We were exhausted; the rainy season was miserable— so many malaria cases. And then, miraculously, he survived. Charity thought of him almost like a son. The next week she brought me a meal to thank me. We were alone in the hospital after hours. I made a mistake."

"If it was a mistake, why did you keep sleeping with her?"

He shrugged. "I'd never met anyone like her. I was with her as long as I could be."

"Why didn't you marry her? You could have made a life together."

"That would have been impossible."

The truth suddenly dawned on her. "Your family wouldn't have approved."

He glanced at her obliquely. "My parents are not racists. But it was 1996. The tensions in the region were extraordinary. No one would have understood."

"So you left her. You got the job in Cape Town and you walked away."

He shook his head. "I did something worse than that. She went to Lusaka because of me."

"*What?*" Zoe demanded. "What do you mean? Frederick Nyambo took her."

"Yes," he nodded, "but I was the one who suggested it."

All at once the whole story made sense. Everyone who knew Charity had been right and wrong at the same time. "How did it happen?" she asked.

"Frederick came to the hospital from Victoria Falls," he explained. "He had an advanced case of leptospirosis—a severe bacterial infection. He'd seen an *nganga* and gotten some potions that did nothing. By the time I saw him, he was a mess. I managed his case, but Charity tended to him. He was there for ten days. I saw the way he looked at her. So I started talking to him about her. I told him about her family, about her grandmother's stroke. I told him how bright she was. I thought if I got her a good job in Lusaka—something better than she could have gotten out of nursing school—she would go there and forget about me."

"You did it so you could live with yourself," Zoe said. "You bribed your conscience and then you broke her heart."

"An elegant summary," he replied, taking no offense. "Yes, I did it for selfish reasons. To be fair, she wasn't guaranteed a job out of school. The economy in Zambia was turbulent in those years. But she was the best student in her class. She wouldn't have starved."

Zoe pictured Frederick Nyambo convalescing in a hospital bed and chatting with Jan Kruger about Charity's future. "Did you convince him, or did he convince himself?"

"We convinced each other. He promised me that he would take care of her. I believed him. So I convinced her." Jan's voice trailed off, and he stared intently at the surface of the pool, as if the still water might conjure a reflection of Charity's face.

"In case it matters to you, he *did* take care of her," Zoe said. "He put her up in a nice flat, made her his personal assistant. Your plan might actually have worked." She took a deep breath, bracing herself. "There was only one problem. She was carrying your child."

Jan sat back against the bench and closed his eyes. In the silence that ensued, nature reasserted its dominance. Water trickled down the rock, clouds sailed the sky-sea overhead, and birds called to one another. At last he opened his eyes again. "How do you know?"

She pointed at the journal still in his hands. "Read it for yourself. I dog-eared the page."

His fingers trembled as he opened the cover. He found the marked passage near the end of the volume and scanned the text. When he finished, his shoulders slumped. "It's possible I am the father," he said slowly. "But it's also possible she was wrong."

"There's a way to be certain," Zoe replied, and outlined her plan.

He looked toward the pond. "I need to think about this."

She struggled to contain her impatience. "We don't have much time."

"Give me until morning," he said.

Chapter 26

Lusaka, Zambia
April, 2012

Three days before the trial of Darious Nyambo, Dunstan Sisilu appeared outside the CILA office driving the gray Prado. He parked on the opposite side of the street and watched the parking lot, making no attempt at concealment. Joseph was the first to see him, and he informed Zoe and Mariam. Mariam, in turn, called an emergency all-staff meeting. Ten minutes later, all twenty employees took seats at the conference table. Most were perplexed; a few were unsettled.

"It's obvious they want Anna back," Mariam

said, glancing out the window toward the gate. "But what lengths will they go to to find her?"

Joseph spoke up. "I suspect their focus will be on Zoe and me, but I wouldn't be surprised if they watch the rest of the legal team."

"I'll alert the guards," Mariam replied. "I don't want anyone leaving here unescorted until the trial is over. Travel in twos or threes. If you have security at home, put them on notice." She paused. "What do you think we should do about our witnesses?"

"If we tell them, they won't testify," Niza said. "It would be one thing if we had knowledge that they're in danger. But we don't."

Zoe nodded. "I agree. He's known where they live for months. They're as safe now as they were before."

Sarge leaned forward. "I suppose there's a bright side to this. They aren't certain Flexon Mubita is on their side."

Joseph looked dubious. "The magistrate isn't their only concern. If Anna talks publicly, her story could damage the Nyambos' reputation. Mubita is still a wild card."

Silence descended upon the room. Zoe saw the weight of uncertainty in her colleagues' eyes. She felt it as much as they did, but she felt something else, too—anger. It gave her the will to fight. She almost spoke up, but a glance at Mariam made her hesitate. Instead of doubtful, the field-office director looked determined.

"You know," Mariam said, putting her hands on the table, "at the beginning of all of this, Niza predicted that the Nyambos would treat this case like an act of war. That's exactly what they've done. There's no way we can control them. We can't control their thugs. We can't control the Court. But we don't need to. Our task is to prosecute Darious. If we do that, we dignify Kuyeya and every Zambian girl who lives in fear of rape."

As she spoke, heads began to nod, including Zoe's.

"I've been in this seat for seven years," Mariam continued. "I can't count how many times my heart has been broken. This case might break it again. Then again, it might not." She paused, looking at each face around the table. "Let's make this the best trial we've ever put on."

★ ★ ★

At the end of the workday, Joseph drove Zoe home in his truck. Sisilu shadowed them, keeping his distance. The next day and the day after that, they followed the same routine, as did their stalker in sunglasses. As Joseph had predicted, Sisilu was not alone. Sarge and Niza also noticed strange vehicles shadowing them by day and watching their houses at night. The mood among the legal team was tense. In the crucible of trial preparation, patience wore thin and tempers flared. Even the unflappable Sarge seemed agitated.

The evening before the trial, Zoe and Joseph joined the Prentices on the terrace for a feast of lamb kebobs and couscous and cucumber salad. The autumn air was cool, and the sky was full of stars. Tom and Carol kept the conversation lively with tales of their misadventures in Africa. Zoe chimed in with memories of her mother, and Carol picked up the narrative thread, sharing stories about Catherine's life that Zoe had never heard—her meeting with Nelson Mandela before the fall of apartheid; the pressure she had put on the Clinton administration not to interfere with African countries distributing generic ARVs in violation of American pharmaceutical patents; the Deputy Secretary of State who had hit on her at a party after too many drinks; the ambassadors who had loved her and those who had despised her. Through all of this, Joseph seemed distracted. At one point, Zoe caught him staring at a cypress tree across the yard.

"What's the matter?" she asked.

"Nothing," he said and returned to his food.

After the Prentices went to bed, Zoe and Joseph walked through the bungalow as they did every night, checking the locks on all doors and windows. Then Zoe led him to the bedroom and tried to entice him with a kiss. Joseph, however, showed no interest in sex. He changed out of his clothes and slid under the covers, pausing only to say "goodnight" before his head hit the pillow. In less than a minute he was asleep.

Zoe slipped in beside him, enjoying his warmth. She lay awake and listened to the night birds and the gentle sound of his breathing. She thought of the future as it ought to be—of Kuyeya safe from men like Darious; of Trevor and Jenna tying the knot; of Joseph and love and what? A long-term relationship? A lifetime commitment? Was it possible? Sensible? What would that even look like? By midnight, her eyelids grew heavy and she, too, fell asleep.

The next sound she heard was a scream.

Her eyes flew open and her addled brain struggled to wake up. She heard a crash in the far reaches of the house. She glanced at Joseph and was struck with a blinding terror.

A human shape was leaning over the bed.

This time it was Zoe who screamed. The shape stiffened and she could almost see it looking at her. Then it vanished. In the grip of fright, she couldn't think, couldn't speak, could only react. Her hand shot out and threw back the mosquito net while her other hand found her glasses. Whirling around, she saw Joseph reaching for his rifle.

"Stay here!" he hissed and bolted toward the door.

To Zoe, however, staying behind felt like a death wish. She leapt off the bed and ran after him—down the hallway, through the guest quarters, and into the living room. She heard another scream and recognized the voice of Carol Prentice. A man shouted: "*No!*" Then something heavy hit the wall and Carol screamed again.

A moment later, Zoe saw a shape emerge from the hallway to the Prentices' quarters and retreat into the darkened kitchen. Something glinted in its hand.

"He's got a *weapon!*" Zoe yelled, as Joseph raised his gun into firing position.

She was utterly unprepared for the foot that appeared out of nowhere and tripped her. She sprawled headlong across the tile floor, losing her glasses. Before she could recover, strong arms lifted her off the ground, and she felt hot breath on her neck. The breath was followed by a blade.

A voice spoke loudly beside her ear. "No move! I kill!"

"Help," she choked out even as the knife bit into her skin.

Joseph's reaction was instantaneous. He pivoted on his feet and trained his rifle on the man who held her life in the balance. She looked down the barrel of the gun and shivered uncontrollably.

"Let her go," Joseph commanded.

Her assailant tightened his grip. "Where is woman?" he barked.

At once Zoe understood. The intruders believed Anna was in the house.

"She's far away," said Joseph.

"Where?" the man yelled.

The next two seconds seemed to happen in slow motion—Joseph taking a step backward and saying, "Okay, okay, I'll tell you"; the blade on her neck relaxing; the sudden muzzle flash; the momentous report of the blast; the searing pain at the tip of her ear as the bullet shot by a fraction of an inch off-target; the smell of acrid cordite and coppery blood.

Zoe shrieked and twisted out of the dead man's grasp as he crumpled to the floor. Her mind was frozen in a state of shock, her ears ringing. She wanted to collapse on the couch and weep. But the second intruder was still at large.

She shoved her glasses into place and focused on the outline of Joseph's face. They ran together toward the kitchen. The room was lit by a dim glow: the servant's door was open. They stopped on the threshold beside a bank of light switches and scanned the shadows for movement. The night was perfectly still—no voices, no footsteps, not even a hint of wind.

"Where is the guard?" Joseph spat, as Zoe's heart hammered in her chest.

He threw the switches and flooded the yard with light.

"Let's go," he said, leaving the house and sprinting toward the gate, his gun out in front of him. Zoe took a deep breath and ran after him.

They found the guard crumpled on the ground. Zoe felt for a pulse. "He's alive," she said.

Joseph checked the gate and found it locked. "They got in another way."

She followed him around to the back of the house. The pool and terrace looked ghostly in the pale light. He stopped at the base of a tall cypress tree and cursed. The ground wire atop the wall had been cut. A carpet hung over the other wires, weighing them down. At once Zoe recalled his preoccupation at dinner. She put the pieces together. *They entered from the neighbors' yard. But how did they get into the house?*

The answer came to her suddenly. "*Rosa!*" she cried.

The door to the servant's cottage was ajar, and the living area was as dark as a crypt. Zoe entered the cottage, ignoring Joseph's commands to stay back. She blinked her eyes against the gloom and made out a couch, a stove, and a bed. A woman lay motionless on the mattress, her arms splayed out at an unnatural angle. Zoe ran to her side, fearing the worst. She pressed her fingers against Rosa's neck and let out the breath she was holding.

"Thank God," she whispered, feeling a strong heartbeat.

"I need to check the rest of the grounds," Joseph said.

Zoe nodded quickly. "I'm coming."

She ran with him into the false brightness of the yard. Together they scoured the walls and vegetation for a hint of movement. Twice Zoe thought she saw motion in the chiaroscuro of light and shadow. But each time it was a phantom, a trick of the mind. After searching the carport, Joseph led her back to the gate and unbolted the latch. He pointed his gun down the street toward the spot recently occupied by the gray Prado. Zoe looked over his shoulder.

Dunstan Sisilu was gone.

Joseph secured the gate again, and they returned to the servant's entrance.

"I'm going to search the house," he said. "You check on Tom and Carol."

The lights were on when they entered the bungalow. Carol was standing in her nightgown by the stove, her face wet with tears.

"Is Tom okay?" Zoe asked, embracing her.

"He's out cold," Carol said.

Zoe walked down the hall to the Prentices' bedroom. The place was a wreck—a table lamp shattered beside the bed, the desk chair upended, clothes strewn about, and Tom lying in a heap. Suddenly, the magnitude of the attack hit Zoe and she fell to her knees, a wave of guilt sweeping over her. *This is all my fault! They protected me and they got hurt.*

After a while she felt a hand on her shoulder. "The police are coming," Carol said softly.

Zoe blinked. "I'm so sorry," she whispered.

When Tom regained consciousness, Zoe helped

Carol move him to a chair in the living room. The Kabulonga authorities arrived a few minutes later and spent two hours collecting evidence. The dead attacker carried no identification. His clothes were nondescript, as was his knife. His nationality was a mystery. Joseph guessed he was Congolese; the chief investigator thought he was Angolan; they agreed he was not Zambian.

The gate guard was the first to revive. He stumbled into the house wearing a look of profound bewilderment. The police questioned him, but his recollection was almost completely blank. Rosa appeared soon afterward, holding her head. Carol directed her to the couch and sat beside her while the police made their inquiry. The housekeeper remembered waking in the dark and hearing scratches on the floor. Then a hand pressed something over her mouth. She recalled the smell of chemicals, but after that, nothing.

As soon as the police removed the body, Tom composed himself enough to call the security company. Carol took a Valium and scrubbed the floor with bleach until the bloodstain was nearly invisible. Zoe, meanwhile, went to the bathroom and washed her face until her skin turned pink. The laceration from the knife had already dried, but her ear continued to bleed.

She stared at herself in the mirror, overcome by emotion. Pain welled up within her and she slumped to the floor and began to cry. She didn't know how long it was before Joseph found her and guided her to her bedroom. She crawled under the covers, shivering uncontrollably.

"Are they gone?" she asked.

"Yes," he said. "I made some calls. Everyone at CILA is okay."

He wrapped her in his arms and began to whisper-sing an African lullaby—in Nyanja or Tonga or Bemba, she didn't know. The soft cadence of the words soothed her shattered nerves but did little to console her. She couldn't bring herself to think about the trial that would begin in just a few hours. She couldn't fathom sitting in the gallery while Darious swore his innocence and Frederick looked on like a man with nothing to hide. Yet that is exactly what she would have to do. The case would not be delayed on her account.

She closed her eyes and forced the memories of violence out of her mind. She focused on Joseph's song, the quiet rhythm, the unfamiliar words.

At last, she drifted off to sleep.

Chapter 27

Just before nine the next morning, Zoe took her seat in Courtroom 10, anticipating and dreading the appearance of the judge. Like actors waiting for the curtain to rise, the players in the trial were subdued, pensive. Lawyers doodled mindlessly on notepads; the witnesses from Kanyama—Given, Dominic, Wisdom, Agnes and Abigail—sat as still as statues; Dr. Chulu shifted his weight around and rubbed his hands together repeatedly; even Benson Luchembe, dressed in his Savile Row suit and surrounded by a coterie of associates, appeared nervous.

Or so Zoe wanted to believe.

The events of the night before had shaken her confidence deeply, and she was struggling to stay composed. In addition to the break-in at the Prentices' bungalow, intruders had ransacked the CILA office, tearing apart case files, and sabotaging computers and office equipment. Had Sarge and Niza not taken their trial materials home with them, the prosecution almost certainly would have been derailed. The night guards were as shocked as the staff to learn what had happened. They claimed they had heard no sounds, seen nothing suspicious. Niza and Zoe suspected otherwise, but there was no way of proving their complicity.

Zoe fingered the scab on her ear and glanced at Frederick Nyambo. He was alone, as he had been at every hearing since the arraignment, his wife apparently having contented herself to exercise her influence behind the scenes. His face was a picture of imperial calm. He met Zoe's eyes and smiled slightly. *The deck is stacked*, he seemed to say. *We own this game.*

Suddenly, the door to chambers opened and Flexon Mubita appeared with a young man who looked like a law clerk. The judge ascended the bench and ordered the courtroom deputy to bring in the accused. Darious sat in the dock and stared at Mubita blankly. His lack of visible remorse fueled Zoe's rage. After all she had done, after the mountains CILA had moved, his fate rested in the hands of a judge whose integrity was in doubt.

"Good morning, everyone," Mubita intoned, nodding cordially to Sarge and Benson Luchembe. "This is the trial of Darious Nyambo, who is charged with the defilement of a child under the age of sixteen. Are there any matters I need to address before we move forward?"

Sarge stood slowly, looking a bit wobbly on his feet. "Your Worship, last night armed intruders broke into the home where Zoe Fleming has been staying since the attack on her flat. One of the intruders was killed in the skirmish, but he has yet to be identified. Intruders also broke into our office and destroyed files and equipment. As you know, this prosecution has been marred by obstructions of justice, but this level of violence is unprecedented. We don't yet have evidence linking the attacks to the accused, but there is no other explanation."

Mubita looked genuinely shocked. He glared at

Benson Luchembe. "Do you have any knowledge of this?"

The defense lawyer shook his head vehemently. "Of *course* not, Your Worship. I'm as horrified as you are. And I resent counsel's accusation. Without evidence of complicity, he should hold his tongue."

The judge glowered at Darious. "If I ever learn that the defense was involved in this campaign of lawlessness, I will personally throw all of you in jail for contempt." He turned back to Sarge. "Are you requesting a continuance?"

Sarge hesitated. "No, Your Worship. We are prepared to try the case today."

The judge nodded. "As disturbed as I am by these developments, I don't like the thought of further delay." He looked at Zoe. "Ms. Fleming, I'm very sorry for what happened to you. I assume you will be tightening security at your home?"

"It's already been done, Your Worship," she said evenly.

"Good," Mubita replied, picking up his pen. "I'm ready for opening statements."

* * *

Sarge and Benson Luchembe made quick work of their openings. Sarge summarized the facts the prosecution would establish but remained coy about Darious's motive and his family's history with Charity Mizinga. Luchembe, on the other hand, enumerated the weaknesses in the prosecution's case—Kuyeya's inability to name the accused and the prosecution's failure to produce an eyewitness to the rape. Afterward, the judge directed Sarge to call his first witness.

"I call Given Sensele," Sarge said.

The examination of a minor child was always a sensitive matter, but Sarge handled Given with practiced grace. He showed her photographs of the alley where she saw the silver SUV and photographs of Darious's Mercedes, and she identified the Lusaka Golf Club crest on the rear of the SUV. Luchembe objected when Sarge asked Darious to stand up and turn around, but the judge overruled the objection. After Darious complied, Sarge pointed at him.

"Does the accused resemble the man you saw in the alley?"

Given's answer resonated in the chamber. "I

didn't see his face. I only saw his back. But, yes. He looks like the man I saw."

When Sarge yielded the floor, Luchembe smiled politely at the girl. "Ms. Sensele, you said you were on your way home when you saw the silver SUV. How fast were you walking?"

The girl thought for a moment. "I was walking quickly."

"You were walking quickly because you were alone and it was dark outside?"

Given nodded.

"You were walking quickly when you observed the silver SUV?"

"Yes. But I stopped when I saw it."

The defense attorney frowned. "May I ask why you did that?"

Given looked temporarily confused. "It was an expensive car. I wondered who was in it."

"But you didn't see who was in it. You testified you didn't see his face."

"He looked like the man in the dock," the girl rejoined.

Luchembe shrugged. "You don't know that for certain, do you?"

Given seemed to bristle. "I already told you what I saw."

The defense lawyer pursed his lips and asked no further questions.

Next on the witness list was Wisdom. The teenager sauntered through the bar, a caricature of adolescent bravado. He sized up Darious, cast a confident look at the judge, and focused on Sarge, who led him through the night of the rape—the TV program he was watching, the sound of an engine on the street, seeing the taillights of a silver SUV. Sarge also showed him a hand-drawn map of his neighborhood and asked him to mark the location of his house.

Soon, Sarge turned the young man over to Benson Luchembe, who promptly made mincemeat of his testimony, establishing that he had no idea about the make and model of the SUV let alone who owned it, who was driving it, whether there were any passengers in it, where it had come from, or where it went after it passed his house. "In summary, then," Luchembe sneered, "you didn't really see *anything* that night, did you?"

Wisdom gave Luchembe a sullen look.

"I'll take that as a 'no'," said the lawyer, sitting down again.

Next, Sarge summoned Dominic. "The boy speaks very little English," Sarge said, escorting him to the witness stand. "His language is Nyanja."

The judge waved to his law clerk. "Timothy will interpret."

When Timothy stationed himself beside Dominic, Sarge led the boy through a series of questions about the court process and the nature of truth-telling. Dominic's answers were uncomplicated, but he seemed capable of holding his own in a chamber of lawyers.

"I don't believe the boy is qualified," Benson Luchembe objected. "My client's freedom shouldn't be imperiled by the unreliable memories of a seven-year-old child."

The judge shook his head. "The boy seems lucid. I'd like to hear what he remembers."

Luchembe sat down heavily while Sarge began to question Dominic. The boy was bright and seemed to enjoy the chance to tell the judge his story. He spoke in short bursts of Nyanja, and Timothy translated. Sarge showed Dominic the hand-drawn map he had presented to Wisdom. The boy struggled to point out his house until he understood that the bush-like symbol at the center represented the tree in Abigail's yard. He pointed to a house just down the street.

"I stay there," he said.

Sarge showed Dominic the photographs of Darious's SUV and the Lusaka Golf Club crest, both of which the boy identified. He also identified Kuyeya playing in the yard at St. Francis. "It is the girl I saw," he said. "She looks happy here. That night she was crying."

Instead of cross-examining the child on his feet, Luchembe moved his chair over to the witness stand. "I'm Benson," the lawyer began, affecting a fatherly tone. "You told Mr. Zulu that it was dark when you saw the truck and the child, isn't that right?"

Dominic fidgeted in his chair. "The night is dark."

Luchembe smiled. "Indeed it is. Dominic, you said that the man you saw looked like the man over there, correct?" The lawyer pointed at Darious, sitting in the dock, and the boy nodded. "Do you recognize the man sitting in the front row of the gallery? He is wearing a gray suit."

The boy looked toward the man in question, and Zoe followed his gaze. The man—a member of the defense team—stared back at Dominic. The boy frowned and shook his head.

"Are you saying you have never seen him before?" Luchembe inquired.

"I don't remember that man," the boy said, sounding confused.

"Are you certain? Why don't you think again?"

Zoe glanced between the boy and the man, feeling genuine concern. Dominic's testimony was crucial to the case, yet the defense lawyer appeared poised to neutralize it.

"I don't think I have seen him," the boy said, less sure of himself.

Luchembe raised his eyebrows. "You don't remember meeting him about three months ago outside your house? You were playing a game with a few other boys."

"Objection," said Sarge. "Counsel is assuming facts not in evidence."

Luchembe stood up and shrugged deferentially. "Your Worship, I'm not assuming anything. I want nothing more than to know what the boy remembers."

The magistrate looked at Sarge. "Objection overruled. The inquiry is appropriate."

The defense lawyer faced the boy again. "You said you haven't seen the man in the gray suit. I want to know whether you remember meeting him outside your house in Kanyama."

"I don't think I've seen that man," he said in a voice barely above a whisper.

The defense lawyer nodded gravely. "Do you remember seeing me that day?"

Dominic looked flummoxed. "I see you now."

"Indeed," Luchembe replied, catching the judge's eye. "That's all I have, Your Worship."

Mubita regarded Sarge. "Anything further?"

Sarge stood up slowly. "Dominic, do you remember meeting the *muzungu* woman who is also sitting in the front row of the gallery?"

Please say yes, Zoe thought, as the boy turned toward her.

To her overwhelming relief, he began to nod. "I

have seen her. She came to my house. She showed me a picture of a girl."

"Was the girl in the picture the same as the girl you saw that night outside your house?"

Benson Luchembe leapt to his feet. "I object. The question is leading."

The judge nodded. "Sustained."

Sarge sidestepped the objection. "Who was the girl in the picture, do you remember?"

Dominic smiled brightly. "It was the girl who was crying."

Sarge nodded, looking satisfied. He glanced at his watch. "Your Worship, I'm finished with this witness. Perhaps we should break for lunch."

Mubita put down his pen, looking relieved. "This Court will be in recess for one hour."

At half past one, the lawyers reassembled in the courtroom. The judge appeared promptly and took a seat on the bench. Sarge began the afternoon session with Agnes and Abigail. He moved through their testimony chronologically, eliciting only the essential facts—the location of their houses, the engine and drumbeats Agnes heard, Abigail's discovery of Kuyeya on the street, her examination of the child, and the blood she saw on Kuyeya's leg. On cross-examination, Luchembe limited himself to a few questions designed to clarify that neither woman saw Darious or his SUV on the street. Sarge declined to redirect and called Dr. Chulu to the stand.

The physician sat in the witness chair and placed a folder on his lap. After qualifying him as an expert in pediatric medicine, Sarge asked him about the nature of Kuyeya's injuries.

"She had bruising and tearing in the vaginal area," Dr. Chulu said. "She had lesions on the skin. I took samples of blood and semen and a handful of photographs with the colposcope, but she was in no condition for a more thorough exam."

Sarge handed Mubita the photos from the colposcopy, and the judge looked through them. "Compared with the worst cases you've seen," Mubita said, "how bad is this?"

"The child was in great distress," Dr. Chulu answered, "but the physical damage was on the surface. There was no evidence of fistula—the tearing of the wall between vagina and rectum. In this sense, the child was fortunate. Her body healed reasonably quickly."

Nodding, the judge asked Sarge to proceed.

The prosecutor leaned against counsel table. "Given the evidence you gathered that night and your medical training, what was the cause of Kuyeya's injuries?"

Dr. Chulu looked at the judge. "There is no doubt in my mind that the girl was raped. The blood, the semen, the surface injuries are consistent with nothing else."

When Sarge sat down, Benson Luchembe rose to his feet. "Dr. Chulu, your experience in these matters is impressive, but there is a gap in your testimony. Beyond saying that the girl was defiled, can you say anything about who might have committed this terrible crime?"

The physician raised an eyebrow. "The biological evidence I took from the victim could have been analyzed for DNA, but it was stolen before we were able to compare it with a sample of the defendant's blood."

Luchembe held out his hands reasonably. "There

are 1.7 million people in Lusaka. Why would you think my client would be a match?"

"Perhaps because a number of eyewitnesses placed him at the scene of the crime."

"The scene of the crime? You mean someone saw my client defile the victim?"

"No," Dr. Chulu admitted. "I'm not aware of anyone who saw the defilement itself."

"Precisely. And this is the problem, is it not? No one knows who *actually* defiled the child? All you can say is that the child *was*, in fact, defiled, am I right?"

Backed into a corner, the doctor barely contained his rage. "In the past ten years I have handled at least five thousand cases of child sexual assault. Every time I testify, you lawyers say the same thing. DNA was supposed to change that. Conveniently for your client, the evidence vanished. At this point, the best I can say is that *some* man raped Kuyeya."

Luchembe took his seat, looking supremely satisfied, and the judge dismissed Dr. Chulu from the stand. On his way out of the courtroom, the doctor mouthed a silent apology to Zoe. She mustered a reassuring smile that patently belied her feelings. He had done his best to pin the rape on Darious, but it hadn't made a bit of difference.

The trial resumed after a brief recess, and Sarge called Joseph to the stand. They quickly dispensed with the basics—Doris's police report, finding Given, collecting the doll and glasses from the alleyway and returning them to Kuyeya—and then moved into the heart of the prosecution's case against Darious.

"When did you decide to focus your attention on the accused?" Sarge asked.

In crisp, straightforward language, Joseph described his discovery of the Lusaka Golf Club crest, Zoe's encounter with the silver Mercedes at the Intercontinental Hotel, and their pursuit of Darious to his home in Kabulonga. He got into a tussle with Luchembe over the relevance of Darious's visits to Alpha Bar and his affinity for prostitutes, but Mubita allowed the testimony on Sarge's certification that its relevance would soon become apparent.

"When you were observing the accused at Alpha, did you notice anything peculiar about him?" Sarge asked, honing in on a critical link in the case.

Joseph nodded. "He was very thin. He only drank two beers, but he used the bathroom four times. He also had markings on his face and his neck consistent with Kaposi's sarcoma."

"Objection!" Luchembe cried. "The officer is not a physician."

The judge narrowed his eyes. "Officer Kabuta, please confine yourself to observations, and leave the opinions to experts."

"Did your *observations* have any significance to you?" Sarge asked.

Joseph took a deep breath. "The accused looked sick. My sister had the same symptoms before she died."

Sarge softened his voice. "How did your sister die?"

"She had AIDS," Joseph said simply.

Luchembe exploded to his feet. "Your Worship, this testimony is *scurrilous*. I will not permit the prosecution to impugn my client's reputation with this horrid speculation."

Mubita regarded Joseph with a mixture of annoyance and sympathy. "I'm very sorry about your sister, but I'm going to disregard your surmise about the accused's health. I meant what I said about confining yourself to observations."

Joseph stared at the judge for a long moment, his eyes clouded with mistrust. Then he turned back to Sarge, who redirected the conversation.

"You were the officer who made the arrest?" asked the prosecutor.

"I led the arresting party, but there were three other officers with me."

"You did so without a warrant?"

"The statute doesn't require a warrant. But I'm very careful. I never make an arrest until I have evidence that will hold up in court. In this case, I took pictures of the accused and his SUV and showed them to Given and Dominic. They told me what they told you today."

"When you made the arrest, did the accused say anything to you?"

Joseph nodded. "He laughed at us."

Sarge raised his eyebrows. "He *laughed* at you?"

"He said our guns were so old they would probably explode in our hands."

"Did he resist arrest?"

Joseph shook his head. "He came to the station and answered my questions. He claimed to have an alibi for the night in question."

"I have nothing further for this witness," Sarge said.

Benson Luchembe stood and began to pace at the edge of the bar. For a moment, Zoe worried that he had something on Joseph, some devastating secret that would discredit the entire investigation. But her concern was dispelled when Luchembe began to speak. His cross-examination was an exercise in sniping. Like a song stuck in an endless loop, he repeated variations on the refrain "you have no way of being certain" so many times that Zoe began to fidget. Joseph, however, parried each thrust, using his answers to reiterate his prior testimony. By the time Luchembe realized his miscalculation, it was too late: Mubita had heard Joseph make the same points twice.

When Luchembe relinquished the floor, the judge checked his watch wearily. "It's nearly seventeen hundred hours. Sarge, how many more witnesses do you have today?"

"Just one, Your Worship."

Mubita took a breath. "In that case, we will take an hour recess for dinner." He rose from his seat and lumbered down the steps, preceding Timothy into chambers.

Joseph sat down beside Zoe. "How'd I do?"

She smiled encouragingly. "He didn't touch you."

He grazed her knee with his fingers. "An hour gives you more time to prepare Doris."

She nodded. "I have a feeling she's going to need it."

"Pass along a tip for me. Tell her to imagine Luchembe as a baboon."

Zoe began to giggle. "Is that what you did?"

Joseph grinned wryly. "The surest way to defeat an interrogator is to mock him."

When the trial resumed, Sarge called Doris to the stand. Zoe walked swiftly to the exit, ignoring

Frederick Nyambo's stare, and texted Maurice. Seconds later, the driver walked down the lamp-lit arcade with Doris. Dressed in an elegant *chitenge* dress, she could have passed for a politician's wife. Her face, however, was haggard and lined with apprehension.

All eyes focused on them when they strolled into the courtroom. Darious, who had been slouching in the dock, sat up straighter and needled Doris with his eyes. *The leopard is afraid of the genet because the genet also sees in the dark*, Zoe thought, handing Doris off to Sarge.

"Please tell the Court your name," he began after she sat in the witness stand.

Doris clasped her hands in her lap and spoke in a clear voice. "I was born Priscilla Kuwema, but people like Darious call me 'Doris.'"

Sarge affected surprise. "You are familiar with the accused?"

"He was once a client," she replied, giving the judge a nervous look. "I am a *mahule*. I do not like what I do, but I am poor and the men who gave me daughters refused to marry me."

Whispers broke out among the defense team, but the judge silenced them with a glare.

"When did you first meet the accused?" Sarge asked.

"Years ago. He was not my client at first; he was a client of a woman who stayed with me. Her name was Charity, but the men called her Bella. Kuyeya is Charity's daughter."

"Objection," said Benson Luchembe. "This case is not about the child's mother."

"Your Worship," Sarge replied, a trace of irritation in his voice, "this case has *everything* to do with the child's mother."

The judge frowned at Sarge. "My tolerance has limits. Make the connection soon."

Sarge regarded Doris. "Please tell the Court about Bella's relationship with the accused."

Doris closed her eyes and began to speak. She told Mubita about meeting Charity on the street; about her relationship with Darious and the abrupt manner in which it ended; about the name she called him—*Siluwe*, the leopard; and about her sickness and premature death.

"Did Bella keep any record of her relationship with the accused?"

Doris nodded. "She wrote in a journal. It was her most prized possession."

Sarge handed her the third volume of Bella's journal. "Is this the journal?"

"Yes," Doris said. "I kept it after she died."

Luchembe stood. "Your Worship, I haven't had a chance to review the journal, but I'm sure it is full of hearsay."

The judge gave Sarge a skeptical look. "Are you offering the book into evidence?"

"I am," replied the prosecutor. "There is no reason to doubt the truthfulness of statements Bella made in her private diary."

"Even if counsel is right," Luchembe rejoined, "they are irrelevant to the case."

Mubita confronted Sarge. "My patience with this line of inquiry is wearing thin. What does the journal have to do with the defilement?"

Sarge bristled. "It helps to establish the motive of the accused. We have evidence that this was not a random crime, that Darious knew Kuyeya and raped her for very clear reasons."

Luchembe responded quickly. "Your Worship, defilement is a strict liability crime. Motive is irrelevant."

The judge glared at Sarge. "I will not allow hearsay to undermine this trial; nor will I permit speculation about matters that do not concern the Court." He paused. "*However*, on your certification, I'm going to take the objection under advisement and decide later."

In the gallery, Zoe glanced at Joseph, her eyes forming an unspoken question. Mubita's behavior on the bench made no sense. One moment, he lectured Sarge; the next moment, he gave him a gift. *What are you up to?* she thought, searching Mubita's face and seeing nothing.

"Did you see the accused again after Bella died?" Sarge inquired.

"A few times," Doris replied without elaboration.

"When was the last time?"

Doris cast a wary look at Darious. "A few weeks before Kuyeya was attacked. He was sitting in a truck not far from my flat."

Sarge glanced at the judge. "Did he see you?"

"It is possible."

"Had he been to your flat before?"

"Many times."

"Was Kuyeya there when he came to visit?"

"Always."

Sarge paused. "What happened on the night of the defilement?"

In clipped, wary sentences, Doris told the judge what she had disclosed to Zoe in their first meeting. This time, however, she didn't hide the fact that she had left Kuyeya with Bright and Gift and gone to the market with a client.

"Do you know how Kuyeya escaped the flat?" Sarge asked.

Doris nodded. "My daughters left the door open." She looked down at her hands, sorrow etched on her face. "I should have taken better care of her. Lusaka is a dangerous place for girls like her. I should have made sure she was safe."

As soon as Sarge sat down, Benson Luchembe went on the attack. Doris, however, seemed invulnerable to the onslaught. He accused her of being a criminal, and she replied that if she had committed crimes, so had the police officers, politicians, and lawyers who paid her for sex. He then made the mistake of turning a question about Bella into an argument about the irrelevance of her relationship with Darious. Sarge quickly objected, and the judge sustained it with a frown. After a few more questions—all of which Doris met with an unflappable calm—Luchembe abandoned his inquisition and took his seat again.

When Sarge declined to redirect, Mubita allowed himself a rare smile. "We will begin again at eight thirty tomorrow. Until then, this Court is in recess."

Watching the judge walk wearily down the steps, Zoe realized the depth of her own exhaustion. Dizzy from sleeplessness and stress, she was tempted to rest her head on Joseph's shoulder. She waited until the deputy removed Darious from the dock and Luchembe departed with his entourage before joining Sarge and Niza in congratulating Doris.

Doris appeared overwhelmed by the attention. "Can I go home now?" she asked Zoe.

Zoe nodded and led her toward the exit. "I

know that wasn't pleasant," she said, "but you were wonderful."

Doris gave the faintest trace of a laugh. "I did what you told me. I pictured that lawyer as a baboon. After that, it didn't matter what he said."

When they reached the arcade, Doris put a hand on her arm. "I have something for Kuyeya." She rummaged in her bag and took out a ring studded with small emeralds. "It was Bella's. She used to put it on Kuyeya's finger before we went out at night."

Zoe's heart clutched when she saw the way the emeralds gleamed in the lamplight. She took the ring, appreciating its immense significance.

"I'll give it to her tomorrow," she said.

Chapter 28

The next morning, Joseph and Zoe drove into Kanyama to fetch Amos, the *nganga*. The rising sun gilded the edges of the compound with molten light, but the spiderweb of lanes remained in shadow. Joseph turned left at the sign bearing Amos's name and navigated toward the house with the red door. The lane was a hive of activity— pedestrians walking, children playing, old men lounging, women hanging clothes on the line— but the house with the red door was quiet.

"Wasn't he supposed to be ready?" Zoe asked as Joseph parked beside Amos's car.

"I texted Bob Wangwe yesterday," Joseph said, grabbing his rifle from the back seat.

Zoe followed him to the porch. He knocked on the door and called out the *nganga*'s name. When they heard no movement, he grabbed the doorknob. The door popped open.

"*Amos!*" Joseph cried, barging into the hopelessly cluttered living room. Close on his heels, Zoe nearly doubled over in disgust. The place smelled like a charnel house.

"*Amos!*" he called again, aiming his rifle into the dimly lit kitchen.

When no one appeared, they moved toward the back of the house, taking care to avoid the tables littered with herbs and animal parts. The stink became so overpowering that Zoe held her nose. Joseph aimed his gun into the bedroom, and Zoe peered into the gloom of the consultation room. She clutched Joseph's arm. On the floor were two misshapen heaps.

One was the charred carcass of a bird.

The other was Amos.

Joseph went to the window and threw open the curtains.

"Dear God," Zoe gasped, staring at the deep cut in the *nganga*'s neck.

Joseph knelt down to examine the corpse. He manipulated one of the *nganga*'s fingers. "He's been dead a few hours. It must have happened overnight."

"What does the bird mean?" she asked softly, dread churning in her gut.

He looked at the carcass in distaste. "It's a spell of protection."

She walked with him into the living room. "At least we have the recorded confession."

Joseph looked dubious. He punched in a number on his phone. At the sound of the message he clenched his teeth. "Mr. Wangwe, this is Officer Kabuta. Your client was murdered last night. I don't know where you are, but you need to meet us at the Subordinate Court right away to vouch for the recordings. If you don't appear, we'll ask the judge for a contempt order."

Joseph slid the phone into his jeans, his face fraught with tension.

"He's gone, isn't he?" Zoe asked.

Joseph nodded. "He must have found out."

"You and I can authenticate the recordings," she said hopefully.

"We can try," he replied. "But I'm not sure it'll be good enough for the judge."

The trial reconvened precisely on schedule. After taking his seat on the bench, Flexon Mubita summoned Darious to the dock. "Call your next witness," he said to Sarge.

"Your Worship," the prosecutor replied, barely suppressing his anger, "we just learned that the witness we had scheduled to testify this morning—a critical witness in our case—was murdered last night. Officer Kabuta found him in his home."

Mubita's jaw went slack and he stared at Sarge transfixed. The fear that haunted his eyes appeared genuine. "Do you have any evidence linking this murder to the accused?"

Sarge shook his head. "We do not."

Mubita took off his glasses and massaged the bridge of his nose. "In all my years on the bench,

I've never seen anything like this. Do you want an adjournment? I'll give you one."

Sarge shook his head. "No, Your Worship. Officer Kabuta recorded the witness's testimony months ago. We wish to offer the recordings into evidence."

Mubita raised his eyebrows in surprise.

"Your Worship," said Benson Luchembe, leaping to his feet, "the violence we have seen in the past two days is reprehensible. But counsel's proposition has grave implications for my client's defense. If the witness doesn't appear, how can I cross-examine him? The accused would be sorely prejudiced by the admission of an unverified recording. And it is my client's freedom, not the prosecution's, that is at stake in this proceeding."

The judge glared at Luchembe, but he offered no rebuke. Instead, he asked Sarge, "How do you propose to verify the recordings?"

"Four people were present when they were made," Sarge replied. "The deceased, his attorney, Bob Wangwe, Officer Kabuta, and Ms. Fleming. Mr. Wangwe had agreed to appear at this hearing, but it seems he's disappeared."

"Disappeared?" Mubita said, narrowing his eyes.

"We haven't been able to reach him. The best I can do is offer the testimony of Officer Kabuta and Ms. Fleming. Both of their voices are on the tape."

The judge cleared his throat. "If the officer certifies the authenticity of the recordings, I'll accept them under advisement. I need to look at the law on this."

Sarge sighed visibly. "Very well. I call Joseph Kabuta to the stand."

In the end, the judge allowed the recordings to be aired in open court. Sarge placed the recording device on counsel table, turned up the volume, and pressed play. The static echoed in the vaulted space, then Joseph made his introductions. When he identified the witness by name—Dr. Mwenya Amos—Darious motioned hastily to Luchembe, and Zoe caught the worry in his eyes. *You didn't know?* she thought, fascinated. *That means your parents are calling all the shots.*

Luchembe seemed off balance, but he righted himself quickly. "I was not aware the witness was a physician," he objected, as Sarge paused the recording. "I'm concerned that this testimony invades the doctor-patient privilege."

"Your Worship," Sarge interjected, "the privilege is subject to judicial discretion. If the testimony relates to irrelevant matters, you can disregard it. But I repectfully request that you permit the recording to be played in its entirety. It is critical to our case."

The judge furrowed his brow wearily. "Go ahead."

Luchembe settled into his chair and didn't speak again. Darious, however, grew increasingly agitated as Amos recounted his concern about AIDS, the course of his treatment, the fears he harbored about his father, and his hatred of the unnamed *mahule* who had bewitched his family with "strife and pain" and left him with a deadly disease.

In the midst of the testimony, Zoe glanced at Frederick in the back row. He looked irritated but unconcerned. She tuned in to the recording again as Amos described Darious's last visit, only a month before the rape—his obsession with the curse of the *mahule*, his fixation on virgin cleansing, and his uncompromising resolve to "bewitch the witch."

"Those were his exact words?" Joseph asked, his voice echoing in the courtroom.

"It is not the sort of thing a person forgets," Amos replied.

When the judge asked Sarge to call his next witness, the prosecutor nodded at Zoe. *Here we go*, she thought, standing up and walking toward the exit. Over her shoulder, she heard him say: "I call Kuyeya Mizinga to the stand."

At this declaration, war broke out between the attorneys over Kuyeya's capacity to testify. Luchembe cried foul, citing Dr. Mbao's initial evaluation, and Sarge defended on the basis of her more recent conclusions. He offered the Court an affidavit from the psychiatrist stating that Kuyeya could answer simple questions. Luchembe demanded a chance to cross-examine the psychiatrist, and Sarge countered, arguing that the affidavit was sufficient.

Zoe left the courtroom and met Sister Irina on the courthouse steps. The St. Francis van was idling at the curb, Sister Anica behind the wheel.

"How is she?" Zoe inquired, looking at Kuyeya through the window.

"She wet the bed last night," Sister Irina said. "And this morning she was disoriented. But she is happy now. She is listening to your music."

"We need to get another opinion about her health. I'll talk to Joy Herald about scheduling an appointment at a private clinic. Do you have the doll?"

The nun lifted the bag she was carrying. "I also brought a wheelchair. I'm concerned about her falling again."

"Good idea," Zoe responded, opening the van door. She greeted Kuyeya and helped her out of the seat, taking care not to tangle her headphones. As soon as the girl was situated in the wheelchair, Zoe pushed her up the ramp and down the arcade to the courtroom.

A hush fell upon the gallery when they entered. From the satisfied look on Sarge's face, Zoe knew that Dr. Mbao's affidavit had opened the door to Kuyeya's testimony. Zoe maneuvered the wheelchair to a spot beside the witness stand and gently removed the headphones. She took off the girl's glasses, too, handing everything to Sarge. It was a move they had prearranged. They didn't want Kuyeya to see Darious too soon.

"Your Worship," Sarge said, "for the child's comfort, I ask that you permit her principal caretaker, Sister Irina, to sit beside her."

"I will allow that," said the judge. "Come forward, Sister."

After the nun took her seat, Sarge moved his chair close to the stand. "Hello there," he said to Kuyeya. "You're wearing a pretty dress today. Can you tell me your name?"

The girl rocked a bit and then said, "Kuyeya."

Zoe let out the breath she was holding. In the past month, she and Sarge had visited Kuyeya three times to prepare her for trial. The girl had been distant at first, unwilling to look at Sarge or answer his questions. Over time, and with urging from Dr. Mbao, she had opened up to him. But a courtroom full of strangers was a world away from the garden at St. Francis. Zoe had feared she would freeze.

"That's a nice name," Sarge said softly. "What is your mommy's name?"

Kuyeya brightened. "Mommy is Charity."

Sarge nodded. "Did your mommy tell you stories?"

"Mommy tells stories," she said. "The bee-eater and hippo are friends."

Sarge smiled. "Was there a river in your mommy's stories?"

Kuyeya clutched her monkey and didn't answer.

He tried a leading approach. "Is it the Yangtze?"

The girl thought about this. After a moment, she shook her head.

"Is it the Zambezi?"

Kuyeya's eyes caught the light. "The bee-eater and hippo live on the Zambezi."

Sarge faced the judge. "Your Worship, I submit that the child is capable of answering simple questions. I have only a few that I wish to ask."

Benson Luchembe stood. "For the record I must object. Does the prosecution plan to put all of the answers in the child's mouth?"

The judge looked at Sarge. "You may only lead the witness to establish a foundation. Beyond that, you have to abide by the rules of evidence."

Sarge nodded and focused again on Kuyeya. "Your mommy taught you stories. I bet she taught you a lot of things. Did your mommy teach you about men?"

Kuyeya's eyes crossed, then resolved. "I don't like men."

"Why don't you like men?" Sarge asked, keeping his voice gentle.

Kuyeya began to rock again. "Men are bad."

Zoe leaned forward. This is as far as the girl had ever been willing to go in talking about the rape. *You can do it. Tell the judge what he did to you.*

"Why are men bad?" Sarge asked.

Kuyeya's rocking increased and she let out a groan.

Sarge persisted: "Did your mommy tell you that men might touch you?"

Suddenly, the girl found her voice: "Men not supposed to touch. Mommy can touch, but men not supposed to touch."

"Kuyeya," Sarge went on, using a soothing tone, "did a man touch you where only your mommy was supposed to touch?"

Kuyeya's groaning took on greater urgency and Zoe grimaced. She had heard the sound before—in the examination room on the night of the rape.

"Do you have the doll?" Sarge asked Sister Irina.

It was then that Zoe remembered something. She couldn't believe she had forgotten. She launched to her feet and said, "*Wait!*"

All eyes in the courtroom focused on her. Sarge frowned. The judge squinted at her. A couple of Luchembe's underlings began to whisper.

"Your Worship," Zoe said, breaching every protocol in the book, "I request a brief recess to confer with counsel."

Mubita's squint deepened into a scowl. "Ms. Fleming, must I remind you that you are not a member of the Zambian bar? I do not appreciate interruptions."

Heart racing, Zoe adopted her most unctuous tone. "I understand, Your Worship, but it's very important that I have a word with Mr. Zulu before he proceeds. Five minutes is all I ask."

Mubita stared at her for a long moment, then shrugged. "I'll give you grace this one time. Five minutes then." He departed the courtroom in a flurry of robes.

Zoe ignored the sniggering of Luchembe's legal team and wheeled Kuyeya out to the arcade. Sister

Irina, Joseph, and the two CILA lawyers followed in her wake. They regrouped in a quiet spot beside a patch of grass.

"That was quite a stunt you pulled," Niza said.

Zoe nodded, feeling the weight of her gamble. "Hear me out. If you give her the doll, she'll get upset and say what we expect: 'The man is bad. Baby is not bad.' It's dramatic and worth some sympathy, but it won't point the finger at Darious."

Zoe reached into her pocket and took out the emerald ring. "Doris gave this to me last night. It was Charity's. I want to give it to Kuyeya now, and then I want you to put her glasses on and let her confront Darious. I have no idea what she'll do, but it may be our only chance to get useful testimony out of her."

Sarge looked skeptical. "Let's see how she responds to the ring."

Zoe knelt down in front of the wheelchair and brought her face close to Kuyeya's. "I have a present from your mommy," she said, holding up the ring. "It's pretty, isn't it?"

Kuyeya's reaction surpassed all of Zoe's hopes. Her mouth stretched into a wide smile and laughter bubbled out of her. She cupped the ring in her hands as if it were a living thing.

"Mommy loves me," she said between chuckles. "Mommy will be home soon." Her voice trailed off, but she whispered the last two words over and over again like a prayer. "Home soon . . . Home soon . . . Home soon."

Zoe pictured Charity speaking the promise to her daughter as she prepared for another night in the embrace of strangers. She saw Kuyeya rehearsing it as she fell asleep in the room she had scored with her fingernails. She imagined Charity's thoughts as she followed Doris out the door: *Everything I do, I do for you.*

Zoe touched Kuyeya's face. "Yes, your mommy loves you. She loves you very much." She looked at Sarge and saw the light of understanding in his eyes.

"Let's introduce her to Darious," he said.

"Your Worship," Sarge began, when everyone had reassembled in the courtroom, "I have only a few more questions for the child. But for the inquiry to be meaningful, she must be able to see the accused clearly. I ask that you order him to stand before her."

Benson Luchembe stood so quickly he nearly knocked over his chair. "I object! My client is not a . . ." He searched for the right word. ". . . *marionette*. And this trial is not cheap theater."

"I don't like it," Mubita snapped at Sarge. "I indulged Ms. Fleming's unprecedented motion, and now you ask me to modify the dimensions of this chamber." He scribbled a few notes on his pad. "However, if the child can't see . . ." He waved toward the courtroom deputy and barked, "Escort the accused to a spot beside counsel table."

Zoe held her breath as Darious walked across the floor and stood before the witness stand. Sarge slid Kuyeya's glasses into place and stepped aside. The girl blinked once, then twice, startled by a world suddenly in focus. *What if she doesn't react at all?* Zoe thought. *What if she doesn't remember his face?*

"Kuyeya," Sarge said softly, "your mommy's ring is pretty, isn't it?"

The girl nodded.

"Remember what Mommy said?" he went on.

"Men are not supposed to touch." He gestured at Darious. "Did this man touch you where only Mommy was supposed to touch?"

Kuyeya cast a glance at Darious and looked away. For excruciating seconds nothing happened. No one in the courtroom moved. No one dared to speak. The silence was complete.

Then Kuyeya looked at Darious a second time. Slowly, she started to rock. Then she began to groan. Finally, the dam broke and words poured out of her in a torrent.

"Giftie is gone, Auntie is gone," she said, staring at the floor. "The door is open. The street is noisy. The boy is running. The car is loud. The man has sweets." The cadence of her rocking increased. "Men not supposed to touch. Not supposed to touch."

Zoe sat riveted, knowing how close they were to a breakthrough. Yet the last push was also the most delicate. If Sarge missed the mark, even slightly, he could lose her.

"Kuyeya," Sarge said with consummate gentleness, like he was trying to wake her from sleep, "Did this man touch you? Did he hurt you?"

The girl faced Darious and her groaning ceased. Her mouth moved but no sound came out. Zoe studied her lips and gripped Joseph's hand. *Come on, Kuyeya, say it! Say the words!*

Suddenly, the girl blurted out, "He touched me. He wasn't supposed to touch. He touched me. He wasn't supposed to touch." She repeated the accusation a third time, as if to seal the truth of her words.

Her testimony transformed the courtroom. Instantly, Darious lost his smugness; Benson Luchembe slumped in his seat; his team sat motionless; Sarge beamed; Niza's eyes shimmered with tears—something Zoe had never seen before; Sister Irina looked astonished; Timothy, the law clerk, stopped his scribbling. Zoe caught the harsh light in Frederick's eyes, the absolute determination. She faced the judge and her joy turned sour. He sat on the bench like a potted plant, looking unimpressed. *Don't you dare take this away from her*, she thought, struggling to contain her indignation.

At once Mubita waved toward Darious. "I've heard enough. Get back in the dock. Sarge, I assume you have no further questions."

"I'm finished, Your Worship," Sarge said.

The judge looked at Luchembe. "Do you wish to cross-examine?"

The defense attorney shook his head.

Mubita sat back in his chair. "By my count the next witness is your last."

"That's correct," Sarge replied.

"Get to it then."

Sarge pushed Kuyeya to the bar and Zoe took over from there, wheeling her out of the courtroom. The girl's hands were folded tightly in her lap, and she was whispering something about her mother. When they reached the arcade, Zoe prised the ring from the girl's grasp and slipped it on her middle finger—the only finger large enough to fit it.

"You did so well," she said, kissing Kuyeya's head. "I'm very proud of you." She looked at Sister Irina. "Take her home. The music and the garden will soothe her."

"I hope so," Sister Irina replied quietly.

Zoe saw Jan Kruger watching her from a bench nearby. Her first thought was unkind: *You kept your distance*. Her second was more charitable: *At least you're here.*

"Dr. Kruger," she said, walking toward him.

He stood up. "Call me Jan. The formalities seem a touch out of place."

"Do you have the paperwork?"

"It's all here." He held up a leather satchel.

They entered the courtroom together, and Zoe escorted him to the bar. Then she turned around and stared at Frederick. The elder Nyambo looked stunned.

"Your Worship," Sarge said, "Dr. Jan Kruger is my final witness."

After the judge swore him in, Sarge ran through the doctor's credentials. Jan answered confidently, yet cautiously, his diction exacting.

"You are a university professor and a medical doctor?"

"I teach epidemiology, yes. And I do clinical work in the townships."

"I'd like to focus on your activities in 1996. What were you doing in March and April of that year?"

"I was wrapping up a study at the Livingstone General Hospital. We were seeking to identify discernible links between HIV infection and the incidence of common childhood illnesses—pneumonia, malaria, TB, and diarrhea."

"Did you do any teaching alongside the research?"

Jan nodded. "I taught a practicum course at the nursing school."

"Was there a nursing student with whom you worked closely during that period?"

"There was. Her name was Charity Mizinga."

Sarge glanced at the judge to make sure he was paying attention. "How close were the two of you?" he asked.

Jan took a moment to answer. "We were intimate."

Whispers broke out in the gallery and the judge's temper flared. "Quiet in the courtroom!" He turned his frown toward Jan Kruger. "Go on."

"When you say intimate," Sarge continued, "what do you mean?"

With the precision of a clinician, Jan summarized his affair with Charity—their rapport as doctor and nurse, their brief romance, and the way he broke her heart.

"When did you last see her?" Sarge asked.

"In April of 1996. Before she moved to Lusaka."

"At that time, did she have a child?"

Jan shook his head. "She did not."

"You say she moved to Lusaka. Do you know why she did that?"

"I'm afraid I suggested it."

Zoe glanced at Darious and saw his confusion. *This is part of the story you've never heard before.*

"Why did you suggest it?" Sarge inquired.

"Because Frederick Nyambo had offered her a job and promised to take care of her."

Shock registered on the judge's face. "Explain yourself," he demanded, ignoring Sarge who was on the verge of asking another question.

Jan faced Mubita, a look of resignation in his eyes. "Frederick was a patient of mine," he said, and then proceeded to tell the judge the rest of the story.

When he finished speaking, Sarge asked, "Do you know what happened to Charity after she left Livingstone?"

"I do. Frederick hired her as his personal assistant and had an affair with her."

"Your Worship!" Luchembe objected loudly. "Frederick Nyambo is not on trial here!"

"That's quite right," Mubita agreed. "I may not admit any of this testimony. But Dr. Kruger has come all the way from South Africa. I want to hear what he has to say."

"Have you seen this before?" Sarge went on, holding up a spiral-bound notebook.

The first volume of the journal, Zoe thought. *The courtroom is about to explode.*

"I have," said Jan. "I've read every word of it."

Sarge handed him the journal. "What is it?"

"It's Charity's diary from her first year in Lusaka."

Zoe heard footsteps in the aisle. She turned around and saw Frederick striding toward the bar, his eyes full of loathing. "Your Worship," he said forcefully, "the document is a forgery. You *must* inquire how the prosecution obtained it."

Luchembe stood up. "I request a recess to confer with my client."

Mubita ignored the defense lawyer and focused on Frederick. "Mr. Nyambo," he said in an even tone. "I appreciate your concern, but this disruption is inappropriate. Please sit down."

For a long moment, Frederick locked eyes with the judge. Then he nodded and returned to his seat. Zoe's heart began to race. *Did they just communicate something?* She turned around and stared at Frederick. He met her eyes, his face a mask.

"Please proceed," said the judge.

Sarge directed Jan's attention to the notebook in his hands. "I've marked a passage in the diary. Would you read it out loud?"

Zoe watched as Jan found the prescribed page. His fingers shook as he opened the volume. She closed her eyes and listened to him read the letter that explained so much.

Dear Jan,

A few weeks ago I gave birth to a baby. I named her Kuyeya, which is Tonga for memory. My grandmother said that memory is the only power man has over death. When I was pregnant, I was afraid the baby would be Field's. Frederick thinks the baby is his. I did not think so because the birth came too soon. Then she was born and I saw her face. Her skin is lighter than mine. I am certain she is your child.

This gives me joy and fear. What will happen if Frederick finds out? I am afraid he will take away my job. I am afraid he will hurt me. I think sometimes I will go back to nursing school. But I cannot return to Livingstone. I would die of disgrace.

Kuyeya has not been well. Frederick's nganga *said there is a hex on her. I don't believe it. She is beautiful. I wish you could see her. I wish she could know you. I should stop thinking that way. It is foolish, just as I was foolish to think you would marry me. Kuyeya and I are together. We will survive.*

Zoe opened her eyes and watched as the revelation settled on Mubita's shoulders.

"Sarge," the judge said, "I'd like to ask the doctor a few questions." He fixed his eyes on Jan. "Who is Field?"

"Charity's uncle. I believe he had been raping her."

Mubita shook his head reproachfully. "Do you admit the child is yours?"

Jan shifted in his chair. "I can't deny it. I've seen the proof."

"You have proof of paternity?" the judge demanded, taken aback.

Jan nodded wearily. "Her DNA is mine."

At that moment, Sarge stood up, holding a sheaf of papers. "Your Worship, the test was conducted in Johannesburg. I have the report here, together with an affidavit from Officer Kabuta, who transported the blood sample to the lab, and an affidavit from Dr. Chulu certifying the accuracy of the report. The probability that Dr. Kruger is Kuyeya's father is 99.99 percent."

"I object!" Luchembe cried, lurching to his feet. "The defense knew nothing of this."

The judge cleared his throat. "Neither did the Court." He took the paperwork from Sarge. "Everything appears to be in order. Do you have any further questions for this witness?"

"Two more," said Sarge. "Dr. Kruger, since Kuyeya is your child, what is her age?"

Jan gave a straightforward answer. "If she was conceived in March or April of 1996, she was born in January or February of 1997. That means she is fifteen years old."

Sarge nodded, barely suppressing a grin. "Finally, do you know what happened to Charity Mizinga after she wrote the letter you read to the Court?"

Jan looked grave. "I can't say with certainty. But I know she ended up on the street, working as a prostitute. She died not long ago. From what I understand, she had AIDS."

"That's all I have," Sarge said, returning to his seat.

Luchembe's cross-examination was brief and formalistic. He forced Jan to concede that he knew nothing of Kuyeya's defilement and—again—that he had no idea what happened to Charity after she realized the paternity of her daughter. But the damage had been done. Jan had shored up Amos's recorded testimony and established Kuyeya's age beyond doubt.

When Luchembe sat down again, Sarge spoke: "Your Worship, the prosecution rests."

"In that case," said the judge, "we will take an early recess for lunch and begin again at half past twelve with the defense witnesses."

Zoe met Jan at the bar and walked with him to the arcade. He looked spent from the ordeal, but he carried himself with dignity.

"Thank you," she said, offering him a smile.

He shrugged. "I said what I came to say."

She watched Frederick Nyambo stroll toward the lobby, talking on his mobile phone. "Are you leaving today?" she asked.

"This afternoon," he said, looking away.

"Have you thought about her future?"

"Yes," he replied guardedly. "I don't see how it makes sense for me to be a part of it."

Zoe bristled. "You're her father. How can you say that?"

"Fatherhood requires a relationship. My only connection to her is genetic." He backtracked, as if realizing how selfish he sounded. "Look, I don't mean to deny my responsibility. I'd like to help with her care. It's just that . . ."

"You don't want to deal with the messiness of her life," Zoe said.

He inhaled sharply. "I wouldn't put it that way."

"How *would* you put it?"

"Look, I knew Charity fifteen years ago. Kuyeya

has never met me before. I'm not what she needs. She needs someone to care for her. To her I'm just a *muzungu*."

Zoe shook her head. "I'm not talking about taking her home with you. I'm talking about being present in her world. Kids like her need two things: consistency and love. You can't give her consistency, but you sure as hell can give her love."

He flinched. "I'll think about it."

With that he turned and walked away.

The defense's case was blunt and unambiguous. Benson Luchembe kept his witnesses within the family, calling Frederick first and then Darious. Much more irritating—and suspicious—to Zoe was the abbreviated nature of their testimony. Leaving whole swaths of the prosecution's theory unchallenged, the Nyambos told a story about a dinner at the Intercontinental on the night of the rape, a dinner Frederick had proposed and Darious had accepted. Trading on the burden of proof, they offered Mubita nothing more than a technical basis for reasonable doubt.

Luchembe's approach gave the defense a tactical advantage. Since the rules of procedure limited the scope of cross-examination to the scope of direct examination, Sarge was unable to interrogate the Nyambos about Charity, about Darious's affection for prostitutes, or about Amos and HIV. In the two hours it took Luchembe to build Darious's alibi, Zoe sat stewing in the gallery, thinking of all the questions Sarge couldn't ask. One question, in particular, drove her mad: how had Darious discovered that Bella had been Frederick's mistress? Zoe thought she knew the answer—that Kuyeya's name had been the clue—but she had no way to be certain.

At three o'clock in the afternoon, Mubita dismissed Darious from the stand.

"The defense rests," Benson Luchembe intoned.

"Argument?" the judge asked.

"Yes, Your Worship," Sarge said, standing again. As he had done with his opening, his closing statement was a model of succinctness. He ticked off the requisites for defilement—the age of the victim, the fact of penetration, and the identity of the perpetrator—and spent the majority of the time connecting the dots of the past, emphasizing Darious's motive.

"Our burden is clear," he said, "and we are convinced that we have met it. Listen to the testimony of our witnesses, read the diary of Kuyeya's mother, remember the words Kuyeya herself spoke when confronted with the accused, and watch as Darious Nyambo takes shape before you. This was not a random crime. This was a premeditated act of wickedness. Kuyeya deserves justice. I trust that you will deliver it."

When Sarge sat down, Mubita regarded Luchembe over his glasses. "Benson?"

The defense lawyer stood and adjusted his tie. "Your Worship, the prosecution has spun a grand illusion for this Court—the illusion of Darious Nyambo, the monster. In *fact*, my client is a television producer in Lusaka and the son of esteemed parents. His father is a former cabinet minister. His mother is a High Court judge. We don't deny that the child was defiled. But by whom? Her caretaker—Doris—doesn't know what happened to her after she wandered out of the flat. It could have been anyone who picked her up—a neighbor, a friend, a stranger. And it was. It was anyone but the accused. Frederick Nyambo has corroborated his alibi."

Luchembe paused. "Crimes like this are a dark spot on Zambian society. But the horror we feel is no justification for putting an innocent man in prison. The prosecution has not met its burden. Justice demands an acquittal."

Once again, silence enveloped the courtroom.

"This is an important case," the judge said after a time. "I have much to consider. I will issue a written judgment after I complete my deliberations. Thank you all for your participation. I know it has been a trying experience. This Court is adjourned."

When Mubita retreated to chambers, Zoe spent a moment in reflective silence. Around her conversations broke out among the lawyers. Sarge shook hands with Benson Luchembe. The courtroom deputy escorted Darious out of the dock. Niza filled her briefcase with documents. Zoe stared at the empty bench, feeling a turbulent mixture of emotions. They had moved heaven and earth to put on a compelling case. But would any of it matter in the end?

"I need some air," she said, touching Joseph's hand.

She led him out of the courthouse into the bright sunshine of the parking lot. She took a deep breath, allowing her lungs to fill to capacity, and then exhaled slowly. "This is the part I hate—the waiting game."

Joseph gave her an empathetic look. "You have to let it go. It's out of your control."

"I know," she said but felt the tension just the same. She saw the gray Prado on the far side of the lot, Dunstan Sisilu behind the wheel. "Are we ever going to be able to do something about the asshole in sunglasses?"

Joseph shrugged. "Not without evidence."

She allowed her frustration to show. "I can't believe he's going to get away with all of this: two break-ins—three, actually, counting the one at the office—the theft of evidence, a murdered witness. At times like this I wish we didn't have to play by the rules."

Joseph glanced at her. "I feel that way almost every day."

She laughed drily. "Did I ever tell you what he said to me on the Zambezi?"

Joseph shook his head.

"He told me to be careful who I offend. What he didn't realize is that I couldn't care less."

As she watched, Joseph's frown turned into a smile. "Let's get out of here," he said.

PART FIVE

That which is good is never finished.
—*African proverb*

Darious

Lusaka, Zambia
August, 2011

The spirits of the ancestors had smiled on him. *Kuyeya had left Doris's flat alone and wandered down the street into a deserted alley. It was as if the stars had aligned to ensure his success. He closed the hatch over the girl and scanned the buildings around him. No one was watching from the windows. No one was paying attention on the street. The neighbors wouldn't remember anything.*

He climbed into the Mercedes and headed east on Chilimbulu Road, thinking back to the beginning of all of this. It was a school day and he had come home early, entering the house by the back door, as he always did. The sound of the argument had shocked him. He had never heard his mother yell at his father before. He had crept down the hall and seen them in the living room: Patricia holding the notebook aloft like a weapon; Frederick sitting silently on the couch. Years later, he could still hear his mother's allegation, still feel his father's shame. To fall for a girl with a mongrel child? Frederick's *mukwala was* legendary. How was it possible?

Darious had waited until the middle of the night to search for the notebook. He thought his mother might have thrown it away, but there it was, in her closet. He stole back to his bedroom and read for hours. The letters filled him with rage. The Frederick Nyambo described in the pages bore no resemblance to the man Darious had admired for sixteen years. According to the girl—Charity Mizinga— his father was a petulant cad obsessed with sex, a hapless fool who believed he had fathered her child when she had been sleeping with another man. It was the grossest kind of fiction. Yet a doubt persisted: what if some of it was true?

That night had changed Darious's life. Within a month he had purchased sex from a prostitute. Within a year he was soliciting twice a week. He had girls on the side. He loved to surprise them with his intellect, to lavish them with gifts. He never considered violence until one of his girls cheated on him. It was rage that drove him to rape her. But the act awakened something in him. Rape gave him power. Its mukwala was absolute.

Darious drove north to the Lusaka Golf Club, then east toward Kabulonga. Fortune was on his side. His father was on a business trip and his mother had gone to visit relatives. The house was empty except for Anna, and she lived in a cottage at the back of the property. The sedative would last an hour, then Kuyeya would wake up. He would wait. He wanted her to feel the pain. It didn't matter if she saw him. She didn't know who he was. He would drive her into Kanyama at midnight and dump her. If his luck held, she would disappear without a trace.

He waved to the night guard and pulled into the drive-way, parking in the garage. He shut off the engine and sat unmoving, surrounded by darkness and silence. He thought of Bella as she was on the night he first saw her— the red dress, the sultry moves she made on the dance floor. He hated her for her deception, for the madness she had evoked in his father, and the rift she had driven between his parents. He hated her for the disease she had given him, for the shame he never ceased to feel.

He left the SUV and walked quietly across the grounds, entering the house by the side door. Down the hall and across the living room he went, turning on no lights. His parents' bedroom was in the far wing, forbidden territory, at least officially. As a teenager, he had cased the bedroom in the night, watching his parents sleep. A few times he had been there when his mother had awakened to use the bathroom. He had stood utterly still, a shadow among shadows, and she had never seen him.

He found the notebook in the closet exactly where Patricia had left it years before. He opened it in the darkness. He didn't understand how Bella's medicine could have been stronger than his father's. But he didn't need to understand. He needed to harness it, to turn the curse back upon itself. Holding the notebook he felt invincible. With it he had exposed Bella's identity, connecting her child in life with the child in the letters, by way of her name.

He put the notebook back in its place and stifled the urge to cough. He walked back the way he came, steeling himself against the sickness that consumed so much of his energy now. He glanced at Anna's cottage beneath the stinkwood tree. A light was on in the window. Had she seen him? For the first time that night, he felt a tremor of doubt. He shook his head quickly, banishing the weakness.

Kuyeya. Memory. It was time to settle the score.

Chapter 29

Lusaka, Zambia
April, 2012

A week after the trial concluded, the *New Yorker* published Zoe's article under the title "The Future of Generosity." It had taken Zoe three extensive revisions to satisfy Naomi Potter, but in the end her persistence paid off. The piece was sharp, edgy and humane, and it quickly attracted the attention of readers, generating over two thousand shares on social-networking websites within forty-eight hours. By the third day, other outlets in the American media had picked up on it, as had Jack Fleming's campaign. Zoe received three emails in rapid succession. She read them at the office. The first was from Trevor.

Sis, I saw your article. It was brilliant, of course. I loved the stories about Mom, and I admire the way you talked about Dad. Ironically, you might have even won him some points with independents. But you should have told me about it in advance. Dad interpreted it as a challenge to his candidacy. I'd be prepared for a bumpy ride.

Zoe closed her eyes and confronted her instinctive guilt. *I wrote about him as charitably as I could. But the truth needed to be spoken. If he gets his way, real people will die.*

She braced herself and opened the second message. Her father had written:

Zoe, I don't know what to say. I was under the impression that I had instilled in you a basic sense of loyalty. Hold your views, express them freely, but don't take them public in the middle of a campaign without talking to me first. I've been getting calls nonstop. I have to make a statement.

* * *

Her father's words stole the wind from her lungs. She wasn't surprised by his feelings, but she hadn't anticipated how much they would affect her. She stood up abruptly and fled the office for the sanctuary of the bottlebrush tree. *Was I wrong? Did I make a mistake?* She thought of Kuyeya and the corruption-riddled African justice system; of Joseph and Charity and AIDS treatment among the poor; of the women and girls across Zambia whose rapists were exonerated because prosecutors lacked affordable access to DNA technology. She found a measure of solace in her indignation, but peace eluded her.

She wandered back to her desk and read the third email—a breathless missive from Naomi Potter.

Dashing off to a meeting, but I've started to hear from reporters. Everyone thinks the piece is a shot across your father's bow. I told them it isn't, but they didn't buy it. They want interviews. What do you want me to do?

Zoe typed a hasty reply: "*Please tell them the article is all I have to say.*"

Five minutes later, Naomi wrote her again:

Understand completely. I just heard from CNN. They want you on Piers Morgan. Be glad you're in Africa.

Zoe responded to her brother next:

Dear Trevor, I didn't tell you because I knew you would try to talk me out of it. I wanted to stay on the sidelines, but I found that I couldn't. The America Dad is talking about isn't the country I believe in. I love you dearly. I hope I haven't hurt our relationship.

Last, she replied to her father:

Dad, I'm sorry you didn't like the article. It breaks my heart that it's come to this. Sometimes I think if Mom were still alive everything would have turned out differently. As for a statement, say what you must. But remember that history will judge you not for the power you wield but for the way you wield it to improve the world. About that, at least, I'm sure we can agree.

She scanned the email again. She had borrowed the line about history from an op-ed her mother had written for the *New York Times* in the early 1990s, a piece Jack himself had quoted in speeches over the years. She knew he would recognize it.

When she hit "send," she shelved her misgivings and joined Niza and Joseph in discussing a new case. Her efforts at distraction lasted until the conversation ended; after that, they failed spectacularly. She slid into such a deep hole of introspection that by the end of the workday three people had asked if she was okay.

On the drive home, Joseph added his voice to the chorus: "Something happened," he said. "You haven't been yourself all afternoon."

She reacted with exasperation. "What *is* it with everyone? Am I leprous or something?"

He regarded her thoughtfully. "The article came out, didn't it?"

"I don't want to talk about it."

"Okay," he replied.

"Yes, it's the article," she conceded eventually. "The press is asking for interviews; my father is angry and he's going to make a public statement; even my brother is irritated with me."

"What are you going to do?"

Her eyes blazed. "I'm not going to talk to them."

"I don't mean the media."

"What am I *supposed* to do? I'm his daughter, for God's sake, but I hope he loses the election. What does that make me? Benedict Arnold? Judas?"

"No, it makes you honest."

"Sometimes honesty is a curse," she retorted, staring out the window at the Intercontinental Hotel and remembering her father's words: "*Talk to me like you did when you cared what I thought.*" She felt a tear break loose, then more followed; she couldn't hold them back. It seemed as if the wedge of the past had turned into a chasm between them. Yet the fault for their estrangement was no longer Jack's alone. The mess of pain and blame and misunderstanding was hers to share.

Joseph reached out and took her hand. "Whatever you do, I'm with you."

In the storm of her emotions, the touch of his

warm skin felt like an anchor. "Thank you," she said, realizing how much she meant it.

* * *

Over the next four days, Zoe amassed over a dozen emails from journalists. Some praised her courage; others questioned her motives; but everyone wanted something from her—more details about her work in Africa, a glimpse into the Fleming Randall financial empire, prognostication about the election, a family biopic, a photo shoot for a glamor magazine, the list was endless and diverse. More than anything, however, the press wanted a reaction to her father's statement, delivered in a televised press conference, which she had watched on the Internet.

The Senator's remarks had been brief and largely oblique, deflecting attention from her and highlighting his commitment to restore fiscal discipline to Washington. Near the end, however, he had dealt her argument a glancing blow, reiterating that the sacrifices necessary to stave off the long-term insolvency of the United States had to be shared by everyone, including recipients of foreign assistance in the developing world. It was this statement to which the media demanded a response, and the sheer repetition of the inquiry tempted Zoe to break her silence.

On Tuesday afternoon, she left her desk and called Naomi Potter in New York.

"Zoe!" the editor exclaimed. "The woman of the hour. Your piece has generated tremendous interest. We're thrilled. What can I do for you?"

"I think I might like to do an interview," Zoe said.

"Let me guess," Naomi replied. "The critics found your email address."

Zoe expelled a breath. "Yes."

"Welcome to the big leagues."

"So who can I trust? I want someone credible who isn't interested in shock or spin."

Naomi chuckled. "You're asking for a fossil. Not many of them left." She took a breath. "Look, you need to be realistic. If you go on television, you're going to hear the same questions you're getting in your inbox. You could do something in print."

Zoe hesitated. "I'd prefer live. It's more personal."

Naomi thought for a moment. "All right, I may have something for you. I got a call last week from Paul Hartman, Chairman of the Senate Foreign Relations Committee. Apparently, your article inspired him. He's sponsoring a hearing on foreign aid in the debt crisis, and he was hoping you'd join the panel. It could be a political stunt, since your father is on the committee. But I've known Paul for a long time. He sounded genuine."

Zoe conjured an image of herself testifying before the Senate. The media would be present; the TV cameras would record her every word. But the format would allow her to tell her story without interruption. There was little risk that she would lose control of the message.

"I'm interested," she said at last.

"Why don't you give Paul a call?" Naomi suggested. "See what he has to say."

She passed along the Senator's phone number, and Zoe dialed without delay. Waiting for the connection, she thought of Alice and the rabbit hole.

The Senator picked up on the third ring. "Paul Hartman."

"Senator Hartman," she began. "It's Zoe Fleming."

In the middle of May, Mariam called a meeting to discuss the status of Kuyeya's case.

"As you know," she said, "we're still waiting on a judgment from Flexon Mubita. The delay is very uncharacteristic of him. He's always been a decisive judge. He ruled on the DNA issue in a matter of days. He moved the trial date forward over Benson Luchembe's objections." She paused. "Unfortunately, it appears that our concerns about him may be true. Three days ago, Judge Ngwenya announced his retirement from the High Court. This morning, my husband obtained the short list of replacement candidates. Guess whose name is at the top?"

Zoe felt acid churning in her stomach.

"We've looked at this from every possible angle," Sarge said. "We can't do anything to take the case out of his hands. Our only option is to leak the story to the media. It may not change the outcome, but at least people will know the truth."

"What if Mubita doesn't get the appointment?" Niza interjected. "We can't afford to make a permanent enemy of the Principal Resident Magistrate."

Zoe channeled her anger into words. "Why don't we dish the dirt on the Nyambos and let the press run with it? If they pursue a corruption angle, we won't get the blame."

Mariam thought about this. "I like it. Sarge?"

He nodded. "I have a friend at the *Post*. I'll give him a call this afternoon."

"Just one thing," Zoe said. "It's probably best if you don't mention my name."

Sarge gave her a puzzled look. "Why?"

"It might be . . ." Zoe searched for the right word. ". . . distracting."

Niza frowned. "What are you talking about?"

Zoe traded a glance with Mariam. "Have you ever heard of Jack Fleming?"

Two days later, Joseph drove Zoe to the airport. The air was pristine, a cradle for the sun, and the trees were resplendent with the colors of fall. Zoe checked her side mirror but saw no sign of Dunstan Sisilu. He had appeared only once since the trial—shortly after she and Joseph had removed the GPS units from their vehicles and crushed them with a sledgehammer. He had shadowed them for two days and then disappeared again. Joseph guessed he was gone for good.

They made a brief stop at St. Francis. Joseph stayed in the Land Rover, and Zoe followed Sister Anica to the courtyard where Sister Irina was reading a story to the children.

"How is she doing?" Zoe asked, catching sight of Kuyeya.

"She's in pain," the nun replied. "She's always talking about bee stings."

Zoe shook her head. "I'm sorry it took me so long to schedule an MRI."

The nun gripped her hand. "It's a miracle it's happening at all."

As she had promised, Zoe had solicited a second opinion from a number of private clinics. She had quickly learned, however, that the barriers to medical care for poor children with special needs were not limited to the public system. Two of the clinics had informed her that they only treated expatriates—a euphemism for "whites"—and a third had asked for a referral from UTH. Disgusted, Zoe had called Dr. Chulu and demanded an MRI. The doctor had hesitated until she told him of Kuyeya's disorientation and bed-wetting. He had scheduled the exam for May 17, the same day as the Senate hearing.

Zoe walked toward the children and greeted Sister Irina. "You don't need to stop reading," she said. "I just brought something for Kuyeya."

The girl made the balloon sound when Zoe sat down. "Hi, Zoe. Look." She held her mother's ring up to the sun. "Green like the Zambezi."

Zoe smiled. "Did your mommy tell you that?"

The girl shook her head. "No, Irina."

"Did your mommy tell you about Victoria Falls?"

Kuyeya bobbed her head. "Falls make the sound like thunder."

Zoe laughed. "That's right. Listen, I'm going on a trip, but I thought you might like a new friend." She handed the girl a stuffed cheetah she had bought in Cape Town.

Kuyeya clutched the animal. "He has spots like the leopard."

"He's a cheetah. He runs very fast."

Kuyeya began to rock. "I don't like to run."

Zoe glanced at Sister Irina. "Does it hurt to run, Kuyeya?"

The girl nodded. "Sting goes the bee. Mommy say don't cry."

Zoe kissed Kuyeya's forehead. "We're going to figure out what's going on, I promise." She walked with Sister Anica back to the Land Rover. "I wish I could be here for the exam."

"She'll be all right," the nun replied.

"Send me a text as soon as the results come in."

Sister Anica nodded. "Go now."

It took them fifteen minutes to reach the airport. Zoe was silent on the drive, pondering the drama awaiting her on the far side of the ocean. The media attention surrounding her *New Yorker* article had not abated in the month since its release. If anything, the queries had increased, thanks to Jack Fleming's now commanding lead in the primaries—many were calling him the "presumptive nominee"—and Senator Hartman's press release announcing the hearing and its celebrity panel. The publication of the witness list had ignited a new wave of criticism from her father's supporters, including a stinging on-air rebuke from the hyper-partisan radio host Ben Slaughter that had gone viral on the Internet.

The most disturbing fallout of the media frenzy was not the attention itself—Zoe quickly learned how to tune it out—but the reaction of her family. Trevor had been the first to contact her about the hearing. He went out of his way to express his support, even opining that Catherine would have been honored to testify, but his confusion was plain, as were his concerns. He couldn't understand why she was doing it.

Then came the email from Sylvia. Brief and blunt, her words triggered a seismic tremor of doubt that Zoe could still feel.

Zoe, I know why you're doing this. It isn't about your mother or generosity or the global poor. All of that is window-dressing. You're angry about the past. I have a question for you: is getting even worth the price of alienating your family? You're only twenty-nine. Think about it.

Zoe had attempted on multiple occasions to draft a reply, but in the end she sent nothing. She spent days in turmoil, harboring a wild hope that her father would reach out to her and make amends. Jack, however, left her in silence. At a low point, she considered withdrawing from the hearing, but she couldn't bring herself to do it. She held tightly to one of her mother's axioms: "*Speak the truth, consequences be damned.*" But the doubt persisted because Sylvia was partly right. When it came to her father, the past was implicit in everything she had said and done for twelve years. She didn't know how to let go of the anger. In truth, she wasn't sure she wanted to.

Joseph pulled to a stop outside the airport terminal. "Are you ready for this?" he asked, touching her hand.

"I don't know," she replied honestly. Over the weeks, they had discussed the hearing from every possible angle, but she hadn't told him about Sylvia's email.

"Nervous?"

"A little. Do you think I'm doing the right thing?"

He gave her a small smile. "Sometimes people have to be reminded why they should care. You have a voice. You must use it."

His affirmation of purpose offered Zoe a lifeline. She brought her face close to his. "I love you, Joseph Kabuta," she said, kissing him with all the passion and uncertainty in her heart. She left him there and walked into the terminal, her words replaying in her mind.

I love you, Joseph Kabuta.

I love you.

Chapter 30

Washington, D.C.
May, 2012

The flight from Johannesburg landed at Washington Dulles International Airport at six thirty in the morning. After passing through customs, Zoe met Trevor outside the baggage claim and gave him a long hug. He escorted her to his black BMW M5 and tossed her luggage in the trunk.

"You like the car?" he asked, opening the door for her. "I got it last month."

"It's nice," she said, slipping into the plush leather seat.

They stuck to small talk on the drive into the

District. Zoe asked about his wedding plans and he rolled his eyes and gave her a rundown of all the hilarity and hysteria. The wedding itself was scheduled for January 1 in Aruba. Jenna, too, came from wealth, and her parents had agreed to fly three hundred guests to the island for the event. Zoe did the calculations in her head but kept quiet with her reservations. In the world of her birth, nothing surprised her anymore.

Trevor found a spot on the street just off Dupont Circle and showed her to his flat. "Do you want to take a nap?" he asked. "We have five hours before we need to leave."

"I slept on the plane," she replied. "I wouldn't mind a shower, though."

He carried her suitcase to the guest room and excused himself, explaining that he had work to do. She threw her backpack on the bed and stood before the window overlooking Q Street. The upscale neighborhood was an oasis of calm in a city of indefatigable ambition. She pictured Joseph's face and recalled the taste of his kiss. *What would you say about this place?* she wondered. *Would it make sense to you? Does it make sense to me anymore?*

She left the window and took a shower. Afterward, she dressed in a gray pantsuit and sky blue shirt that complemented her eyes and took her MacBook to the bed. She had rewritten her speech four times, striving for a harmony between authority and poignancy that would reframe foreign aid as a philanthropic partnership between the American people and their leaders, not as a retirement plan for dictators or a diversion of resources from the domestic poor. Her heart quickened when she reached the addendum. She had almost deleted it numerous times, but whenever her finger hovered over the button, she had stopped herself. She didn't know what she was going to do with it, but she wanted to keep her options open.

At noon, Trevor reappeared in the doorway. "Are you hungry? I'm making a sandwich."

"I'll help you," she replied, leaving her computer on the bed.

She followed him downstairs to the kitchen— an urbane blend of dark marble and stainless steel— and fixed her own lunch. The air was charged with all that was unspoken between them.

At last, Trevor said, "Are you sure you want to do this? You may lose Dad for good."

She sliced her sandwich in half and laid it on a plate. "I have to finish what I started. People like Ben Slaughter have grossly distorted my motives."

"Don't be naive. They don't care about you. They care about controversy. Testifying today will only make things worse."

"You don't understand."

"Then *make* me understand. Dad loves you. Do you really want to hurt him?"

Zoe looked away, unable to bear the pain in her brother's eyes. "It's complicated, Trevor. There are things you don't know."

"Then *tell* me. Don't destroy the only family you have."

His words cut her to the heart. She took her plate to the table and sat down, eating in stubborn silence. For the first time in her life, the gap between them seemed unbridgeable.

At a quarter past one, they left Trevor's apartment and walked to the Dupont Circle Metro Station. The skies of late spring were clotted with cumulus, and the humid air carried more than a hint of the summer heat to come. Trevor bought her a day-pass and swiped his SmarTrip card, leading the way to the Red Line. They took their place beside the tracks just as the headlamp of the approaching train broke free of the tunnel.

Trevor nudged her shoulder. "You don't get service like this in Zambia."

Zoe laughed, grateful for the olive branch of affection.

The trip to Capitol South via Metro Center took fifteen minutes. They emerged on First Street and joined the stream of pedestrians hurrying in the direction of the Capitol. After passing the Library of Congress and the Supreme Court, they made their way toward Dirksen Senate Office Building, the home of the Foreign Relations Committee.

On the cusp of Constitution Avenue, Zoe saw a herd of reporters and cameramen milling outside Dirksen's public entrance. She turned abruptly and faced the Capitol, the gravity of the moment settling on her shoulders. Trevor put a protective arm around her, reverting to the role he had played since they were children.

"They're here for Frieda Caraway, too," he said. "Ignore them and they'll let you pass."

She nodded, warding off her doubts. "Let's go."

They crossed the barricaded tarmac and entered the throng of journalists. For a second or two the reporters didn't recognize her, but then someone spoke her name—"That's Zoe Fleming!"—and the sidewalk erupted with noise. Zoe allowed Trevor to take the lead and walked forward step by step until at last they found shelter inside the doors.

After clearing security, they took the elevator to the fourth floor and traversed the marble hallway to the hearing room. The crowd outside was dotted with journalists, but the atmosphere here was more sedate. One reporter—a man Zoe vaguely recognized—pressed close to her and asked, "Ms. Fleming, isn't it true that your appearance today is a vote against your father's campaign?"

She engaged him despite herself: "This isn't about politics or the election. It's about America's relationship to a billion people around the world who live in conditions we would never tolerate for our own children."

She slipped into the wood-paneled hearing

room and kissed Trevor on the cheek, leaving him to find a seat in the gallery. She walked up the aisle and found her place at the head of the witness table. The card beside hers read: "Ms. Frieda Caraway." Zoe smiled apprehensively. That Senator Hartman had given her the pole position ahead of an Academy-Award-winning actress was either a reflection of admiration or the basest political opportunism.

She settled into her seat and surveyed the dais, focusing on her father's nameplate three chairs down from Senator Hartman's. "Mr. Fleming," it read. She closed her eyes and allowed her mind to drift back in time to the day when all of this had begun.

She remembered the boyish face of Clay Randall, drawing her into the lonely dunes of East Beach on Chappaquiddick. The sand had blown with such fierceness that she had suggested turning back, but he had led her into a lee with a view of the Atlantic, and she had relented. Then the blanket came out, and the bags of red grapes and cheese. After that came the poetry and the kissing and the hands that had disregarded the boundaries of her bikini, causing her to squirm and protest, then to slap him in the face. She had nearly escaped. But nearly was not enough. Afterward, through a veil of tears, she had whispered: "*Why?*" Clay had looked her up and down and sneered: "*You know you wanted it.*" Ten days later she had summoned the courage to tell her father. She could still hear his words if she listened closely enough: "*It sounds like the two of you had a misunderstanding. I think it's best that you forget about it and go on with your life.*"

The next forty minutes in the hearing room passed in a blur—the noisy admission of the media; the assembling of the photographers; the arrival of the other panelists, including Frieda Caraway, aglitter with diamonds; the dance of congressional aides and security officials; the entry of Senator Hartman, followed by a steady trickle of other members; the sudden appearance of Jack Fleming with his senior aides a few minutes after two o'clock; and, finally, Hartman's long-winded introduction. Zoe endured all of it with a deliberate composure that belied her nervousness. Even the confident smile she gave her father was a fleeting thing.

As the chairman concluded his remarks, Zoe blinked away the glare of the lights and glanced at Frieda Caraway beside her. The actress was seated primly, her posture erect and her face impassive despite the cameras trained on her. For a moment, Zoe imagined her mother sitting there, and asked the question again: *How would you handle this?*

Suddenly, Zoe heard her name.

"Ms. Fleming," Senator Hartman said, "the committee is grateful for your excellent article in the *New Yorker* and for your deep personal commitment to the poor and vulnerable around the world. We welcome your remarks."

Zoe hesitated for a moment, her mind distracted by the cameras. Then the words came to her without thought. "Senator Hartman, members of the committee, I'm honored to be here with you today. My mother, Catherine Sorenson-Fleming—whom many of you knew—dedicated her life to the proposition on the seal behind you. '*E Pluribus Unum*'— 'Out of many, one.' She saw America and the globalizing world as a melting pot united by more than the sum of what divides us. But she was not a utopian. She understood the power—and to some extent the inevitability—of the age-old distinctions in human society. She didn't believe that the world should become homogeneous, but she *did* believe passionately in two notions—justice and generosity."

Zoe looked at the senators around the dais. "I could speak to you today about justice—economic justice between the rich world and the poor world, about the moral obligations created by centuries of slavery, colonialism, and avarice. But if I took that approach I would disparage my mother's legacy. I would rather talk to you about generosity. Unlike justice, generosity isn't hard to define. When confronted by the one who has not, the one who has either offers a helping hand or walks by. We all know the kindness of the Good Samaritan and the parsimony of the priest and the Levite who preceded him. The difference could not be starker."

Zoe took a breath. "When I was six years old, my mother took me to Africa for the first time. We stayed with a diplomat in Nairobi who lived in a bungalow built by the British. My first memories of the continent came from the lush gardens in his backyard. Then we went into Kibera, one of Africa's largest slum communities, and I met children who had nothing. Actually, they had less than nothing—they had disease, dead parents, polluted water, nutrition-depleted food. I didn't know what I could do to change their circumstances. But I knew one thing instinctively—the only thing separating me from them was the accident of birth."

"My mother took me back to Africa seven times before she died," Zoe went on. "She loved it as much as a person can love a place. She was on the vanguard of AIDS relief. She championed microfinance before it became a buzzword. She built water systems and bush clinics and funded medical trips into conflict zones. She worked with anyone who cared about genuine philanthropy—the love of human beings. She had only two enemies: cynicism and greed.

"If my mother were alive today, she would praise Africa's economic growth and fledgling middle class. She would encourage the expansion of free enterprise and support efforts to make aid smarter and more efficient. She would hold high the banner of trade as a rising tide that lifts all boats. But she would *not* abandon our system of foreign assistance. Indeed, she would argue that generosity will always be necessary because the profit motive that drives trade has no mechanism for meeting the needs of the poor. The reason is simple: the poor cannot pay."

Zoe's voice took on a stronger cadence. "Today, around the world, the poorest people struggle to feed their children and keep them in school. They have no way to afford life-saving medicine, no way to fund an adequate justice system. Those of us who have the means must help them. We in America are not blind to this. Generosity is one of the great legacies of our nation. But some among us are suggesting that we close our eyes."

"We are in a position to all but *eliminate* the transmission of AIDS within a generation, but we're scaling back PEPFAR. We've saved countless lives through the Malaria Initiative and the Global Fund, but we're retrenching on our commitments. In Zambia where I work, hundreds of children are brutally raped each year, but their abusers get away with it because prosecutors don't have access to

DNA. These are problems that money *can* solve, but the market alone won't solve them because there is little in it for the businessman. Generosity must deliver them."

Zoe glanced around the panel. "Confronted with the crises of debt and deficit, we face an equally momentous crisis of conscience. On one side are our fears. On the other is our humanity. It is at moments like this that we prove our true character."

She hesitated on the threshold of decision, her heart racing with adrenaline. She could conclude cleanly or toss a hand grenade at the dais. She fixed her eyes on her father and saw the stillness in his frame. The blankness of his expression pushed her toward the precipice.

"I know the inconvenience of humanity. I know what it feels like to be . . ."

Suddenly, her father winced and she saw pain in his eyes. She paused ever so slightly and softened her words.

". . . to be alone in a vulnerable place. Today in Africa and all around the world there are people whose names will never make it into the history books—people living on the margins of society, amid war and famine, violence, and disease. We will never meet them, but we are no different from them. They do not need welfare or dependency. They need generosity and empowerment. We are in a position to offer that. If we do, history will judge us kindly. If we do not, God help us."

When she spoke the last word, Zoe sat back in her chair and retreated inward to a place she could not define. She heard the speeches that followed and the questions and answers, but the rest of the proceeding carried the faded edges of a dream. Occasionally, she glanced at her father, expecting to see anger, but his eyes held only sadness. He declined to question the panel and left the hearing room as soon as the adjournment was announced.

Zoe followed suit, pausing only to shake hands with Senator Hartman and to give Frieda Caraway a hug. Trevor met her at the exit and guided her through the horde of cameras and journalists. They left Dirksen by a side exit and walked around the Capitol to the National Mall. The wide grass of the commons was half-dead, trampled by tourists, but the clouds had broken up and left the sky full of light.

"There's something I want to know," Trevor said, sitting beside her on a bench. "What did you mean at the end? When were you alone in a vulnerable place?"

The pain in his voice made her cringe. "If I tell you, it'll be worse."

He took a sharp breath. "It's that bad?"

She nodded slowly.

"Tell me anyway."

Zoe watched a young father throwing a Frisbee with his daughter. The girl was seven or eight years old, and her smile was frank, uncluttered by the world. "It happened the summer you left for Harvard," she began, and told him the whole story.

When she finished, he massaged his face with his hands. "Clay Randall. I should break his kneecaps. Why didn't you say something?"

Tears came to her eyes. "There were times I almost did. But it never seemed right."

He shook his head wearily. "Sometimes I wish Dad never got into politics. Partisanship turns friends into enemies."

"I never wanted to be his enemy. I just wanted an apology."

Trevor looked resolute. "I should break *his* kneecaps."

"Please don't," she said, laughing softly.

"The press is going to have a field day with the hearing."

If only you knew what I was about to say, she thought, feeling an overwhelming relief that she had stepped back from the ledge. The word in her notes, the word she almost used, was the word "betrayed."

"I'm going back to Africa," she said. "It won't matter."

"You can't hide there forever."

She frowned. "I'm not hiding."

He looked into her eyes. "Did you hear yourself today? You were magnificent. You'll be thirty in a few months. The trust will be yours. Imagine what you could do with it."

Zoe turned away and saw the girl running to catch the Frisbee, her blonde hair flowing behind her. *I can't*, she thought, picturing Joseph's face, but the idea stuck to her like a burr and would not let her go.

Chapter 31

The next morning, Zoe awoke in the goose-down warmth of Trevor's guest bed. She grabbed her iPhone off the bedside table and checked her messages. More than twenty-four hours had passed since Kuyeya's MRI, and Dr. Chulu had promised her quick results now that the chief radiologist was back from leave.

She saw a text from Joseph, sent at 4:07 a.m. D.C. time: "*Good to talk yesterday. Happy the hearing is over. Call Dr Chulu ASAP.*"

Her pulse quickened as she searched for the

physician's number. She reached him on his mobile. "What's going on?" she asked. "Is something wrong?"

"There have been complications," he said guardedly. "Kuyeya needs surgery."

"Why?" she asked, sitting upright in the bed.

He took a breath. "Children with Down syndrome sometimes have laxity in the ligament that separates the bone of the atlas—that is, the top cervical vertebra—from the spinal cord. It's called atlantoaxial instability. Most of the time it doesn't become symptomatic. But trauma can trigger it, such as a fall or a violent incident—"

"Like a rape," Zoe interjected.

"Yes. It can take months to manifest. But when it reaches an advance, stage—when the cord itself is threatened—the only way to correct it is to perform a spinal fusion."

"Shouldn't you have caught this before?"

"An MRI is much more revealing than an X-ray."

That's why I wanted one before now, she thought. "So when is the surgery scheduled?" she asked, forcing herself to stay calm.

"That's the problem. A fusion requires a neuro-surgeon operating in theater with an orthopedic surgeon. The closest hospital equipped to perform the procedure is in Pretoria."

"Why can't UTH do it?"

"We have qualified surgeons," he answered a bit defensively. "We lack a proper facility."

"So medevac her to Pretoria. Get the South Africans to do it."

He cleared his throat. "That would involve sub-stantial expense."

"How much?"

"Pretoria Wellness Hospital is a private facility. With the medevac, it will cost at least one hundred thousand dollars, perhaps more."

Zoe was stunned. "How soon does this need to happen?"

"She needs to be operated on immediately. Her spinal cord is in peril. If she were to fall again, it could kill her."

Dear God, Zoe thought, chills racing through her. "I'll see what I can do."

She hung up and placed a call to Atticus Spelling.

The octogenarian was both a compulsive work-aholic and a habitual early riser. His secretary—an old bird named Harriet—greeted Zoe officiously and transferred her to Spelling.

"Zoe," he said. "Such a pleasant surprise."

She dispensed with pretense. "Atticus, we've had our share of disagreements, but I know how much you love your grandchildren."

"That goes without saying," he agreed cautiously.

She told him a boiled-down version of Kuyeya's story. "I need a hundred thousand dollars from the trust to save her life. I can put you in touch with Dr. Chulu if you want confirmation, but that's the number he gave me."

Spelling sighed. "I sympathize with the plight of this child, I truly do. But there are thousands of others just like her around the world. You would squander the trust principal quickly if you tried to cover all their bills."

Zoe's temper flared. "I'm not talking about *every* child. I'm talking about *one* child."

The trustee didn't break stride. "I'm sure there are charitable programs in place that can assist

her. Find me one that has appropriate account-
ability structures, and I will consider a disbursal
of that magnitude."

Zoe exploded: "*Damn* you, Atticus. I'm asking
for one half of one percent of the principal balance
six months before it's mine anyway. Please give me
the money."

"I'm sorry, Zoe, I can't do it," said the old man.
"I have a fiduciary responsibility to fulfill. Call
your father if you like."

The next thing Zoe heard was the dial tone.
She took a deep breath, struggling to maintain her
composure. Then she threw on jeans and a T-shirt
and went to find Trevor. He was in the dining
room, eating a plate of scrambled eggs.

"Did I make the paper?" she asked.

He laughed wryly. "The front page of the *Post*.
Below the fold, but still prominent."

The noose around her neck tightened. "What
did they say?"

"They were complimentary. But it isn't the last
we'll hear of it."

She sat down across from him. "Have you
talked to Dad?"

Trevor regarded her frankly. "A few minutes ago. He isn't happy. He thinks the media is over-playing the story. It's not like you said anything damaging." He paused, looking conflicted. "I'm sorry. This has put me in an awkward position."

"I know," Zoe said apologetically. "Look, it's simple. He should just let it go. It'll blow over in a week, and the press will find something else to talk about."

"It's *not* simple," Trevor disagreed. "You opposed him in a very public way. It doesn't look good to the voter on the street."

Zoe allowed her pain to show. "He should have thought of that years ago."

Trevor ran a hand through his hair. "This is such a mess."

"Not to change the subject," Zoe said, doing exactly that, "but I need a hundred thousand dollars." She told him about Kuyeya and the door Atticus Spelling had slammed in her face.

Trevor shook his head slowly. "You are one complicated human being. The most I can give you is ten. I maxed out my savings to buy the M5."

She shook her head. "I wasn't thinking of you. I was thinking of your trust."

He looked perplexed. "I transferred all the money to Mom's foundation. I told you that."

"Yes, but that puts you in the Founders' Circle. You could talk to Monica."

"I barely know her. You're the one with the relationship."

For the first time that morning Zoe smiled. "Then come with me to Manhattan."

The Acela Express train from Washington to New York was a pale shadow of its European cousins, but Zoe preferred it to flying. After stops in Maryland, Delaware, and New Jersey, the train deposited them at Penn Station just before one in the afternoon. Zoe and Trevor navigated the crowded underground corridors and emerged on Seventh Avenue not far from the taxi stand. They climbed into a cab, and Zoe gave the driver the address.

Fifteen minutes later, the taxi pulled to the curb outside the Park Avenue headquarters of the Catherine Sorenson Foundation. Zoe introduced herself to the doorman, who ushered them to the bank of elevators. They got off on the tenth floor and entered the foundation's elegant wood-and-glass reception area. The receptionist greeted them by name and escorted them down a hallway lined with photographs to the office of the Executive Director.

Monica Kingsley rounded her desk and shook their hands affectionately. At just under sixty years of age, she had the look of New York high society without the affectation. "It's so *good* to see you again," she said, gesturing toward a pair of leather chairs opposite her desk.

"Thanks for working us in on short notice," Zoe replied, taking a seat.

"I always have time for you," Monica said.

Zoe traded a glance with Trevor. "We need your help. It's a bit unusual." She summarized Kuyeya's story and outlined her prognosis. "There are a number of charities in Lusaka that are assisting her, but they don't have funding for something like this. I—we—were hoping the foundation could cover the cost of her treatment."

Trevor chimed in: "I would have put the money up myself if I still had my trust."

"Of course," Monica replied. "I'll be perfectly frank with you. If Catherine were sitting in this seat, she would call the bank and they would wire the funds. I don't have that power. I have to take it to the board. I'll do my best to make the case, but I don't know how they'll vote."

"How long will that take?" Zoe asked, struggling to suppress her discouragement.

"I'll need a couple of days to call a meeting." Monica looked quizzical. "Can't you talk to your father? Surely he would help."

Zoe listened to the hum of traffic far below. She couldn't believe how spectacularly her plans had backfired. In challenging her father, she had not only succeeded in damaging their relationship, likely beyond repair, but also—and far worse—she had endangered Kuyeya's life.

"I'll talk to him," Trevor said suddenly. "He might listen to me."

She regarded him in surprise. "He'll think you're taking sides."

"It doesn't matter. I'd rather be with you anyway."

She reached out and squeezed his hand. "Please

talk to the board," she said to Monica. "We don't have much time."

Monica nodded. "When are you leaving the country?"

"Tomorrow morning."

"I'll send you an email as soon as I have an answer."

"Thank you," Zoe said, standing up.

"Wait," Monica said. "I have something for you." She reached into a drawer and extracted a yellowed envelope. "This doesn't seem like the right time, but I doubt I'll see you again before your birthday. It's from your mother."

At the mention of Catherine, Zoe's pulse quickened. "I don't understand."

Trevor touched her shoulder. "It's all right. I got one, too."

Zoe gave him a baffled look.

"It's a letter," Monica explained. "She left it with her will."

Zoe's spine tingled when she took the envelope. The sight of her name traced out by her mother's flowing penmanship triggered a cascade of emotions—astonishment, grief, nostalgia, and love. She fingered the flap. "Should I open it now?"

"I'd save it for a quiet moment," Monica said.

Zoe shook her hand and walked with Trevor to the elevator.

"Is Dad still in D.C.?" she asked.

He shook his head. "He's on the Vineyard. He needed to get away."

She took a sharp breath, wondering at the irony. "I'm coming with you."

Her brother grimaced. "It could get ugly."

"I don't care. I need to be there."

Chapter 32

Martha's Vineyard
May, 2012

The Gulfstream III executive jet touched down on Martha's Vineyard a few minutes before six in the evening. The plane was the oldest in the triumvirate that made up Jack Fleming's fleet. The "Three," as they called it, was Sylvia's favorite, but Trevor had no difficulty requisitioning it from Westchester County Airport for the short flight to the Vineyard.

They rented a car at the airport and drove east through the plantations and pine groves of the island, reaching Edgartown just as the sun fell behind the trees. Zoe inhaled the moist air rolling in through the open window and allowed the tranquility of the village to soothe her nerves. As pristine as a museum piece, Edgartown was both the haven of her childhood and the scene of her worst memory. She cherished the place and resented it at the same time.

Trevor made a series of turns and took them toward Eel Pond. Zoe saw the gray-blue sea through a break in the trees. Then the water became the horizon, presided over by blushing clouds. She saw the house next—the gabled roofline, the gray clapboard siding and white casement shutters. Two members of the Senator's security team greeted them at the gate. The men recognized Trevor and admitted them without delay.

They drove up the winding drive and parked behind Sylvia's Porsche and the Senator's Mercedes. Zoe took a breath, wishing she could still her trembling hands.

"Why don't you go for a walk?" Trevor said, sensing her mood. "Let me talk to him."

"No. I'm not going to run from this."

"Suit yourself."

He led the way to the porch, where a third security officer was sitting in a lounge chair.

"The door's unlocked," the man said, making no move to get up.

They entered the foyer together. Built just after the turn of the century, the house was a throwback to a simpler architectural era—low ceilings, square rooms, and wide-plank floors minimally polished. Over the years, Sylvia had begged Jack to remodel it, but Jack had resisted, prompting her—out of his hearing—to nickname the property "the shrine of St. Catherine."

Zoe inhaled the familiar scent of lavender and spice. She heard voices coming from the kitchen. A fluffy white Bichon Frisé lapdog skittered up to them and sniffed her toes.

"Maria, is that you?" her father called out when Trevor pulled the door closed.

"It's me, Dad," Trevor announced, glancing furtively at Zoe.

Zoe braced herself at the sound of her father's footsteps. When he reached the foyer, he stopped and blinked, staring at her. Zoe looked back at him, her heart pounding like a charging horse. From the floridness in his cheeks, she could see that he had been drinking.

"Hey, Dad," Trevor said, trying to affect non-chalance.

"A family reunion," the Senator said ambivalently.

"Who is it, Jack?" Sylvia called. Seconds later, she appeared beside her husband and stopped cold. She scooped up the dog and stared at Zoe without a word.

"We're here to talk," Trevor said. "There are some things I need to understand."

"Let's talk then," the Senator replied, leading the way to the living room.

Zoe walked to the bay windows and looked out at the scene that lived in so many of her memories—the sugar maple that shaded the servant's cottage, the path through pines and thistles that led to the marsh at the edge of their land, the sandy beach where she had learned to swim, and, beyond, the Atlantic, restless beneath a darkening sky. After a moment, she went to the couch and sat beside Trevor. Her father took a seat in his favorite leather chair, and Sylvia remained standing, petting the Bichon Frisé.

"What do want me to tell you?" the Senator began.

"Clay Randall," Trevor said. "I want to know why you didn't do anything about it."

Jack gave his son a deliberate look. "It wasn't clear what happened."

Trevor squinted in disbelief. "What are you talking about? Rape is a simple concept."

"Oh, Trevor, nothing is simple," Sylvia interjected. "They had a relationship. They were infatuated with one another. I was there; I saw it with my own eyes. I was certain they were having sex. That's what teenagers do. I did it, you did it, I'm sure. When the lines aren't clear, things can happen."

Trevor regarded her indignantly. "You were *not* there. You didn't see what he did to her."

"Trevor," the Senator cut in. "Look at me, son. I never meant to hurt your sister. You're right— we weren't there. We didn't see it. The only thing I knew for sure was that her heart was broken. Harry Randall is my best friend. I wasn't about to accuse his son of rape unless I was absolutely certain of it."

Despite her best efforts, Zoe began to cry. Suddenly, she was seventeen again, wounded, confused, and incapable of comprehending why her father had chosen not to believe her.

Trevor squeezed her hand. "Zoe's sitting right here, Dad. Look her in the eye and tell her she made it up. If you can't do that, then the last twelve years of your life are a lie."

The Senator stood abruptly. "I can't believe it. I've given you both privileges I never *dreamed* of when I was a kid, and this is what I get in return?" He faced Zoe. "Do you know how many calls I've gotten since the hearing? My party, my campaign, no one knows what to do with the footage on TV. I have to tell them something, but what I am supposed to say? That my daughter opposed me in my own committee because of something that happened a decade ago?"

"Stop it," Zoe said, tears streaming down her face. "I didn't want this. I don't care about the White House. I hate politics. I hate what they've done to us. I never asked you to punish Clay. All I wanted was for you to believe me, to say you were sorry and that you'd do whatever it took to make it right. But no, you couldn't do that. You had too much to lose."

She took a breath and tried to calm down. "The irony is I'm not even sure *you* really *care* about politics." Seeing her father stiffen, she forged ahead. "Tell me I'm not right. You were spinning after Mom died. You needed a distraction, and Sylvia gave you a mountain to climb. You convinced yourself it was your idea because you needed to escape the guilt."

"What guilt?" the Senator asked in a near whisper.

"That you weren't there to save her."

"That's absurd," he said unconvincingly.

"Look, I don't care what you tell people. Lie to them if it makes you feel better. I have no intention of speaking about this ever again. I'm here for one reason. There's a girl in Zambia who has a medical condition that could kill her. The doctors in Lusaka can't perform the surgery. The nearest hospital that can do it is in Pretoria, and it's going to cost a hundred thousand dollars. I asked Atticus, and he won't give it to me." She leaned forward. "So here's your chance at redemption. You can change what happens to this girl. But the clock is ticking."

Silence enveloped them when Zoe concluded. She heard the calls of gulls playing in the wind and the distant sound of the surf. To her surprise, it was Sylvia who spoke first.

"Jack, can I talk to you for a minute?"

The Senator nodded and joined her in the hallway. Instantly, Zoe was struck by déjà vu. *I've been here before. Is it possible it could happen again?* When her father reentered the living room, she noticed a change in his countenance. In confronting the subject of Catherine's death, he had seemed human, even vulnerable. Now the steel of the candidate had returned.

"We can help each other," the Senator said. "I'll give you the money, but I need you to close Pandora's box. I'll make a brief statement to the press that you will attend with Trevor and Sylvia. I'll talk about our family's commitment to philanthropy, and you'll show the world that you respect me and support my candidacy."

His words pierced Zoe like a knife in the back. "I can't believe you want me to bargain with you." She shook her head. "It's amazing, Dad. After all these years, you still can't say it."

He narrowed his eyes. "Say what?"

Zoe knew what decision she had to make, but still she hesitated. In the end, her legs were stronger than her heart. "You can come, or you can give me the keys," she said to Trevor.

"I'm coming," he replied, following her toward the door.

"You're really going to walk away from this?" her father called after her.

Zoe turned and met his eyes. "No, Dad. I walked away a long time ago."

Trevor drove her to the airport in a silence as deep as the dark Vineyard sky. Zoe looked out at the forest and felt something inside her break. A jumbled torrent of memories and fears cascaded through her mind—the day her father won the Senate race and she understood why he had not defended her; Kuyeya playing at St. Francis, a misstep away from paralysis; Amos lying in a pool of blood; Clay Randall watching her cry; Flexon Mubita meeting with Patricia Nyambo; cameras flashing in the Senate chamber; the pain in her father's eyes; the black mamba slithering across the floor; Joseph's HIV. She leaned her head against the window, overwhelmed by it all.

"Are you okay?" Trevor said.

She took a moment to answer him. "I'm not sure."

"What are you going to do about the girl?"

She shrugged. "I'll figure something out."

He stared at her in the darkness. "I'm sorry, Zoe. For everything. If I could change it . . ."

"I know, Trev," she said, touching his arm. "It's not your fault."

When he focused on the road again, she rolled down the window and leaned into the slipstream, allowing the island air to envelop her, to whip through her hair and fill her lungs as she had when she was a girl. She could see the brightest stars twinkling through the sea haze. Their names came to her like a fragment from a long-forgotten lesson: Castor, Pollux, Capella, Regulus. She smiled at them in an easy way and felt her confidence beginning to return.

In the airport parking lot, she had an idea. She took out her iPhone and called a number in South Africa. She listened as the phone rang and rang, waiting until a male voice delivered a sleepy greeting in Afrikaans.

"Jan," she said, "it's Zoe Fleming."

"Zoe?" He sounded bewildered. "It's one thirty in the morning."

"I'm in the United States. Your daughter needs help."

"My daughter?"

"Kuyeya," she said impatiently. "Do you know anyone at Pretoria Wellness Hospital?"

"No," he replied, still fuzzy. "Why?"

She outlined the situation and made her request. He hesitated, and she heard only static on the line. *Come on, Jan*, she thought. *Be a man.*

Eventually, he spoke. "I've heard of AAI. Dr. Chulu says it's progressive?"

"Life-threatening. She needs an operation right away."

"I know a medevac outfit in Johannesburg that does charity flights."

"That's a good start, but we're still well short. Do you have savings?"

He hesitated. "Ninety thousand rand, but that's not nearly enough."

"And your parents?"

His reaction came swiftly. "They don't know anything about this."

"What about a loan? You have friends. Somebody will help."

"What about you?" he countered. "You have connections, too."

His words fell like salt on her open wound. "What do you mean?"

"Zoe Fleming, daughter of Jack." He paused. "It seems both of us had secrets."

She gripped the phone. "This isn't about me. It's about your daughter's life."

He sighed, sounding weary. "I'm not denying that. Let me see what I can do."

"Start with the medevac and your savings. I'll work out the rest."

Her words seemed to embolden him. "When are you flying back?"

"I'll be in Johannesburg on Sunday morning."

"Good," he said, speaking with sudden conviction. "With any luck, so will she."

Chapter 33

Johannesburg, South Africa
May, 2012

Zoe spent the fifteen-hour flight from New York sleeping and scheming—making a list of influential friends and acquaintances and compiling numbers to call on the ground. Somehow, six miles in the air, her frame of reference had changed. It no longer mattered that Atticus Spelling had turned her down, that the decision of the foundation board was a crapshoot, or that her father had asked her to put on a show for the media in exchange for Kuyeya's life. She would find a way to pay for the surgery. She couldn't afford to fail.

When the plane parked at the gate, she checked her iPhone for email, hoping for a missive from Monica Kingsley. Instead, she found a handful of queries from reporters, which she deleted. She collected her bags and followed the crowd to customs and immigration. Thirty minutes later, she entered the cavernous terminal and saw Jan Kruger waiting for her.

He surprised her with a hug. "I just got a call from the orthopedic surgeon. She goes into theater in two hours."

"You did it," she replied. "You came through."

He showed her the way to the parking garage and a black Audi coupé. "I've been thinking, assuming all goes well, I'd like to spend some time with her."

"You'll have to work at it. She's never had a decent man in her life."

"Any advice?"

"Bring her Johnny Cash. She'll love you forever."

They left the garage and drove into a world alive with sunlight. Jan navigated the N12 to the Eastern Bypass and sped north to the N1, paying no attention to the speed limit. As they flew across the bronze hills of Gauteng, Jan surprised Zoe again. Beginning with the day he met Charity in a classroom in Livingstone, he told Zoe the story of the girl she was before he broke her heart, before Frederick Nyambo and Lusaka and prostitution and AIDS. Listening to him, Zoe knew that he had loved her and that in some ways he still did.

They left the expressway on the south side of Pretoria and drove through Wingate Park to Pretoria Wellness Hospital. Ultramodern in its design, the medical center sat on a sprawling, tree-shaded campus within sight of a golf course. They parked in the lot and entered the atrium-like lobby. Zoe was immediately struck by the warmth of the place. The walls were decorated with artwork and the air was full of natural light.

A woman at the reception desk directed them to a waiting area not far from the operating room. They walked together down a corridor lined with floral prints. Zoe imagined Kuyeya in theater, sleeping beneath the lights, a team of surgeons working to fuse her vertebrae and relieve the tension that could have severed her spinal cord. *You're going to make it*, she thought. *I know you will.*

She found Joseph and Sister Irina in the waiting area.

The nun embraced her. "God will bless you for this."

"Thank him," Zoe replied, introducing Jan. "He made it happen."

She turned to Joseph and all but ran into his arms. She had only been away for four days, but it felt like a month. "I missed you," she said, nestling her head against his chest.

"I missed you, too," he said, kissing her forehead.

After a while, he led her to a pair of chairs beneath a window. "Guess who I put in jail a couple of days ago?" he asked with a grin.

She felt a rush of excitement. "Dunstan Sisilu?"

"Unfortunately, no," he said, shaking his head. "His name is Eddie Mpungu—the leader of the gang that attacked us in Kanyama."

Her eyes widened. "You found him."

"At Soweto Market. I charged him with assaulting a police officer and told him if he ever touched another girl without permission I'd turn him into a eunuch."

Zoe laughed, feeling a deep measure of satisfaction. "What about the *Post*?" she asked. "Have they done anything with the story Sarge gave them?"

Joseph nodded. "It was on the front page yesterday. The reporter asked a lot of unflattering questions about the Nyambos and raised a hint of doubt about the Court. What is it you say in English? He smelled a rodent."

She smiled brightly. "A rat."

"Right. Sarge is confident he'll continue to dig. Who knows what he might find?"

Around two o'clock, a fair-haired doctor entered the waiting area. He introduced himself as Dr. Jacobs, the orthopedic surgeon.

"Dr. Kruger," he said, spotting Jan. "It's an honor to meet you."

"Pleasure," Jan replied. "How did it go?"

"She's lucky to be alive," the surgeon replied. "The subluxation of the atlas was so pronounced that she could have been crippled getting out of bed. She'll be in a hard collar for three weeks and a soft collar for several months, but she should be okay."

Zoe closed her eyes, her relief complete. "When can we see her?" she asked.

"She's sleeping now," the surgeon said. "The nurse will let you know when she's awake and can take visitors."

After he left, Zoe gave Sister Irina a long hug.

"I was afraid we would lose her," the nun said. "I don't know what I would have done."

"She'll be back in the garden soon," Zoe said.

She sat down beside Joseph and checked her email again. Her heart skipped a beat. She had a new message from Monica Kingsley. She opened it with trepidation.

Zoe, I had a conference call with the board this morning. It pains me greatly to say this, but they voted against us. They were very sympathetic, of course, but they were concerned about the precedent it would set. I'm so sorry. In lieu of institutional support, I would like to make a personal contribution of $2,000. Best of luck putting together the funding for this very worthy cause. I have no doubt you will succeed.

"Damn it," Zoe said under her breath. Though the board's decision didn't shock her, it disappointed her greatly. She stood up and turned to Joseph. "I need to make some phone calls. Text me when the nurse says we can see her."

She ignored his questioning look and grabbed her backpack, heading to the lobby. She took a seat in a coffee shop just off the atrium and opened her MacBook, pulling up the list of contacts she had assembled on the plane. At the top she typed: "Trevor Fleming—$10,000. Jan Kruger—R90,000 / $12,000. Monica Kingsley—$2,000."

She made her first call—to a friend from Stanford, now the founder of an Internet company worth half a billion dollars. She got his voicemail and left him an urgent message. Her second call went to her childhood best friend whose mother presided over a society club that hosted regular benefits for charity. She left a second voicemail. On her third call, she finally got through. Sam Rutherford was a retired real-estate tycoon who sat on a number of nonprofit boards. He and his wife were in the Founders' Circle of the Catherine Sorenson Foundation.

"Zoe," he said, "it's been years. How are you?"

After a bit of small talk, she got down to business. Sam listened carefully, dropping little phrases that indicated interest—"poor girl," "sounds like a great cause," "glad to see you following in your mother's footsteps"—but at the end he posed the unanswerable question: "I imagine your father has pledged his support?" When she offered a lame answer, he seemed to vacillate. "I need to talk to Margaret. You know how she is. I'll get back to you."

Zoe scrolled to the fourth number on her list, but the thought of her father kept her from placing the call. She brought up the Senator's campaign website on her computer. It had been two days since she left the Vineyard—enough time for him to sell a story about her to the press. When the "Media" page loaded, she read the top line of text. Instead of a hyperlink to a press conference, she found an interview announcement. The Senator and Sylvia were scheduled to appear on *Piers Morgan Tonight* on May 21—tomorrow. Zoe sat immobilized, wondering how her father would spin her appearance in the Senate. Suddenly, she caught herself. *He can say whatever he wants. I don't care anymore.*

She picked up her iPhone and placed two more calls—to a psychotherapist and bestselling author who was also a childhood neighbor, and to her roommate at Stanford who was the daughter of a Hollywood director. When no one picked up, she left two more messages.

She looked at the sixth name on her list and felt suddenly queasy. What if her friends didn't return her calls? What if they found excuses not to help? It was an implausible scenario. She knew too many people with money to fall short of such a modest goal. But the stress of the moment made her waver. At last, she dialed the number, praying for an unscripted voice.

"*Pronto!*"

The emphatic Italian greeting brought a smile to her face.

"Alex," she said, "it's Zoe Fleming. Let me guess: you're in the Adriatic."

Alex Denver was a child prodigy—fluent in seven languages, a celebrated concert pianist, and the holder of three patents in biomedical technology. He was also the son of the fifth richest man in America. After earning a master's degree from

Stanford at the age of eighteen, he had set sail around the world while ostensibly working on a PhD. He had never come back.

"Zoe!" he exclaimed. "*Amore mio*. Tell me why we aren't still together."

She let out a wry laugh. "If I recall, you found a new girlfriend."

"What was her name? I don't remember. You, I can never forget."

She stifled another laugh. "I have a favor to ask," she said, and told him Kuyeya's story.

"How much do you need?" he asked, turning serious.

She did a quick mental calculation. "Around $50,000. I'm not sure yet."

"It doesn't matter. I'll cover it."

"All of it?" She was astonished. At Stanford, he had talked about poverty as if it were the fault of the poor. It was one of many reasons they had broken up.

"Of course," he replied. "I just put in at Sardinia. I can get it to you inside a week."

"What happened to you?" she had to ask.

"You mean to the kid who gave bums foreign

change?" He laughed at himself. "I met the real world. It gave me a heart." He paused. "I signed the Giving Pledge."

Now she was stunned. The pledge was a commitment by some of America's wealthiest individuals to give at least half of their wealth to charity.

"Dad isn't thrilled," he went on, "but his opinion won't matter when he's dead."

"You're beautiful, Alex," she said, surprised by the affection in her voice.

He laughed. "If you ever want a holiday, I'm always looking for a pretty first mate."

Some things never change, she thought.

When the call ended, she sat back in her chair. She had done it. She had covered Kuyeya's costs without her trust, without her father, solely by appealing to the decency of people with means. It was the alchemy her mother had so prized: turning nothing into something so that something else—a disease, a famine, a war—could be negated.

She went to the receptionist and asked for an estimate of charges for Kuyeya's surgery.

"It will take me a few minutes," the woman replied. "Do you wish to wait?"

Zoe shook her head. "I'll take a walk."

She left the hospital and wandered down the hill, making a slow loop around the parking lot. Ten minutes later, she approached the receptionist again.

"Here it is," the woman said, handing her a printout. "The cost for the hospital stay will be 279,000 rand. The doctors charge separately, but the total should not exceed 425,000 rand."

It was less than Zoe had expected. She turned away, thinking to send an email to Alex, when the receptionist stopped her.

"By the way, a man came by a minute ago and asked about Kuyeya. He looked rather flustered. If you see him wandering around, perhaps you can show him the way."

"What did he look like?" Zoe asked, confused.

The receptionist turned curious. "Actually, he looked a bit like you."

Zoe was thunderstruck. It had to be Trevor, but his visit made no sense. She had left him at JFK airport less than two days ago. To reach Pretoria so soon, he had to take a flight immediately after hers. *Or maybe he took one of Dad's jets*, she thought. It was possible, but it only deepened the enigma.

She walked quickly down the corridor, passing two doctors deep in conversation and a woman bouncing a baby. At the top of the steps, she froze. In the hallway below her were three men. Two of the men were dressed in bulky suits straight from central casting, and the third man was tall with graying hair and the build of an athlete past his prime.

It was her father.

"Zoe," he said. "Will you take a walk with me?"

She stood motionless, staring at him. He looked exhausted, like he hadn't slept in days. His skin was sallow and his blue eyes were clouded like an overcast sky.

"What are you doing here?" she asked softly.

"I had to see you. A phone call wasn't good enough."

She gave him a puzzled look. "What do you mean?"

"Walk with me," he said again, gesturing down the hallway. When still she didn't move, he turned imploring. "I had a speech scheduled for tonight, a primetime interview tomorrow. I rescheduled them. I flew nineteen hours to be here. Please."

"Okay," she said at last. She walked beside him away from the waiting room, away from Joseph and Sister Irina and Jan and Kuyeya, toward a glass door that led to a courtyard with trees and a fountain and a few scattered tables. She sat down at one of them, trying to ignore the pounding of her heart.

"I told Harry Randall," he said when his bodyguards were out of earshot.

She looked at him in shock. "And?"

"He wasn't surprised. There have been other allegations."

Her eyes flashed. "All swept under the rug, I'm sure."

His guilty look confirmed the truth.

"And the press?" she asked. "What are you going to tell them about me?"

"I'm not going to say anything. Neither is Sylvia."

She let out the breath she was holding and waited for an explanation. His words, when they came, seemed disembodied, almost trance-like. She had seen him like this only once before—on the night the call came from Somalia.

"There are some things you don't know," he began. "I offer them not as an excuse, but as an explanation. Your mother and I were an unlikely couple. I don't know how it happened that we fell in love, but we did. There were a lot of things about her that I didn't understand. She was selfish. When she set her heart on something, she didn't let anything get in the way. Even you and Trevor. But she had this gift, this glow. When she was around, she made me feel alive."

He took a breath. "It wasn't Sylvia who suggested I get into politics. It was your mother. I'll never forget the night she told me I could be President of the United States. She gave me that earnest look—you know the one—like she had a secret to tell. 'Jack,' she said, 'imagine how much good we could do in the Oval Office.' We planned it all out. She was supposed to be with me when I ran for the Senate." He choked up. "She was supposed to be with me now."

Zoe stared at him in shock. So many of her assumptions had been wrong.

"When she died," he went on, "I promised her on her grave that I'd make it to the White House. What I didn't realize is how many concessions

I'd have to make, how many things I'd have to say that I don't really believe. It's ironic: your description of me in the *New Yorker* was spot on. It's who I've always been. But the political climate right now is more toxic than I've ever seen it. It's impossible to run as a moderate. People don't want to hear about the benefits of co-operation. They want you to tell them how right they are and then beat up the other side."

He ran his hands through his hair. "Please hear me, Zoe. I never intended to put politics before you. But when you told me what happened with Clay, I was blindsided. So much was at stake. I didn't think. I reacted. I knew you had a crush on him. Sylvia told me how affectionate you'd been. I figured there must have been a misunderstanding. I thought you'd get over it."

He shook his head wearily. "I don't know if it means anything now, but I'm so sorry. I should have believed you. I should have defended you. I was wrong."

Tears spilled down Zoe's cheeks and collected on her chin. She saw a shaft of sunlight on the ground and walked toward it, allowing the light to warm her skin.

"I don't understand," she said, turning back to him. "The other night . . ."

He hung his head. "When you walked out the door, I finally realized what I'd done. I couldn't bear the thought of losing you forever. Not you and your mother both."

She felt an ache deep inside, a mixture of empathy and sorrow. She went to him and touched his hand. "Thank you," she said. "For coming here and telling me this. It means a lot."

He met her eyes and nodded. "I'm glad."

Suddenly, her iPhone beeped. Joseph had texted her. Kuyeya was ready to take visitors. "I need to go," she told him.

"Wait," he said quickly. "You asked for—"

"It's done. The bill is covered."

He gave her an inquiring look. "Then you'll have to find something to do with the money. I got the wire confirmation when I landed."

She couldn't help but smile. "Thank you," she said again.

"The little girl," he ventured. "Can I . . . meet her?"

She examined his face and saw his sincerity. "Of course," she said.

She led him down the hallway, past the theater where Kuyeya's vertebrae had been fused, to the now empty waiting room. His bodyguards trailed twenty feet behind. She saw Joseph walking toward her. He slowed in astonishment, staring at her father.

"Joseph," she said, "meet my dad. Dad, this is Joseph Kabuta."

"Jack Fleming," the Senator said, taking Joseph's hand. "It's a pleasure."

"Likewise, Senator," said Joseph, glancing at Zoe. "Right this way."

They found Kuyeya in a private room with a sitting area and a television. Her bed was on the left, configured like a recliner. She was resting quietly, her neck in a stiff brace. Sister Irina was at her side and Jan was lounging in a chair. He stood up quickly when he saw the Senator. Sister Irina looked confused until Zoe made the introductions. Then her eyes went wide.

Zoe approached the bed and touched Kuyeya's hand. "Hi there. I missed you."

At the sound of her voice, Kuyeya blinked and focused on her. She tried to speak, but the words came out in a barely discernible whisper. "Hi, Zoe," she said.

"Dad," Zoe said, "meet Kuyeya."

She stepped back and watched as her father squeezed Kuyeya's hand—the hand that held Charity's ring. It was a scene she could never have predicted in a hundred lifetimes, a vision of the world that could be, the world of the possible.

Suddenly, she noticed something in the girl's arms. "Where did that come from?" she asked, pointing at a brand-new doll.

"I brought it," Jan replied. "From what I understand, her old one wasn't too friendly."

Her smile broadened. "You didn't need my advice after all."

"It is good to see her at peace," Sister Irina said quietly. "If only an operation could make the rest of her whole."

"'The chains of the body are often wings to the

spirit,'" Zoe replied. "Mandela wrote that on Robben Island, but it's true for her, too."

Sister Irina nodded. "You're right. She's perfect in her own way."

Chapter 34

Lusaka, Zambia
June, 2012

At the end of May, Flexon Mubita received an official appointment to serve on the High Court of Zambia. Two days later, he announced he'd reached a decision in Kuyeya's case. On a bright morning in early June, the legal team drove to the Subordinate Court to receive his judgment. Sarge and Niza rode with Maurice, and Zoe and Joseph followed in her Land Rover. The mood among the lawyers was gloomy; the timing of the hearing suggested a quid pro quo with the Nyambos. Their only recourse was to ensure the press would be on hand to document the miscarriage of justice.

When they pulled into the parking lot, Zoe saw a ZNBC television crew waiting on the courthouse steps along with an army of pad-wielding journalists. They entered the judicial complex by a side door, bypassing the horde that had descended upon Sarge and Niza. They walked the length of the arcade and took their seats in Courtroom 10. Darious was already present in the dock. He gave Zoe a confident smirk. It was the first time he had acknowledged her directly. She looked away, enraged.

Before long, the lawyers took their places at counsel table—Sarge and Niza on the right and Benson Luchembe on the left. Luchembe's entourage sat on the bench beside Zoe, and the press crowded noisily into the rear of the gallery. Frederick and Patricia Nyambo made their appearance at the last minute. They took seats immediately behind Zoe and Joseph, ignoring the swirl of hushed gossip among the journalists. Zoe glanced over her shoulder and saw the smugness on Frederick's face. Patricia, by contrast, was a model of neutrality.

Moments later, Flexon Mubita took the bench. He peered over his glasses at the packed courtroom. "In the matter of Darious Nyambo," he began, "I have reviewed the evidence presented at trial and recorded my findings and conclusions in a written judgment. Copies will be furnished to counsel and any interested third parties." As he said this, he looked toward the press. "Are there any preliminary issues that I must address before I pronounce my judgment?"

Sarge and Luchembe both shook their heads.

"Very well," said the judge, folding his hands on the bench. "This case troubles me deeply. As the father of two daughters, I am horrified by the crime of defilement. As a judge, I am angered by the violence that has attended these proceedings. Yet the law is not about my morality or feelings. It is about the conscience of our society. And society in its collective wisdom has placed a high burden on the state to establish the guilt of any man accused of raping a child. It is not enough for a victim to be found in a state of defilement. It is not enough that the accused knows the victim, not enough that he wishes her ill. The state is obligated to prove beyond a reasonable doubt that the accused *in fact* defiled a victim under the age of sixteen."

Reasonable doubt, Zoe thought, her heart sinking into the mire. *He's going to hand the case to the Nyambos and look Solomonic while he does it.*

The judge glanced at Darious. "After reviewing the evidence, I find that Kuyeya Mizinga was raped on the night of August 20, 2011. I find, moreover, that she was underage. I had hoped that DNA would establish the identity of the perpetrator with the same degree of certainty. Alas, we must wait for another case to bring Zambia into the modern age. In the absence of scientific evidence, this case boils down to the credibility of witnesses and the burden of proof."

Mubita took a breath. "The prosecution presented a great deal of evidence about historical relationships between Darious Nyambo and the victim's mother, Charity Mizinga, and between Ms. Mizinga and the accused's father, Frederick Nyambo. This evidence was offered to establish the motive of the accused in committing this particular crime. While I find the prosecution's theory highly intriguing, it is irrelevant to the question before the Court. Defilement is a strict liability crime. The thoughts in the head of the accused are immaterial. It only matters whether the evidence shows he committed the act alleged.

On that ground, I have excluded from consideration the following evidence: the journals of Charity Mizinga, the testimony of Dr. Amos, the testimony of Dr. Kruger, except as it pertains to the paternity of the victim, the testimony of Officer Kabuta about the accused's state of health, and the testimony of Priscilla Kuwema, also known as Doris, except as to her observations of the accused shortly before the incident in question."

He just eviscerated our case, Zoe thought, horrified. *I can't believe I'm listening to this.*

"Concerning the eyewitness accounts," the judge went on, "I see no reason to doubt that the children saw a silver SUV and a man who resembled the accused. I also find no reason to quibble with the testimony of the women from Kanyama. They saw and heard what they saw and heard. The question is whether this evidence is sufficient to prove beyond a reasonable doubt that Darious Nyambo defiled Kuyeya Mizinga on August 20 of last year. I find that it is not."

Zoe closed her eyes and felt the pain down deep. How much she had risked for Kuyeya. How much they all had risked. They had built a persuasive case out of fragments buried in the past. They had defied their fears and spoken truth to power. And now a corrupt judge was dismantling their handiwork, piece by piece. She imagined Darious's smile, the warmth in Frederick's stomach. *Check and checkmate*, she thought. *It's all over.*

And then she heard a single word and her heart stopped in mid-beat: "However—" She opened her eyes and stared at Mubita. His countenance had transformed. No longer was his expression matter-of-fact. He glowered at Darious like an avenging angel.

"*However*," he said, "there is a witness whose testimony I found compelling. The child herself confronted the accused. She did not equivocate. 'He touched me,' she said. 'He wasn't supposed to touch.' The truth could not be spoken any plainer. Taken together with corroborative evidence from the children and old women and the medical evidence offered by Dr. Chulu, and setting aside the unbelievable alibi offered by the accused, I find that Darious Nyambo *in fact* defiled Kuyeya Mizinga, a child under the age of sixteen, on August 20, 2011."

Zoe watched in shock as Mubita delivered the coup de grâce to a terrified Darious. "Let this be clear: *no one* is above the law, not even the son of a former cabinet minister. In accordance with the power vested in me by the Republic of Zambia, I commit your case to the High Court where you will be sentenced to no less than fifteen years in prison. The evil you have committed will not be tolerated by this nation."

As soon as the judge departed the bench, the gallery erupted with noise. Zoe, however, sat in silence, incapable of believing what she had just witnessed. Nothing made sense. She had seen Mubita with Patricia Nyambo and the Deputy Minister of Justice. His behavior at trial had been inexplicable. He had mollified Frederick at the bar. He had delayed his decision until the Nyambos secured him an appointment to the High Court.

Could it be that he had taken the bribe and walked away from the deal? Could he have defeated them at their own game?

She stood up slowly and accepted Joseph's stunned embrace. She looked for Frederick and Patricia but didn't see them. The press surrounded the legal team when they left the courtroom, every reporter asking a different question. Sarge and Niza offered rapid-fire answers, enjoying the limelight, but Zoe took Joseph's hand and whispered: "Let's go."

They made their escape through the side exit, scurrying across the parking lot and keeping their heads down to avoid attracting the television crew. Joseph climbed into the Land Rover and started the engine, but Zoe looked back. She saw Frederick and Patricia leave the courthouse by the main doors. They forced their way through the cameras and walked quickly in her direction. With a start, Zoe realized that Frederick's Jaguar was only two cars away.

The Nyambos didn't notice her at first, but Zoe continued to stare at them, and the moment when it came seemed inevitable. Her eyes met

Frederick's across a distance of twenty feet. He looked startled, as if the sight of her carried an electric charge. For a split second, Zoe didn't react. Then her expression caught the wind of her feelings, and she grinned.

The Rule of Achilles. We win.

What happened next turned the world on its head. Instead of following Frederick into the Jaguar, Patricia hesitated, her hand on the door. She met Zoe's eyes and her lips curled into a smile. It was a vanishing thing, swallowed quickly by the sorrow that had preceded it, but its meaning was transparent—it was a smile that carried a secret, a smile of complicity. When she followed it with a nod, like a grace note, Zoe realized the truth.

Sliding into the Land Rover, she began to laugh and cry at the same time, as all the doubt and frustration of the past nine months rushed out of her on the current of vindication. The conspiracy of corruption had been thwarted by a conspiracy of mercy. Frederick had betrayed Patricia with Charity, and Patricia had betrayed him back, salvaging the institution to which she had committed her life, even at the expense of her son's freedom. She had executed the deception perfectly, leading her husband to believe that she had set up the exchange with Mubita, making the necessary connections and delivering the High Court appointment. But she had neglected to tell him one thing: the Principal Resident Magistrate had no intention of selling out.

Suddenly, Zoe understood the last piece of the puzzle. Flexon Mubita. His behavior on the bench hadn't been erratic. It had been purposeful. While giving Frederick and Darious the impressions they expected, he had built a blemishless evidentiary record and grounded his judgment on the surest foundation—the accusation of the victim, corroborated by eyewitness testimony and medical evidence. Far from subverting justice, the judge had given them a sublime gift: a ruling the High Court would never reverse.

"What?" Joseph said, giving her a peculiar look. "Something happened."

She laughed again. "I'll tell you on the drive."

Two days later, Zoe awoke to the sound of vervet monkeys chattering outside her guest room at the

Royal Livingstone Hotel. Joseph lay beside her on his back, snoring softly. She kissed his cheek and slipped out of bed, dressing in capris and a white cotton shirt. She grabbed her backpack off the floor and stole out of the room into the coolness of the morning. The monkeys scattered when they saw her, and she watched them go, laughing at the sight of a baby hanging onto its mother for dear life.

She crossed the wide lawn and took a seat on the deck overlooking the Zambezi. In the distance, the mist of Victoria Falls hovered like a cloud on the horizon. She took out the envelope that Monica Kingsley had given her in New York. She had hesitated to open it before now, preserving it on the intuition that she would find a more appropriate moment. Now, studying her mother's graceful penmanship, she knew she had been right to wait.

She breached the seal of the envelope and extracted two sheets of yellowed paper. She looked toward the falls again and took a deep breath. Then she read her mother's words.

Dearest Zoe,

I hope this letter never reaches you. I hope I am with you when you enter womanhood and realize the strength and beauty that dwells in you. But our lives are not in our hands. I am writing you because my work is dangerous and because what I have to say cannot be left unsaid.

I have many regrets as a mother. If you are reading this, I imagine you can name them as well as I can. I've never been great at motherhood—at least the conventional kind. I have long struggled to harmonize my passions with my devotion to you and Trevor. So before I go any further, let me offer you an apology. For the days when I was gone and you needed me, for the times when I was there and my mind was in another place, for allowing others to raise you in your early years, I am sorry. I tried to make it up to you by taking you with me when I could. It hasn't been enough, I know, but it's the best I've known how to give.

I remember the first time I took you to Victoria Falls. I saw the spark in your eyes, and the way it quickly grew into a flame. I knew then that our hearts carry the same beat. I never told you about the beginning of my love affair with Africa. It was a Kenyan poet who convinced me that the stories we tell ourselves about the "Dark Continent" are deeply flawed. Wesley had a better name for Africa.

He called it "The Garden of Burning Sand"—a land of splendor and severity, a land that gives and takes away. I loved him for a memorable season, and then life called me home. The rest you know.

If you are reading this, you are thirty and I am gone. I'm not certain where life has taken you, but I know that the spark I saw in your ten-year-old eyes was not a lie. I am writing to offer you a proposition. Please feel completely free to decline it if you have chosen a different path. But if your future is still open, I ask that you consider it.

Buried in the charter of my foundation is a clause that names my successor upon my death. I chose Monica Kingsley to serve as Executive Director. I trust her implicitly, and that is a rare thing. What you do not know is that the charter allows for the appointment of a Special Envoy who would operate outside the sphere of Monica's control and exercise a discretion that otherwise I have reserved for myself. This position is available to only two people. I offered it to Trevor first, but I asked him to consider leaving it to you. I suspect he did. His passions are elsewhere. I offer it now to you.

Perhaps you have wondered why I left you with a charitable trust. Perhaps you have questioned my judgment in naming Atticus Spelling as trustee. I created the trust for a reason—to train you to think of your life as an instrument of good. Even Atticus I chose for a purpose, though I never told him why. I wanted you to learn the traditional rules of philanthropy so that when you have gleaned their wisdom and been frustrated by their rigidity you will know exactly how and when to break them. Human problems must be met with human compassion. The person, not the system, must be preeminent.

If you are interested in my offer, let Monica know. She will explain it in more detail. Suffice it to say that you will be endowed with all the powers and privileges that I have, and you will ride on my reputation as you build your own. In the midst of politicians and bureaucrats and institutional players, you will be that rare person with allegiance to none but the truth and vast resources at your disposal. Truth and resources alone cannot change the world. But the world cannot change without them. If I have trained you well, you will know exactly what to do with them, and change you shall see.

The thought of you reading this breaks my heart. But if I am gone, know that I am never far away. Go to Cape Point and watch the breakers of the circumpolar current, stand in the rainforest at Victoria Falls, and I will whisper to you. The spirit of love that binds us in life is *indestructible in death. Give yourself as a gift to others, and you will know a joy that never fails.*

Never doubt that I love you.

Below Catherine's signature was a date: July 20, 1996. She had written the letter less than two weeks before she died. Zoe carefully folded the pages and placed them back in the envelope. Her face was a mess; it seemed she had an endless reservoir of tears. She saw Joseph walking toward her across the grass, clad in a long-sleeve shirt and jeans.

"Hey," she said, wiping her eyes. "I was wondering when you were going to get up."

"I'm on vacation," he replied with a lilt that died quickly. "What's the matter?"

She hesitated and then handed him her mother's letter. She watched as he read it, worrying that he would judge her for considering Catherine's offer.

When he reached the end, he regarded her reflectively. "What are you thinking?"

"I don't know. What should I be thinking?"

He gave her a serious look. "That you'd be a fool not to say yes."

Her eyes went wide. "What about us? I love you. I don't want to let this go."

"Then don't," he said softly.

She was incredulous. "You'd come with me to the United States?"

He shook his head. "I can't be Inspector General in America."

"What are you saying?"

A smile rose upon his lips. "How often did your mother visit Africa?"

That night, Zoe asked Joseph if he wanted to go for a swim. He declined with a laugh, saying it was too cold. So she went alone. She threw on pants and a shirt over her one-piece suit, slid her iPhone into her pocket, and strolled barefoot across the grass to the pool. The hotel was lit warmly by lamplight, but the grounds around the pool lay in shadow.

No one was about when she dived into the frigid water. She stroked to the far side and back again, doing ten laps. Afterward, she climbed out of the pool and wrapped her shivering body in a towel. In time, she found her iPhone in her pants.

She typed two emails beneath the canopy of stars. The first she sent to Monica Kingsley:

I read my mother's letter. I've decided to accept her offer. Let me know what needs to happen next.

The second she sent to her father:

Dad, I've been thinking about what you said. If you're really serious about using the presidency as Mom imagined, then I will support you as your daughter, politics aside. Send a plane, and I'll join you on the stage at the convention. As for forgiveness, it is a journey. But I promise to try.

She dressed again and followed the short path that led to the river. The sand was cold on her bare feet, and the boat launch was deserted. She knelt down at the water's edge and placed her fingers in the gentle current of the Zambezi. Words came to her then, and she spoke them to the night and the river and the land beneath her.

"I'm going home for a while. But I'll be back."

Author's Note

The Garden of Burning Sand is a work of fiction, but it was inspired by real issues and by my love for Africa and its people. Kuyeya's story offers an authentic glimpse into the horrifying world of child sexual assault in sub-Saharan Africa. As a father, I am profoundly troubled by this epidemic. My heart breaks for the children who suffer such predation and for the families who agonize with them in the aftermath, wondering whether their wounds can ever be healed. As a lawyer, I am equally troubled that most perpetrators are never punished for their crimes.

There are many reasons for this injustice. Some are cultural and difficult to change. One, however, could be eliminated almost overnight. If every African country had a DNA laboratory, prosecutors like Sarge and Niza could convict more criminals, and girls like Kuyeya would walk the streets in greater safety. In countries like Zambia where doctors, scientists, lawyers, and judges have the skills necessary to employ DNA in the prosecution of rapists and pedophiles, all that is missing is funding and political will.

Kuyeya's story also highlights the disenfranchisement suffered by African children with intellectual disabilities. In Zambia, four in five children born with an intellectual disability die before their fifth birthday, and disabled girls are more likely to be raped than their non-disabled peers. Again, there are many cultural obstacles to progress on this issue, but the greatest obstacle is the lack of effective assistance. Although many organizations offer support to people with disabilities, the common practice of lumping intellectual disabilities (i.e. cognitive impairments) in with physical disabilities (e.g. a missing limb) ensures that many of the more difficult cases like Down syndrome and cerebral palsy fall through the cracks. Thankfully, the NGO community is beginning to address this problem, but they need our help.

Much has been said and written about HIV/ AIDS in sub-Saharan Africa. I particularly benefited from *Sizwe's Test* by Jonny Steinberg, *28: Stories of AIDS in Africa* by Stephanie Nolen, and *Africa: Altered States, Ordinary Miracles* by Richard Dowden. Two things struck me as I researched the novel. First, despite the attention the issue has received, the stigma associated with HIV remains entrenched around the world. Second, despite the extraordinary success of PEPFAR and the Global Fund in curbing the AIDS pandemic and saving millions of lives, Western nations, including the United States, are retrenching on AIDS relief at the same time that researchers are telling us that early ARV treatment can dramatically reduce the transmission of the virus. What once seemed impossible—a future without AIDS—is now conceivable. But it will not happen without the ongoing commitment of the rich world to humanitarian aid.

The good news is that private foundations,

large net-worth individuals, and charitable organizations are taking up some of the slack left by governments. Indeed, it is possible that the foreign assistance of the future will be dominated by smart, innovative private giving. The source of the funding doesn't matter. What matters is that we in the developed world maintain the spirit of magnanimity that has defined our relationship with the developing world for generations.

It is up to all of us to ensure that this happens.

Corban Addison
March, 2013

Acknowledgements

I could not have written *The Garden of Burning Sand* without the help of many people around the world. My wife deserves the greatest credit—both for infusing the concept with her own sense of inspiration and for enduring (once again) the seemingly endless litany of days when I was absent either in body or in spirit during the research, writing, and editing of the book. With small children in the home, this was no easy task. Marcy, without your love, encouragement and faith, many of the best things in my life—including this novel—would not exist.

Just as most of the narrative is located in southern Africa, so are the majority of people to whom I owe gratitude. In Zambia, I wish to thank the amazing team of lawyers and social workers at the International Justice Mission (www.ijm.org) for giving me a tutorial of the law of child sexual assault and for your gracious hospitality during my time in the office. I continue to be inspired by your devotion to the work of justice and your commitment to care for the needs of the poorest victims of violence, young and old.

Many thanks to Eric and Holly Nelson and Elizabeth Bailey of Special Hope Network (www .specialhopenetwork.com) for educating me about the plight of Zambian children with special needs and for devoting your lives to meet those needs. Thanks to Wesley Ngwenya for giving me an insider's tour of Lusaka and Livingstone and for sharing your stories with me. I could never have gotten Zambia right without your help. Thanks also to Allen and Marcia Craig, Dan and Kate Bridges, and the Nelsons for opening your homes to me and for bearing with my incessant questions about expat life in Africa.

I wish to extend special thanks to the experts I interviewed during my research in Zambia—Dr. Jonathan Mwansa at UTH; two VSU officers from the Zambia Police; Brenda at YWCA; Clotilda, Lucy and three former sex workers at the Tasintha Programme; Professor N.K. Nkanza of Nkanza Laboratories; Namuchana Mushabati at Women and Law in southern Africa; friends at USAID and CDC; and Rob and Kay Baer. Without your knowledge of medicine, law enforcement, forensic evidence, prostitution, gender-based violence, and the cultural context of southern Africa, I could never have written this book.

In South Africa, my thanks go to Arnie, Emay, Abigail, and the team at Oasis for hosting me, showing me Johannesburg, and educating me about HIV/AIDS; to Annatjie Cilliers for instructing me in the clinical aspects of ARV treatment; to Professor Patricia de Witt for giving me a tour of Wits University; to Razelle Viljoen for information about Pretoria East Hospital; to Philip and Sandy Barlow for introducing me to Cape Town; and to Mike and Alyson Guy, Dr. John and Isobel de Gruchy, and the Reverend Barry Wood for your hospitality at Volmoed.

In the United States, I wish to thank Holly Burkhalter at the International Justice Mission for sharing your expertise in congressional procedure, Beltway politics, and foreign aid, and for inspiring me with your passion for justice in the African context. Thanks also to Michelle Conn for opening so many doors within IJM.

Huge thanks to my savvy and compassionate team of agents, editors, and publishers at Creative Trust, Baror International, Quercus Books, Harper-Collins, and publishers around the world for everything you do to support my artistic vision, improve my craft and get my stories into the hands of readers. Special thanks to Dan Raines for brokering connections in Zambia and to Jane Wood and Lorissa Sengara for bringing out the shine in my work.

Last but certainly not least, to my readers, thank you for your messages and notes of encouragement and for your concern for the cause of justice. I write my stories for you.